# Second Chance

# Elizabeth Grey

**Please visit www.elizabeth-grey.com to sign up to Elizabeth Grey's newsletter and for more information on her books.**

Facebook: www.facebook.com/elizabethgreyauthor
Twitter: www.twitter.com/elizabethjgrey
Instagram: www.instagram.com/elizabethgreyauthor

Second Chance – The Agency Book 3

Published 2019
ISBN-13: 978 1098999834

Copyright © Elizabeth Grey 2019

The right of Elizabeth Grey to be identified as the author of this work has been asserted in accordance with sections 77 and 78 of the Copyright Designs and Patents Act 1988.

All the characters in this book are fictitious and any resemblance to actual persons, living or dead, is purely coincidental.

Condition of Sale

This book is sold subject to the condition that it shall not, by way of trade or otherwise, be lent, re-sold, hired out or otherwise circulated in any form of binding or cover other than that in which it is published and without a similar condition including this condition being imposed on the subsequent publisher.

Set in 12 pt, Times New Roman.

Cover designed by Elizabeth Grey Art & Illustration of South Shields, Tyne and Wear, UK.

Copy Edited by Kia Thomas Editing of South Shields, Tyne and Wear, UK.
www.kiathomasediting.com
www.twitter.com/kiathomasedits

"Women speaking up for themselves and for those around them is the strongest force we have to change the world."

*Melinda Gates*

# TABLE OF CONTENTS

Dedication
Acknowledgements

Prologue
Chapter 1
Chapter 2
Chapter 3
Chapter 4
Chapter 5
Chapter 6
Chapter 7
Chapter 8
Chapter 9
Chapter 10
Chapter 11
Chapter 12
Chapter 13
Chapter 14
Chapter 15
Chapter 16
Chapter 17
Chapter 18
Chapter 19
Chapter 20
Chapter 21
Chapter 22
Chapter 23
Chapter 24
Chapter 25

Message from Gunther
Elizabeth's Books
Cast of Characters
About the Author

# 1

"FINALLY. THE WOMAN OF THE MOMENT. What took you so bloody long?"

Where to start? Today has been an absolute twat of a day. It started badly when my colossally fuckwitted neighbour decided to throw a house party at three a.m., then it got progressively worse. I spilled an entire cup of coffee all over my living room rug, and a power cut meant it took me an hour to towel-dry my hair. The last thing I needed after that was a note through my letterbox from colossally-fuckwitted-neighbour telling me I need to stop spoiling his fun and get a life. Seriously, you'd think he was fifteen not thirty-five. If I hadn't been futilely attempting to scrub Italian Roast espresso from my hand-tufted wool rug when he shoved his inexplicably unapologetic note through my letterbox, I'd have shoved it where the sun doesn't shine.

Or maybe, on reflection, I wouldn't. He smells of wet dog on a dry day and his hair looks like it's been styled with bird shit. And if that wasn't bad enough, he once dropped his keys outside his front gate, bent over and gave me very good reason to believe he doesn't wash his underwear. I imagine shoving the note in his grubby arse-cleavage and a wave of queasiness washes over me. Ew. Why do I do this to myself?

"Dealing with a very long and unpleasant list of domestic disasters took me so long," I say to my friend Violet as I walk over to the bar and order a very large mojito. Then I do a double take. *Åh nej. Allerede*? Already? It's only half past nine and she looks fit to drop. I love her dearly, but she has the drinking stamina of a Tibetan Buddhist monk. This means she rarely sees the end of a good night out. "Violet, how on earth are you hammered already? What time did you get here?"

She tucks her arm around her fiancé Ethan's as her body sways. "We've been out since six thirty and I'm not apologising. I've had a bloody awful week."

With his free arm, Ethan pulls me into a friendly hug. "Huge congrats, Freja. You've got Best TV Ad in the bag. I'm calling it now. You're going to get Tribe our first big win at the AdAg Awards this year. And if it's any consolation," he says with a hint of mischief in his lovely Scottish accent, "if Violet had been nominated this year, she'd be in a much worse state tonight."

Violet's crystal-blue eyes register the horror. "It's all true. When I was nominated last year I wanted to kill myself. I ate my way through five tubs of strawberry cheesecake Häagen Dazs in a twenty-four-hour period in a vain attempt to cheer myself up. The thought of going on stage with everyone looking at me . . ." She rubs her brow, and I'm not sure whether her grimace is due to her traumatic memory or her alcohol fog. "But I'm *so* happy for you, Freja. You deserve this so much."

"Thank you."

Violet, our agency's creative director, is a textbook introvert, while her fiancé, Ethan, who is my and Violet's boss at Tribe advertising agency, loves the limelight. They're two opposite cosmic forces, yin and yang, different in every way yet totally perfect together. As for me? I haven't had a proper relationship since my actor-boyfriend decided to bang his co-star five years ago. I caught them half naked in the front seat of his Volkswagen Golf, and what they were doing with the six-speed gear shift knob will be forever etched into my memory. But strangely, that wasn't *really* what made me swear off relationships. I realised I didn't give a shit that Richie was secretly screwing his daytime-soap co-star. In fact, I was relieved. No more domestic drudgery. No more squabbles over whose turn it was to wash the bloody dishes. No more having to watch his god-awful 1970s sitcom DVDs. *Åh Gud*, the sitcoms. A whole bookshelf in our house was dedicated to the sitcoms, and every Friday night Richie would put one on and pray to the gods of all things racist, sexist and homophobic.

I finish my mojito just as Tribe's whacky designer, Max Wolf, bounds over to join us.

"Why are you dressed like Ozzy Osbourne?" asks Ethan, taking in Max's too-tight trousers and burgundy velvet jacket.

"And Dame Edna?" adds Violet, her bright eyes fixed on her friend's diamanté choker and feathered brooch.

"And Dita von Teese?" I say with a laugh, as I spot his leopard-print corset belt. Where on earth does this man shop? Has he won a trolley dash through a stripper's closet?

"I don't have time to explain my style tonight." Max's tone is serious and urgent as he wedges his gangly six-foot-four frame between Ethan and Violet, his arms draped around their shoulders. "I need you to settle an argument for me. Will says Stella will instantly promote him to creative director if he wins best ad campaign at the AdAg Awards. I say she won't seeing as she's just promoted Harry."

"No, ah-ah, I'm not touching that." Worry dulls Ethan's eyes as he steps out of Max's hold. He's been one of Tribe's junior partners for six months now, but the tightness of his shoulders shows that he still feels uneasy managing his former friends. I follow his nervous gaze to the group of guys huddled at the far side of the bar. "Just tell Will that I don't have any real power and that Stella makes all the important decisions."

"If I had any power, then I'd have promoted Will over Harry bloody Hopkins," says Violet. She takes another large swig of wine, and my insides churn. Violet knows I've had a "friends with benefits" arrangement with Harry for the last couple of years. It's strictly sex only – no sleepovers, dates or commitment – but I still feel hellishly awkward when she voices how much she can't stand him.

Violet notices my unease. "I'm sorry, Freja. I know you guys are close, but Harry deliberately ruffles my feathers ten times before breakfast every single day. Actually, he doesn't just ruffle my feathers; he plucks them – every last one of them – and then he stuffs cushions with them."

"I don't understand the duck simile," says Max. He's German and he's lived in the UK longer than I have, but he has a far poorer grasp of British humour. "Anyway you *do* have power. You're sleeping with *him*, aren't you?" He jerks a thumb in Ethan's direction.

"It's a metaphor, not a simile," Violet says with a

hint of schoolteacher in her voice. "And I'd have to be sleeping with Stella to have any power, not *him*."

A lascivious smirk creeps over Max's face. Ethan laughs.

Violet narrows her eyes at both of them. "Max, are you imagining me sleeping with Stella?"

"Yeah." Max's grin gets wider. "Thanks for putting it in my head."

Ethan mirrors Max's grin. "Oh great, now it's in my head too."

"Right, I've had enough." Violet pushes the pair of them in the direction of Will and the other guys. "Shoo! Go away. Go and tell Will he's not getting a promotion because Tribe only promotes people who annoy me."

When we're alone, Violet sidles up to me, rests her head on my shoulder and sighs. "I've had the worst work week ever, Freja. I'm a thousand per cent sure Stella hates me. Ever since she made Harry creative director, she's given him all the best campaigns and totally overlooked me. He got JET Financial, our biggest client by considerable millions of pounds, in his first bloody week, and what did I get? A series of literally painful haemorrhoid-awareness ads for the sodding NHS. You couldn't make it up, could you?"

"Violet, we've been through this, honey. This is just your paranoia. And you're overthinking. And you're also . . ." I look at her hurt face and my heart sinks. She can't help who she is, and it isn't my place to tell her that her feelings aren't important. "I know Harry getting JET Financial upset you, but you have to let it go." I take her over to a quieter corner of the bar and we sit down at a high table.

"Harry got JET because he worked on the bid, helped with the pitch *and* because the client wants to ramp up their digital presence. Harry specialises in digital advertising and you don't. It really is as simple as that. You must know deep down in that weird little brain of yours that it made perfect sense for Stella to assign Harry to the campaign."

She bows her head, her gaze concentrated on her wine glass, which is as empty as mine now. "You must think I'm a crackpot."

"I think you desperately need to embrace some *hygge*."

Her dark, perfectly sculpted eyebrows twist into a frown. "I need to embrace my hoo-ha? My vagina has nothing to do with this conversation, Freja."

"*Hygge*, not hoo-ha, you twit. And I've told you about *hygge* before, the last time being only yesterday. I knew you weren't listening. It's my Danish happiness philosophy, remember?" She looks at me with blank eyes, and I resist the urge to pinch her.

"I *was* listening when you told me," she says. "It's all about drinking hot chocolate and having cosy nights by the fire, isn't it?"

"Something like that." Normally I'd take Violet to task about her infuriating habit of pretending she's listening intently to conversations she's tuned out from, but she can barely stand up, so I change the subject instead.

"Anyway, listen – it's awesome that Tribe has received three AdAg nominations when we're only six months old. You were creative director on the Sunta campaign, so you should be really proud. Will and Pinkie are your team, so this is your nomination too." She smiles a stiff smile that doesn't reach her cheeks. "Although now I know you'd rather face a game of Russian roulette than walk onto a stage to collect our industry's top award—"

She grabs my arm tightly. "Oh my god, don't say that word!"

"What word?"

"Russian."

I'm confused. "Um, okay . . ."

"I'd almost erased this afternoon's disastrous Subway pitch from my mind. I've been drowning out the sheer terror that was on the client's face with wine, but . . . oh god, why did you have to remind me? I have to drink more wine now." She tries to get up from the stool but thinks better of it and sits back down, holding her head in her hands. "God, I can't even . . ." she says, rubbing at her brow. "This is all Ethan's fault. He knows me better than anyone, so why on earth did he think assigning Rasputin's long-lost half-crazed, weed-obsessed great-great-granddaughter to my team was a good idea?"

She must mean her new Russian art director. "Natalia is obsessed with weed?"

"Not that kind of weed. Don't worry, she's no competition for Max's Colombian connection. I mean dill."

"Dill? As in the plant?"

"It's a weed, not a plant, and it shouldn't be food, yet she eats it in everything and on everything. And she grows it. I wouldn't be surprised if she smokes it. It smells awful. I can't go near her desk at lunch time and . . . she's just odd.

Very odd. Don't tell me you don't think she's odd."

I smile because there wouldn't be much daylight between Violet and Natalia in an oddness contest. "I think she's interesting."

She scrunches her beautiful face into a scowl. I'd kill for Violet's flawless porcelain skin and sparkling blue eyes. Even when she's drunk and in a bad mood she still manages to look like a fairy-tale princess. "That's because you don't have to work with her."

"But I *do* have to work with her."

She yawns and slumps forward onto the table, making it wobble. "I meant manage her. You don't have to manage her. I do. Every bloody day."

"Natalia is a free spirit. She says what she thinks and she's confident in who she is. There's a lot to be admired in that." Why am I even attempting to reason with Violet? Her brain fell asleep five minutes ago and her body isn't far behind.

"There you are, sweetie." Our friend Georgie totters over to me in sky-high fuchsia-pink heels which look like they were designed with the feet of a Soho drag act in mind. "Sorry I'm late. Mitchell has gone to Switzerland to hook up with his tobogganing team again. He's only just got back from spending a whole season in the Alps, so I'm not at all pleased about it." She flings her arms around me and gives me a peck on the cheek. "Congrats on your nom, darling. I am totally beyond excited for you. And sorry for being miserable. I solemnly swear I'm going to try to be more fun."

"Thanks, George." She gives me another kiss. "What's with the shoes? You don't usually wear heels."

"They're Jimmy Choos." She looks proudly down at her feet. "I'm trying to be more fashionable, but they're absolutely killing me. How have you spent your entire life wearing these things, Frey? They're the fashion equivalent of medieval torture devices. I think I've left it far too late to start wearing nice shoes. My feet just won't comply. What's up with Violet? She doesn't look good."

"She's had too much wine. Which doesn't have to be very much for Violet."

Before I finish my sentence, Georgie has enveloped Violet in her arms. She places one hand on Violet's forehead, looks into her eyes, then starts stroking her hair. "Violet, sweetie. How are you feeling? Do you need anything, hmm? Can you hear me, sweetie? Should I get Ethan?"

Violet rests her head on Georgie's shoulder. "I've had the worst week ever. It's all down to dill, you know."

"There, there, darling," purrs Georgie. "I don't have a clue what you're talking about, and I'm not at all sure you do either, but why don't we go outside and get some fresh air so you can tell me all about it?" She links Violet's arm and starts to lead her to the exit. "Are you coming, Frey?"

"No, you're good. I'll just get another drink or six."

Georgie looks disappointed, but I hold strong. I'm always the person everyone talks through their problems with, but tonight I'm allowing myself to be a little bit selfish. It's Saturday night – I want to celebrate and I want to have fun. I head for the bar and search the crowd for anybody I recognise with a smile on their face. Thankfully the first people I find are Anaïs and Rachel.

"You look like you need a drink, Freja." Anaïs is Tribe's public relations manager. She's a stylish Parisian and one of my oldest work friends. "What would you like?"

"Something with a double shot of anything strong. I arrived late so I'm playing catch-up."

Anaïs gives my arm a squeeze. "Say no more. There's three for two on cocktails tonight." She walks over to the bar, giving me a great view of her backless dress. I'll never understand why Anaïs isn't a stylist for an incredibly famous person. I need her to dress me. Hell, she needs to dress the entire planet.

"Freja, I need to talk shop with you for a moment." Rachel, a film producer on my team, is my newest recruit and is fast becoming a friend. She's bright, bold and popular, with a filthy sense of humour, and she brightens up my studio every day. "I can't stop thinking up ideas for the JET Financial ad. What do you think about filming inside a fighter jet?"

Is she serious? "*You* want to go up in a fighter jet? Rachel, I love you, but you almost passed out when you had to shoot in a cornfield for Miller's Muesli Bars."

"There was a huge pile of dung in that cornfield. I'm a London girl. Everything to do with the countryside offends me." I can't help laughing as I remember that infamous shoot. Wendy, our post-producer, saved all the best outtakes, which mostly consist of a terrified Rachel yelling a cacophony of four-letter words behind the camera as she struggled not to barf.

"I know what you're thinking. However, I have two words for you: *Top Gun*."

"*Top Gun*? Rachel, the creative team isn't going to refocus three months of intense planning with the strategy department just because you want to shoot some fit guys in sexy uniforms."

She places her hands on her enviably curvy hips. "The fit guys would be a bonus, but focus on the message. We can't do an ad for a company called JET Financial without linking the JET to a jet."

"JET is an acronym for Jared Eugene Taft, the company's founder." The excitement fades from her face. Damn it. I didn't want to quash her enthusiasm. "So, that's probably going to be too literal."

Her lips thin to a pensive line. "I admit that *did* cross my mind."

"I'm not saying it wouldn't work, but you know how creative teams would rather turn out shit than run with a producer's idea. It's our job to translate *their* vision, not push our own."

"I know, I know." She turns up the excitement, and the volume, again. "But I just told Harry Hopkins about my idea and he thought it was great."

"You've already run this past the creative director?" Again, I don't want to quash her enthusiasm, but she's new and she's young, and I'll be the one for the high jump if she starts stepping on toes. And since when was Harry here? I scan the bar and find him in deep conversation with a pair of breasts belonging to a blonde with orange skin and drawn-on eyebrows. Typical. "I also don't know who's going to be producing the JET Financial ad yet. There's a lot to consider. I have to consider workloads, the creative brief and our skills base . . . and I'm bracing myself for the client requesting Jadine."

Rachel's eyes roll under her heavily made-up eyelids. "Jadine? Why on earth would they request Jadine? JET is Tribe's top client. They deserve better than Jadine. *I'm* better than Jadine."

"You may well be, but you aren't the part-time shag-buddy of JET's millionaire CEO."

She almost drops to the floor just as Anaïs rejoins us with three pina coladas. "You're kidding me. Why don't I know this? Did you know about this, Anaïs?"

"Know about what?" Anaïs passes me one of the bright yellow drinks.

"Jared Taft is screwing Jadine Clark."

"Ew, no I didn't." Anaïs's face twists with disgust. "Freja, you're absolutely shit at gossiping."

"That's because I'm not interested in Jadine Clark's love life."

"Why wouldn't you be interested?" Rachel screws up her nose. "This scenario is absolutely crying out for a bitching session including a generous portion of judgement and bitterness." She closes her eyes and sucks so much pina colada through her straw that she almost empties the glass. "God, if this is true, it's such a waste. Jared Taft is far too hot, rich, gorgeous and charming to be with Jadine Clark. Have you felt how hard his thighs are? He accidentally nudged me in the lift and my knickers dropped three inches—"

"Oh my god." I almost choke on my drink.

"Rachel, you really need to stop reading trashy romance books."

Anaïs nods her head and laughs. She knows what I'm talking about. Rachel's appetite for almost-but-not-quite-pornographic literature is legendary.

"My expert knowledge of fantasy hot, sexy millionaires means I have expert insight into real-life hot, sexy millionaires. Trust me on this. Jared Taft could have any woman he wanted, so why in the name of Christian Grey's delicious arse would he pick Jadine Clark? She's bloody awful. And she doesn't have any tits."

Anaïs looks down at her own flat chest and sighs. "Tits aren't everything."

"Who says tits aren't everything?"

Oh, for crying out loud. Could Harry Hopkins choose a worse time to join us? His bright-blue eyes sparkle as his gaze sweeps over me, settling on my boobs. Clearly he had no luck with the orange girl he was drooling over earlier.

"Is this our cue to leave?" Rachel asks me.

"It is *my* cue," declares Anaïs. She's hated Harry for years, and the feeling is mutual.

A flash of mischief lands in Harry's eyes. "Oh, don't be like that, *Anus*."

Anaïs's light-brown skin darkens, and she shoots him a glare that would strike fear into the hearts of most men, but not Harry. This is because Harry reaches peak euphoric happiness when he's tormenting the life out of people who don't like him. Anaïs tells Harry to go fuck himself, then she turns on her heel and disappears into the crowd.

Rachel stands awkwardly for a moment. Her green eyes flit between Harry and the group of colleagues her friend just joined. "I'd best go check on Anaïs."

"Sure. We can talk about your fighter-jet idea on Monday if you like," says Harry.

An excited squeal escapes from Rachel's throat. "Oh my god, do you mean it?"

"Of course," Harry says.

Rachel's round cheeks turn into bright shiny apples, then she squeals again and heads off in the direction of her friend.

When we're alone, Harry sweeps his hand around my back and grips my hip firmly. "I haven't had the chance to congratulate you on your nomination yet." He's standing so close to me that his beard rubs softly against my neck. He suits his beard. Together with his biker clothes, floppy blonde hair and infamous attitude, it fits with his bad-boy image.

"Why do you have to be so rude to Anaïs?"

"She's a moron and she hates me, so—"

"So, she's my friend, Harry." I pull out of his hold and spin around to face him.

"I'm your friend too."

"Seriously? You sound like you're jealous that I have other friends."

"I'm the only friend you sleep with, so I'm not jealous."

"Maybe you are, or maybe you're not." I say it teasingly, but if he thinks he's sleeping with me tonight, he's got another thing coming. I hate it when he's presumptuous. I drain my glass and head over to the bar to order another cocktail. But Harry doesn't take the hint and follows me.

"Do you remember my friend Lola?"

A surge of desire swirls low in my belly. What a night that was. "How could I forget?"

Harry's eyes sparkle and he leans in close to me again, his hand returning to my hip. "She's attending a banking conference in Frankfurt next week and has a stopover in London tomorrow, for one night only. What do you say we all get together again?"

The bartender passes me a red wine spritzer and I immediately take a huge, nervous drink. "Lola was a one-time thing, Harry. I try everything once, not twice."

"But if you enjoyed it once, you'll enjoy it twice." His Aussie accent makes his voice growl with a sexy purr. "Do you think about that night as much as I do? Watching you with Lola is my brain's top-rated download whenever I fancy a wristy."

"You did more than watch, if I remember correctly." With a rush of excitement, my mind takes me back to that night. Despite spending my student years in the company of liberated, free-thinking acting types, it was my first threesome. And it was pretty spectacular. "Lola *is* an amazing kisser."

Harry frowns. "Better than me?"

"Well, she doesn't have a beard."

Harry smoothes his hands over his wiry chin. "You told me my beard heightened your pleasure."

"Yeah, I did," I say flirtatiously. "But I wasn't talking about pleasuring my mouth when I said that."

Harry's skin flushes pink. "Fuck. You have no idea how much I need this again. You have to come over tomorrow night. Can I call you in the morning when I find out when Lola's plane lands?"

Do I want to go there again? I think back to Lola's kisses, and I figure why the hell not. "Yeah, you can call me."

At that moment, the door swings open and Violet reappears, slumped around Georgie's shoulder. She looks like she took a bath in the river of the dead. Ethan immediately rushes to her side, his brow pleated in a concerned frown.

"Looks like Violet's had a gutful of piss again," says Harry.

I give his arm a sharp nudge. "Leave her be. She's had a tough week."

"Every week's a tough week for her." He glares at her with barely contained contempt, and I fight an overwhelming urge to knee him in the balls. Harry's my friend, but I'm here for my girls first, and I'll protect them with claws if necessary. Harry drains his beer bottle and plonks it down on the bar. "If Stella assigns Klein & Co to Violet, then she's an even bigger mug than Ethan Fraser is."

My heart skips a beat.

I must have heard wrong.

"If she assigns who?"

"We signed Klein & Co last night. I doubt Stella will give me another high-profile campaign, but she fucking should. I can easily handle JET Financial *and* Klein & Co. Violet's skills are better suited to smaller, less important clients."

For a second I can't hear anything but the sound of my own pulse sloshing around in my ears. I spent January worrying and praying this wouldn't happen. Then I spent February trying to find a secondment somewhere . . . anywhere. Then, a few weeks ago, I got my reprieve. I thought I was out of the woods.

"What's up?"

"Erm . . . nothing . . . I . . ." The tremble in my voice elicits a look of concern on Harry's face. I take a deep breath and try to focus. "I just thought Klein & Co had signed with BMG."

"They almost did, but then the chairman of our board got himself knighted in the New Year's Honours and he's suddenly best pals with Lord Klein. They sealed the deal with cognac, cigars and a handshake in some poncey Mayfair gentlemen's club."

A sickly swirl of nausea rises into my throat. It tastes of bile mixed with alcohol and fear. I need to get out of here. I need to breathe different air. I need to feel safe. I need to clear my mind and plan what the hell I'm going to do.

I wait until Harry goes to the toilet. I don't say goodbye. I just leave.

# 2

I DIDN'T SEE HARRY YESTERDAY. I didn't see or speak to anybody. I rarely need alone time, but I turned my phone off, unplugged my Wi-Fi and spent the entire day grappling with thoughts I didn't want in my head. This is not how I deal. Do I even need to "deal"? It's been eight years, after all. Surely, I've got this.

*It didn't happen.*

That's what I've been telling myself for the past eight years.

*It didn't happen.*

I had no choice but to kill every single memory from back then. I had to kill *her* too – the person I used to be. The waitress who worked ten-hour shifts in roller skates so she could afford to pay for college, the actress who took her clothes off for money because she thought it would lead to greater roles, the girl who loved someone so much that the only way she could save him was to let him go and never see him again.

That girl doesn't exist anymore. I killed her so I could live, and I became who I am today by refusing to allow the shadows of my past to creep into my future.

I won my war years ago. Nothing needs to change. I *have* got this.

\* \* \*

I arrive at my office early and occupy my brain with as much work as I can find. This is an opportunity for me to put my multi-tasking skills to the test. My animation team needs me to look over their preliminary work on bringing a 2D toothbrush to life, and my line producer needs me to sign off her costings for Sunta's next TV ad. I message Andrew, my character animator, to suggest the toothbrushman he created might work better if he had a full set of sparkly teeth, then I open an email from Rachel. Wow! She's been busy. She's outlined three entire storyboards for her fighter-jet idea, and one in particular looks really great. My gut is telling me that Rachel deserves her first big break based on enthusiasm alone. She may have less experience than Zain, and she isn't an all-round creative genius like Neil, but she's certainly very talented and crazily ambitious. Is she ready for this? Yes, I think she is. If my gut is telling me Rachel can do this, then she can. I reply telling her to set up a meeting with the JET Financial creative team. I type with a huge smile on my face because I know she is going to explode with excitement when she reads it.

As soon as I've cleared my inbox, I pluck up some courage and call through to Ethan's all-knowing secretary, Lucille. There's a slight tremble in my voice as I talk to her; the pit that's been in my stomach since Saturday night clenches with dread at the prospect of hearing news I don't want to hear – something that might knock my confidence and make me doubt myself.

"I thought you were Tribe's resident authority on celebrity clients," says Lucille, when I ask her about Klein & Co. She still has a gorgeous Barbados accent despite living in London long enough to raise four children and, on the last count, eleven grandchildren. "Why don't you already know everything there is to know about the Klein family, girl?"

"That's precisely why I called you. I just need a quick refresher, um, in case I've mixed up the name of Klein's wife or something."

Lucille sighs, and for a second I imagine her breath rushing through the telephone, hitting me square in the chest and making my heart drop through my stomach. I imagine she knows the real reason I'm calling her. *Kom igen, Freja. Come on. Hold it together.*

"Davina. Lady Klein's name is Davina. She designs hats for rich white ladies."

"Ah, yes, thank you. I can't believe I forgot about those hats." And I'm not even lying here. Lady Klein's hats are outlandish, yet instantly recognisable. They have sombrero-sized brims, and plumage plucked from ostriches, peacocks and even, if *Hello* magazine's fashion editor is correct, Royal Palm turkeys.

"Davina is Klein's second wife. The first one died in a car crash following some scandal back in the eighties. Wasn't she a princess, or the daughter of a princess? You'll have to google that as I can't remember. And his son, the eldest one, is a judge on a panel reality show on Channel Four. *Beat the Boss*, I think it's called. I don't know if it's any good because it clashes with *Strictly Come Dancing* and you know nothing comes between me and my *Strictly*."

For the last eight years I've flipped my TV

channel, switched off my radio or stopped reading newspaper articles every time the name "Klein" has appeared. I haven't seen *Beat the Boss*. I was too afraid of how I would feel when I heard his voice or saw his face.

"You know Klein & Co own KTech and BuzzPay, right?" asks Lucille.

"Yes, of course I do."

"Well, BuzzPay spends four times more on advertising than Klein & Co, and KTech isn't far behind. The partners want to win all of the business, but there are existing contracts still in play. They also own Cask & Cork, which exports spirits and craft beers, and a chain of whisky bars called Statten."

Ugh, this I didn't know. I enjoyed a fabulous night out at the Leicester Square Statten a few weeks ago. Ah well, that's the first and last time I'll be experiencing their over-inflated drink prices. "Do Klein & Co need TV work?"

"No, just print and digital. But if Stella closes on BuzzPay there'll definitely be some meaty TV work for you to get your teeth stuck into. They'll be our largest client for sure."

Shit. Time to start praying. *Åh nej. Ikke panik, Freja. Don't panic yet. One day at a time.* "Okay. Thanks, Lucille." I put the phone down.

"What the fuck happened to you yesterday?"

I look up as Harry strides into my office, closing the door with a hard slam. I haven't given Harry a second thought all morning. I'm a terrible friend. "If this is about Lola I'm—"

"Of course it's about Lola!" His yellow beard shakes like a field of wheat battling a strong wind.

"If you didn't want to come over, why the hell didn't you just say so? You made me look like a right galah."

"I'm sorry. Something came up."

"I tried to call you all day. Did you switch your bloody phone off?"

"The battery died. I was busy. I forgot to charge it."

"Why don't you have a landline?"

"Because I don't need a landline."

"Well you did yesterday!" Shit, he's really mad. Boiling, hopping, red-faced mad. "What the hell 'came up', anyway? You usually can't go two seconds without checking your phone."

"Nothing major." I start opening apps on my computer. He'll give up the interrogation if he thinks I'm busy.

"I need to talk to you about JET Financial."

Christ, that was easy. Maybe he isn't as mad as I thought, or more likely, he cares far more about himself than my shit weekend. "I've already assigned Rachel Hart to shoot the ad. Her ideas need fleshing out with your team if they want to run with them, but she wants the gig and I know she's ready."

Harry sits down in the chair opposite my desk and pushes up his sleeves. As a creative with minimal client interaction, he's permitted to dress casually, but today he looks like he's borrowed my scruffy pot-head neighbour's clothes. "Rachel's idea isn't half bad, but what the hell were you thinking giving her JET without running it past me first?"

"Excuse me? Harry, I think you might be

overreaching here." I adopt a light tone and a smile, but my patience is already wearing thin. Alpha-asshole behaviour from Harry Hopkins is the last thing I need today. "My staffing decisions don't need your approval."

"This time they do," he snaps. "You may be able to ride roughshod over Violet, but you're not pulling that shit with me. JET Financial is my first big campaign as creative director. I helped pitch for the business and I know what the client wants. I also know what they don't want, and that's Rachel Hart, so you need to pull her, pronto."

"Harry, I honestly have no idea why I'm having this conversation with you. We've worked together for five years and you know how I operate. Don't question my judgement on this."

"I'm not questioning you; I'm telling you what the client wants." Harry's tanned skin notches back up to boiling point again. He's a hothead with everyone he works with, and we've had far too many humdingers of arguments to count, but he's always respected how I run my team.

"Last time I checked, Lennox Jackson is the client account manager, so if anybody gets to tell me what the client wants, it's him and not you. But make no mistake, if he came into my office making the same demands, I'd be kicking his ass too."

"Freja, for fuck's sake, get your head on straight." Harry's brow ripples and bends into a very angry-looking concertina. "You really think a client paying us high six figures doesn't get input into who works on their account?"

"Yes I do." I answer without missing a beat, but when Harry rolls his eyes dismissively at me, I wonder if I'm being naïve.

"Well, far be it from me to argue with you when you're never wrong, but it actually does give them a say. Jared Taft wants Jadine Clark on his team, so you'll have to find a way to give her to him."

*For helvede skyld.* I bloody knew it. "Jadine is neither skilled nor experienced enough to shoot an ad. I'd be putting my professional reputation on the line, and frankly you'd be doing the same."

Harry shrugs. "Not my problem. Jared personally requested her."

"Because he's screwing her."

"Is he? Well, blow me." He shrugs again, takes out a packet of gum and pops a piece into his mouth. He starts to laugh and chew at the same time, which results in a very unattractive slavery cackle. Not for the first time I wonder why I chose him to tend to my sexual needs. How on earth did I get so desperate? "If you ask me, Jadine can do better."

Has he lost his mind? "You think Jadine is the one who could do better in that pairing?"

"Sure. She's fit and Jared's a dirty root rat."

"He's a what?" I speak five languages, but Harry's Australian slang often evades me.

"A root rat. You know – he'll root around with anything."

"Well, Jared Taft's love life is nobody's business but his own." I concede it's probably also the business of whomever he's "rooting" with. "How do you know so much about him anyway?"

"I worked on the JET bid with Ethan and Lennox. We had a few meetings over a few beers, and he reckons he's got at least five women on the go at any one time. Most of them in different countries. It's not surprising, is it? I mean the guy became a millionaire at twenty-two. When you surpass the life goals of the average man before your balls have fully dropped, then odds-on you're going to turn into a prize whacker."

I'm just about to ask what the hell a "whacker" is when Harry helps me out with a hand-wank signal. Nice. "You're giving me even more reason to refuse his demands. I'm not putting the reputation of my department on the line just because Jared Taft is screwing my unqualified trainee." My blood starts to boil as the reality of the situation sinks further under my skin. I've never liked Jadine. She's the queen bee of Tribe's mean-girl clique and has a discernible cruel streak. "Jadine got on my team because her father was one of Tribe's founding partners, but now that he's been booted out of the agency, I'm free to say what I think. The truth is, I've been wanting to switch Jadine's position for weeks now. I've tried with her, but she just doesn't have what it takes to be a film producer. And, after what she did to Violet, she's lucky she's still here at all."

Harry laughs, and his chewing gum clacks against his teeth, producing a nerve-jarring squelchy sound. "So this is about Violet?"

"Of course it isn't. Aren't you listening? I've already told you that Jadine isn't cutting it."

"Come off it, Freja. I've been around the block a few times. I can spot girl-code stuff a mile off. You hate Jadine because Violet hates her, and Violet hates her because she made a move on Ethan. You and Violet have been as thick as thieves ever since we started at Tribe. You want to oust Jadine to stick it to her for upsetting your friend."

And this is the moment I give up trying to keep the red mist under control. "Harry, you should know me better than that. How dare you come into my office and tell me how to run my studio? I suggest you think very carefully about what you say next—"

Our argument is interrupted by three soft knocks on my door, followed by the entrance of Rachel. "Freja, I'm sorry to intrude, but I need a word. It's quite urgent." She looks fed up. Please let it be something minor – like her favourite Quality Street has been discontinued.

"Sure, what is it, Rachel?"

She glances nervously between me and Harry, and I feel a prickle of unease. Rachel is never nervous about anything. "What's going on with JET Financial? I thought I was shooting their ad."

Oh for god's sake. "You are shooting their ad."

She places her hands firmly on her hips. "Then why is Jadine packing up her things and heading out for a meeting with the creative team?"

I practically leap to my feet. "I have no idea, but I'm bloody well going to find out."

I march out of my office and onto the studio floor, with Rachel and Harry following behind me. Thankfully, most of my team are busy filming on stage set two, but Zain and my post-producers, Wendy and Jimmy, are working at their desks. Jadine, meanwhile, is putting on her coat.

"Jadine, where are you going?"

"I have a meeting." It isn't unusual for Jadine's demeanour to bear an aura of superiority, but today there's so much conceit radiating off her she could power a streetlight with it.

"You have a meeting where and with whom?"

Her cat-like green eyes smile smugly, and I'm reminded of all the reasons I dislike her. She's calculating, combative and entirely self-absorbed.

"With JET Financial's creative team." Jadine drops a folder into her Tuscany leather messenger bag and fastens the buckle. "Lily and Sean invited me over to JET's offices, so if you'll excuse me, I only have thirty seconds to get out of the building and into a taxi."

"You're going nowhere." I turn around to find Harry wearing the expression of a man who would like to be strapped to a rocket and blasted to space. "Care to explain?"

He shrugs. Then he clacks his chewing gum against his teeth again. It's all I can do to stop myself pulling the gum from his mouth and shoving it up his nose. "Nothing to do with me."

"Really?" I run my hand through my hair and shake my head. He must think I was born yesterday. "So our conversation of two minutes ago is entirely coincidental to these events?"

He responds with another shrug. He's an absolute nightmare to work with sometimes.

Jadine wraps a silk scarf around her neck and throws her waves of long golden hair over her shoulders. "Freja, I really need to go. Lily and Sean are expecting me."

"They should be expecting me," says Rachel.

"Yeah, I am sorry about that, Rachel. Genuinely sorry." There is no empathy in her voice; her tone is pure ice.

Rachel steps forward, head held high and shoulders straight. "This is my gig, Jadine, so get your coat off and sit your bony arse back down in your chair."

I think I hear Jadine gulp. She may be a good few inches taller than Rachel, but she's built like a blade of grass. Rachel, on the other hand, is made of far more robust stock, with power hips and a cleavage she once lost her mobile phone in.

"I was just telling Freja there'd been a misunderstanding," says Harry.

"What do you mean by misunderstanding?" Rachel takes the words straight out of my mouth. Her skin is getting redder by the second. I'm reminded of what she looked like after a few too many vodka cocktails the night she picked a fight with a brick wall.

I take a deep breath and summon some calm. "Jadine, I think you probably know this already, but Rachel has been assigned to produce JET's TV ad. How exactly did you get invited to the creative team meeting?"

"She invited herself," Rachel mutters under her breath.

Jadine scowls at Rachel. "No, Rachel, I didn't invite myself. Lennox Jackson called me. Apparently JET Financial personally requested that I work with them."

I mentally sign and serve Lennox's death warrant. "Who is responsible for assigning film producers to ad campaigns?"

"Well, um, usually you are, but this time—"

"This time *I* still assign film producers to ad campaigns, and this morning I gave JET to Rachel."

I fold my arms and hold Jadine's frosty glare until she looks away. "Harry, can you call down to your team and tell them Rachel will be joining them?"

Rachel marches to her desk, picks up her things and stomps across the floor towards the stairwell, but Harry doesn't budge. "I'm going to have to speak to Stella first," he says.

"Stella is in South Korea negotiating Tribe's Far East expansion. Do you really want to bother her with a staffing dispute?"

"What choice do I have?" Harry holds up his arms in exasperation. "I can't talk to Ethan Fraser because he'll take your side. He always does."

"He doesn't, but he will on this. And that's because I'm right." The look on Harry's face tells me this probably wasn't the smartest thing to say. He's had a colossal Ethan-sized chip on his shoulder since before Tribe's launch. Harry hates Ethan because he's younger, richer, more popular and more successful than him. He can't admit this, of course, so he hides his resentfulness beneath an ingrained surliness. I wonder how long he's going to be in a huff over Ethan this time, and I wonder if I'll ever stop sleeping with him. Don't get me wrong, Harry is a great-looking guy – if you can see past the beard – and he's blessed with the body of a Roman gladiator – if you can see past the scruffy heavy-metal t-shirts he wears. But he's also a prize-winning ass.

"I'll come with you when you speak to Ethan." Jadine's jaw is tense and her lips have thinned to an angry line.

"No thanks, sweetheart," says Harry. He sinks his hands in his pockets and starts to walk away.

"It'll be better if I talk to him on my tod given what I'm likely to say."

As if I care. I watch him skulk away, then I turn back to Jadine. Her shoulders are slumped and her eyes are glassy, so although I'm seriously pissed off with her, I don't want to humiliate her any further. "I'm sorry, Jadine, but Lennox shouldn't have gone over my head like this."

"Are you sorry?" She shuffles out of her coat and shoots me a glare that would dull sunbeams. And the tiny bit of empathy I was feeling towards her disappears quicker than it arrived.

"I don't say things I don't mean, Jadine. Of course I'm sorry."

She rolls her eyes and slams her laptop shut. "I'm going to take an early lunch."

She picks up her coat and heads for the stairs, and for reasons known only to my persistent feet, I follow her. "We need to finish this conversation."

"What's the point?"

I've half a mind just to let her go. When it comes to grown-ass adults stomping off in huffs, I'm rapidly running out of fucks to give. "What would you have me do, Jadine? I can't kick Rachel off a campaign just because you're sleeping with our client."

She stops still, then swings around to face me. *Is that steam billowing out of her ears?* "How dare you insinuate that's the reason JET Financial want to work with me?"

Is she for real? I do a quick scan of her expression and body language: she's standing tall, shoulders raised, brow pleated in manufactured offence. Hmm. I know where my gut is going with this, so I trust it. "I'm not insinuating that's the reason; I'm stating it quite clearly. You have neither the skill nor the experience to head up a high-profile ad campaign."

"Well, Jared thinks otherwise, and it's his money," she snarls. "I want this more than Rachel, and I *am* ready. I wonder if Jared's money would follow me if I found a new agency to work for."

Would the board fire me if I tell her to pack up and go? To think I was feeling sorry for the bratty Veruca Salt wannabe a minute ago. Now, I think I'd be overjoyed if a pack of hyper-intelligent squirrels threw her down a rubbish chute. She's definitely a bad nut. "I can't stop you leaving, but I'd be happier if you appreciated the chances you'd been given following the stunt you pulled last year."

"So this is about Violet?" She looks to the ceiling, laughs and flicks her golden hair. "Oh my god, I can't believe this is *still* about Violet."

I hear a clip-clop of high heels coming down the stairs, and my stomach leaps into my chest when I see who the shoes belong to. Violet steps down the last few stairs then walks over to join us. "Well, I wish I could say this wasn't awkward."

"You two deserve each other." Jadine meets Violet's mischievous grin with a look of sheer contempt, then the former model glides up the stairs as if they were her own personal catwalk.

"Do I need to know what that was about?" asks Violet.

"It's Jadine, so no."

We walk back to my office and I close the door behind us. Then I look at Violet. She's chewing her bottom lip and fidgeting with the buttons on her dress. This is not good news. I sit down in my chair and Violet sits opposite me. "What on earth is it now? Please don't tell me I'm going to have to take up yoga to deal with workplace stress again, because the new instructor looks like Beavis and Butthead's even more badly drawn older brother, and it's very off-putting."

She frowns at me. "Why is that off-putting?"

I feel a pang of shame at my shallowness. "I slept with the last instructor, so . . . it's a bad reminder. Just tell me what's up."

"Have you met Madeline Westgate yet?"

"The new account manager?"

She nods, then holds her head in her hands. "Oh god, you won't believe it."

"What have you done now?"

"Me?" she asks with a gasp. Why is she surprised? Her lack of brain-to-mouth filter is as legendary as Robin Hood's fondness for green hosiery. "Why do you always assume it's me who's upset the apple cart?"

"Honey, you know I love you, but you've burned more bridges than Caesar on his way back from Gaul."

Her mouth falls open, then her forehead creases. I wonder if she'll ever realise how easy she is to read. "Okay, you have a point, but this time it isn't me. It's Rasputin's crazy great-great-great-great-great-granddaughter. She's just refused to work for Klein & Co because Lord Klein wrote a frothing article in his shitty *Sunday Herald* newspaper column last week likening vegans to the Bolsheviks."

My blood runs cold at the mention of *his* name. I

quickly take up arms against the memories and force them back into their cage. "I'm guessing Natalia is a vegan?"

"Of course she is. Didn't her polyurethane shoes, hemp trousers and obsession with dill give it away?" Violet rubs her brow and takes a deep, exasperated breath. "I don't mean to be intolerant, but refusing to work with a massively important client because they criticised a lifestyle choice you subscribe to is pretty much career suicide, isn't it? I don't know how to handle her. Could she sue Tribe for constructive dismissal if I found a way to blackmail her into working for Klein?"

I can't help but laugh. Violet is a phenomenal copywriter, but her transition to creative director hasn't been easy. She wasn't so much at the back of the queue when patience was handed out as tucked up in bed blissfully unaware that the queue existed. "Can you assign another team?"

She shakes her head. "Will and Pinkie are far too busy with Sunta, and Tom and Ruby have six small campaigns on the go. If I can't get Natalia to relent on her principles, Madeline says she's going to ask for one of Harry's teams instead. I'll riot if he gets another top campaign, Freja, honestly I will. Please, you have to help me."

Helping a friend in need is what I do, but where Klein & Co is concerned, I daren't risk it. "Can't Ethan help? He's the creative managing partner after all."

"I don't want to keep asking Ethan to sort my problems out for me. I hate that people think I get special treatment as it is." She puts her head in her hands again, and I feel like crap because I want to help her more than I want to breathe. "I can't keep track of how fast we're expanding. Madeline Westgate is the fourth new account manager we've recruited this year and she's an absolute dragon. A Prada-wearing dragon. Or is it a devil? Anyway, she's got 'nightmarish corporate automaton' so nailed down that if there's ever a movie of her life, casting Meryl Streep to play her wouldn't be a stretch."

I start to relent. Violet's a great fixer of other people's problems, but she's hopeless with her own. She needs me. "Okay, do you want me to work my Freja-skills on Madeline or Natalia?"

She glances at her silver bangle-watch. "Neither. I have a meeting with Klein & Co in five minutes and I want you to come with me and help convince them I can make Natalia behave herself."

I close my eyes as my pulse skyrockets. I don't think I can do it. "I . . . I can't . . . I'm sorry, but I can't."

She looks desolate. "But it's just a meet-and-greet. If I have to convince Klein & Co that Natalia is our best art director, when I know she's really our best pain in the arse, I need your help. You know I'm utterly hopeless at lying, and you're the most persuasive person on the planet."

"I'm sorry, I can't. I'm just really busy right now."

"Urgent-busy or can-spare-a-minute-for-a-friend-busy?" The usual sparkle in her bright-blue eyes is dulled with suspicion as she locks onto me. "I don't think I'll be able to keep my mouth in check if Madeline goes all Cruella de Vil on me again. Please, it'll only take five minutes. Ten max."

Panic settles into my throat. I take a bottle of water from my desk drawer. "I can't. I'm sorry."

"There's something wrong, isn't there? What is it?"

I shake my head as I drink. "Nothing. I'll catch you later. Something urgent has cropped up about the Ice-Brite toothpaste ad and I need to talk to animation. You'll be fine with Madeline – just be firm and stick to your guns. Honestly, I've had disagreements with every single account manager I've ever worked with. It's par for the course. Our creative brains are wired differently to theirs."

"Okay." She stands up to leave, and I hate myself for lying to her even more than I hate myself for letting her down. I manage a smile, which she returns laced thick with cynicism. "I know you're not being straight with me, Freja."

"I'm sorry. I, um, really have something urgent I need—"

"It's fine." She opens the door, then reaches out and gives my arm a light squeeze. "We'll talk later."

# 3

*"I DON'T KNOW WHO I AM! Woooh-oooh-oooh."*

"I'll tell you who the fuck you are!" Violet yells at the top of her voice as the horrendous singing and guitar-playing of Derrick, my insufferable neighbour, invades my living room. "How the hell do you put up with him, Freja?"

I sigh wearily because I don't put up with him. I call environmental health most weekends, and I'd sail the Baltic Sea on the back of the Kraken if it meant I could get my old neighbour back. I miss Shirley. She moved in with her boyfriend four months ago, at the ripe old age of seventy-two, leaving me with current tenant-from-hell. Shirley was my kinda girl. She was a roadie for the Rolling Stones and flashed her tits at the Home Secretary during a feminist rally in the sixties. "I hate Derrick. And I hate that I hate him. Hating people is very bad for my *hygge*."

"Why does he have to be so whiney?" Georgie asks as Derrick continues to "woooh-oooh-oooh" from behind my wall. She curls her legs up on my sofa and sips at her wine. "I can't imagine Simon Cowell will be breaking his door down anytime soon."

"Oh my god, I hate those TV talent shows. They're so fake and voyeuristic," says Violet. She stretches out next to Georgie, and I giggle at her fluffy kitten slipper-socks. Talk about making yourself at home. Violet would choose a girls' night in over a girls' night out every time. "But I agree.

He's absolutely horrible. Don't tell me he's moved to London to make his fortune. He has all the talent of Max's cat's left bollock."

I laugh as I top up my glass. "According to Shirley, making his fortune in the music business is precisely why he's here."

"Oh god, really? He's like a modern-day Dick Whittington then." Georgie screws up her nose in disgust.

"Sounds like he's nailed the 'dick' part of that," adds Violet. She gets up off the sofa and heads to the kitchen.

"Well I for one am praying he does succeed," I shout after her.

"You're kidding?" says Georgie. "The only success that guy deserves is winning a one-way ticket back to wherever the hell up north he came from."

"No, I'm not kidding," I say honestly. "Think about it. If he became an overnight sensation, made millions of whiney records and sold out the O2 Arena, then he'd move out of Shirley's place and buy a mansion somewhere. In short, he'd be far away from me."

Violet returns from the kitchen with four jars of dips, a bottle of wine under each arm and a jumbo bag of paprika-flavoured nacho chips between her teeth. She offloads the snacks and drinks onto the coffee table. "Why does your rent-a-dickhead have to ruin our girls' night in?"

"He *is* ghastly, Frey," Georgie chimes in. "If he was better-looking and built like an African god, he'd remind me of my beautiful Didier. He was a terrible singer too."

I share a bewildered glance with Violet. I've been friends and workmates with Georgie for seven years, but I've never heard her mention that name before. "You dated a guy called Didier?"

Georgie nods, and her silky bobbed hair swishes around her jawline. "He was from the Côte d'Ivoire and he played three seasons of football for Paris Saint-Germain before being signed by Chelsea. He was gorgeous. Sadly, he was a terrible, horrible singer. And, much worse, he had zero interest in art. I tried to tolerate it, but can you honestly imagine me dating a guy who thinks Gustav Klimt was a racing driver?" She rolls her eyes and simultaneously flicks nacho crumbs off her frilly shirt. "I often think about Didier. His body looked like it was carved from marble, and his biceps were like hard, shiny chestnuts. He was so dark and delicious . . . even his cock was a masterpiece."

I almost choke on a nacho. "Good god, George. Why haven't I heard about this guy before? Please. Tell us more."

"Okay, but I can't be too graphic," she says, screwing up her nose. "Mitchell is away for four weeks and talking about Didier's manhood makes me hornier than a very lonely unicorn."

Violet bursts out laughing. "Oh my god, what? Wait. I have to programme my brain to remember this line for possible future use."

"Don't you dare turn my sex-starved state of mind into ad copy, Violet Archer," says Georgie. Her eyes lose focus and she sighs deeply. "I do miss Didier's cock though. It was magnificent."

I consider holding my tongue for all of five seconds before I give up. "Erm, Georgie. Are you trying to tell us Mitchell's cock *isn't* magnificent?"

Violet erupts into giggles. Georgie shoots me a glare. "If you must know, it's adequate. But . . . it's a little bit . . ."

"Jesus Christ, George, don't leave us hanging. I need to know how Mitchell is hanging." My eyes go wide as she makes a very worrying shape with her hand, indicating Mitchell's penis has problems I'm not at all sure I want to hear about.

Violet holds her sides and screeches with laughter into a cushion.

Georgie folds her arms. "If you're going to be crude, Frey, then I'm not telling you."

"You can't clam up now." Why am I not surprised that boring toboggan-obsessed Mitchell is hung like a circus sideshow?

Violet wipes streams of tears from her face. "Georgie, I don't think you should tell us. I'm worried we'll have to bleach our brains as well as our eardrums."

"It's not *that* bad," says Georgie.

"So spill," I say, passing a very tasty chilli dip over to her. "You've been with Mitchell for six years, so there must be something appealing about him, despite the weird-shaped thing that lives in his pants."

I catch a glint of hurt in Georgie's doe-like brown eyes and I check myself. Georgie and Mitchell are childhood friends who obviously care deeply about each other, but I've never been able to shake off the feeling that they're hopelessly mismatched. I love Georgie. She's one of my oldest, dearest friends. She's a sweet idealist, and a little bit ditzy, but she has the integrity of a high court judge. Mitchell, on the other hand, is so boring that if I ever got trapped up a mountain with him I'd rather eat my own head than endure the wait to be rescued.

"Maybe you shouldn't tell," Violet says sympathetically. This surprises me. Violet is worse than any of us for gossiping.

Georgie's pet lip appears and she sighs again. "I was only going to say his penis is a little bit bent. To the left."

"I'm surprised it doesn't bend to the right, given his questionable political views." Oh god. Someone tape my mouth shut.

She huffs out a breath. "I knew I shouldn't have said anything."

"Bent in what way? Broken-bent or kinky-bent?" asks Violet, crunching on a mouthful of nachos. "Because I shagged a guy with a bent dick once and I didn't mind at all. Maybe that was because I'd eat a banana over a courgette any day of the week."

"Banana? I wish," says Georgie, her eyes fully expressing her disappointment.

"George, I think Violet may be right for possibly the first time ever when it comes to gossip," I say. Violet gasps, then pauses for thought before nodding in agreement with me. "So unless you're finally ready to throw off your comfort blanket and find a boyfriend who's worthy of you, perhaps you shouldn't be sharing."

Georgie's body relaxes into the sofa as she takes a sip of wine. "I *am* getting tired of Mitchell," she says sadly. "I'm thirty-four years old. All of my sisters are married and have children. I don't want to be the family's spinster aunt, and I don't think

I'll ever want to marry Mitchell. But he's my friend and . . . well, he's always been there."

"He's always been up a mountain, George." Am I being unfair? Maybe I am. I just want her to realise she could have better. "If you can't see a future with Mitchell, then just keep him as your friend."

"You never have this trouble, do you, Frey?" she asks.

"No, because I don't do relationships. But you do, so please have one with the right guy."

Georgie places her glass on the coffee table. I move to top it up, but she places her hand over it. "No. I've had enough. I have to be up at five thirty for a conference tomorrow morning. It's in Wolverhampton. And you know how train travel confuses me."

Violet starts to laugh. "What part confuses you? The getting-on-the-train part, or the getting-off part?"

"If you must know, I really don't like sitting next to strange train people. And trying to navigate station timetables gives me a headache. Then there's the worry of whether I've got on the right train." She grimaces and adjusts the cushions behind her back. "Trains are just awfully stressful for me. That choo-choo thing they do lulls me to sleep. You must have heard about the time I woke up in Edinburgh when I should have been in York." She grimaces again as she tries to get comfortable, then she pulls something out from behind the cushions . . . Oh god, it's *that* parcel.

"Don't open that." The shame of my latest internet buy will be burned into my brain for eternity. Considering I work in advertising, you'd think I should have an understanding of how easy it is to flog utter crap to clueless people, but I don't. My home is where the most horrific of internet fashion horrors come to die.

Georgie pulls the teensy-tiny white bikini from the parcel. "Jesus Christ, Frey! Have you taken up lap dancing?"

Violet bolts upright, her eyes lit up in horror. "Or prostitution?"

"I bought it for Anaïs's birthday spa weekend, and I swear it looked nothing like that in the Facebook ad. Sadly, I've been duped again." This is only half true. The bikini looked awesome on the model in the ad, but there's no denying that it looked small – just nowhere near as small as it is in real life.

Georgie stands up and pulls the high-cut string bikini bottoms on over her jeans. "Freja, I love you and you're beautiful and have the figure of a very tall Greek goddess—"

"A Viking goddess," I correct her, but she's too busy pulling at the thin piece of cheap Lycra that is hugging her crotch to respond.

"I love you too much to allow you to wear these." Her dark-brown eyes are filled with worry and pleading. "If you cough, you're going to lose these bikini bottoms until your next smear. Think of the poor NHS, darling."

"Obviously, I'm not going to wear them," I manage to say before erupting into laughter.

Georgie bends her knees and stands with her feet wide apart, and the vagina-covering part of the bikini bottoms swings loose between her thighs.

"Oh my god. I've never seen – or worn – anything this offensive in my life."

"I'm a ginger, so imagine what those knickers look like on me." Both of their jaws drop. "Between waxes, my vagina would look like a squirrel's tail trapped under a twig."

Violet, in a fit of giggles, makes a grab for the bikini top. "No woman could have designed this thing." She pulls the halter-neck strap over her head, then she adjusts the shiny Lycra strip over her boobs and frowns. "Worrying about nip-slips is a given with swimwear, but no girl needs to worry about clit-slips."

"Whose lady garden is this small anyway?" Georgie asks as she tests out the knickers by contorting her body into even more strange shapes, just as Derrick's awful whiney singing starts up again.

"You have to help me to stop buying crap off Facebook, girls. My wardrobe is full of clothes I can't wear in public. Remember that snood I thought would be a great idea until it almost strangled me in a high wind?" I've already checked the returns procedure on the bikini. The part that isn't written in Chinese is deliberately confusing and convoluted, so I already know the eighty-pound monstrosity is headed for the bin rather than back to the woman-hating bastard who made it.

"Would stapling the bikini to your laptop stop you impulse shopping?" asks Violet, removing the top from around her neck.

"I honestly wouldn't mind if you did that." I pour myself another glass of wine as my neighbour cranks the volume even louder on his electric guitar.

The sound sets my teeth on edge. Why am I putting up with this? The weekend is one thing, but everyone needs sleep on a Monday night. Everyone other than the useless, jobless, Dickhead Whittington arsehole that lives next door. I shoot to my feet. "Right, I've had enough. That idiot isn't so much impinging on my *hygge* as driving a chainsaw right through it."

Before I know what I'm doing, I'm charging into my hallway and opening the front door.

"Wait!" Violet calls.

"What are you going to do?" shouts Georgie.

I'm not at all sure what I'm doing, or whether I'm sober enough to be doing it, but as I start hammering my fist on Derrick's front door, it seems I'm about to find out.

Seconds later, the music quietens down, the door swings open and I stare into the bloodshot, soulless eyes of my musically challenged neighbour. "Yeah?" he grunts, wafting the aroma of stale weed into the night air.

I try not to look at his hair, which is even greasier and dirtier than usual. "Any chance you can turn the noise down?"

He rests his back on the doorframe and glances at his watch. "It's only ten fifteen, so no."

At work, my powers of persuasion are legendary. If I'm ever up against a difficult client or demanding account manager, then I get under their skin, find out how they operate and convince them that I know what's best for them. But Derrick is different. He's immune to reason, devoid of compassion and lacks any level of human decency. "Look, I'm getting really tired of calling out environmental health every night. How about I call the police instead? Maybe they'll want to investigate whatever it is you get high on every night. Greenwich Borough Council will find it easier to bring charges against you if you have a criminal record."

He laughs, pulls an almost-new joint from behind his back and takes a long drag. "Marijuana's fine for personal use. Nobody cares, love."

"Love?" Red-hot anger swirls in my belly. "I'm not your fucking love, you greasy, talentless, self-centred pig!"

He looks over my head to my friends. "I think you better get her inside. She's had a few too many gins."

Georgie steps forward and links my arm. "We agree with her. You have no respect for other people with that awful singing. Can't you plug in headphones or something?"

Headphones? Jesus, she's not helping.

"Looks like you've got your knickers in a right twist there, Posh Spice." Derrick lowers his gaze. Oh crap. She's still wearing the bikini bottoms. She pulls them off and stuffs them into my hand.

"Posh Spice?" she says, placing her hands on her hips. "Is that all you've got?"

"Yeah, have you heard your stupid accent?" He turns to Violet and narrows his eyes. "So, we've got Posh and Ginger. Which one are you?"

"How about Tired-of-my-friend-having-to-put-up-with-dickheads Spice?" says Violet, straight off the cuff. I'm relieved, because I'm not sure Violet could name any of the Spice Girls. She's so completely oblivious to pop culture it's like she's been teleported from the Victorian times. "Why don't you do the world a favour and give yourself a laryngectomy?"

"A laryn-what?" Derrick asks, as his spaced-out body sways against the doorframe. "What's that?"

"I could show you with a scalpel and preferably no anaesthetic," she says. I mentally high-five her. She's like lightning with the comebacks tonight.

"Ooh, looks like we've got a live one – Smart-arse Spice," Derrick says with a scoffing laugh. "You need to loosen up, love. Chill out and enjoy the vibes."

"The vibes? Are you kidding me?" I can feel my blood pressure start to rise. "Why do you feel the need to force me to listen to your noise every bloody night?"

"At least it drowns out the noise coming from your bedroom."

"Excuse me?" If he's suggesting I snore, I'm going to knee him in the balls because I know I don't.

"You heard, love. Where's bearded lover-boy tonight? Have you given him the night off?" He takes another drag of his joint, and I resist the urge to smack it clean out of his hand. "I wouldn't be surprised if you'd worn the poor guy out. But you don't have to worry about that with me. I prefer my girls a lot less slutty."

What the hell? I take another step forward, determined that he isn't going to get the better of me. "That's funny, because you've lived next door a couple of months now and I haven't noticed a stream of women at your door. Understandable, given you're a talentless waster who doesn't know how to bathe or wash his hair." In the absence of hot molten lava to throw over his head, I swing my arm back and throw the bikini bottoms. Luckily, I throw with enough force that the cheap shiny Lycra whips his face and he yelps in shock. "This is your last warning. Shut the noise down, or I'll shut you down. When I get pushed to my limits, you have no idea what I'm capable of."

He laughs, but there's a hollow edge to his voice and a slight hint of apprehension in his eyes. Good. I've rattled him. "My music is my work, and you'll be singing another bloody tune when I make it big."

I give him my most condescending eye-roll. "Yeah, I won't hold my breath on that." I start to walk away. Violet and Georgie follow me. "You can keep the knickers. They probably fit you better than they fit us, you prickless loser."

# 4

ONCE WE'RE BACK INSIDE MY house, Georgie calls a taxi. "I'm sorry, girls. I really need an early night tonight if I'm to get through a day with Max tomorrow."

"How are you two getting on?" Max Wolf works in the agency's art department, as Georgie's senior designer. He's the most eccentric man I've ever met, but he's a very good friend of Violet's, so that makes him a good guy. It's just a shame that he irritates the life out of Georgie.

"Fine," she says with zero sincerity in her voice. Violet clears her throat. Obviously something is up. "What's he said to you?" asks Georgie, catching her awkward expression.

"Nothing," says Violet, although she's already given the game away – as usual. She's a hopeless liar. "Okay. He just feels overlooked and said he should have been chosen for the Klein & Co rebrand. You know what he's like. He's insecure in so many ways, but when it comes to his work he has the confidence of a charging bull."

My stomach sinks at the mention of that name again. *Klein*. Will it ever stop doing that?

Georgie shrugs. "Max *is* the best branding designer, but the client asked for me. I'll talk to him about it tomorrow and explain this wasn't down to me. For a client, Klein & Co are awfully demanding."

"Ethan said our newly knighted chairman of the board is *very* eager to impress Lord Klein," Violet says. "They frequent the same gentleman's club, apparently."

"Ah, that explains it," says Georgie, just as her phone pings. "That'll be my Uber." She opens the front door but doesn't stop talking. "Ethan told me Klein & Co demanded to see the CV of every department head and senior creative. They wanted to check over our credentials and select who they wanted to work with. They asked me to lead purely because I'm the studio head, but can you believe Stella is putting up with this?"

My stomach sinks further. Does this mean they have my CV? Oh fuck, it does, doesn't it? He'll know – they'll know. My head starts to swim. I can't think. Maybe they've forgotten . . .

"I do find that odd," says Violet. "I can't imagine anyone telling Stella Judd what to do – even if he's a multi-millionaire with a peerage."

Georgie gathers up her purse. "When Hexian Holidays demanded to recruit their own team, Stella went nuclear. I hope Klein & Co aren't getting their own way just because Sir Arthur smokes cigars and drinks cognac in a Mayfair club with Lord Klein every Friday night. If that's the case we'll definitely have a gigantic power struggle to look forward to somewhere down the line. What do you think, Freja?"

"Hmm?" My brain snaps slowly back into gear. They're both looking at me as if I've grown three heads. "Oh, um, I don't know. Maybe Stella is just preoccupied with our Asian expansion." I thought I could do this. Can I do this? God, I wish I could stop feeling so ridiculously helpless. Freja Larsen does *not* freak out. Ever.

Georgie's phone pings impatiently. She shares a totally obvious "what the fuck?" glance with Violet, then she says her goodbyes and heads for her taxi.

I close the door, return to the living room, and brace myself for the inevitable.

"What's the deal with you and Klein?"

My stomach stops sinking and starts to churn. Usually, I'm a fan of getting straight to the point, but not when the point involves my innermost secret feelings. We both sit on the sofa. I pull my feet up and wrap my arms around my knees. And then I cringe at how defensive I must look. "It's nothing really . . ." I sound pathetic. And I can tell by the way Violet is looking at me that she isn't going to give up.

"Ethan said you had a run-in with Madeline Westgate earlier."

"You talked about that?" I hug my knees tighter. Violet usually does everything she can to deter us from assuming she and Ethan have work-related pillow-talk. "She wanted my help on something, but I was too busy, so she thought coming at me with a crappy attitude was appropriate. Needless to say, it wasn't."

"He said you snapped at her for no reason."

I think back to this afternoon's meeting and cringe. Madeline has only been with us a week, but she's ruffled everyone's feathers already. She's blunt, forthright, outspoken and knows how to stand up for herself. Usually that's a combination of personality traits I admire. I like confident and I like honest, but when she insisted – and persisted – in asking me for help in putting together a TV advertising bid for BuzzPay, I did snap at her. Not a brilliant move when the absolute last thing you want to do is draw attention to yourself.

"Everyone can have a bad day, Violet. Even me." I give her half a smile, but the pleat in her brow tells me she isn't buying my excuse. "Look, I had a fight with Harry first thing, then I had to practically pull Rachel and Jadine apart on the studio floor, and . . . well, you had a run-in with Madeline too, so you know what she's like. You even called her Cruella de Vil."

"That's different. I don't get on with people." She reaches for a half-full glass of wine, then thinks better of it. Crap. If Violet is refusing drink, she's in the most serious of serious modes. "But you always get on with everybody. So, I'll ask again. What's going on? You're not yourself. When I asked you to help me with Klein & Co this afternoon, you were *really* weird."

The game is up. Violet may be one of my more socially challenged friends, but she's also one of my smartest. It's been eight years. I haven't told anybody the whole truth of what happened in Los Angeles. My ex, Richie, who was just my roommate back then, knows some of it – but not all. I couldn't tell him everything. It's always been easier to lock it all away in a cast-iron cage inside my brain. Before I forced myself to forget, I let it tear me apart. But I've always known the cage would unlock one day. I needed time for the pain to numb. I needed years. Are eight years enough?

"Remember I told you that we all have that one guy?" I say. "The one who we can never forget?"

Violet nods. "You said you loved someone, but you let others take him away from you. Is that what this is about?"

"Yes and no," I say truthfully. She moves closer to me, resting an arm on the back of the sofa. "We only knew each other for two weeks. It's ridiculous really. How can you fall in love with someone you've only known for two weeks?"

She reaches for my hand and smiles. "Of course it isn't ridiculous. That just means he meant the world to you."

"He was more than my world." The words leave my mouth before I have a chance to decide if I want to say them. "I've never felt that way about anybody before. Not Per, or Richie, or Harry. Definitely not Harry. Men have come and gone in my life since him, but he's always been with me. He's like a beautiful, painful ache."

Violet's bright-blue eyes glisten with sadness. "How did it end with him?"

"I'm not even sure anymore. I was a student in California with high hopes of becoming an actress. And I was good. *Really* good." I smile as I think back to the girl I was. I used to serve pancakes in a diner every morning, study film production at UCLA most days, and attend every single audition my agent could find for me. "My American dream was just a dream. All I ever thought about was glamorous film roles, celebrity parties and dates with hot Hollywood actors. I shared a house in Santa Monica that had a view of the pier and the funfair. I wasn't looking for him, but suddenly he was there and my life was . . ." Red-hot tears prick at my eyes as a rush of anger soars through my veins, making the muscles of my neck ache. This is what I was afraid of. If I let this thing out – this monster – what will happen? I inhale a sharp, shaky breath as Violet's grip on my hand tightens. "They say you never know how much somebody means to you until they're gone, but I knew. I knew right from the start."

"So what happened? Didn't he feel the same way?"

What do I say? I can't tell her everything. Maybe if I tell her part of the truth, she'll still be able to understand. "He loved me, but I had to give him up. I had no choice. He lived in London and was only visiting California. He said he'd come back, but he didn't. I hoped he'd find a way, even though I knew it'd be practically impossible. And then I heard he had a new girlfriend and was living in China—"

"China?" Violet gasps as her brain quickly catches up with my words. "Wait a minute. Are you talking about Nate Klein as in Klein & Co?" I nod and watch her jaw drop. "Oh my god, Freja, he's . . . Shit, he's like totally gorgeous. And rich. Really, really rich. And famous. Me and Ethan have watched every episode of his reality show. He's so funny and . . . bloody hell, I can't believe you haven't said anything before now."

"Like I said, it was a long time ago."

The glint of excitement in her eyes dims. "You're not telling me everything, are you?"

"When did you get to be so perceptive?"

"Since you became my friend and I learned from you."

I reach over to the coffee table and fill up a glass with wine, wishing I had something stronger. "Nate was Richie's best friend from uni, and he came to LA on business. We met, fell in love, and everything was going great until his father decided I wasn't good enough for him." I close my eyes as a swirl of nausea twists my gut. I wish I could tell her everything, but I can't. Not yet and maybe not ever. "He was controlling and he was cruel and I hated him. I let him come between us, and I wish with everything I have that I'd been able to fight him off, but I couldn't."

Violet's face blanches. "I knew it. I guessed he was an awful man right from the start. The newspaper column he writes is vile. Only the *Sunday Herald* would put out his brand of poison, which says everything anyone needs to know about him and his shitty newspaper."

"I've never read it."

"Well, you've missed out on immersing yourself in everything that is wrong with Britain. That rag has a reading age of six and a half, helped by the fact their writers wouldn't know the truth if it jumped out of a bush, knocked them to the ground and kicked their lying teeth out. All of their journalists have the integrity of rattlesnakes." Her body shudders as a look of disgust washes over her face. "I just knew he'd be horrible."

"This is why I couldn't go to your meeting this morning. I'm sorry for not being straight with you."

She waves away my apology. "I understand, but Lord Klein wasn't there. Ethan says his ermine-covered carcass spends every hour on the golf course these days. Either that or grabbing power in the House of Lords. To think that cretin helps make our country's laws."

"I just don't want anything to do with him, and I certainly didn't want him to know I worked for

Tribe, so when you said he asked for all our CVs..."

Violet's eyes grow wide. "Oh shit."

"Precisely." The full horror of my predicament registers in Violet's expression. "I'm so sorry you have to work with him."

"Hopefully our paths won't cross," says Violet. She yawns and checks her watch. "Claire Hill, his marketing person, is lovely."

"You should be thinking about getting home. It'll take you the best part of an hour to get to Kilburn at this time of night. Unless you want to brave the Tube."

She shakes her head. "I might crash here again actually. I'll text Ethan to bring a change of clothes from my drawer to work."

"You still haven't evolved your drawer into a full wardrobe, then?"

"Are you kidding?" She rolls her eyes and I try not to laugh. "He says there's no space, and he's right, but will he move out of Soho? Like hell. Renting somewhere just a square foot bigger in the same postcode would cost my entire year's salary. And unless we find a few spare millions lying around we can forget buying. Honestly, Freja, if he thinks I'm moving into his teensy-tiny cupboard when we get married, he's in for a huge shock."

I start to get up, but she makes a grab for my arm. "Where do you think you're going?"

"To make up the spare bed."

"You can do that when we've finished talking."

I sit back down on the sofa, my back sinking into the cushions. "There's nothing left to say, Violet. Help me avoid Lord Klein, and I can get through this."

"What about Nate?" she asks eagerly. "Would you want to see him again?"

My heart balloons in my chest. "Sometimes I think there's nobody in the world I'd want to see more, and for that reason, I shouldn't. That's part of the reason I lost it with Madeline this afternoon. I can stay under the radar with Klein & Co, but Nate is BuzzPay's CEO. If she wins the bid they'll want TV work, and I don't know what I'm going to do if that happens." I bite my lip as my brain whirrs with possibilities. "This has totally knocked me off my game, and the fact that it bothers me so much is *really* bothering me. I don't like feeling afraid."

She rests her hand on my arm and gives it a squeeze. "Hey, look at me." Her beautiful china-doll face is tense, showing just how much she cares. Violet is messy and conflicted and totally, adorably unsure of herself. She'd be the first to say she needs me, but if I told her how much I needed her, she wouldn't believe me. "We'll get through this together. I'll ask Ethan to help."

I shake my head. "No, I don't want Ethan to know. Violet, you have to promise me not to pillow-talk about this with him."

"I promise," she says quickly. A flash of hurt lands in her eyes. "I'd never tell him unless you wanted me to, but he's best placed to make sure yours and Klein's paths don't cross. And if we get BuzzPay, he can see to it you don't have to see Nate."

I consider the implications of this for a moment. As film production director I'm responsible for every TV commercial the agency produces. Nothing leaves the film studio without my approval. It wouldn't be right or professional to abdicate my responsibilities to somebody else. "No, Violet. I need to get some perspective. My career is the most important thing in my life, and all that other stuff happened years ago. If we get the chance to do a BuzzPay commercial, it's going to come with a huge budget. It'll be much bigger than JET Financial or Sunta even. How would it look if I passed the production of the agency's most prestigious TV ad onto someone else?"

"And if you have to be in the same room with Nate?"

My stomach does another horrible flip-flop. *Min Gud*, I hate my stomach so much right now. "It's been eight years. He's probably moved on a long time ago, and I have to do the same. He probably won't even remember me."

"How could anybody forget you?" she says with a smile that lands a turquoise glint in her eyes.

I smile back. I hope he remembers. I hope he still feels something. And I hate myself for it.

I leave her to make up the spare bed while she heads for the bathroom. For somebody who would describe herself as definitely not a people person, Violet spends a lot of time sleeping over at my house.

# 5

"HEY, FREJA. JUST THE PERSON I wanted to see."

Lennox Jackson's shiny shoes tap loudly against the tiled lobby floor as he practically jogs to catch up with me.

"What can I do for you, Lennox?" I take a sip of my triple espresso but don't slow down my pace. It's already eight and I have a full schedule today. I'm also still pissed off with him for going over my head with Jadine and JET Financial.

"I wanted to talk to you about a couple of things. First and foremost, I wanted to apologise about overstepping with Jadine Clark. I should have come to you first."

I keep walking. "Yes you should, but the time to apologise to me for that was two days ago."

"Better late than never. You know me, Freja. My priority is getting my clients what they want."

"Even if they ask for Spam dressed up as steak?"

He laughs lightly. "Yes, even then."

I reach the top of the stairwell, stop walking and turn to face him. His black eyes look up to meet mine and I spot a flash of apprehension. Lennox, one of our senior account managers, was snatched from Barrett McAllen Gray, along with over half of Tribe's current staff complement. He's an ambitious Londoner with a solid work ethic and a very large wardrobe of impressive designer suits. He's always confident, assertive and charming, but this morning he's definitely a little bit twitchy. "You want something."

He smiles broadly, making his neat beard rise up around his dimpled cheeks. "Freja, did I ever tell you you're my absolute favourite production team member?"

"Yes, you told me that the last time you wanted something."

He sinks his hands into his pockets and gives me a guilty smile accompanied by a deep belly laugh. "Sounds like I'm bang to rights."

"You are, so spill. My espresso isn't going to drink itself."

His dark-brown skin shines with a light blue tint from the bright lights in the stairwell, making it suddenly appear as if he's glowing with confidence. "I need you to help me present a bid for BuzzPay. My source at BMG tells me they're making a revenge move to snatch them out from under our noses. I'm not going to let that happen, but nearly all the execs are in Seoul and I need to act quick. Ridley Gates, BMG's attack dog, has already fixed a meeting with Nate Klein. If we win BuzzPay, there's going to be a shit-ton of TV ads coming your way, so will you help me?"

My brain, heart, body and soul are screaming "No", and not just because of Nate. Madeline asked me to help her do the exact same thing two days ago. With our top execs in the Far East, it seems nobody is keeping an eye on the accounts team. The last thing the agency needs is a turf war. "Have you asked anybody else for help?"

"No," he says quickly. "You're the best, so I'm

coming to you first."

"You don't think you should run this past Ethan? He's the only managing partner in the country at the moment, so he's the guy in charge."

He shakes his head, but looks awkward. "I like Ethan. I've worked with him for years. He was a great art director, but . . ." I raise my eyebrows, and Lennox responds with an almost audible swallow, his Adam's apple bobbing against the stiff collar of his sage-green shirt. "Ethan is a creative and he's just a kid. He's not a salesman. Stella likes him, and that's fine, but I was in this game while he was still at school. I've worked my backside off to get where I am, without the luxury of a fancy degree. I'm a grafter. I know how to sell and I work damn hard for my clients. I need to act fast on this, so I need to know if you're with me."

"No, I'm not," I say plainly. Lennox straightens his back and his glow fades to dull. "I'm sorry, Lennox, but I'm one deal you're not going to close today. Get your plan sanctioned by Ethan, or remotely by Phillip or Daniel, and then we can talk again."

He narrows his eyes in frustration. "I'm a senior account manager. I don't need Ethan Fraser's approval."

"That may be so, but two days ago I had this exact same conversation with Madeline Westgate, so if you're not talking to your teammates and you're not talking to your bosses, then you probably need to check in with somebody even higher up the food chain."

Lennox's face develops tense lines. "Sounds like Madeline needs an introduction to the way things run around here."

And off he goes, leaving me with my lukewarm coffee and the feeling I'm going to have a rotten week.

* * *

Churchill House's cafeteria officially serves the worst coffee in the whole of London. I know this because Euan, my sound guy, conducted a building-wide survey and posted the results on TripAdvisor, which prompted a war between the building's facilities manager, David Amory, and Tribe's HR department over whether Stella could fire him for it. David eventually backed down, but point blank refused to replace his shitty coffee. Which is why I'm thoroughly miserable and massively regretting not having the foresight to pick up some lunch from Pret this morning. My chicken salad sub tastes like rubber sandwiched between cardboard on a bed of toilet paper.

"Is this seat taken?"

Madeline Westgate's light-brown eyes smile down at me as she pulls up a chair. Clearly she wasn't waiting for me to answer. She rips the cellophane off a tub of creamy pasta salad and stirs the contents around with her fork.

"I'm afraid this place isn't exactly the Ritz."

She pulls her fork out of the tub and we both watch as watery creamy liquid drips back into the bowl, leaving a congealed clot of yellow mush behind it. "Ugh, this is like some horrific mix of pasta and pease pudding," she says in her strong north-eastern accent.

"Pease pudding?" I ask, wondering if she's talking about food or using a euphemism for something gross.

"It's a..." She stops abruptly, her thick eyelashes flicking upwards to reveal puzzled eyes. "You know, I have no idea what it is. I ate it all the time when I was a kid. At a guess, I'd say it was mushed-up peas."

"Ah." I don't have a clue what she's talking about, but I'm imagining something squishy and yellow.

She pushes the pasta tub to the other side of the table and opens a bottle of mineral water. "I wanted to apologise for the other day. I didn't make the best first impression."

I'm an expert at reading people, but Madeline evades me. When we had a run-in two days ago, I didn't observe any changes in her expression or body language that gave me an indication of who she is. And today is the same. Her voice is even and balanced, her eyes are warm and focused, and her temperament is cucumber-cool. "Let's start from scratch then," I say, offering my hand. "I'm Freja. I'm passionate about my job, I love old movies, cocktails, Denmark and coffee, but I'm not so passionate about the state of the food in this place."

She shakes my hand. "Hi, Freja, I'm Madeline." She smiles and her cheeks dimple. "I'm passionate about my job too. I love kick-boxing, rock music, Newcastle... oh, and I also love coffee. *That* coffee, however..." She screws up her nose and points at my drink. "I tried it last week and vowed never to touch it again. You've worked in this building since forever. Why do you keep torturing yourself?"

Madeline's smile reaches her eyes, but I'm still unsure of her. When we first met, she was blunt and demanding, with a demeanour reminiscent of the great Stella Judd's. I don't mind people who have sharp edges. I don't find them intimidating because at least you always know where you stand. But there's just something about Madeline's manner that doesn't quite sit right. It's as if she's consciously presenting an image of a person she wants to be, as opposed to the person she is. It feels as though I'm trying to connect her dots, but they aren't numbered right. "I keep hoping the coffee will get better one day."

"You're an optimist then," she says.

"Definitely. And what are you?"

Our eyes meet for a moment, but it doesn't take long for her to break the connection. Interesting. My question was a simple one, but that's the first time I've seen her confidence wobble. It seems she doesn't like to talk about herself.

"Lennox said you told him I was preparing to bid for BuzzPay's advertising." She folds her arms, elbows resting on the table, and her change in tone, from warm to cool, slices through the air between us. Is this the real Madeline? Was I right the first time after all?

"Yes, I did tell him that." I push my sub to one side and remind myself not to eat here again for probably the seventy-sixth time today.

"I got the jump on everyone, including BMG, but now they'll know I'm coming and that's down to you." Her plump blood-red pout thins to an angry line. "Why are you screwing with my career?"

"Excuse me?" I can barely believe what I'm hearing.

"Look, Freja, when I said I loved my job, I wasn't exaggerating. This job is my life. I've been in sales since I was sixteen. I was with Bright Star Advertising for seven years, where I managed Toyota and Sky TV. I know how to close a deal. I want this business. I need to win this contract." She tucks a strand of bobbed platinum hair behind her ear and her steely glare intensifies. "What I don't need is people interfering in the way I do things."

"The fact that without knowing the first thing about me you assumed I wanted to hurt your career says far more about you than me."

And there it is. She breaks focus again – just for a moment – but I notice it. "I was basing my assumption on you snapping at me when I asked for your help two days ago. Everyone talks so highly of you around here. 'Freja Larsen gets things done', 'Freja Larsen is the best TV ad director in the city', 'Freja Larsen is everyone's friend'. I was looking forward to working with you, but so far I'm disappointed."

Oh god, she makes Violet look like a professor of people-pleasing. "Well, like I said, Madeline, your reactions say more about you than me. I wasn't aware your BuzzPay bid was confidential, and I told both you and Lennox that I wasn't going to help until you got your plans green-lighted from above."

I pick my half-drunk coffee and half-eaten sub off the table and toss them both in the bin.

"I did get my plan green-lighted. Ethan okayed my going after BuzzPay because Lord Klein is my client already and he's more than satisfied with me and my work. Have you any idea how important the Kleins are?" She stands up and her fierce eyes connect with mine again. "The partners are looking for major investors to fund our global expansion ambitions. With both Kleins, father and son, on board, they'll be our star client. Lord Klein and Sir Arthur have already started talking about a possible investment deal."

My irritation with Madeline evaporates. Investment deal? Why did this have to happen? Why now? Since when was I scared of my future? Hell, I never even used to think about my future. I could leave. I have contacts all over the city. I could get a new position tomorrow if I wanted one. My brain races with dozens of possible escape routes, but then I feel my heart start to crack. I don't want to leave. I have friends. This place is my home and I'm happy.

Madeline's expression changes as I struggle to regain my composure. Her steel bends and is replaced with uncertainty. "What is it?" she asks in a much softer tone.

I quickly pull myself together. "Nothing." I take a couple of steps away from the table. "I need to get back to work. I'll talk to Ethan."

She doesn't answer me. I can feel her eyes boring into me as I walk away.

\* \* \*

I bump into Ethan on the way back to my office. "Thanks for letting me in on your investment plans," I say with a horrid bite in my tone. Ugh, this isn't good. This isn't Ethan's fault.

He does an about-turn in the middle of the lobby. "Um, what investment plans?"

I rub my brow and mentally kick my own ass. "I'm sorry. I've just . . ."

"Bad day?" he asks.

"Bad week."

He leans forward and lowers his voice. "Don't worry, we all get them. This may be the first time Freja Larsen is experiencing the metaphorical equivalent of a kick in the bawbag, but her boss has one weekly. At least fifty times a year."

I laugh. "So what happens during the other two weeks?"

"I'm on holiday somewhere hot," he says, nudging my shoulder affectionately. "Don't get me wrong, shit is probably still happening to me, but I'm drinking so much beer I won't notice a thing."

I can always count on Ethan to throw me a little sparkle when I need it. He's the best boss I've ever had in every way that counts. "That sounds like a holiday I'd like to go on."

"And you'd be more than welcome, but let's get back to where we started. What investment plans are you talking about?"

I nervously chew on my bottom lip, wishing I'd been chewing on it two minutes ago instead of blasting my insecurity out of the bag. "I have some history with a client."

"Ah. Roger that." He gives me a funny little salute.

"I like how you're automatically assuming what you're assuming," I say as we walk through the lobby doors and into the stairwell.

"C'mon, Freja. You're like a female version of

six-months-ago me, but even more fun-loving and impulsive."

"Don't let Violet hear you say that," I say with mock outrage. "You guys have been together almost a year."

"A year already?" There's a glint of mischief in his lively blue eyes. "It seems like only yesterday."

We stand at the top of the stairs. I'm not sure how much I should tell him, but when he cocks his head to the side and gives me a knowing smile, I remember he's my friend, as well as my boss, and I trust him. "This goes no further than you, me and Violet—"

"If Violet knows this must be girl-zone stuff," he says with raised eyebrows.

"It is, and yes, you can be an honorary girl. And yes, you're both sworn to secrecy, okay?"

He nods. "Okay."

I take a deep breath and brace myself for his reaction. "When I lived in the States, I had a relationship with Nate Klein."

His eyes almost pop out of his head. "Wow, he's hot. Nice one, Freja."

"Ethan, be a boss!" I say with a measure of frustration. I usually adore his playful side, but now isn't the time.

"I'm sorry." He clears his throat and switches up to serious-mode. "I'm guessing things didn't end well."

"No, they didn't." I'm far from being a closed book and I don't embarrass easily, but I hate the fact I'm having to brief my boss on the one relationship in my life that totally floored me. "Madeline told me that Stella is trying to get Lord

Klein to invest in Tribe's expansion."

"Yeah, that's right. Sir Arthur has been in serious talks with him for several weeks now. They're both Etonians with some kind of 'old boys' thing going on. I'm fucked if I understand posh people's behaviour, but apparently it's good for business."

"*For søren!*" I drop my gaze to the floor and kick the stairs' glass balustrade. And I don't care that I look deranged.

"Freja, if you're swearing in Danish, then I'm worried. Tell me what you need me to do."

Boiling-hot waves of anger charge through my body, making me lightheaded. He has my CV. He knows I work here. He's doing it again. "This is what Lord Klein does, Ethan. You can't let that man have a piece of this agency."

His face blanches. "Why not?"

"He controls people. He'll stop at nothing to get what he wants, and if anybody stands in his way then he'll hurt them." Ethan's eyes fill with terror, but there's just enough suspicion in his expression to crinkle his brow and make his neck flush. I'm not surprised. I must sound like I should be living in a padded cell.

"Can you tell me what he did?" he asks cautiously.

I shake my head. "If Klein's going to be an investor, I can't work here anymore." Saying the words out loud makes my voice tremble.

"Jesus. It's that bad?" I nod and he exhales a heavy, anxious breath. "There's nothing I can do to stop the deal." He runs his hand through his hair. "Unless he's committed a crime."

I close my eyes and try to breathe my rage out of my body. "I wouldn't be able to prove what he did."

"Okay. If you're telling me he's a bad guy, then of course I believe you, but he's due to seal the deal with Sir Arthur this afternoon. The other senior partners are arriving in the next hour to complete, and Stella's asked me to be her proxy as she's tied up in Seoul." He holds his hands up. "I don't know if I can stop this."

Two of my producers, Neil and Zain, barge through the double doors leading from the lobby, filling the small space with their loud chatter. I lose my train of thought. They say hi, then they hold the doors open for a young woman I don't recognise, who's carrying a huge box full of files. "Can I give you a hand?" asks Neil, pushing in front of Zain to get to the door first.

The pretty, warm-skinned woman smiles sweetly at Neil, then tells him she's fine and heads up the stairs. If I wasn't feeling sick to my stomach, I'd enjoy a scene with this many romantic possibilities.

Still holding the door wide open, Neil declares that the young woman, an accounts junior called Sophie, is "into him" and my romantic dreams evaporate. I hear Zain start to tease him over his unfounded claim, but their voices turn to white noise when I notice the group that has just arrived in our lobby.

A group of ten, maybe a dozen, men and women. And him.

He mostly looks the same: slight build, grey hair, olive skin, wiry beard. His eyes sweep over his surroundings as his people swarm busily around him. Then I feel his eyes on me. We're yards away from each other, but I can see him. He can see me.

And then the doors close between us. Neil and Zain continue bickering playfully as they walk past me and descend the stairs to the studio. Ethan is talking to me, I think, but the white noise in my head is louder than ever and I can't hear him. He grips my arm for a moment; he says he has to go. I want to ask him to stay, but it feels like something has crawled down my throat and died. I give him a smile instead. Then, I watch him walk away from me, back through the double doors. I snap my eyes shut because I don't want to see *him* again.

And I don't want this to happen. Again.

*Please no. Please not now. Not after all this time.*

I stumble to the stairwell, blood pounding in my ears and my chest feeling like it's being crushed under the weight of a tombstone. The stairs below me blur into the glass balustrade and I can't . . . fuck, I can't even walk down the stairs. I need my office. I need safety. I need to hide. Could I reach the toilets?

I put one foot in front of the other as my heart continues to thud. I take off my heels and almost drop to the floor trying to pick them up. Damn my stupid brain. Damn my ridiculous life. Most of all damn him.

I clatter through the door and head straight for a cubicle. I throw down my shoes, lock the door and practically fall on top of the toilet seat. Gripping both sides of the cubicle walls, I bow my head and try to remember how I used to get through these attacks eight years ago.

I want to cry out as my heart heaves through my

ribcage. My skin is hot. My head, my chest, the tops of my legs – every part of me is burning up. My stomach is churning with dread and my bare feet tingle as if they're being pricked with tiny needles.

Terror rises in my throat as I struggle for air. It feels like I'm drowning. What if I can't breathe anymore? What if I just die here? My lungs frantically grapple for oxygen. This is just like before. I've locked this all away for almost a decade, but now it's back. Angry tears stream down my face as the unfairness of it all sinks into my bones.

I don't want to go back under the sea. I don't want to be her again.

I hunch over and wrap my arms around my knees, turning my face to the side. I close my eyes and I start to swim. I pull everything back inside the iron cage, then I lock the door.

My lungs inhale one sharp painful breath after another. Slowly. Softly. I pick my feet up off the floor and tuck my head between my knees. Then I wait in silence for it to pass.

# 6

I HAD MY FIRST PANIC attack when I was twelve, shortly after my mother left us to live with her new boyfriend in Spain. It took years of expensive therapy sessions to learn how to keep my feelings under control and lock down the panic before it had a chance to consume me. Then years later, when Nate left, I started having them again. Anything could trigger an attack: a call about a movie audition, a taxi ride past the Beverly Wilshire hotel where he stayed, the Santa Monica Pier where we had a date. I learned to avoid so many things that reminded me of him. I stopped acting. I stopped dating. I retreated into myself for months. I couldn't afford therapy. I could barely afford a trip to the doctor when I lived in California. So, the feelings of worthlessness and uselessness crept into my brain and stayed there until I learned, just like when I was a kid, to shut them out. And it worked. No more anxiety, no more nightmares and no more sadness. Well, it worked until two days ago.

The shame crept back under my skin silently and purposefully. I'm ashamed of feeling afraid and I'm as annoyed as hell for even considering running away. This isn't me. I am not weak and I am not timid. I don't want to be the person I was, and I don't do "what ifs", but what if my past escapes from the dungeon I've locked it up in and brings all of those thoughts and feelings back? I know it's always been there. Lurking and waiting. Pushing it away was always a short-term fix.

Yesterday, I had a much better day. I had dinner with non-work friends, and we talked and drank into the night, the ghost of my memories drifting away on a cloud of alcohol and laughter. For the first time in months I felt like myself, and I let my stubborn determination take control once more. If I decide the past is dead, then it's dead, right? It's up to me. I have the power to control this.

This morning I put my resolve to the test. Ethan came to my office to tell me I was expected to attend an impromptu drinks gathering to celebrate Klein & Co's investment in Tribe. I immediately felt the panic rise up from my belly, but I took a deep breath and shut out the fact my heart was hammering in my chest and my pulse was thudding in my ears. I crushed the feelings before my brain had a chance to let them settle. I refused to let fear seep into my veins and rot my life from the inside out. I told him I could do it.

I can't expect Ethan and Violet to understand that this is more than just me not wanting to be in the same room as a former lover's father. I haven't told them everything. I wouldn't be surprised if they think I'm silly for avoiding somebody they view as a dusty old man who lives on the golf course when he's not postulating to rows of other dusty old posh people in the House of Lords.

So here I am, in Heron Tower's private club, mingling with the top executives of Klein & Co and their subsidiary companies. Lord Klein isn't here. After this morning's presentation, he flew out to his home in Spain for a golfing weekend. As Tribe's PR manager, Anaïs is hosting the swish evening, together with Klein's large team of executives, advisors and equity partners. I listen to the ambient music, wishing it was edgier, funkier and a hell of a lot louder. I also wish there was a dance floor. I may be in my thirties, but I'm in absolutely no hurry to be an adult.

I'm drinking my sixth dry martini of the evening when Violet and Georgie's attempts to outdo each other with complaints about their team members really start to irritate me. I know they're only making small talk, but the alcohol in my blood is driving my negativity tolerance level lower than a snake's belly. To make matters far worse, they both have nothing to complain about. I'd swap Jadine Clark for Violet's art director, Natalia, and Georgie's designer, Max, in a hummingbird's heartbeat.

"It's Frank who I feel sorry for, the poor bloke." Violet rests her elbows on the table of our extremely comfortable corner nook, heaving a genuine sigh of pity. "He's my most gifted copywriter. He can pluck the most beautiful words out of thin air at a moment's notice. He's sweet and gentle and has the soul of a poet." Georgie nods her head as Violet gushes about Frank, who is a quiet man best described as "nice". "Frank has four little boys, you know. All of them are under seven, so you can imagine how much sleep he gets each night. I honestly don't know how he functions most days. Then, on top of all that, he has to work with Rasputin."

"Violet," I say admonishingly. "You shouldn't call her that."

The ridge between Violet's eyebrows crumples. "I know, but I just can't warm to her. She's so self-important, she doesn't have a clue how to work in a team. Today, she spent almost four hours in the brainstorming area, refusing to talk to anybody. I gave Frank permission to take a long lunch. Creative teams work together, not on their own."

"At least you managed to persuade her to co-operate with Klein & Co," says Georgie. She rests her hand on Violet's arm. "I commend her for sticking to her principles, and Klein's column on veganism was deliberately inflammatory, but still . . . she works for an advertising agency, not the RSPCA. We operate by the rules of capitalism, so she really can't afford to have such an inflexible moral code."

Violet takes a huge gulp of her wine. She's drinking red, which means she'll be completely out of her skull by the time she finishes her fourth glass. "Her surrender was Madeline's doing." She glances in the direction of the enigmatic blonde standing at the entrance to the garden terrace, commanding the attention of Klein's executive team. She must be warm-blooded, because it's a rather icy night and her red sheath dress is thin and sleeveless. "Don't get me wrong, she's clearly a gigantic pain in the arse, but over the last few days I've been pleased to have her in my corner. She frightened the living daylights out of Natalia last Tuesday."

I look over to the group and watch Madeline talk animatedly. Kenneth Ives, one of Tribe's silent senior partners, and Patrick Grainger, a big-time capital investor, laugh along with her conversation. She looks at ease, but there's still something about the way she's standing, a glass of red wine hugged close to her chest, that intrigues me. I want to know her story. I want to know why she's abrupt and standoffish with her colleagues, yet the epitome of charm with her clients. "What did she say to Natalia?"

"It wasn't so much what she said as how she said it." Violet sounds impressed, which is intriguing considering she wanted to kill Madeline earlier in the week.

"As in . . . ?" I ask.

Violet finishes her wine. "As in, she threatened to win contracts with Aberdeen Angus Steakhouse *and* Sellafield nuclear power plant, then force Natalia to work on their accounts."

Georgie gasps, then she starts to giggle. "Oh my god, she didn't."

"You know, as funny as that is, you should have Natalia's back," I say. Violet looks up and hurt flashes in her eyes. I can't believe how puritanical I just sounded. My twenty-year-old self wants to jump into a Tardis, seek me out, and choke the life back into me. "I'm sorry, Violet. I don't want to be a bore, but Natalia is on your team and Madeline isn't."

As Violet sits back, her small waist is almost enveloped by two plump cushions. "Okay, I take your point, but let me ask you this – would you have Jadine's back?"

"It would be hard," I say honestly. "But in this scenario, if she was up against it with Madeline? Then yeah, I think I would."

"I wouldn't have Max's back." Georgie grits her teeth as she twirls her straw between her fingers. "I'm sorry, Violet. I know he's your best friend, but he called me a champagne socialist yesterday, in front of the whole department, and I'm bloody sick of him."

"Just threaten him with a pay cut," says Violet, with a smile that doesn't quite flush the disappointment from her eyes. Crap, I've really upset her. I know I must have come across as judgemental, but I can't help it. People need to be able to count on their boss. We share an uneasy moment of silence.

"How was the Klein & Co presentation this morning?" Georgie asks.

Violet sucks in her cheeks. "Not great." Her eyes shift nervously between me and Georgie.

"Why? What happened?" asks Georgie, a look of pure dread sweeping across her face. "Please don't say they're unhappy with my designs, sweetie. I've put in fifteen-hour days all week so I can finish their ad sets on time. Ethan should never have agreed to such a tight schedule."

She runs her fingers down the stem of her empty wine glass. "No, it's just . . . um . . ."

"Spit it out," Georgie says. Violet gives me another worrying look. I start praying. Georgie doesn't cope well with criticism. She's been known to launch Twitter tirades against anonymous members of the public if they dare to hate her art.

"It isn't that he doesn't like your designs." There's a hint of appeasement in Violet's voice that would have made Chamberlain proud. "They just want a couple of changes – well, around a dozen specific changes, but I know Claire, their marketing director, loves what you've done, so it isn't her. It's just *him*."

"Who?" asks Georgie. My stomach feels like it

drops through my pelvis when I catch the regret in Violet's eyes. I know who she's talking about.

"I'm sorry – both of you. I wasn't going to say anything tonight, but you were totally right about him, Freja." A glass collector approaches our table. I quickly down the last of my martini and he leaves with our three empty glasses. "Lord Klein is a pig. He spoke to me like I was shit today, questioning my qualifications and belittling my experience. He looked at me like he'd just scraped me off the sole of his shoe. He's just horrible. I can't wait until I'm done with his campaign, and I am really pissed with Ethan for letting a man like that invest money in Tribe."

My blood feels like ice. And so it starts. Despite my best efforts to keep this thing buried, it just won't stay in the cage. "I thought we, I mean *you*, wouldn't have to see him."

"He's a client," says Georgie, completely in the dark about our previous conversation. "And an investor. Why wouldn't she see him?"

"Ethan said he was semi-retired and had very little to do with his businesses." Violet glances over to the group surrounding Madeline, which has grown to include the senior execs from Klein & Co who she's been working with. "Kevin Conroy is really great," she says, her eyes fixed on the CEO of KTech, Lord Klein's flagship IT company, who appears to be deep in conversation with Madeline. "He's bright, engaging and hot too – in a squeaky-clean kind of way."

"I wonder if Madeline knows he's married." Georgie narrows her eyes suspiciously as Madeline leads Kevin onto the lantern-lit garden terrace with views across the entire city.

Violet coughs. "Sorry. I was about to say something highly amusing, but also highly disparaging."

Georgie laughs. "So what's stopping you?"

"I don't know whose side I'm supposed to be on," she says, no doubt contemplating whether or not I'll scold her again.

My twenty-year-old self rolls her eyes at me. I deflect the conversation. "Kevin seems nice."

"He is, except he's got a hard-nosed, capitalist-poster-boy vibe," she says, adequately describing Lord Klein's second-in-command. "He communicates solely in incomprehensible business-speak too, which is annoying, and I think he must have sold his soul to the devil – literally – to get where he is at such a young age."

"By 'the devil' I suppose you mean Lord Klein?" says Georgie. She roots through her handbag, produces a crumpled twenty pound note and shuffles out of the nook. "I'll get the next round."

As soon as we're alone, I turn to Violet and lower my voice. "Please be careful with Klein."

Her face blanches. "I will. I can't tell you how much I hope I'm done with him already. This morning was really unpleasant. He speaks to Claire, his marketing director, like shit too. He's probably the same with all women. And I didn't want to tell Georgie this, but he hates her designs. Like, *really* hates them. He says the web interface she and digital worked on looks like it's been put together by a primary-school kid with access to Microsoft Paint."

"Hey, Freja, you got a minute?"

Harry Hopkins suddenly appears behind my left shoulder, one arm draped across the back of the nook. I feel like swatting him. "That depends how long your minute is."

He nudges my arm. "Won't take long."

He looks over to Violet, and they share a smile as fake as a three pound note. I mouth "I'll be back" to her and follow him into the private lounge.

"What can I do for you?" An alcohol-infused buzz spreads across my skin as I stand. I feel my cheeks flush, and I wonder how much money I'd have to give the snooty club receptionist to swap the classical mood-music for the Ministry of Sound's Friday-night playlist.

"You know our agreement?" His tone is different. His usual tease has been replaced by a shaky discomfort. Please don't let him try to renegotiate our agreement. For over two years, the terms and conditions have been perfectly clear: no dates, no sleepovers, no strings and definitely no mess.

"Yes, I may be familiar with it."

He shoves his hands into his jeans pockets. "I've met someone."

Wow. I wasn't expecting that. His sapphire-blue eyes sparkle and a smile lights up his face.

"I'm happy for you, Harry."

"You are?" He takes his hands out of his pockets and folds his arms across his hard chest.

"Of course I am. Why wouldn't I be? When did you meet her?"

"Um, last year . . . sometime last year."

What the hell? I swear to god, if he's been two-timing I'll kill him. "Harry, please tell me you haven't been having a relationship with someone you care about whilst also fulfilling your part in our agreement. Please tell me you haven't made me the kind of woman that women hate."

"No," he says unconvincingly. I shoot him a death glare and his eyes become infused with guilt. "Okay, okay. There may have been some overlap. But I wanted to be sure with her."

Oh for fuck's sake. "How long ago did you break our agreement without telling me?"

"I didn't break it," he protests. "I met Melissa a year ago, but we've only been dating since Christmas."

He's unbelievable. "So the answer is three and a half months." I try not to raise my voice, but I fail. "Why on earth didn't you say something to me sooner? For crying out loud, you wanted me to have a threesome with you and Lola only last weekend."

His beard twitches. "Can you keep your voice down?"

"No, I can't! I'm too busy concentrating on stopping myself from ripping your tongue from your throat."

He takes a step back and holds his hands up. "You sure this is about how long I've been seeing Melissa, and not—"

"If you want to live past tomorrow, don't finish that sentence."

He sniggers. "I'm not a complete galah, Freja. It's obvious you're jealous."

He's such an idiot. And I don't have the energy for this. "Okay, Harry, you got me. Nail hit squarely on the head."

His smile briefly returns before fading just as

quickly. "So you're not bothered I'm ending our agreement?"

"Why would I be?"

"You know that means no more sex, right?"

As if he was my only option. "I think I'll survive."

He tucks his hands in his pockets again and waltzes off, and not for the first, or third, or fiftieth time this week, I wonder why I ever entered into that "agreement" with him in the first place. No-strings sex was the draw, but you can only have so much of that before you work out Ann Summers' best battery-operated products deliver far more satisfying results.

I go back to the nook in the corner of the club to find Violet and Georgie deep in conversation about Klein & Co's biggest rumour. Yeah, I really need to be wondering whether Lord Klein is the father of his executive advisor's two children. "I've heard the boy doesn't look like him," Violet says in a hushed tone. Georgie's eyes widen at the intrigue. "But the girl is his double. Same grey eyes and olive skin." As if I want to hear this. I drink a huge gulp of martini, then I head off to the toilets, hoping they'll be finished gossiping by the time I return.

On my way back to the lounge, my body sways slightly as I try to balance on my delicate Francesco Russo heels. These are definitely not the best shoes to wear whilst teetering between level three (slurring) and level four (toppling over) on the getting-pissed scale I created when I was seventeen. I wonder if I'll make it to level five (semi-conscious) tonight? I'm just about to head back to the bar and give it my best effort when Violet appears in front of me looking like she's been in a fight with the Grim Reaper. And lost.

"Oh god, you look dreadful. What the hell has happened now?"

Her crystal-blue eyes dull. "He's here."

"Who?"

It hits me the second the word leaves my lips. A whirl of dread knots inside me as I quickly connect the "he" with her freaked-out expression. I thought he was in Spain . . . I thought I wouldn't see him. I need to leave. Adrenalin catapults me into action. I can't remember where the exit is. Fuck. It's at the other side of the club. Is there a fire exit? I turn back to Violet, ready to plead for her help, when my eyes meet his.

And the world stops turning.

Because I'm not looking into the cold grey stare of the man who ruined my life. I'm looking into the warm dark eyes of the man who broke my heart eight years ago. I've superglued the pieces back together since then, but as I stand frozen before him, his gaze locked on me and his chest rising and falling at the speed of a galloping racehorse, I feel my heart start to crack again. The pressure pulls the fragments apart, pain swelling inside my torso as I try to remember how to breathe.

He's surrounded by people, his gaze briefly flicking to Kevin Conroy, then to Madeline, both of whom are vying for his attention, but then his eyes reconnect with mine and he looks as if he's mentally pinching himself. He rubs at his neck, and his jaw tenses, popping a vein at the side of his head.

*Hvad tanker du på? What are you thinking?*

The years have been kind to him. He must be close to forty now, but his olive skin still looks just as warm and soft, and his brown hair is still highlighted with flecks of natural gold. The shock slowly fades away from his face. His jaw relaxes, and a smile – that old familiar smile composed entirely of sunshine – lights up his eyes and sends shockwaves of confusing energy rippling through me.

When Ethan approaches the group, shaking Nate's hand then striking up an animated conversation which draws his attention away from me for a second time, I immediately want it back. The pain in my chest evolves into the familiar burn of panic. I force my eyes shut, and it's all I can do to concentrate on staying upright.

I feel Violet's hand on my arm. I hear her ask if I'm okay. I nod. For a second I worry that I'll completely humiliate myself by crashing to the floor, but then I find my equilibrium and do the thing I've always done. I swallow my heart, my pain, my fear, my memories – everything that hurts – back inside me. I let it sit, locked in the cage in my brain along with the certainty that I'm still her and it did happen.

I haven't been dealing with any of it for the past eight years at all; it's been dealing with me. And if now is the time to unlock the cage door, I know I won't be able to stop it.

# 7

"DO YOU WANT TO LEAVE?"

Do I? I don't know anymore.

He's gone now. Probably mingling with his father's execs in another part of the club. The space where he stood, and the bar behind, are deserted now. I can hear the soft drumming sound of distant chatter, interspersed with occasional bouts of loud laughter, coming from the garden terrace. That'll be where he is. He was always the centre of things. People were always drawn to him.

Violet touches my arm. "Freja, I'm getting a bit worried . . ."

I force a smile onto my face and cover her hand with mine. "I think I'm feeling okay. And I'm amazed that I'm okay."

"Oh my god, he is so hot. Like steaming hot." Georgie appears from the lounge, playfully wafting the air in front of her face. "How is he far hotter in real life than on TV? He's so tall and tanned . . ." Her eyes sweep over us and she instantly drops her swoon. "What's going on?"

I take Georgie's arm and walk to a secluded corner between the lounge and reception. "Remember I told you about that one guy I fell in love with years back? The one who was different to all the other guys?"

She nods. "The heartbreak guy?" I answer her with my eyes and watch as realisation slowly spreads across her face, ending with a jaw-drop so big I can practically see her tonsils. "You mean . . ."

"Yes. And I didn't know he'd be here tonight and I haven't seen him for years and—"

"You're totally blown away by how hot he still is?"

Georgie's excited words cut through me. "Something like that." Crap, I *am* blown away by him, aren't I? After all these years. I let happier memories tumble into my brain: corndogs and Pepsi cola on Santa Monica Pier, hot steamy nights in the Beverly Wiltshire hotel, stargazing at the Griffith Observatory. Los Angeles became all about him, and when he left me behind I hated everything that existed in the city, including myself.

"If we're talking about being blown away," says Violet, resting her back against the wall, "did you see the look on his face when he saw you?"

"He didn't know I worked for Tribe and that I'd be here, did he?" I'm pleased I didn't imagine the way he looked at me. He looked lost and found all at the same time.

"No chance of it," Violet says, her eyes sparkling eagerly. "You knocked the air out of him."

I feel a flicker of hope somewhere inside me. "I hope that's a good thing."

"Doesn't matter, so long as it's a thing." Violet absently fiddles with her sapphire engagement ring. The stone catches the light and twinkles. "If you're still doing that to a guy after all these years then the flame hasn't died."

I'm definitely in the wrong company right now. Georgie has always been a gushy romantic, and Violet, who is usually the world's biggest cynic, has been flying the flag for all things hearts-and-flowers ever since Ethan popped the question.

"Are you going to talk to him?" Georgie casts a quick glance around the club. We can only see the empty bar area from where we're standing. "I could go get him—"

"No!" My heart leaps at how loudly I shouted that, but Jesus Christ, is she trying to kill me? "No, just get me a drink."

"Water?" she asks, and I wonder if she might be going mad. "You look like you need a huge glass of iced water, sweetie. If you sober up a bit, you can talk to him tonight and be in with a shot of remembering the conversation tomorrow."

"Are you kidding me?" I rub the back of my neck; my muscles are tense through either drink or stress. "I have never needed a strong drink more than I need one right now. Please don't give me water, Georgie."

She clacks her tongue disapprovingly, which sends very unwelcome memories of my mother spiralling through my brain. "Okay, I'll get you a double shot of something, but don't blame me if you do something stupid because of it."

After Georgie returns with the drinks, we all sit down in the lounge bar on a large grey corner sofa lined with cushions in lime and aubergine. There's a small billiards table behind us, and a glass coffee table strewn with artsy hardback books in front of us. I haven't been in The Heron before, but its residents' club is gorgeous. And it reminds me of Nate: classy, cool and smooth with state-of-the-art design, yet an undeniable softness making me want to stay here forever.

"So, how rat-arsed will you have to get before you realise you're only putting off the inevitable?"

asks Violet. She's twiddling her ring again. This means she's subconsciously spreading the love. Do I really have to tell her that her ridiculously expensive Tiffany engagement ring does not possess superpowers? I honestly wouldn't be surprised at this point if she started to call it "my precious".

"I'm not putting anything off, because there's nothing to put off."

"It does seem like you're working up some courage, sweetie," says Georgie.

I shake my head. "No, I just don't know what to do. This is weird. I *think* I'm freaking out, but I'm also feeling pretty good. I've been dreading this for months, but seeing him again hasn't killed me." I take a huge gulp of something fruity, purple and strangely medicinal. Christ, what has Georgie bought me? Vodka and vermouth mixed with my Aunt Alberte's homemade cough syrup?

Violet laughs softly. "If you're freaking out, then I'm in awe of how calmly you freak out. If it were me, well, I've been known to overthink things and make a scene."

"This I know." I recall all the Violet-shaped problems I've helped fix since we met, with certainty there'll be many more to come. "But don't be fooled by my exterior." I take a sip of my drink while I try to make some sense of how I'm feeling. But this doesn't feel like me. I shouldn't be sitting here thinking. I should be walking onto that terrace like I own it, pulling Nate to one side and demanding he tell me why he cut me off all those years ago. I'm the person everyone comes to for advice because I know how people tick. I'm also not afraid of anything. So what the hell am I doing sitting here overthinking the "could haves" and "should haves" whilst numbing my ridiculous emotions with alcohol?

"Why don't you go over and ask him why he's here?" Georgie asks tentatively.

"Because it's obvious why he's here. This is his dad's work celebration do."

Violet takes her iPhone out of her bag. "I know!" she says with a little jump that splashes wine onto her black linen skirt. "I'll text Ethan and tell him to think of an excuse to send Nate over."

"No. Just no." I snatch her phone out of her hand. "A round of text messages about the love of my life is the last thing I need."

They both fall silent.

A tall man in a suit the same colour as Nate's strides past us towards the toilets. Clearly we all thought it was him. I inhale a huge lungful of air and force my heart back into my chest. "Ugh, it's no good, I can't deal with this. I need the bathroom."

Georgie moves her legs to the side, allowing me to sidestep the coffee table, but I misjudge the distance, wobble on my heels and collide with the billiards table, knocking three balls and a cue to the floor with an almighty clatter. Shit and hell! Talk about drawing attention to myself. I bend down to try to pick them up, but of course I miss, topple over and land on my ass. I think I just passed level four on the getting-pissed scale. This is great news because that means I have level five, aka semi-unconsciousness, firmly in my sights. Violet and Georgie rush to my side and help me to my feet.

"I'll take you home," says Violet. "I hate work

dos anyway. I'll text Ethan and tell him I'm staying over at yours again."

I grab onto her shoulder as the walls start to melt around me. "You don't have to."

Georgie retrieves my bag from a potted palm. "I'll come too. You need a lovely glass of water and a good night's sleep."

"Don't start with the water again, George. Please. I haven't needed a mother since I was twelve, and I don't need one now." I run my hand through my hair and – ew – find a sticky clump of something horrible at the base of my ponytail. I pull as hard as I can, then I screech because the whatever-it-is decides it isn't coming loose without ripping a million hairs out of my head in the process. "Oh shit. Oh yack . . ." I try again, gritting my teeth and squeezing my eyes shut, until the gooey matted object finally falls into my hand. "Oh my god, it's a tumour!"

Georgie clamps her hand over her mouth. "I'm going to be sick."

I drop the reddish-pink gelatinous blob, wrapped up in orange hair, onto the carpet. "What the hell is it?"

Violet prods it with the toe of her shoe. "It could be anything, but I don't think it's alive."

"What? Why the hell would it be alive?" Is she seriously being serious?

"Let's retrace our steps," Georgie says in a poor attempt to take charge of the terrifying situation. "Where have you been?"

"You know where I've been. Here."

Violet prods it again. "It could be poop."

I almost gag as I'm reminded of my smelly

neighbour's filthy greasy hair and perma-stained underwear. "Pink poop? Done by what, a freaking unicorn? As far as I'm aware, I haven't been in any situation tonight that would have enabled an animal to shit on my head."

"It looks like a skinned bollock," says Georgie unhelpfully.

I run my fingers through my long hair again to check it's all gone. "Ugh, it's all gummy. It feels like someone's jizzed in it." Could I have had a good time in the toilet earlier and forgotten all about it? Have I drunk that much? I summon the courage to sniff my hand. "Smells like drink . . . Oh, wait a minute." I reach down, but my head-spin almost throws me to the ground again. I grab the nearest thing I can find – Georgie's hip – and lower myself onto my hands and knees. I prod the tumour with my finger. "Ah-ha," I say triumphantly, slowly peeling my hair from the blob. "Two morello cherries stuck together with a slice of passion fruit. I picked it out of my drink and it must have got tangled in my hair."

"Your hair gets everywhere," says Violet, pulling a strand of copper off her flouncy black skirt.

"At least it's not a bollock, darling," says Georgie.

"Or unicorn shit," I add, but my attention is diverted as a familiar face enters the room. It takes me a moment to place him. Bright blue eyes, a dusting of freckles, smart suit. I can't work out if he's pleased to see me or terrified. "Sam?" I ask, wondering why on earth I hadn't realised Nate's brother, the CEO of Klein's whisky export company, might be here too.

"Freja Larsen?" I can tell by the slight tremor in his voice that he's only pretending to be surprised to see me. He extends his hand, which I shake whilst scanning his face for clues.

"So, um, how've you been?" I pinch myself. Yes, Freja, you're really standing here making small talk with Nate Klein's little brother. While rat-arsed. With your hair matted in sticky, fruity clumps.

"Great. You?" I don't think I had one conversation with Sam back in LA. He was the highly dependable, yet extremely forgettable, second son. I feel bad for not noticing anything about him aside from the fact he existed.

"Well, as you can see, I've had a career change." Violet and Georgie pick up on the scene and head back to the sofa. I want to join them. Not just because this is hellish awkward, but also because the earth is spinning off its axis.

"Yeah, I guess you work for Tribe then. What do you do exactly?"

He knows what I do, and every inch of his body – from slumped shoulders to twitching hands – tells me he knew I'd be here. His father requested to look over every director's CV, including mine. "I think you know what I do already, Sam, so can we just cut the bullshit and get to the part where you say what you want to say?"

Sam's blue eyes dart around the still-empty room behind us. "Look, I swear this is the truth; we didn't know you worked here until after we signed the advertising contract with Tribe. Dad and Sir Arthur are friends and—"

"Would it have made a difference?"

He tilts his head. "Honestly? I think it might."

I wasn't expecting him to say that. My stomach whirls, making me feel even more nauseous than I do already. He's telling the truth. Or at least he believes what he's telling me is true. If his father had known I worked for Tribe before signing with them, it's likely he'd have jumped at a chance to fuck up my life. But he wouldn't have wanted to risk me seeing Nate again. "Maybe you didn't know before signing the advertising contract, but you did know before making the investment. What does Klein & Co know about the advertising business anyway?"

He pauses for far too long. "As I said, Dad and Sir Arthur have become good friends, and we've made lots of investments in non-tech businesses over the years."

The room-spin picks up speed, so I rest my back against the nearest wall. "Did either of you think to tell Nate? Because he almost fell through the floor half an hour ago."

"So I heard." Sam stares at his feet. The fluffy purple carpet has almost swallowed up his shiny black shoes. "Dad said there'd be no need to make a fuss. You're part of our past. Nate moved on a long time ago."

My insides slump at the certainty in his voice. I've been deluding myself. He said he'd never forget me, but of course he did. My eyes become glassy, and I'm grateful that I'm too drunk to fully feel the sharp sting of humiliation. "So how do you want to proceed? This isn't the first time your father has thrown money into a business connected to me.

I'd be happy having absolutely nothing to do with your family, but unfortunately I'm head of film production, so keeping out of everybody's way isn't going to be possible."

"No, I guess not," says Sam, his wide face flushing various shades of pink. He doesn't look much like Nate. Or his father. He is fairer, stockier, and has light blue eyes instead of dark. The one thing he does share with Nate is a twitching, anxious jaw. "Freja, I know how this looks, but it isn't how it was with your movie. Everything we've done with Tribe, the advertising contract *and* the investment, has been purely a business move."

"Because I'm old news, right?"

He nods in agreement. Then he takes a step closer and lowers his voice. "I just wanted to say . . . well, I guess Dad wanted me to say, that Nate has moved on. He's finally happy and settled, and we don't need anything, or anybody, upsetting the apple cart. Nate has been living between London, Hong Kong and Shanghai for eight years, but he's back for good now. This is where he lives," he says, gesturing to the space around us. "He has a penthouse suite here and he's a member of this club. He's made a name for himself on TV, which has been great for business as well as for him." His eyes flick to his feet again. "Everything that happened in LA needs to stay there."

The club's cushioned brown wall tiles melt into my back, and it's all I can do to stop myself sliding down them. How are the walls slippery? I should lie down before I pass out. I should keep my mouth shut before I say something catastrophic. I should go home. I "should" do a number of smart things, but all the things I "shouldn't" have done take up arms inside my head instead. *I shouldn't have let it happen. I shouldn't have let him go. I shouldn't have shut this all up for so damned long . . .*

"How about you tell your father he can kiss my ass?"

"Look, Freja, I know what you're thinking—"

"No, Sam, you don't. You don't know anything. You don't know anything about me, and I'm not so sure you know Nate either."

"Oh please," he says, folding his arms. "You knew him for a couple of weeks almost a decade ago. He's my brother."

All of a sudden, I rush through level four-point-five on my getting-pissed scale, which means I start yelling at the top of my voice whilst not giving a fuck who can hear. "And *you* know how he feels, do you? You know everything about me? About us?"

"I'll tell you what I know." Confrontation isn't Sam's style, I can tell. His flushed skin is mottled and he looks like he could fill a bathtub with sweat. "I know he barely spoke to me, or Dad, or the rest of the family for years. I know you broke him."

My throat contracts. I almost choke on air. Not once did I ever imagine that Nate would be suffering in the same way I was. All these years I've hated him for not fighting for me. Was he hating me for the same reason? I feel an uncontrollable urge to run onto the terrace and blurt out everything, but most of all I want to tell him I'm sorry. Why didn't he tell me? Why did he cut me off?

"He's fine now." Sam's tone becomes more reassuring, but it fails to take the edge off my shock.

"He threw himself into his work, and he had Evelyn for a while, then he slowly came back to us."

Evelyn. I forgot about Evelyn. She was introduced as Nate's friend back in LA, but her name was later joined with his in the *Time*s Forthcoming Marriages section. That was the weekend I binge-drank my way through Georgie's thirtieth birthday celebrations, fell down her stairs and ended up in A&E with a broken wrist and a golf-ball-sized bump on my head. "I was surprised to hear about Evelyn."

"He was surprised to hear about Richie."

I rack my brain, trying to remember who came first. Did I hook up with his best friend before he hooked up with her? "Is that why he cut Rich off? Because of me?"

Sam doesn't answer my question, but the dullness in his eyes and the ever-present jaw twitch speak volumes. Of course it was. "I just think you should know that Nate has been through a ton of really bad stuff, but he's happy now. He's slogged his guts out to make BuzzPay Europe's most used online payment system, he's part of a TV show he loves, and he has Lucy."

Please let Lucy be his dog. Like, *please*. I will sell my soul to the hordes of hell and happily give up my place in Valhalla if Lucy is his dog. I mentally cross fingers, toes, teeth and every moveable body part I possess. "Who's Lucy?"

"Lucy Tonner, his girlfriend."

My brain screams *Fuck!* Double fuck. I know her name. "Lucy Tonner? As in *General Practice* actress Lucy Tonner?"

"Yes, that's her."

"The same crap BBC2 drama Richie acts in?" Christ, this is so messed up. And I think I'm going to hurl.

He nods his head and joins the dots of my thought process. "Nate and Richie got back in touch a year ago. Nate and Lu get on really well with Richie and his wife, so—"

"So you really are warning me off?" My eyes fill with angry tears just as the spinning room makes me stumble into the wall again. Gravity is such a bitch when you're hammered. One minute it's keeping you from flying off into the sky, the next it's dragging you to the ground. And who the fuck calls themselves "Lu"? Is she a toilet?

"You don't look okay. Shall I get someone?" He glances over to where Georgie and Violet are sitting.

"Don't worry, I haven't reached level five yet."

"Level five?"

"Never mind." I push myself off the wall with my palms, kick off my heels and head for the toilets. "Just let my friends know I'm puking in here."

# 8

MADELINE CLOSED BUZZPAY ON TUESDAY.

Somehow I knew it was going to happen, even though Nate knows I work for Tribe and our paths are bound to cross. Maybe this was just the direction my life was headed. Or maybe the universe has decided my time is up. For the last two days it's felt as though a boa constrictor is slowly strangling me to death from the inside out. I haven't been sleeping properly, I've been living off cupboard food, and my skin is so dry I want to work from my bathtub. Didn't Cleopatra used to bathe in milk? Hmm, that sounds like a great idea. Maybe the pressures of Mark Antony returning from an eight-year-long battle with the Gauls made her feel exactly the same way I'm feeling.

Last week Sam Klein's words seared into my brain, scorching to ashes the tiny fragment of hope that I didn't even realise I was hanging on to. But as the days have gone on, I've realised that working with Nate mightn't be such a bad thing. If we can get on professionally, it could bring closure. I could move on. Finally. He's always been my "one", but letting go of him is long overdue. I have a job that I love, I have a support network of great friends and, best of all, I have myself – and I feel like I'm the person I was always meant to be. I cringe at my own cheesy thoughts. I didn't "find myself"; I "created myself". I'm who I want to be and who I should be, and I love my life.

The signing of BuzzPay has made our entire agency "buzz" with excitement. And it's all because of him. Nate's reality TV show, which I've deliberately avoided, broadcasts late on a Wednesday night. I didn't know it, but he had already acquired a cult following in our agency, never mind the world at large. From what Twitter tells me, women of a certain age are drawn to his good looks and undeniable charm, while guys admire his drive, success and no-nonsense attitude. I don't think I'll ever get used to how other people see him. To me he's always going to be the sweet, funny guy with the sad past who gave me the most beautiful two weeks of my life.

My colleagues' reaction to Nate surpassing Jared Taft to become our biggest, hottest and most famous client has been intriguing. Earlier this week, Rachel and Jadine put their differences to one side to pore over all the Nate and Lucy content in *OK* magazine. I found them huddled together in the break room, flicking through page after page of inane gossip and glossy photographs. For at least a day and a half, they bonded over their mutual dislike of her. Trashy-soap-opera-loving Rachel told me *General Practice* has gone downhill ever since she joined the cast, while ex-model Jadine, who knows Lucy personally, says she's dull and wears ballet pumps out of season. The fashion faux-pas seems to be the far worse fault in Jadine's eyes. Thankfully Georgie brought something else to my attention. Whilst *OK*'s sycophantic journalist gushed praise over Nate and Lucy's mutual good looks and B-list celebrity status, a writer for *Femail Online* cited a "source" who said they've broken up three times already due to his work schedule and her high-maintenance demands. For reasons I don't wish to contemplate, the *Femail* article made my soul jump for joy, but Violet reminded me that gossip magazines are, without exception, a steaming pile of untrustworthy vapid junk. You can always count on Violet to bring a huge dollop of reality to a story your jealous green soul desperately wants to be true.

I switch off my non-work-related thoughts and switch on my business brain. Who could I delegate BuzzPay's million-pound advertising contract to? Zain Haddad, my senior film producer, is the most obvious choice, but he's due to go on paternity leave in two months and has a heavy workload to get through before that. Rachel is far too busy with JET Financial. Jadine is a great big fat "nowhere near qualified". This leaves Neil Dawson, Violet's former protégé who moved from art direction to film producing at the beginning of the year. I like Neil. He's whip-smart, imaginative and buys me exotic caffeinated beverages whenever he wants to share one of his always amazing concepts with me. Best of all, he has an enormous heart and I trust him. I open up my email to schedule a meeting between Neil and Violet's creative team when I hear a knock at my door.

"Come in," I call without looking up from my computer screen.

The door opens with its usual creak, but the loud, excited background noise that follows is unexpected. My head snaps up, then it feels like all the air is sucked out of the room as Nate walks into my office. He closes the door behind him, then slowly turns around to face me.

I try to catch my breath. He appears to do the same. Hot, sexy memories of Nate's hard, naked body flash inside my brain. My thighs throb and my cheeks burn as I imagine locking my office door, helping him out of his suit and . . . fuck, this is bad. I have no doubt that I'd have sex with him here and now if he made a move.

"I, um, thought I should come . . . I . . ." His eyes leave mine and dart around the room. For a second I worry that I might have something in here I don't want him to see, like a dartboard with a photograph of his dad's face attached to it. Thank heavens I didn't follow through on that daydream. "It's a bit yellow in here."

What an odd thing to notice. "Um, yeah, I like yellow." I glance at the row of collectable plastic figures on my shelf, suddenly realising that maybe my office does look a bit crazy. "I can't even remember how the Minion thing started. Maybe it's because they're obsessed with bananas." Crap. Why did I have to mention bananas? They're the rudest, most sexually explicit of fruit. I want to die.

"Well at least it brightens up your underground office. You must never see the sun."

"Yeah," I say with a laugh. "I was definitely last in the queue when Tribe were assigning rooms with a view. My team call it the dungeons down here." I watch his cheek twitch the way I remember it always did when he was nervous, then his hands dip into the pockets of his light-grey expensive-looking suit and he stares at the floor. He looks terrified. "You've been working on coming to see me for the past week, haven't you?" I ask him.

Recognition lights up his dark-brown eyes and he smiles. "I forgot how well you read people." My ovaries flutter because even though some things have faded over the years, his sunshine smile never left my memory. Sunshine? I wonder if my yellow thing started subconsciously because it reminded me of his smile.

I sit back in my chair and let his presence invade my senses. There's a lot that's different about him. His shoulders seem broader, his body stronger, and he seems more polished. Is this what success has done to him? Back in LA he wore fitted shirts, turned-up jeans and deck shoes, but now he's the living embodiment of accomplishment, standing tall in a suit which looks like it could be a Tom Ford, or even a Brioni. But all the things I loved about him are still there: his perfectly styled hair with the flecks of gold, his warm tanned olive skin and, of course, his smile. The important things are just as I remember.

He sits down opposite me. He's still finding it difficult to make eye contact, which is strange given how confident and successful I know he is. "So, I don't really know where to begin."

I tilt my head to one side, following his gaze until it finally meets mine. "You could start with 'hi'."

He smiles again; this time it reaches his beautiful chocolate-brown eyes and stays there. "I'm sorry. This is all a bit strange. I never expected I'd see you again." His voice trails off and catches, making my heart jump. He clears his throat again.

"Me neither."

"How long have you lived in London?"

"Seven years."

He looks surprised, but I don't know why. His brother said he'd reconnected with Richie recently. Hasn't he talked about me?

"Do you still act?"

I shake my head. "No, I finished my film production studies at UCLA, then I answered a few job ads for film crew around the world, and ultimately found myself here. It could have been anywhere though."

His smile grows wider, the corner of his mouth curling into a cute kink. My pelvis goes all fluttery again. "Still as spontaneous as ever?"

I laugh. "Well, I was back then. Now that I have a mortgage to pay and a whole department to run, my need to adult suppresses my spontaneity and glues my feet firmly to the ground."

"I hoped you'd make it in Hollywood one day, but you've done really well in advertising. Do you regret ending up here?" There's a grain of sadness in his voice. Does he have regrets about his life? My mind races with questions I want to ask him.

"No, I don't regret anything. Every decision I've made has been exactly what I wanted at the time. I love my job and I love London."

"Then I'm really pleased for you." He's still smiling, but the sadness that was in his voice has spread to his eyes.

"What about you?"

He swallows hard. "Huh?"

"Any regrets?"

"Not with my career," he says, which obviously leaves me to assume he has personal-life regrets. Shit, this is torture. I'm torturing myself. Even if he has personal-life regrets, that doesn't mean they're connected to me. "I broke out on my own like I always wanted. KTech was mine. I launched the company in Shanghai on that little piece of tech I bought from your friend Aaron back in LA. KTech is part of Klein & Co's portfolio of companies now. I sold it to Dad for capital to start up BuzzPay."

"And now BuzzPay is a Klein & Co company too."

He laughs softly. "Yeah, that came about when I needed more capital. The TV show is all me though."

I mentally hold my tongue by physically chewing my lip. He wants to break away from his father's control, whilst still using him to bankroll his business projects? That's so infuriatingly typical of their relationship.

"I know what you're thinking," he says, scanning my face. "Truth is, Dad and I never really got back on track after . . . well, after you. There have been a few times we've come close to rebuilding what we had, usually where our business paths have crossed, but splitting with Evelyn was the final nail in our coffin." He pauses and his eyes lock onto me for a moment. Does he want me to ask him about Evelyn – the woman his father said was Chanel, while I was Walmart? "I couldn't go through with it in the end."

I'm confused. "You couldn't go through with what?"

"Don't you know? Sorry, I assumed you knew, but why would you? I *may* have jilted Evelyn on our wedding day, after her father spent two hundred grand to host it at the Landmark Mandarin in Hong

Kong. If you remember, Sir Cuthbert is my dad's oldest friend and business partner. He's also my godfather. And he's also never forgiven me."

Holy crap. And here's me worried about tackling the fact I ended up rebounding with his best friend. "Don't tell me you left Evelyn standing at the altar?"

He nods, a pink tinge of shame warming his cheeks. "I felt like I was drowning. I loved her, but I couldn't love her in the way she needed. I've known her all my life, but she's like a sister. She wasn't the one."

My heart starts to race. No, scrub that – my heart starts to rocket into space. "I'm sorry to hear that."

He brushes off my apology with a wave of his hand. "No need. The relationship was a shitshow from beginning to end, and it was all my fault. I should never have rushed . . ." His voice gets lost in his memory. Is he stopping himself from revealing too much? "I'm guessing it was the same thing with you and Richie. What happened there?"

"Richie didn't tell you?"

He shakes his head. "I didn't ask him."

"Oh. Why not?"

The skin of his neck reddens. "We've only seen each other a couple of times since LA. He works with Lucy, my girlfriend. His wife, Alyssa, seems really nice. I hear they're expecting their first child."

"Are they?" I ask, trying to recall the last time we spoke and deciding it must be far too long ago. "That's great news. I must give him a call to congratulate him."

"So you're still on good terms with Rich?"

"We're on okay terms. It's a bit hard to remain on good terms with your ex-boyfriend after you've caught him screwing another woman in his Volkswagen Golf." I laugh at the memory. Of course, it's ugly and horrific in so many ways, but finding Alyssa pumping Richie's gears in more ways than one saved me from ending things with him. It adds a touch of dark comedic value to the whole sorry tale.

"He did what? I'm going to wring his neck when I see him. No wonder he was so bloody quick to agree not to talk about . . ."

"About me?" Did he really just say that? My stomach falls flat, matching the expression that settles over Nate's face. "You asked him not to talk about me?"

His jaw tenses and his eyes become steely. "Look, Freja, what I came here to say – what I've been working up to telling you – is that there's no reason why things have to be awkward between us. Eight years is pretty much a lifetime ago."

*It isn't for me.* I want to say that. I want to scream the words out, but of course I don't. "Sure. I mean, you have your business and your TV show and Lucy and, well, my life is pretty great too."

He smiles, but he doesn't look convinced. "Good."

"Good." I sit forward and rest my elbows on my desk. If he wants us to develop a professional relationship, then that's what we'll do. "I was actually just about to assign one of my best guys to work with you. He's called Neil Dawson and, as luck would have it, he worked in Hong Kong before settling in London. I'm pretty sure you'll like him.

Maybe you can bond over China."

"He sounds great. I'm really looking forward to seeing what Tribe comes up with for my company. This will be our first international ad campaign, and I want to hit TV stations all over Europe. The first ad is going to tie in with the product launch of our new card reader. My goal is to capture a bigger slice of market share. I want your client rep, Madeline, to work in sync with my marketing team, making sure the entire process is streamlined. We've already started the direct marketing drip on our business customers ahead of hitting the general public. I'm expecting inbound leads to start rolling in well ahead of going live."

Holy shit, he's really forcing himself into Mr-Corporate-Businessman zone, isn't he? I try to stop a smile exploding onto my face, but I fail spectacularly when it turns into a giggle.

"What's funny?"

I feel like I've been caught passing notes in class. "I'm sorry, I guess I wasn't expecting all the work talk. Which is stupid considering we're at work."

"Like I said, there's really no reason we can't be professional."

His eyes are pleading. He wants an easy ride out of here, but I still have so many questions. Sam said I broke him. Part of me doesn't want to push him if that's true, but the other part of me wants an answer. And I think I deserve an answer. "Why did you cut me off?"

His jaw locks and his eyes immediately break the connection. Silence. The seconds roll by. Has it been a minute yet? It feels like an hour already. "It was easier that way." He looks at me, and my throat swells when I see his deep dark-brown irises glisten under a veil of water.

"I know it was a long time ago, Nate. I know we've both moved on. I respect that your life is great now and you're happy, but . . ." I notice it immediately. His back stiffened and his shoulders rolled back when I said the word "happy". He isn't happy at all. "I guess I need some closure. Even after all this time has passed. Seeing you again last week knocked the wind out of my sails, and today has made me realise how much never knowing why has affected me."

"Freja, I really don't want to do this. Not here, not now." He tugs his expensive suit jacket down just a little too forcefully, then he stands up. He's running away. *Min Gud*, he's literally running away.

"Fine, if you don't want to talk about me, tell me why you cut Richie off. He was your best friend."

"Like I said. It was just easier." He starts to walk towards the door.

"Well it wasn't easy for me!" I yell at the back of his head.

He stops still but doesn't turn around. "You mean you didn't seek solace with Brett?"

"Who?" I have no idea what he's talking about. "Who the hell is Brett?"

He swings around. "Brett Kirkman? The guy you were screwing around with behind my back."

*Hvad taler han om*? What on earth is he talking about? My eyes fill with frustrated tears. "Nate, I have never lied to you in my life and I have no reason to lie to you now. I don't know anyone called Brett." Is this his father's doing? Is this . . .

*Nej.*

*Nej, vær venlig.* Please, it can't be.

Nate shakes his head and sighs. "For years I've racked my brain wondering how you even met him. I can't remember being in a room with you both. Brett is my dad's chief strategist now. He'd only worked for us for a couple of weeks when you slept with him. I saw the photographs, Freja." His voice breaks painfully as a tear falls slowly down his cheek. He lets it fall onto his jacket collar, and I want to reach over and wipe the wetness from his face. "I was all set to go back to LA to get you back. I wanted you in my life so badly. I never stopped thinking about you, not for one moment. Hell, if I had to, I'd have thrown my dad under a bus if it meant I could be with you. As for Brett, I couldn't stop myself taking a piece of him when I found out what you did, but it wasn't his fault, was it? He didn't know you were with me."

I can't think. I can't feel. I can barely process what he's telling me. *Brett.* That was the guy's name. I never knew his name.

"Dad didn't want to show me the photographs, and he sure as hell couldn't predict what seeing them would do to me." He tenses as the words leave his body. It's as if he's been wanting to let it all out for years, but I'm too stunned to speak. My throat is dry and I feel numb all over. Klein showed him. I let Nate go, just like he demanded, but he still showed him. "It was eight years ago. It's in the past now and I'm happy to let it stay there. Nobody will hear a word about Brett from me. All I want from you is a cracking TV ad that will make my company a stack of money. Can you do that?"

My voice leaves my battered chest in a croak. "Yes. I can do that."

As I watch him leave I realise how easily I could have had it all. If only I'd spoken up eight years ago. If only I'd told somebody – anybody – what Nate's father did to me.

# 9

THIRTY SECONDS AFTER NATE DROPS his gut-wrenching bombshell, Rachel thunders into my office, her round hips swaying heavily underneath a figure-hugging pencil skirt. "Oh my god, girl," she pants excitedly. "How did you get a one on one with Mr GQ?"

I try to switch my brain into gear but it's firmly stuck in reverse. "Mr . . . who?"

"Mr GQ, you know, Mr Epitome of all that's good-looking, charming and successful. That guy is a walking, talking parcel of hot . . ." Her voice disappears inside my head. At least I think it does. Maybe she's just stopped talking. "Freja?"

"Hmm?"

"You look like you've seen a ghost." She walks toward me and I scramble to compose myself.

"It's nothing. I just heard some news I wasn't expecting, that's all." I can hear my heart beating and, crap, my eyes are wet. I didn't realise . . . Shit, I must look a complete mess. I blow some air onto my face. "Did you want something?"

"I did, but I'm more concerned about you right now. What did he want?"

"Oh, it isn't important."

Her hands flex around a bundle of folders. I notice that her silver-blue glittery nails perfectly match her eyeshadow. Rachel must spend more hours maxing out on the sparkle each morning than all of the other women in my team combined, and I love her for it. "Do you know him?"

I don't say anything, and the fact I don't say anything makes her jump to the right answer.

"Oh my god, you know him! Why the bloody hell didn't you say? How do you know . . . Oh wait, this is you, so . . ." Her big blue eyes double in size and she almost drops her stack of files. "Have you? With him? You have, haven't you?"

I'm usually proud of my conquests, and under any other circumstances I'd be cracking open a bottle of prosecco over lunch and telling her all the thrilling details, but not this time. "No, it's not like that," I say, shoehorning some "boss" into my tone. "Can we change the subject? I've a stack of work to complete this morning. What can I help you with?"

Her body deflates and I instantly regret putting out her spark. "I just wanted you to check over my blocking for tomorrow's shoot. It's for the scene in the aircraft hangar with the fit *Top Gun*-era Tom-Cruise-a-like. I've sketched it all out and I have some photos of the set, so hopefully you'll get an idea of what I'm aiming for."

"Sure, let's get to it." I follow her onto the studio floor. "How are you finding working with Lily?"

"She's really great, although I'm worried she might snap in a strong wind. I swear her thighs are smaller than my wrists. When I stand next to her we look like the number ten."

I laugh at Rachel's turn of phrase. Art director Lily Xu is an enigmatic soul whose physical fragility is at odds with her creative brilliance. By comparison, Rachel thunders through life with the might of a thoroughbred stallion. I grab a spare chair and wheel it over to Rachel's desk.

"So I was thinking we could block the initial shot

like this . . ."

I spend the next hour looking over Rachel's plans for her shoot, making suggestions that would make best use of the low sun that will accompany her six a.m. start. I'm grateful to have something to take my mind off earlier. Knowing the truth has filled in a blank, but I'd sooner have learned that Nate simply moved on, or he genuinely fell in love with Evelyn, or he just didn't love me enough. Any of those options would have been preferable to this.

"This is fab, Freja, thank you." Rachel bundles her files back together. "I'm going to show Lily and Sean, then we're dodging over to Surrey to set up for tomorrow. Who knew my teenage obsession with *Top Gun* would take me to this moment in my life?"

"Hey, how do you fancy going out tonight? You, me, the other girls, copious amounts of cocktails . . . ?"

Her jaw drops. "Tonight? On a work night?"

I shoot her a massive eye-roll. "How old are you, grandma?"

"A very young-for-my-age twenty-six," she replies, a light smile curling at the corner of her plump burgundy lips. "So if I'm a grandma, you must be a corpse."

"Well, I remember what twenty-six feels like, so if I tell you filming hot actors in fighter-pilot uniforms will be a lot more fun if you're experiencing the morning-after glow of a good night out, you should believe me."

"Freja, cut me some slack here. I have a four a.m. wake-up scheduled for tomorrow," she says with a sigh of disappointment. "Last two times we've been out I haven't seen my bed till three." She catches another of my eye-rolls. "I can cope with five hours' sleep, but not one, and not before the most important ad shoot of my career so far. Jesus, you're supposed to be my boss."

She has a point. "Okay, but I was aiming for a level five on my getting-pissed scale of shame tonight, and I haven't done that since Christmas, so think about what you're going to be missing out on. And don't blame me when you're eaten alive with jealousy after seeing selfies of me with all my fun, non-grandma friends on Instagram."

She makes a silly cry-face. "Now that's just mean."

I spot Violet walking onto the floor and I hit the guilt-inducement up a notch. "Violet, just the girl I needed to see. What do you think about hitting a level five tonight?"

"A level what?" she says in a weird half-daze. Why are my friends suddenly so crap? Granted, Violet was never a bastion of debauchery, but still. "Oh, you mean your getting-drunk scale? Er, sure. But wait . . . isn't level five completely shit-faced, falling on the floor in a stupor of semi-consciousness?"

"Yes, that's the one," I say gleefully. "Are you up for it?"

"On a week night? Not a chance."

I hate her. "Fine, be boring." I poke out my tongue. "I'll call Anaïs. She won't let me down." This is true. Being French, Anaïs has a ten-year head start on drinking the rest of us under the table. She was having wine to accompany her food when her food consisted of mashed-up bananas and breastmilk. This is not a national stereotype. These are Anaïs's own words.

"Before you do that," Violet says urgently. "I need a word, in private."

She actually looks exhausted. As if she's carrying the weight of the world. I should have noticed that. Rachel gathers up her bag and mobile phone and heads off to meet the JET Financial creative team while I beckon Violet into my office. "Is everything alright?"

"Yes, I, um . . ." She closes the door, letting her hands linger for a moment, flat against the wood. "I just wanted to be here . . . and to make sure you were here."

Something twists deep inside me. "Violet, what is it? You're worrying me."

"He's here."

"Who's here?" Does she mean Nate?

"Lord Klein." She presses her back against the door, subconsciously securing the barrier, as a wave of nausea rushes through me. "Klein & Co's campaign is complete. Ethan is signing off on Georgie's rebrand and paperwork. It was only supposed to be him and their marketing rep, Claire, but his top execs have turned out too. Kevin Conroy and Julia Hinckley. And Nate was here earlier."

I feel her eyes scan my face. "I know Nate was here. We've talked already."

She practically leaps to attention. "Oh my god, what did you talk about?"

"This and that." I wince at my stupid words and cringe all the way down to my toes. As if she's going to buy that.

"Really? Can you be a little bit more specific?

Because I've just seen him with the others in the lobby and he looked pretty much like you do right now – drained, washed out, devastated. As if he'd had all the air blasted out of him."

Sadness courses through me when I think about how he must be feeling. "Honestly? It was mostly small talk. Our careers, our past . . . some stuff about our friends and a bit about Lucy." My nerves jar when I speak her name. I know she's beautiful and probably perfect, but he shouldn't be hers . . . and damn, listen to how jealous I am. This is not a good feeling.

"I don't believe you. I don't have your empathic superpowers, but I'm not stupid and I'm not blind." She comes closer and gives me a look full of kindness. "What's got the both of you in this state? What did he say to you?"

I feel my eyes well up. "He told me why."

She takes a few steps closer. "Why he cut you off?"

The tears that have been threatening to fall all morning finally roll down my cheek. "It was all down to his father. I should have guessed . . . I shouldn't have let him . . ."

Her perfectly sculpted eyebrows bend into a frown. "What did he do back then? Can you tell me?"

I breathe and my body involuntarily lets out a sob. "I wouldn't know where to begin."

"People tend to start at the beginning."

I wipe the last tear from my face and, for a moment, consider telling her. "I can't. I don't want to open the cage."

Her frown deepens. "What would you say if it

were me?"

"I'd convince you to tell me." I think back to all the times I've been there for Violet. Within the first few weeks of our meeting I was sucked into her and Ethan's relationship woes. They were both stupidly in love but also stupidly poised to destroy one another. "There's nothing in the Freja rulebook which says I have to follow my own advice."

"What is in your rulebook then? Because *this* – how you've been the last couple of weeks – isn't you."

"I know it isn't me." More tears fall because Klein's in this building – my building – and he's probably going to be here indefinitely. I don't want to have to call ahead every bloody day to make sure I don't see him. I want to be safe here. A rush of panic soars through my veins. I can't make him go away, but I can make my feelings go.

She strokes my arm, then grips my elbow. "Even in that 'not you' brain of yours, you know keeping this thing in a cage isn't working for you."

Damn. Yet again Violet surprises me. "You're right," I say, placing my hand over hers and giving it a light squeeze. Since when did my most socially inept friend become this insightful? "And that bastard's luck has just ran out."

I don't stop to think about whether I'm about to do one of the most reckless things I've ever done in my entire life. I don't have time to engage the sensible part of my brain. I make the decision, and my feet do the rest.

"Wait! Freja, where are you going?" Violet, a few steps behind, follows me to the stairwell.

"I'm putting an end to this." I climb the stairs

two at a time, but when I get to the ground-floor reception, I have no idea where I'm going. "Where is he?"

Violet slows to catch her breath. "Nate? I think he left already. What's going on?"

"I don't mean Nate. I mean Lord fucking Voldemort. Where is he?"

A look of terror sweeps across her face. "He's with Ethan. There's a client meeting up on the exec floor—"

No sooner has she told me than I spin around and run-walk to the lifts. I slam the up button. Then I hit it again, and again, each angry tap reverberating in my ears. We wait in silence until we hear a ping, followed by a swish, then we step inside the metal box and I hit the button for the eighth floor.

"Are you absolutely sure you're doing the right thing – whatever it is you're doing?" Violet asks.

"No, but you were right. Caging up my past isn't working anymore."

She sighs and places her hand lightly on my arm again. "Then I'm with you."

"Thanks, Violet. That means a lot." I place my hand over hers and let the warmth of her touch give me confidence to keep going.

The lift doors swish open, and I lead Violet out onto the polished dark oak floor. Churchill House is a forty-storey tower block in Canary Wharf, with Tribe occupying the lowest eight floors plus my basement film studio. Floor eight, the location of our executive offices and boardroom, is easily the most stylish, with brilliant white walls accented by zesty raspberry and lime accessories.

Lucille Monroe, Ethan's formidable assistant, is

seated at her desk outside Ethan's vacant office. She takes one look at us and jumps to attention. "You can't go down there," she barks, reminding me of Cerberus guarding the door to the Underworld. I'm instantly glad she has one head instead of three, because Lucille is fierce.

Violet stops dead in her tracks behind me. "We can't go where?"

Her black eyes are fixed upon us. "You can't go down the hall. Mr Fraser's in the middle of an extremely important meeting. I should know cos he had me setting up all kinds of techno mumbo-jumbo for his presentation as soon as I hauled my ass in here at six thirty this morning. And that's a whole hour before I usually start work, so I'm grouchy as hell." Her eyes remain glued to us as she starts to tap on her keyboard. "Don't make me come after you." How the hell can she think, talk and type all at the same time? What kind of witchcraft is this?

"Is Ethan in the boardroom or one of the conference rooms?" Violet asks.

Lucille stops typing and her glower intensifies. "Didn't you hear me?"

Violet steps closer to Ethan's guard dog. "Lucille, I know you're the best secretary in this entire building—"

"And I know you're full of horseshit," says Lucille, her melodic Caribbean accent accentuating her no-nonsense attitude. "You ain't going down there."

Violet's hands go to her hips. "You know I could outrun you."

"You could, but you know I keep score. You wanna be top of my grudge list for the rest of your life?"

"Lucille," I say, sidling up beside Violet. "You know me. I wouldn't be here if this wasn't important – life-or-death important."

Her angry expression wanes for a brief moment. "Your life or hers?"

"Mine," I say.

"Why does that matter?" says Violet, her voice full of indignation.

"Cos you're an overreacting drama magnet, and she isn't." I almost laugh at her bluntness. What I wouldn't give for a piece of Lucille in my DNA. Her omniscient eyes give me the final once-over, then she jerks her head in the direction of the boardroom. "Go, but if anyone asks, I haven't seen you."

"Thanks, Lucille."

My heart is in my mouth as I march towards the boardroom's solid oak double doors. With blood rushing through my veins I raise my hand, but then I do nothing. I hear muffled voices from inside the room – shuffling, movements, chairs rolling against carpet. Noise. What on earth will they think? How much do I care?

"Do you want to go back?" Violet asks in a soft whisper.

I shake my head. I've come this far. I grip the metal door handle and start praying that by some miracle the cage inside me has been soldered shut. I never wanted to stay under the sea for this long. I wanted to be under the sun, with him. I wanted my voice back and I wanted to dance again. I wanted my legs to be strong enough to follow him.

I shut my eyes as the pain of calculating how

much I have lost takes hold.

Then I take a deep breath, open the door and stride confidently into the room.

It takes a few seconds to find him. He's sitting at the centre of the table. Greyer. Older. Frailer. To think that this old man could hold so much power over me.

Ethan is standing at the head of the table. As soon as he sees me and his fiancée, all the colour drains from his face. To his left, Madeline shoots an agitated glance between Violet and Ethan, her blood-red silhouette dramatically accentuating her rapidly reddening skin tone. "What the hell is going on?" she shouts across the room.

I step forward and summon my voice. "I need to speak to Lord Klein in private."

Madeline's sleek platinum bob swishes around her shoulders as she takes to her feet. "He's busy, Miss Larsen," she says with an odd formality. "All of us are busy. If Lord Klein agrees to speak to you, it will have to wait—"

"I'll speak to her now." Klein rises from his chair, buttons his suit jacket and slides one hand into his pocket. A middle-aged woman with a neat, pleated up-do tugs his arm. He bends down so she can whisper something into his ear. She must be Julia Hinckley, Klein's most trusted advisor. Kevin Conroy runs his eyes over me and shares a hushed conversation with Klein & Co's plain-looking marketing rep, Claire Hill, whose neck is covered by a fussy blouse tied with a huge bow. Then, at the end of the table, I notice someone familiar. She definitely worked for Lord Klein back in LA. The woman's dark eyes refuse to meet mine, but I remember her. I think her name was Sarah. Or was it Sandy? Finally, next to Madeline is the pretty brown-skinned client accounts junior who Neil declared was "into him" the other day. Heaven help her if Madeline has taken her under her wing.

Lord Klein walks towards me. My veins tremble under my skin as hot blood charges through me to a rhythm of *why the fuck are you doing this?* He extends his hand towards the door and I walk through it. In my heels, I tower over him, and the artificial height difference makes me feel stronger. I follow him out of the room, across a hallway, and into a plush vacant office used by our investors and non-executive directors.

I close the door and press my back against the wall. Lord Klein sits down in an armchair and crosses his legs. "I've often thought about this moment," he says and my body shudders. I'd forgotten what his voice sounds like – rich and plummy, but with the unmistakeable hardness of power.

It's my turn to speak but I don't know what to say. On my way up here I ran several lines through my head, but every scenario ended with me shoving him against a wall and choking the life out of him. I listen to my pulse pounding in my ears and one word – "Why?" – escapes from my shaky vocal cords.

He dips his head. "Why was I thinking about this moment?"

I shake my head. "No."

He watches me struggle to speak, and I cringe because I know he must be enjoying this. "If you mean why am I here, you can relax. I didn't know you worked for Tribe, or even lived in London, when I shook hands on the deal with Sir Arthur Lovett."

I wish I had water. My mouth feels like it's in a climate zone all of its own. "No, I meant why did you lie to him?"

A look of sheer contempt explodes onto Klein's face. "That was a long time ago."

"For all these years, I thought . . ." My voice cracks again. I try to clear my throat, coughing into the back of my hand. "He wanted to go back to the States for me."

"And I couldn't let that happen. I told you back in LA that I would do anything to ensure my son reached his potential. He's lived up to every expectation I had of him, and then some. He's head of a giant multi-national corporation, he's a TV star and the world loves him. He needs to share his future with a woman who is his equal."

"All of your 'not good enough' bullshit may have hurt me when I was a struggling student, but I'm thirty-three years old now and I am his equal. How many women my age become directors in advertising agencies?"

"I don't care about how successful you think you are," he says, shrugging his shoulders. "You could have landed your job whilst lying on your back for all I know."

"Excuse me?" I recoil in horror. Is he really suggesting I slept my way to the top? I've never had a relationship with anybody I worked with, aside from my stupid arrangement with Harry. The dryness in my throat burns as bile rises up from my stomach. I swallow as hard as I can, and I tell myself to aim for his head if I can't keep it down.

"I showed my son the photographs to set him free. I chose to stop him destroying his life. The man he is today wouldn't exist if he'd gone after you. I'm sorry you got hurt, but I did warn you." He stands up and takes a step towards the door. "I have no quarrel with you now. Keep away from my son and your job is safe."

And then he's gone.

Was that it? What exactly have I accomplished aside from not being sick whilst shaking like a scared rabbit? I suppose it could have been worse. I suppose I could have punched him.

I should have said more. I repeat the lines in my head – the words I want to speak into life. Everything I wanted to say but was too much of a coward to follow through. I start walking back towards the lifts.

My throat feels like there's a roll of industrial sandpaper lodged in it, and my nausea is building by the second. When I reach the bank of lifts, I hit the button to take me back down to the basement, then I hear the doors of the lift behind me swish open. I spin around and . . . I almost drop to my knees when I see him.

That face. That name. *Brett.*

I didn't even know his name until this morning. His ice-blue eyes brace when he sees me, as if he's a cartoon character that has just been hit on the head by a coyote brandishing a mallet. I allow his features to drip into my memory. I remember his dark hair, lean build and athletic body, but most of all I remember the flashing lights, the sound of their arguing and his hands touching me.

"Excuse me," he says as he takes a step back. His American accent has been plucked directly from my nightmares. He looks afraid and he looks anxious, but his eyes – those ice-blue eyes that have haunted me all this time – they're still just as frightening.

I don't answer him. I stumble around him and step inside the lift, my body crashing against the back wall. I see him walk away just as the lift doors close and the panic rises in my chest.

I try to crush it. I try to think of other, nicer things. The night out I was planning with Anaïs. The Dior jumpsuit I've been saving up for. My annual trip home for *Sankthansaften* . . .

I try to focus. Can I stay in the lift? What if I hit the emergency button and just stay here until it's over? I try to remember all the aversion techniques I learned as a kid, but as I struggle to drag the air into my lungs, the only thing I want is help from my friends.

The doors ping open and, with daggers slicing through my throat and my brain slamming against my skull, I find my office door and concentrate hard.

One step . . . then another . . . I ignore the muffled voices, I ignore the blurred faces, I just keep going . . . and when I get there it takes every ounce of strength I have in me to close the door. Then I fall to the floor.

# 10

I'VE LOST TRACK of how many panic attacks I've had over the years. That first one, just after my mother left, happened at school. I thought I was going to die, and I wouldn't have cared if I did. The racing heartbeat, the pains in my chest and the frantic need to suck air into my lungs always pass, but sometimes, like right now, the pain is so bad I can't imagine it ending.

I'm sitting in the corner of my office, my back pressed up against the wall and my fingers digging into the bristly loops of the nylon carpet. I consider lying down, but I'm scared to move in case I pass out, so instead I stare at the ceiling, wrap my arms around my knees and just wait.

I must have been sitting here ten minutes when the door to my office swings opens. A surge of frantic anxiety rockets through my body, but when Violet walks into the room the pressure in my ribcage ebbs a little.

"Hey, what is it?" She drops to her knees next to me, not realising what's happening at first, but her concern quickly escalates. "Freja, what's wrong?"

"I . . . I'm . . . it's okay . . . just . . ." Crap! Why can't I speak? I bang my head against the wall three times, hoping it will click my thinking and speaking brain functions back into place.

"I'm calling an ambulance," she says, shuffling back on her knees.

"No!" I shout so loudly that she jumps. "It's . . . happened before. I . . . just need water."

"I'll get some." She touches my arm, then feels her way around my wrist. "Shit, what am I doing? I'm an idiot. I don't even know where your pulse is."

The door opens again, but this time I'm not so lucky. "What the actual hell was that about?" Madeline storms into my office, slamming the door behind her. Doesn't anybody know how to knock anymore? She looks down at me, then at Violet, and her anger is replaced by concern. "My god, is she okay?"

"I don't know," says Violet, getting to her feet. "She can't seem to breathe properly. I was just going to get some water."

Madeline rushes over and my heart speeds up. I rasp desperately at the air as the sharp pain in my chest gets tighter. "Do you have asthma?" Madeline asks as she crouches down next to Violet.

I shake my head. "No . . . it's a . . . panic attack."

She finds the pulse point at the side of my neck. Her dark-brown eyes scrutinise me. I wish Violet had called that ambulance a few minutes ago. I don't trust Madeline and I don't want her here. "Your heart rate is soaring," she says, moving onto her knees to sit closer to me. "You've had these attacks before?"

I nod, wondering if she was a doctor or nurse in a former life. If she was, I dread to think what her bedside manner must have been like. "On and off . . . since I was a kid."

"I'll get the water," says Violet, practically running to the door.

"Do you take medication?"

"No . . . not for years. The attacks are . . .

unpredictable."

"Breathe through your nose," she says, taking hold of my hand. "Inhale deeper, gentler breaths, then breathe out slowly through your mouth."

This is what I've been trying to do ever since the attack started. I follow her lead as she keeps me alert by tapping her fingers against the back of my hand. I focus my mind, then I try to inhale through my nose, but I can't get enough air inside me. Fear starts to build in my chest again, the walls are closing in around me and . . . oh my god, this is it. This is how I die.

"Listen to me. You can do this." Madeline's voice is forceful and commanding, but everything is hurting too much. I can't make it stop. My head, my heart, my throat . . . my body is killing me. I feel tears run down my face and suddenly I can't keep my legs still. My feet jerk against the wiry carpet, my knees shake, and I can feel her soft tapping against my hand again. She's trying to focus me, but I can't calm down. "You're a strong, brave, brilliant woman, and you can beat whatever it is you're afraid of." Violet returns to the office holding a plastic cup filled with water. "Everyone's here for you. You're going to be okay."

Violet kneels next to me and passes me the cup. I shakily take it from her, splashing a few drops over my grey wool trousers in the process. I gulp at the water, drinking so quickly that I feel the cool liquid surge through my oesophagus and rush into my stomach.

"Okay, now it's time to try again," says Madeline. Her tone is firm and her round, pretty face is stiff and serious. "Breathe in through your nose, then count to five."

I do as she says, making great effort to inhale as slowly as I can. I count in my head, then I breathe out.

"Brilliant. Good girl," Madeline says. "Now keep going. Close your eyes if it helps."

I close my eyes. I breathe in. I count. I breathe out. I feel Madeline's hand holding mine and I wonder how a virtual stranger, and somebody I didn't particularly like, could become the exact person I need. After five minutes has passed, my breathing is steadier and my heart rate has slowed, but my head still feels like it's being pecked to death by an extremely busy woodpecker.

"How are you feeling now?" Violet pushes a few strands of bedraggled hair from my face.

I inhale a pain-free lungful of air. "Better, but pathetic and a little bit stupid."

"Don't you dare think like that," says Madeline. "Anybody can suffer from panic attacks." She lets go of my hand, eases herself up off the floor and steps back into her shoes. "You're going to be fine. But take things easy for the rest of the afternoon. I need to get back to work. Um, forget what I said when I came in here, okay?"

I shift around on the floor. Ouch! I feel like I could sleep for a week, but at least my ass has had a half-hour nap. "How did you know what to do?"

"Someone close to me used to suffer from panic attacks. I learned how to help her." A fleeting thought sweeps across her face and lands in a small, barely-there smile which quickly fades. I thank her and she leaves my office, but before she does she smiles at me again. And for the first time I feel like

I want to get to know her better.

Violet helps me get up off the floor. We sit down together on the sofa.

"Freja, you really scared me there." Her voice is soft and her eyes glisten with unshed tears.

"I'm really sorry." I rub her arm gently. "I can remember telling Georgie a few years ago that I used to have panic attacks, but I don't think I've told anybody else. I haven't had one for so long that I thought I was done with them. I'm so sorry for frightening you."

"And I'm sorry for being so bloody useless. Ethan has been telling me for ages to book myself onto a first-aid course. I wish I could have done more. If Madeline hadn't been here, I dread to think . . ."

"Yeah that was, um, unexpected, wasn't it?"

"Totally. I always thought she had a bit of sergeant major in her DNA, but jeez, talk about calm under fire. I thought she was cold and aggressive, but next time I'm in the shit, I want her on my side."

I give her a pointed look. "Really?"

"Yeah, I think so. I mean, I don't want to get ahead of myself because last night she sent me a list of demands for BuzzPay that will probably give me a hundred very good reasons to blow my stack with her over the next few weeks, but there's no denying she was awesome just now."

"She was." I say, realising it's rapidly approaching lunchtime and I've tied Violet up for well over an hour. "You should get back to work."

Her bright-blue eyes scrutinise me as I stand up and walk over to my desk. "I want to stay here but I have a ton of work on. How about I come over tonight?"

"There's really no need."

"Yes, there is." She gets up and walks to the door. "I'll be there at eight thirty."

\* \* \*

I left work earlier than usual and picked up a chow mein ready meal from the Sainsbury's near Greenwich station. I don't know why I had the sudden urge for noodles, but all I could think about on the DLR ride home was stuffing myself with carbs. Comfort food at its finest. Or so I thought until I over-microwaved the meal into a solid brick of congealed mush. My hungry stomach had to make do with toast and a banana.

Violet rings my doorbell at eight twenty. Never in all the time I've known her has she ever been late. I've lost count of how many arguments she's had with Ethan over his punctuality. My lovely, kind-hearted boss is great in so many ways, but he couldn't be punctual if he had his internal body clock surgically tuned to the chimes of Big Ben.

When I open the door I'm met by a casual Violet dressed in a sloppy cardigan, even sloppier wool scarf and a pair of jeggings. "I have wine," she says proudly, waving a bottle of red at me. "I'll just get us some glasses." She heads for the kitchen and I sit down on the sofa, already speculating how this evening might end. The panic attack I had today scared me. It was far worse than the one I had last week, and it's clear that both episodes were triggered by what happened in LA. Confronting

Lord Klein today was part of closing the door on my past, but how can I possibly move on from something I've refused to acknowledge even happened?

Violet returns from the kitchen with the glasses and her uncorked wine. She almost always drinks red, and it suits her; it's just a shame that she gets drunk after one sniff. She sits down next to me, curling one leg under the other.

"So, how have you been?" she asks.

"Truth, or something less ugly?" I wait for her to nod, then I release everything I've been holding inside. "Today was the worst I've ever been, but yesterday was pretty bad too and I actually can't remember the last time I had a good day and I'm tired of holding it all in – pushing it all down deep inside me. This isn't me, Violet. I'm never the one sitting here trying to work out how to unscrew my totally screwed-up life."

"No, that spot on the sofa is usually mine." Violet's long black lashes flutter as she smiles. "But how have you screwed up? If this is about you falling in love with a guy who has an evil dad, then that isn't *your* fuck-up."

"I let him go," I remind her. "I didn't fight for him."

She pulls both of her feet up underneath her and wraps her long cream cardigan around her knees. "Would you want him back?"

I shake my head, but my heart is calling me a liar. "Even if I did, it would be impossible. And way too late. He has a girlfriend and a glittering career."

"*And* he has a dad who makes mine look like

Father of the Year?"

"Exactly." She understands, and it would be easy to leave the conversation here, but I know I have to keep going. "Have you told your family about Ethan?"

Her eyes shift from me to her wine glass as she swirls the dark burgundy liquid around in a soft rolling motion. "I called my grandma. She was really happy. She begged me to visit, just like she always does. I don't know, maybe I will one day. I expect she told my parents, and I expect they won't give a shit. The happier I am, the more they hate me."

Every time I talk to Violet about her family, my heart aches for her. Her parents blamed her for the accidental death of her sister. Knowing she can't ever share her happiness with the people who should love her unconditionally makes my sorry situation seem woefully trivial. "You should go see your grandma."

She smiles briefly, then has a long drink of wine. "Don't think I haven't noticed we're talking about me."

"Hmmm?"

"I came here to talk about you. I'm not on the therapist's couch tonight, remember?"

I laugh as I realise I'm bang to rights. "Sorry, I guess the role of therapist comes a lot more naturally than the role of patient."

"Well it doesn't come at all naturally to me. I usually try to fix things by telling people what to do."

"I *had* noticed." We share a giggle, then I get lost in thought as I wonder if Violet's creative problem-solving could ever fix any of this. "I told you this morning that Nate told me why he cut me off."

She puts her glass down on the coffee table. "You said it was all down to his father."

Brett's name and face slam into my brain, and panic flames in my chest again. *The flashes. The touching. The photographs.* I sip my wine and let the spicy liquid warm my throat and relax my muscles. "I honestly don't think I was expecting to hear what he told me, but I should have. That's something else I pushed out of my mind. Maybe if I hadn't shut out what happened for so long . . ."

"I don't understand, Freja. What did you shut out?"

"The thing that triggered my panic attack today. And the one I had last week—"

"Wait. I thought today was a one-off?" She rests her arm on the back of the sofa and runs her hand through her hair. "Freja, this is really serious. Before today, and last week, when did you last have an attack?"

"Eight years ago." I mirror Violet's position on the sofa, bringing one of my legs up to rest on the other. My eyes connect with hers, and I accept that the universe has decided I'm going to tell her. The feeling in my gut is propelling me towards opening my mouth. And it feels more than mere intuition. It's like a cosmic force. I glance over to my bookshelves and I spot the figurine of the Little Mermaid my dad bought me a couple of years ago. Cast in bronze, it's a mini replica of the statue that sits on a rock in Copenhagen harbour. Dad intended to give me a little piece of home to keep with me in

London, but he had no idea how much the character, and her story, is woven into my past. "Did I ever mention Riley to you?"

Sensing a shift in the conversation, Violet picks up her glass and has another drink. "No, I don't think so. I've never heard that name before."

"Her mum was my roomie in LA, and she was the world's biggest Little Mermaid fan. She would watch the Disney movie on repeat five times a day, dancing around our living room to all the songs in a cute little seashell bathing suit. I once told her that the real-life Ariel came from Denmark, just like me, and her three-year-old brain decided that my Danish-ness and red hair meant I was secretly a mermaid. I may have played along with her on that."

A broad smile lights up Violet's eyes. "Sounds like fun."

"Yeah, it was." I remember Riley's shrieks of laughter when I pretended to brush my hair with a fork. Or rather, a *dinglehopper*. "But the game turned bittersweet when my life started to mirror Ariel's."

She raises her eyebrows, and I worry that I sound completely crazy. "I know I usually don't get your pop culture references, but I have actually seen that movie. What's the connection?"

How do I explain it without sounding dumb? "He took my voice."

The bridge of her nose crinkles into a confused frown. "Who did?"

A lump forms in my throat, but I push past it. "Lord Klein. I never told anybody . . . not Nate, not Richie, not my dad or sister, but he didn't just take

Nate away from me, he took everything. He took my voice, my dreams, my identity and my self-respect. I was trapped under the sea, unable to walk on land. Unable to speak."

She puts her glass down with a clunk and scoots closer to me, resting one hand on my knee. "Can you tell me what he did?" I can feel her warmth through my silk pyjamas and it gives me the strength to continue.

I inhale sharply and shakily as my thighs start to tremble. "I don't know for sure what he did. That's the worst part of it. But in a way I'm thankful I don't know. Not knowing has allowed me to pretend it didn't happen."

# 11

HER FROWN DEEPENS AS SHE searches my face for answers. "He hurt you, didn't he?"

I nod and my eyes fill with tears. "I've carried this around for so long . . . and it's exhausting. It takes so much effort to bury a memory. Klein hated me pretty much on sight. I was a student, a jobbing actress and a Route 66 diner waitress. I didn't have a penny to my name, but I believed in myself, and I was living my best life. He couldn't stand the thought of his son falling in love with someone like me, and that's what made him do it." Violet's hand grips my knee, urging me to continue. I take a huge gulp of wine, a shot of courage, which almost drains the glass. "I got a part in a movie. It wasn't anything major, but it was decent money for a student with tuition fees to pay. There were nude sex scenes involved, but I didn't mind. I'd already done intimate scenes for a TV show back in Denmark."

"Really? My god, Freja, I can't even imagine having the balls to do that." She looks shocked, yet impressed at the same time.

"Well, I don't think many actresses enjoy sex scenes. They're embarrassing and they're a little bit terrifying and you spend the whole time worrying you're going to accidentally touch the wrong body part, but when it's over, you get a buzz out of doing something brave." I recall my co-star's random pop-up boners and how completely mortified he was by his body's reaction to the scenes we shot. Poor

Todd. It was the first, and probably last, time he was ever naked on camera. "In a way, filming those scenes trained me in how to compartmentalise thoughts I didn't want to think about. I just became the character and shut out the weirdness of what I was doing."

"I bet," she says, her eyes still wide with surprise. "Do you miss acting at all?"

"I miss having a dream, but I honestly don't miss the reality. That movie – *Twisted Street* – ended it all for me."

She shuffles closer and her knee touches mine. "Why?"

All of a sudden, my heart starts to pound. I drop my legs to the floor and stand up. "Shit, I thought I could—"

She stands and sweeps her arm around my shoulder. "You don't have to talk about it if you're not ready. It took me years to tell anybody about my sister." My vision is blurred, but I can tell she's looking at me in a way I don't like. Pity. I don't want to be a victim. I don't want my friends to feel sorry for me.

I turn to face her. My eyes connect with hers and I choke out a sob. "Promise we won't change after this."

Her beautiful fairy-tale princess face looks like it's going to crack. I have never seen her look so completely devastated, and I feel bad for making her worry about me. "I don't know if I can answer that."

I sit back down on the sofa and she joins me, gently rubbing my back. I drain the remaining drops of wine from my glass. I hoped talking to Violet would be easier than this. It should be easier. "Klein invested in the movie I was making, then he invaded a closed set without clearance and watched me shoot those scenes. It was all a cruel game – his way of showing me I was powerless."

"Oh my god." Her face crumples with disgust. "You mean he walked onto set when you were—"

"When I was naked and vulnerable and totally humiliated. I haven't acted since that day. I gave up on the dream I'd had ever since I was a little girl because of him."

"And that's why you let Nate go? Because you couldn't tell him what his father did?"

"No, I told Nate about him crashing the movie set. He was so angry, I thought he was going to kill him. He told his father he was quitting the family business and he was choosing me." I don't realise I'm shaking until Violet takes my hand between both of hers. It's a gesture she's made repeatedly tonight, but this time her grip is stronger. Tears roll down my cheeks, and my head feels like it's going to explode. "I walked off the movie, but when I went back to my trailer days later, he was there. He said he wanted to talk to me. He brought a bottle of wine with him. I thought that was odd because it was early afternoon. The last thing in the world I wanted to do was share a drink with him, but at some point I drank maybe a quarter of a glass . . ." Suddenly I can't speak. It's as if I've spent so long under the sea that I don't know how to breathe now that my head is breaking the surface. "He drugged the wine."

I close my eyes, blinking a wave of tears onto my face. I can feel Violet's body tense. Her fingers slide between mine, then lock onto me, while her other hand returns to my back. "Let it out," she says softly.

"I was completely out of it in minutes. My body felt like it was floating. I was calm, but I was terrified. There was another guy with him who I'd never seen before. I've never forgotten his face: ice-blue eyes, cold stare, pale skin that smelled like peppermint. It's funny that I can remember the smell of his skin, but I can't remember what they did to me. My memories of that day are all disjointed: the acrid taste of the wine, raised voices arguing, camera clicks and flashes. Then there's the feeling of him taking my clothes off and moving me around the bed. Tugging and pulling at me. I don't remember if they hurt me. I went to a clinic afterwards and there was no evidence of . . ."

I've never been able to say the word out loud. A girl I worked with at Diablo Brown a few years ago was raped on a blind date. I wanted to help her so badly, but I couldn't even look at her. I was terrified that I might have to speak that word. She left the agency to work in a flower shop a few months later, and I've always regretted not reaching out to her.

"I'll never know for sure what they did to me, but I did ask him. I went to his hotel the day after and he showed me the photographs. I was naked, in bed, with that guy. In some we were covered by a sheet, but in others . . ." I try to clear the swelling lump from my throat as the memory of those images invades my mind. "Even if they didn't do anything, I can still feel their hands on me. Klein threatened to show Nate the photos. They'd act as irrefutable proof that I was a cheat and a slut and not good enough for his blue-blooded ridiculously wealthy family. I had no choice. I let Nate go."

I meet her gaze, and the horror I see embedded in every inch of her beautiful face cuts into my gut. Her grip on my hand tightens, and tears roll down her cheeks, dripping silently onto her lap. "I'm so sorry, Freja. I can't believe you've kept this to yourself for so long."

I thumb a tear from her cheek. "You should know why I chose to forget about it. You didn't tell anybody about your sister."

"Yes, that's true." She sucks in a breath and twists her nose to stop herself from crying even more. "When Laurel died and my parents rejected me, all I could think about was starting over. Keeping Laurel's death inside me meant I could leave tragic Violet in the past and move on." She wipes her eyes with her cardigan sleeve and blows air onto her face. A vein ripples at the side of her head – the one that always appears when she's thinking hard. "I understand why you pushed this away. You don't want what Klein did to consume who you are."

"Yes. And I don't want it to be everything people think about when they hear my name."

"But Tribe has brought Klein back into your life. How can you work in the same office as him?" She picks up her wine glass and downs what's left of her drink in one angry gulp. "I can't believe I worked on that bastard's campaign. I can't believe Ethan let him invest in our agency. If he knew about this he—"

"No, you can't tell him. Please, I don't want him to know."

She meets my panicked gaze, her eyes still glistening with tears. "Ethan could help you. He'd fix it so your paths never crossed. And I know he'll agree that Klein doesn't deserve a seat in the boardroom. He's our biggest investor, but the partners could buy him out or find somebody else. He destroyed your career and your relationship . . . and he sexually assaulted you."

"No, I'm pretty sure he didn't, I mean, I don't think—"

"Freja, no more downplaying this." Her voice is sharp and steady, reminding me of how Madeline brought me back from the brink earlier today. "Klein drugged you, removed your clothes, and you don't know what else he did. He may not have raped you, but he definitely sexually assaulted you. Please tell me you accept that this happened."

"I . . . I want to." Hearing her speak what he did aloud – the words I've never been able to say – makes it more real. "I've been denying it for so long that I don't know how to move on from it. It's only ever been real in my nightmares. I'm terrified that if I let it exist, I'll lose control."

"The panic attacks?"

"Yes. The first one happened last week when I saw Klein in the lobby. I was with Ethan at the time."

"With Ethan? He didn't say anything."

"He doesn't know. It started just as he went over to greet the Klein & Co team. I made it to the ground-floor toilets, then I promptly threw up and stayed there for an hour."

She gets that look I don't like again; I'd place it somewhere between compassion and pity. "And when you saw Klein this morning, you had another attack?"

"No, I had that one when the guy in the photographs with me walked out of one of our lifts."

"Wait, what?" Every trace of pink drains from her face. "The guy who helped Klein hurt you was in our agency today?"

"He's called Brett Kirkman. I never knew his name."

Her eyes darken and her thinking-vein reappears. I can practically hear the cogs in her brain whirring. "I don't think I've ever heard that name, but I'll find out who he is. Madeline will know. He definitely wasn't at any of my meetings with the team. We really should tell Ethan. There's no way you should be dealing with this at work. That guy can't come into our offices again."

I shake my head. "No. I can't risk any of this getting out, so please don't say anything. I'm delegating BuzzPay's ad to Neil, but I'll probably still have to see Nate at some point. And he told me today that his father showed him the photographs. Even though I did what he asked and let Nate go, he still went ahead and showed him. Nate has believed I cheated on him all of these years. He must hate me, but he can't ever find out the truth."

"Oh my god, but why? He loved you, Freja. He loved you. He was your 'one'. He has a right to know his father lied and took you away from him."

"If I tell him, I'll destroy his life, his family and everything he's worked for." I've replayed the same scenario of telling Nate over and over in my mind ever since I first saw him again. It starts with helping myself to heal, but it always ends the same way – with his complete and utter destruction. I love him far too much to hurt him. "Nate's moved on. He's fallen in love and he's successful. I don't think I'll ever forget him, but I let him go so he had a shot at happiness. For the past eight years I've known he was out there somewhere, living his life, growing further and further away from me. It isn't just what his father did or the lie he told that separates us; it's time too. We can't go back, only forward, and I need him to be happy living the life I gave him. Does that make sense?"

She nods sorrowfully. "But what if he wanted you back?"

"I don't even know if I'd want *him* back." I think about the last time I saw him in LA. It was a gorgeous spring day in Griffith Park. We had a picnic, then we watched the stars and he asked me to move to London with him. "I knew he was the one right from the start. He got me. Within five seconds of knowing me, I knew he got me. And then I knew he loved me. But if I found a way to keep him in my life, I'd have to keep his father."

"But you deserve to be happy too. There must be something you can do," she says, before checking herself with a deep sigh. "I'm sorry, I'm in fix-it mode, aren't I?"

"I wouldn't have you any other way." We both yawn and I glance at my clock. It's almost ten and Violet's flat is an hour's taxi ride away. "But it's late. Should I get you an Uber?"

She breaks her hold on me and stands up. "I have a better idea. I'll stay over again."

I'm about to protest that I don't need a babysitter

when another huge yawn climbs up from my throat. "I don't know if my brain will let me sleep tonight."

She rubs my arm. "You're tired, so you should try. But if you can't sleep, come get me. We'll talk into the night if we have to."

I make sure Violet has everything she needs, then I go to bed. I always thought I'd feel an overwhelming sense of relief if I unburdened myself of my terrible secret. But now that I've finally spoken, all I feel is numb. The pain of what happened is still there, and it's still the exact same nauseating, churning, grinding pain that makes my intestines twist into a knot and my chest feel like it's going explode. I hoped talking to Violet would make the pain stop, but it hasn't.

And that's when I realise nothing will ever make the pain go away.

It's always going to be part of who I am.

I've opened up to Violet. I've confronted Klein. The only thing I haven't done is rip Brett Kirkman's head from his shoulders, but although his slow, agonising death would probably bring some short-term satisfaction, it wouldn't be a cure.

I cry into my pillow until my cheek is cold and clammy against the wet cotton. God, I'm tired of crying. And I'm tired of being tired. I cover my mouth with the back of my hand as frenzied sobs rack my body, forcing me to curl up into a ball on my side. Maybe I'll feel better if I cry it out. I bury my face into the pillows to muffle the sound, but I allow my body to do what it needs to do to flush out all the pain. If I do this tonight, then I can start a new chapter tomorrow.

Violet comes into my room so quietly that I

don't notice her at first. Then, the bed creaks as she climbs in next to me, slides under the duvet, and wraps her arms around me. I don't try to stop crying. She strokes my hair, and it's the best feeling in the world. I didn't doubt she'd believe my story, but I worried she might think I was making too much of it. I know some people would think something that happened eight years ago shouldn't still be hurting this much. But, as Violet snuggles against me and makes gentle, soothing noises into my hair, I know she understands. And I know she's feeling my pain with me.

The ache in my chest transfers to my head under the weight of the memories. It's like the truth is growing stronger and stronger inside me, screaming to be let out. My nightmares may have lessened in frequency over the years, but I still have them. And when I do, I'm afraid and ashamed and I'm back in that trailer, on that bed, unable to move, unable to speak, unable to breathe. What will happen when I close my eyes tonight? Will I be back there again?

"It all happened, didn't it? It was real."

Violet brushes my hair from my face and wraps her arms around my waist again. "Yes," she says. "But I'm here for you. And it's going to be okay."

# 12

I WAKE UP TO AN empty bed. The delicious smell of freshly blended coffee fills my room and makes my senses buzz to life. I put on my robe, bundle my hair into a ponytail and head for the kitchen.

"Ah, you're up," says Violet meeting me halfway. She's holding two mugs of steaming coffee, and my stomach responds with a very hungry groan.

"Thanks. You have no idea how much I need this." She smiles and follows me into the living room.

"I know you can't function without it."

"And you know me far too well."

Violet sits down on the sofa next to me. I laugh as she almost trips over the feet of the pyjamas I loaned her. She's six inches shorter than I am, and my Long Tall Sally PJs seem determined to cause her injury. She curls her legs up to get comfortable and sips at her drink. Then she twists her nose up and grimaces.

"Wait a minute," I say suspiciously. "You hate coffee."

"Tell me about it." She puts her mug down on the table. "I went to the kitchen to make you a cup, but I was completely seduced by how amazingly sexy your coffee machine is, so I made myself one too. I was trying to be more sophisticated."

This is music to my ears. "I'm glad you're impressed. It's a Sage Barista and it cost almost a grand."

She almost chokes on air. "You're kidding? You paid a thousand pounds for a piece of kitchen tech?"

"Violet, do you have any idea how much coffee means to me? Imagine living your life without quality ice cream."

"I couldn't, but with a grand I could buy my own herd of dairy cows." The bridge of her nose crinkles as she giggles. "Luckily my local Tesco stocks a full complement of Häagen Dazs's finest, and I'm pretty sure they sell coffee there too."

"You don't understand." I take a long sip and enjoy every second of toe-curling pleasure as the coffee rushes into my system and emits a glorious tingling caffeine high. "Supermarket coffee is crap. I subscribe to a specialist coffee-importing website and they send me a selection of their best beans every fortnight. This . . ." I raise my cup and inhale the aroma ". . . is the absolute finest Pacamara roast from El Salvador. What if every shop in London only sold the ice cream equivalent of Tesco Value vanilla?" Her face registers the hypothetical trauma. "See, now you get it. I take my coffee very seriously." Right on cue, my dickhead neighbour cranks up his horrible music. "And caffeine helps me cope with that prick."

"Oh my god, what time is it?" We both glance at my mantel clock, which says seven fifteen. "What is wrong with him?"

"Aside from being a twat?" I take another gulp of coffee and wonder what it would taste like accompanied by a double shot of vodka. "He's probably just got in from a night smacked off his skull. He'll go to bed soon. This isn't an unusual morning in Derrick's miserable life." I get up and close the living room door, instantly stifling the noise. Thank goodness it's my hallway that shares a wall with him, as opposed to a more important room.

"I like how you say 'twat'," says Violet. "Your accent makes swearing sound sexy."

I raise an eyebrow. "You taught me that word. And everyone knows that swearing is sexy." I have another drink of coffee, then settle the mug on my knee.

"So, I've been thinking," Violet says.

"Me too." I quickly analyse the thoughts that refused to budge from my brain last night. "I think it would be okay if Ethan knew about Lord Klein."

Her body stiffens in surprise. "You're sure?"

I weigh up the pros and cons for the hundredth time. "Yeah, I'm sure. I *do* need his help and he'll be able to keep it all under wraps."

"He definitely would," she says eagerly. "Of course he would."

I take another long drink. Thank the gods of everything for coffee. "And thank you for last night."

"After all the times you've helped me fix my muddled life, I reckon I *still* owe you at least another hundred sleepovers." She twists her long ebony hair into a loop, then lets it all unravel. She always fidgets with her hair when she's nervous. "I'm really glad you talked to me last night."

"Me too. It was a long time coming."

"It was. So, um, do you want to tell Ethan yourself?"

The thought of telling the story again is about as

appealing as a wasp getting trapped in my pyjamas. "Oh, I just assumed you would . . . but I have no right to assume—"

"Of course I'll tell him," she says reassuringly. "Do you want me to tell him everything – I mean, in detail – or should I skirt around the more intimate . . ." She bites her lip, which means she's already overthinking about all the things that could possibly go wrong if she reveals something I mightn't want revealing. "You just need to be sure you're comfortable with Ethan knowing."

"I'm sure. You can tell him everything I told you. He may be my boss, but he's also my friend, and if you trust him, then so do I."

She smiles softly and a spark lights up her bright-blue eyes. I'd kill for her lashes. Even with no make-up on she has lashes Betty Boop would envy. "I think you've made a very brave decision."

"I figured I didn't have much choice." She smiles again, but this time her eyes are telling a different story. "What is it?"

"I was just thinking about something you said last night. When I asked if you missed acting, you said you didn't, but then I realised you haven't stopped acting for the past eight years."

"What do you mean?"

"You've been pretending all this time."

"Acting isn't about pretending. It's about exploring other people's humanity and finding parts of yourself in them." She raises her eyebrows and I let her words sink under my skin. I hear what she's telling me, but I can't quite join up the dots. Was I pretending? She knows I killed the spontaneous, free-spirited girl with a head full of dreams, and created a person I wanted to be in her place. But this is who I am now. The new Freja is all about confidence, ambition and independence. She's the best ad producer in London. She doesn't need men; she needs her friends and crazy nights out and casual hook-ups and coffee. I love who I am, but is she saying that person isn't me?

She shuffles closer and rests her hand on my knee. I turn to face her, and the compassion I see in her eyes knocks the air from my lungs. "When you blocked out what Klein did, you also blocked out who you are. I did exactly the same when my sister died. It took Ethan to show me that I couldn't ignore the huge crack in my heart that losing Laurel caused. Then, it took you to show me how we learn much more from the bad things that happen to us than we do the good. You're made up of so many wonderful things: your friendship; your empathy; your talent and abilities; the love you have for old romantic movies, and coffee, and annoying boggle-eyed yellow cartoon aliens. These are the things that make you special, but you're also made up of what Klein did to you that night . . . and how you lost Nate because of it. Those are two enormous cracks in your heart that are always going to be there. You're an amazing person who had something really shitty happen to them, but you survived, and you became who you are today because of that too."

I kick my brain into gear and try to process her words. I know I don't feel very strong and I'm not proud of how I'm handling this, but deep down my cracked heart knows she's right. The problem is that my head is already wondering if cementing over the cracks is easier than examining their rough, broken and scarred edges. "It sounds like you think I should go live on a secluded island for six months and find myself."

She laughs. "No, not exactly, but you do have to start listening to *her*. After all this time, she's found her voice, so ask *her* what she wants."

"I don't know what she – what *I* want."

"Ask her again. And this time, don't be afraid of what she tells you." She gives my knee a squeeze, then she gets up. "We should get ready for work. Are you coming?"

"Yeah, in a minute."

I watch her leave with dazed, confused and probably still red-from-a-night-of-crying eyes. The grating sound of dickhead neighbour's horrible singing drifts through the door Violet has left open, but then it abruptly stops. Silence at last. An omen?

I close my eyes and take a deep breath.

*What do you want?* I ask her.

*I want him to love me again,* she tells me.

Oh great. That's just what I need. The impossible. Good job, stupid brain.

\* \* \*

It's after nine when we arrive at work. Violet heads straight for a creative meeting with her BuzzPay team, while I go to my desk and promptly drown in the sea of misery otherwise known as my inbox. Rachel's decision to buy custom-made fighter pilot costumes has taken JET Financial's advert over budget, and Lennox is gunning for her over it. Naturally, going after Rachel is Lennox's first course of action despite the creative team having full control of the budget. I have five angry emails from Lennox and two ass-covering emails from Harry. They're all very shouty and include far too many random exclamation marks.

It takes me until noon to save Rachel's skin, appease Lennox, make sure Jadine isn't relaying all the drama to her client-boyfriend, and kick Harry's ass for passing the buck. Then, I get a notification from HR that I apparently have a brand-new part-time music supervisor starting on Monday. I'm just about to fire off an angry email asking how I not only missed my new team member's interview, but also missed writing his job description, oh, and neglected to tell anybody I needed a "music supervisor" in the first place, when I notice the guy's name – Rory Fraser, i.e. Ethan's brother. I'm fine with blatant nepotism as a junior partner perk, but why didn't he tell me before hiring? Definitely not the best of mornings, but at least it's kept my mind off other things.

After lunch I sit down with Neil and run through BuzzPay's brief. This will be his first major campaign as a film producer, although as an art director in Violet's department he was responsible for "Simon the Snail", who helped money-saving website *CashCounter.com* snatch a fifty per cent market-share increase.

It's almost four thirty when Ethan knocks on my office door. Unfortunately he arrives bearing an expression last seen on a fish out of water. He closes the door and sits down facing me.

"I'm guessing Violet has told you." I already know the answer.

"She did." He nods sadly, his blue eyes heavy

and hurt. "I wish I could find the right words and say something meaningful, but I'm a bit out of my depth here. As your boss *and* as your friend."

"There's nothing you need to say." I offer him a smile, which I hoped would register somewhere on his face, but it doesn't.

"If you'd told me all of this earlier, I'd have found a way to stop Klein investing in Tribe. You know that, right?"

I don't have to think for longer than a second. "Yeah, I know you would. I wish my timing was better, but . . ."

"You don't have to explain," he says with a wave of his hand. "But I have to tell you that I'm going to do everything in my power to get that man and his money out of my agency."

"No." I shake my head. "I know you want to protect me, but if you do anything that could risk this getting out . . . I don't want my team, or the partners, or anybody else knowing what he did. I don't want to come to work every day with a huge, pathetic 'victim' sign hung around my neck."

"Nobody would ever think that about you," he says. His eyes are steady and determined, refusing to be swayed. "You're the strongest woman in this entire building. That's why . . ."

My heart sinks as his words get lost inside his throat. "That's why what?"

He sits forward, concentrating his gaze on his interlocked hands. "That's why this is so hard. You're the one person who everybody respects and relies on. Every job I give you, you not only get it done, but you blast the shit out of it. In six months, you've built the most cohesive team in the entire agency, and you did it effortlessly because you're you. Hell, you even managed to fit bloody Jadine Clark into your team." He sits back in his chair and the tension floats from his body. "I've never once had to worry about you. And as for me and Violet? There's a good chance we wouldn't be together if it wasn't for you. Tell me what I can do."

I melt at his kindness. "Just have my back. That's all I need."

He gives my request a moment to register, his eyes fixed intently on mine. "I want to do more."

I let out a small laugh. "And the fact you want to do more means you're already doing more. You're being a friend and a great boss, so thank you." His cheek twitches and he looks away from me. "There's something else, isn't there?"

"I don't think I'll be able to spend five seconds with that man without skelping his ugly head clean off his scrawny neck."

I sigh deeply. "Well, as much as I'd love a front-row seat for that, you mustn't."

He lets out an angry breath. "I just fucking hate guys like him. No matter what shady underhand shit they do, there are always more than enough people licking their arses who'll cover for them. They're just like dogs. Sir Arthur has been Klein's loyal puppy ever since he joined his poncey old-man's crotch-sniffing club, and the other partners, even Stella, have all fallen in line behind him."

A new fear sinks into my chest. What if Ethan can't contain his feelings? He's impulsive and headstrong and pretty much a male version of me. As a hands-on junior managing partner, he has to work with all of the senior partners and investors.

He creates strategy and brings in new business and ensures huge dividends are paid. "I shouldn't have burdened you with this. It's not fair."

"You had to," he says quickly. "Violet was right to convince you to tell me. You have a right to feel safe at work. As your boss, it's my responsibility to not only protect you, but to protect every other woman in this office. Have you ever wondered whether you were a one-off, or if there were others?"

Lord Klein's motivation for hurting me was so specific and personal, I never once stopped to consider if I mightn't be alone. But what if there were others? What if my long silence meant . . . No, it wouldn't be my fault. I'm not spiralling down that road. "He wanted me away from Nate. That's how he justifies what he did. He hated me so much he didn't want me anywhere near his family. I wasn't good enough for his son."

Ethan's face is consumed by anguish. "I can't even comprehend that. I'm not just saying this because you're my friend, Freja, but you're amazing. You're smart and brave and talented and . . . Why on earth wouldn't you be good enough for anybody?"

"I think he had a Mary Sue character in mind for Nate. Inexplicably good, extraordinarily beautiful, an 'English Rose', whatever that means. Men like him hate strong women who break the gender stereotype rules. But my not ticking his boxes wasn't really the problem. His need to control people, especially Nate, was what fuelled his obsession."

"No wonder the poor sod ran away to China."

"You don't know the half of it," I say, wearily shaking my head.

He pauses for a moment, as if he's trying to imagine what his life would be like if he'd had a tyrant for a father. "I've asked Lucille to update me with Klein's whereabouts daily. She's linking up with our own receptionists as well as the building's, and she'll alert me whenever he's here. I'm not letting him within five feet of you."

Crap, I don't know if this is a good idea. "Does Lucille know?"

"No," he says with an emphatic shake of his head. "I mean, Lucille's as astute as hell, you know that, but she never pries. I've no doubt she'll have picked up on the vibe, but I'd trust that woman with my life."

I think back to my encounter with Klein yesterday and resign myself to the fact that Lucille will most definitely be suspicious, but she'll also be discreet. "I'm sure it'll be fine."

"Okay, there's just one more thing." He swallows hard. *Ah min Gud*, what is it now? "Stella Skyped our weekly meeting from Seoul earlier this afternoon. I briefed her on all our major campaigns, and she wants you to film BuzzPay's TV ad."

"You're fucking kidding?" Why is Stella doing this? Neil is new to my department, but I wouldn't have assigned him if I didn't know he could do it.

He shakes his head. "I'm really sorry. I sold Neil as best as I could. I told her Violet had briefed him on the creative team's ideas and he'd started planning the shoot already. I said Violet was happy and comfortable working with Neil as he used to be one of her art directors. I tried everything I could, but she wouldn't budge. She's adamant you oversee the shoot from beginning to end given how prominent the client is. By all means take Neil along as co-producer, but she won't allow him to lead in Italy."

My heart thumps. "In Italy? We're shooting in Italy now?"

Ethan's neck reddens. "Um, yeah, Violet signed off on one of Natalia's ideas this morning, then Madeline presented it to Nate. They originally envisioned the south coast of England, but apparently Nate owns a villa in Lake Como, and BuzzPay are keen for Nate to star in the ad to capitalise on his burgeoning celebrity status. Didn't Violet tell you?"

"I haven't seen her since this morning." I can barely think straight as dozens of horrific potential catastrophes zoom into my brain. Christ, I need to stop this. Violet's overthinking obsession is rubbing off on me. "Is Stella's mind totally set? I know Neil is relatively new to producing, but he's brilliant. Everyone agrees he's brilliant."

"He was a brilliant art director, no question. But he hasn't shot an ad of this magnitude yet, and he's only been in your department for two months. You're our top film producer and BuzzPay is our biggest client. Not to mention, they have links to, um . . ."

"Let me guess, links to Lord Klein, Stella's new favourite investor?" An acrid taste forms at the back of my throat. This is precisely what I've been worried about. I knew I'd have to see Nate at some point, but I was prepared for the odd budget meeting or product review. Shooting an ad in freaking Italy with him is a whole other ball game. How am I going to get through that?

"I'm sorry, Freja. I really tried."

"I know you did."

"Do you think you can work with him?"

"Truthfully? I have no idea."

"I'll talk to Stella again. Maybe if I tell her some of your history."

"No, please, don't say anything to Stella."

I'm actually quite pleased that our formidable CEO is in Seoul while all of this is happening. When Violet and Ethan were having problems last year, she was brutal. Stella Judd does not tolerate personal drama in her ad agency.

"Okay, I'll do it," I say, gritting my teeth. "And I'll make sure it's the best TV ad this agency's ever produced."

# 13

THE BLUE ROOM BAR AT Canary Wharf has become Tribe's regular post-work haunt. It's part of a purpose-built area across from the DLR station which serves the Friday-night needs of the bankers and office workers who occupy the area's glittering skyscrapers. Finding myself here with my friends and colleagues after work isn't unusual. Finding myself rapidly approaching level three on my getting-pissed scale by quarter to nine isn't very unusual either.

"You okay?" asks Violet for probably the hundredth time tonight.

"Yes, I'm still very much okay." I notice she's carrying a very offensive-looking non-alcoholic drink. "What's that?" I say, pointing at her orange juice.

"I think I'm getting a cold," she says solemnly, but I feel my eyes narrowing to suspicious slits. "What are you looking at me like that for?" she asks.

"There's only one reason for a woman to be drinking a soft drink in her favourite bar on a Friday night," I tease.

"Don't you dare," she says, her eyes flashing with horror. "I had a craving for vitamin C, that's all."

My eyes practically explode inside my head. "You're having cravings already?" I try not to laugh as her brain slowly catches up with her word choice and manifests in an even more terrified expression.

"Will you just stop?" she says. "Please, don't make me laugh. My throat is really sore."

"Sure, whatever you say." I snort-laugh into my margarita. "But if you want my advice, I think you and Ethan should think about bumping that wedding up by, say, nine months."

"Oh, for heaven's sake." Violet snatches my drink off me and finishes it. "There, are you satisfied?"

"Oh my god," I say, faking outrage. "I can't believe you're drinking alcohol while pregnant."

"You're doing what now?" I spin around and find Ethan standing behind me, his panic-stricken face resembling a washed-out raincloud. Dilemma time. Do I be kind, or do I keep playing?

"She's just teasing," says Violet, trying to calm her fiancé's shock.

Ethan practically throws an entire shot of whisky down his neck. "Jesus Christ, don't do that to me."

"Wait a minute," says Violet, her expression swiftly moving from mildly embarrassed to slightly agitated. "Why do you look like you've just been told you have six months to live?"

A weary, whiny sound escapes from Ethan's throat. "Um, well, you know . . ."

"I don't know," says Violet. Her voice is croaky, and I start to feel guilty because clearly she really is suffering from the onset of a cold. Not that I ever doubted that in the first place. "Explain yourself."

Ethan looks at me. His eyes are pleading for help, so I give him a get-out-of-jail card. "You probably just want to do big, life-changing events in the right order, don't you, Ethan?"

He nods very slowly. "Yes, that's right.

Engagement, which I've done already, then our first house, then the wedding, then babies about ten years later."

Violet's eyes flash at him. "In ten years we'll be almost forty. I can't wait that long. What if we find out you're firing blanks and it's too late to fix you?"

Ethan looks like he wants to crawl under a rock. His skin flushes scarlet and his jaw drops. "Well that's not going to happen."

Violet laughs. "Oh my god, you're so easy to wind up."

I start to laugh too. "You know, sometimes I wonder why I love working at Tribe so much. You guys are all certifiably crazy." Ethan can usually tease as good as he gets, but this time Violet has really thrown him.

Ethan's colour slowly returns to normal. "Hey, I'll let her do this to me all day long if it makes you laugh again."

A rush of warmth spreads through my body. "I'm actually feeling remarkably good tonight. It's amazing what a few drinks with friends can do." I plaster a smile on my face, but the same gnawing, churning knot of anxiety that has been all twisted up inside me these last few weeks is still there. Maybe it's duller and smaller now. I talked to Violet and I opened up to Ethan, and because I did that, I made this thing real and conquerable.

"What are you drinking?" asks Ethan. "Let me get you another one."

"It's fine, I'll go," I say. Ethan's arm slides protectively around Violet's waist. Her nose suddenly looks like it's been painted with lipstick. "You should go home and get a good night's sleep,"

I tell her. "We're supposed to be scouting locations for BuzzPay first thing tomorrow."

"I emailed everyone this afternoon about the scout. Natalia thinks she's found the perfect . . . " She suddenly grabs Ethan's arm and squeezes her eyes tight. "A-choo!"

"Jesus Christ, Violet, you sneeze like Dumbo." I discreetly check out her ears.

Violet tries to talk but then grimaces and clutches her throat. "It feels like I've been gargling with razor blades." She swallows a huge mouthful of orange juice, then promptly sneezes again. "God, I hate being sick. Like really hate it. Can you remember when I caught flu three Christmases ago?"

"No, because you didn't catch flu," says Ethan.

She glares at him. "I did. I was poorly for a whole week and Christmas was ruined."

"Yes, and I was a fabulous friend to you. I brought you soup and I endured BBC Arts, as well as a load of subtitled movies, for five nights in a row. But you didn't have flu, you had a cold."

"How dare you," she says, clutching her chest in mock outrage.

"It's true, and you're a big baby when you're sick, so I am not enjoying that this is happening right now, because I've just re-subscribed to Netflix and I don't want to watch ballet for a week again. But what was that about tomorrow? I pictured a lie-in followed by brunch out, so why are you working?"

"I have to go. Natalia is on a march," says Violet.

Ethan's eyes pop. "She's on a what now?"

"Something to do with plastic carrier bags," Violet replies. "Or is it whales?"

I interrupt with knowledge I gained from a conversation I had with Natalia in the break room. "She told me she was protesting deep-sea fracking. Apparently it's very dangerous for sea life and she's marching on Downing Street armed with an online petition."

"I don't want people to think I don't give a shit about the environment, but Natalia Salnikova will be the death of me if the flu doesn't get me first." Violet sniffs sadly into a napkin. "We booked Lexi Grant this afternoon, so I need to make sure the location fits with her celebrity persona."

"Woah, back up a minute," says Ethan, making "rewind" circles with his index finger. "I don't think I heard you right. You booked who?"

"I'm positive you're going deaf." Violet gives him a stiff glare. "We signed Lexi Grant, and if you dare tell me you've slept with her, or wanted to sleep with her, I'm going to call her agent and fire her."

"I have never met her, but she's . . . well, she's the hottest . . . okay, maybe I should . . ." He scratches his head to the beat of Violet impatiently drumming her fingers against her glass. "How much did she cost?"

Violet glances at me briefly. "Too much, but Nate asked for her and he's paying, so . . ."

"Oh." Ethan has the same cautious look in his eye. "Does he know her?"

"I think he just liked her in that superhero film she made," Violet says in a hushed, awkward tone.

"The one where she wore the scarlet rubber

catsuit?" Ethan casts a nervous glance in my direction.

"Guys, please. It's been eight years and Nate already has a girlfriend. I think I can cope with him choosing his favourite movie actress to star in his TV ad." I make it sound like I don't care, but the irritating niggle in the centre of my abdomen calls me out. I leave them and go to the bar. A double-shot whisky sour is the only thing capable of drowning out the inconvenient feels.

Gina, my favourite bartender and the owner of London's curliest, most unruly hair, hands me my drink. "There's something different about you tonight," she says as she takes my money and pops open the till.

I'm intrigued. "Oh, what's that?"

She looks me over from top to toe. "You're usually the life and soul of our Friday nights here, but tonight you seem different. Everything okay on the man front?"

I feel my cheeks flush. "Everything's non-existent on the man front actually." I take my change from her.

She frowns. "Sorry if I've upset you."

"You haven't. I'm just really stressed out at work."

Her concentration shifts to the door. "Speaking of men," she says with a nod in the direction of Harry Hopkins, who's just arrived with Lennox Jackson. Harry catches my eye, whispers something inaudible to the always best-dressed account manager, then starts walking towards me. I search for an escape route. Ethan is having an animated conversation with a group of guys, one of whom is

Myles Stanning, who works at Credit Suisse and looks like a flesh-and-bone version of Homer Simpson. Tragically, after I consumed far too many margaritas on my thirtieth birthday, I woke up in Myles's bed fully believing he looked more like Vin Diesel than Homer. I was shamefully deceived by alcohol on that night.

Not wishing to spend tonight fending off the Homer-a-like's advances, I scour the room for Violet and find her languishing in a corner with Georgie. I pick my drink up off the bar, and I'm on my way over to them when Harry grabs my elbow. "I was hoping you'd be here tonight."

"Really? Why's that?" I say with a mixture of apathy and dread.

He leans in too close, and his scratchy beard rubs against my neck. "You mean aside from Rachel Hart blowing half of JET Financial's budget on costumes?"

I'm really not in the mood to talk shop. "Firstly, you're exaggerating. Secondly, your team okayed her decision. And thirdly, if I even needed a thirdly, you shouldn't have signed off on her spending."

"I didn't see it. Sean signed it off. Rachel completely bamboozled him when he was in A&E after having a hypo on the tube. The poor guy was in no fit state to sign off on anything."

"You're kidding me? Did you or didn't you sign off on your team's expenditure?"

He shakes his head. "I've just told you that Sean okayed it."

"So you didn't even look at it?" I take a drink; the strong, spicy liquid warms the back of my throat and the room spins a little. I hope he changes the subject because I'm drunk enough to rip his head off over this.

"I took Sean at his word."

"Then that's your fault for abdicating your responsibilities, you idiot. Stop using your copywriter's diabetes as an excuse."

"I delegated, not abdicated." He steps closer and a familiar look spreads across his face. "But let's change the subject to 'I broke it off with Melissa'."

Already? Christ, he is even more hopeless at relationships than I am. "The answer is no."

He frowns so deeply his eyebrows almost meet in the middle. "What are you saying no to?"

"Rekindling our arrangement. Do you have to be *this* obvious? You've got 'quickie' written all over your face."

"Okay," he says, stepping closer and sliding his arm around my hip. "But I was imagining more than a quickie."

"I don't care what you were imagining. I don't exist to service your needs." I ignore the fact his grip is tightening around me and find Ethan in the crowd again. Myles seems to have moved on, thank goodness, and Ethan's now talking to a really good-looking guy with dark curly hair. I'm intrigued already. "Who's that with Ethan?"

Harry follows my gaze across the bar floor. "No idea. Never seen him before."

"Hmm, maybe I'll go and find out." I take another drink of my whisky sour and start to move in their direction. Good-looking guys come equipped with a homing signal for me when I'm sober, never mind ramping up to a level four.

I feel Harry's fingers lock against mine. "You're

leaving me just like that?"

"Unless you want another threesome."

"A threesome with a guy?" He swallows hard and shakes his head. "No thanks. My arse is a one-way street."

"Good, because I don't like sharing."

I make my way through the crowds to where I last saw Ethan. Luckily for me, what I see now is the back of Ethan as he heads off in the direction of the toilets, leaving the great-looking guy balancing a beer on one of the bar's elbow-high tables.

I don't stop to wonder what I'm doing, or if I should be doing it. I want to feel like myself again, and judging by all of the best moments I've had in my life, there's no better fun than getting to know a really hot guy. I pull my shoulders back, hold my head high and walk over to him. He's tapping away on his mobile, but he looks up as I approach. And oh my god, he has the biggest, darkest, most delicious eyes I think I've ever seen. "You know, for someone I haven't seen in here before, you fit right in."

It's a bullshit introduction, but who cares? I'm wearing my favourite Karen Millen tailored dress, which accentuates every curve of my body, and mystery guy's wandering eyes tells me he's definitely noticed. "It's my first time here," he says in a lovely soft accent that sounds northern-ish. I'm too drunk to be any more precise. English-language accents are extremely puzzling to my Scandinavian ears.

"Do you work around here?" I ask, placing my drink on the table next to him.

"Not yet. I start on Monday." His dark eyes

crinkle at the corners as he smiles. Maybe this guy could be the perfect antidote to Nate popping back into my life. He's casual and relaxed while Nate is dynamic and intense. A cosy cup of hot chocolate versus a thousand-pound bottle of champagne. Surely I'm old enough to know what's good for me by now.

"Well, don't assume this place is all Canary Wharf has to offer." I flick my hair over my shoulder and turn slightly to let my hip "accidentally" nudge his left knee. But then I wobble on my heels, and one of my stupid drunken legs almost forgets it's attached to my foot. I have to grab the table to stop myself from falling over. Hello, level four! Thanks for arriving when I absolutely don't need you.

"Are you okay?" he says, with a little chuckle, as he steadies my arm. *Min Gud*, he's cute! His eyes flash as he beams a huge, almost-sunshine smile. Yes, I definitely like him, and yes, I definitely *would*.

"It's been a very long day, so this is a very much needed night."

His dark, neat beard curves around his cheeks as he delivers another warm smile. "I know the feeling, especially if it's a Friday feeling."

I notice him checking out my body again and I respond by doing the same to him. He's half-sitting on the bar stool, but I think he's definitely under six feet tall – maybe five-eight – which means he's shorter than me. Would that matter to him? He seems totally laidback, possessing a calm and quiet confidence, so I don't think it would. His hard, toned body is encased in a tight-fitting navy shirt, belted into smart black trousers. He knows he's good-looking, and the vibe I'm picking up from the way he's checking me out tells me he thinks I am too. I drink the rest of my whisky sour, place the empty glass back on the table and run the tip of my tongue over my lips. "Why don't you buy me a drink, and I'll let you find out exactly what kind of Friday feeling I'm having?"

He raises his eyes to meet mine. His mouth curls into a smirk. "I think I'd like that. What do you want?"

*You in my bed? Your body on a bed of rice?* No, far too slutty. "How about another whisky sour, and then we'll see?"

"Ah, great, you two are getting to know each other already."

What the hell? Ethan's hands suddenly dive between us and place two bottles of London Porter on the table. I stare at him, and he stares at the guy whose name I never bothered to ask for because I was only interested in the contents of his pants. "Do you two know each other?"

Ethan looks between us, his trademark cheeky grin pulling at his mouth, then he laughs. "Good one."

I have a funny feeling about this. "Good one what?"

He stops grinning and raises a very inquisitive eyebrow. "Wait a minute. What's happening here?"

"*He* was just about to buy me a drink." I jerk my thumb in the mystery man's direction. The guy looks as confused as I am.

"Oh shit, wow, welcome to awks-land," says Ethan. His smirk from thirty seconds ago is replaced by one that screams "beam me up", but there's still a trace of mischief in his eyes. "Um, Freja, let me introduce you to my kid brother."

Oh, for fuck's sake. "Your what?" I thank the gods of alcohol that I'm far too pissed to feel anywhere near as embarrassed as I should, but I'm already dreading work on Monday.

"This is my brother, Rory." Ethan passes one of the bottles of beer to him, and his smirk returns. "Congrats, kid, looks like you've just made a play for your new boss. A feat even I've never achieved."

Rory's dark eyes send Ethan a warning. "We were only talking, but I think now would be a good time to go and get you that drink."

Rory disappears into the crowd. I turn back to Ethan, who is still grinning like a teenager. "Well, this is embarrassing times a fucking million."

"You'll see the funny side tomorrow."

"You're sure about that?" I ask, ignoring the fact that all of my internal organs are cringing. Even my bones.

"No harm, no foul."

"I've been meaning to take you to task for hiring your own brother to work in my team, but I can't do it now because my brain isn't working properly and I might throw up." Do I even feel sick? Or is the swell of nausea in my belly really a swell of shame?

"I hired him on impulse, which is something I do, um, often. Rory needed a break, and he knows music better than anybody on this planet." Ethan nudges my shoulder and throws me a wink. "And you like him, don't you?"

"You're such an idiot."

"I won't argue with that, but I'm also the fiancé of someone who's the absolute worst pain in the arse when she's sick, so I'm going to have to shoot off and put her to bed." He takes a huge swig of his beer then wipes at his mouth.

"You're leaving me?" I say, folding my arms. "I can't believe you're bailing on my night."

Ethan looks around the bar. "You've dozens of friends here. You don't need us." He finishes his beer, then his very irritating smirk returns.

"Don't you dare."

"What?" he says with a laugh.

I brace myself. "Whatever you're going to say, keep it in your head."

He places his hand at the centre of his chest. "I was only going to say that I trust you not to bang my brother."

And there it is. Honestly, if he wasn't such a great boss, I'd knee him in the balls. "Okay, just go. Get out of here."

Rory returns with my cocktail. "You're leaving?" he asks Ethan. A slow crawl of red spreads across his face.

"Violet has work tomorrow and she's coming down with a cold."

"Oh, hell," says Rory. And just like that I match up his non-London accent with Ethan's. How didn't I notice that? "Violet is awful when she's sick. Remember when—"

"I know," says Ethan, his voice drenched in the horrific memory. "Christmas three years ago."

Ethan says goodbye by squeezing my arm, then he pulls me into a hug. "Great to get the Freja we all love back tonight."

He wanders off to retrieve Violet, and I find myself suddenly alone with a guy who's undeniably hot, but also undeniably off-limits. "I think we should put tonight behind us and start again." I offer Rory my hand. "Freja Larsen, Tribe's film production director. I'm not usually this drunk and I'm definitely never this embarrassed."

Rory smiles widely and shakes my hand. "Rory Fraser, musician, bartender and Tribe's new part-time music supervisor. I'm not drunk, but I'm probably even more embarrassed than you."

"You know, I think we'd be within our rights to blame your brother for this."

"One hundred per cent. I love him, but he's such an idiot."

"He is," I say with a laugh. "But he's also a good guy."

"Yep." He raises his glass for me to clink. "One of the best."

"Come on," I say, taking his elbow and stumbling into the crowd. "I'll introduce you to the rest of the gang."

\* \* \*

I strain my eyes open as images from last night hammer into my brain. Too many whisky sours. Far too many Moscow Mules. Laughter. Dancing. Was I in Leicester Square? Fuck, who the hell did I go up West with?

I roll my face to find a cool patch on the pillow and shut my eyes again. I feel like I've been vomited up by the beasts of hell, but I have no regrets. I needed last night. I needed to get back to being me, enjoying my life and having a great time with my friends. I yawn, then I have to stop myself crying out as the dryness in my throat scratches every single nerve in my neck and sends shooting pains soaring into my skull.

I bury my head deeper, but then memory and reality finally separate, and the truth doesn't so much hit me as bulldoze me into an alternate universe. Where am I?

My eyes fly open. Small room, peeling wallpaper, flat-screen TV, bathroom door, plastic fire safety notice. What the shit? How am I in a fucking Travelodge? *Classy, Freja. Very classy. Now think.* Did I pull a cheapskate last night, or somebody who works in a call centre? Oh crap, did I fuck Ethan's brother last night? I seem to remember spending a large amount of the evening appreciating his body. Whilst dancing with him – a lot. And more to the point, where are my clothes?

Shit. Crap. Hell. This is not a great move.

I close my eyes and concentrate hard. I remember going up West with a few people. Rory was definitely there. Neil, Rachel, Euan, and I think Kris came with us too. I have no idea what happened to Georgie. This means I'm a totally shit friend whilst drunk – which she knows – but who else was there? The guy from finance who used to dance on a cruise ship was boring us for a while . . . and flip, so was Myles Stanning.

*Quick, brain, think.* What's worse? Banging my boss's brother, or banging a guy who looks like Homer Simpson?

Or maybe I did both, or neither. Maybe I got here on my own. I look around the room and spot my grey dress folded neatly on the chair opposite. Could I have done that in the state I was in last night? Doubtful.

Just then, the bedroom door buzzes briefly as it connects with a key card. I hear the handle turn. I steady my eyes and brace myself as the apple-chomping carcass of Harry Hopkins enters the room.

"Morning, gorgeous," he says, taking a huge bite of a shiny green apple.

His crunching gnaws at my tender brain. "How did I get here?"

"You were too pissed to make it back to Greenwich, so I thought I'd look after you."

I peek under the duvet. Pants and bra are on, which is a good sign. "Did we, um . . . ?"

His eyes go wide. "Strewth, what do you take me for? I might be a wanker, but I'm not about to screw a woman when she's totally ratted."

"Then how did . . . ?" I feel the coolness of the duvet against my clammy skin. My body is aching all over, from the balls of my feet to the top of my skull, but there's a far worse sensation building in my gut.

Shame. Fear. Panic.

This is just like before.

Harry sits on the edge of the bed and rests his hand on my leg. "What's wrong?" he asks, looking worried.

I pull my knees up to my chest. "My dress. What did you do?"

He looks at me like I've lost my mind. "You were practically unconscious. I put you to bed and watched over you. Think I nodded off around five. I was really worried though. I thought you might hurl in your sleep and choke."

My flesh starts to burn. "You had no right," I say, tears forming in my eyes.

He removes his hand from my leg and sits to attention. His face is a mess of confusion, and my shame evaporates into guilt. I'm not being fair. He's done nothing wrong. "I wanted you to be comfortable. It's not like I haven't seen your body before."

"That's not the fucking point!" I yell. He jumps off the bed, holding both his hands up. "My body doesn't belong to you, and you had no right to touch me."

He looks devastated. "I'm sorry. I thought . . . I was only looking after you, I swear. It was a really tight dress. I didn't think you'd want to sleep in it."

I wipe the tears off my cheeks then fall back onto the pillows. Am I being unreasonable? Am I overreacting? Will I ever not be a complete fucking mess?

"Just leave," I tell him.

"Not until I know you're—"

I raise my voice. "I said leave."

I keep my eyes fixed to the ceiling. I hear the door open and close, then I glance at the alarm clock. My panic soars further when I realise I'm due in Hampstead in ten minutes.

This day is about to get a whole lot worse.

# 14

THIS IS THE FIRST TIME in the history of my entire working life that I've been late for an important location scout. I don't want to think about all the possible psychology-related reasons why today's scout is the one the universe chose to bestow with my lateness, but here I am, a whopping hour and twenty minutes behind schedule. I'm also completely fuelled by maximum-strength espresso, topped up by paracetamol, and wearing the darkest pair of sunglasses I own in a vain attempt to kill one of the worst hangovers I've ever had. I hope we can get done as soon as possible so I can spend the rest of today – and possibly tomorrow – in bed.

I take a black cab from the Travelodge in Covent Garden to my house in Greenwich. As I'm changing my clothes, I receive a text from Neil: *We're at the Chelsea house – would have been nice if you'd filled me in – please hurry!* I feel terrible for being late, but I don't know what he means about "filling him in". I don't think my brain is working yet, so I'll ask him when I get there. Usually in moments like this I promise to never drink again, but I'm realistic, so instead I promise to drink a pint of water every time I get wasted. And swap out the paracetamol in my bathroom cupboard for double-strength co-codamol.

The Uber drops me off at the top of Bywater Street – which I vaguely remember was Violet's first-choice location. Pastel-coloured terraced houses with white window frames and smart black front doors sit neatly on a narrow road lined with delicate leafy trees and parked Range Rovers. It looks like it's been plucked directly from a Keira Knightley movie. I'm imagining her walking out of one of the pretty houses, dressed in a nineteen-twenties silk dress and cloche hat, when Neil appears in front of me with a camera in his hand.

"What the hell took you so long?" He gets closer, and his face crumples into a mess of creases. "Holy shit, you look terrible!"

"Thanks for the compliment." I push my sunglasses further up my nose. "I had a late one last night if you must know. It was Friday, after all."

He scrunches up his eyes. "I know, I was out with you last night."

Oh shit, he's not wrong. "Sorry, I haven't woken up yet. And my head is killing me."

"I'm not surprised," he says, sounding infuriated and impressed all at the same time. "However, I *was* surprised at the number of shots you downed last night. While standing on a bar stool. And while throwing down all the moves to 'Uptown Funk'."

A memory stirs and I cringe. "Oh shit, I assembled an audience again, didn't I?"

"Yep. It wasn't as big as the audience you assembled when you did that twerking thing on our last team night out, but it was still pretty impressive."

"I got four guys' telephone numbers that night," I say proudly.

"I'm pleased for you, but you're not seventeen anymore. If you keep going like this you're going to rot your liver and die a slow, painful death."

I lower my sunglasses so I can give him the glare

he deserves. "Why would you say something like that? What's wrong with you?"

"It's just what happens. My great-uncle Howard died of cirrhosis and I very much doubt he could have downed six vodka shots in thirty seconds like you did in the early hours of this morning."

I poke my tongue inside my cheek and raise my eyebrows. "But could he have danced to 'Uptown Funk' while standing on a bar stool?"

"No, but I'd have paid good money to see him try," he says, with a wry smile which fades from his face as fast as it appears. "But I'm being serious now. You knew we had work today, and I've had to make excuses for you all morning." He takes hold of my elbow and guides me between a tree and a parked Volkswagen Beetle. "Ethan called first thing to say Violet couldn't make it because she has the flu, so we've had no director input all morning."

"You're kidding? Violet has a sniffle. Possibly a cold." I'm going to feel bad if she actually does have the flu, but I know her too well, so I'm going to go with my gut until I see evidence to the contrary.

Neil pushes the sleeves of his jacket up to his elbows. "We could have coped without Violet if you'd been here. I couldn't reach Natalia. She's probably been arrested for chaining herself to the gates outside Number Ten by now. Frank has had to make all the big creative decisions on his own, and if he's messed up, we're going to have Madeline Westgate on our backs for the rest of our lives."

I look over at the group of people standing around outside a candyfloss-pink house further up the street. My eyes are still drunk, but I easily spot the tall enigmatic blonde standing with her hands on her hips. "Why is she here?"

"She has no life," he says in exasperation. "She has no friends, she hates people, she definitely hates me and she probably hates herself. All she does is work, and she's a bloody control freak. Remember when Lennox put his foot down over the FX Jason designed for Heliotrope?"

"How could I forget?"

"Yeah, well multiply Lennox's stubbornness by a million and you'll still fall short of how big a pain in the arse Madeline is." He runs his hand through his muddy-blonde hair, then shakes his head. "She's made Polly cry twice and it isn't even half past ten."

I want to go home. Could I get away with asking Neil to take care of everything for me and disappear into the nearest King's Road coffee shop? "Crap. I'm not in a fit state to manage Polly's meltdowns or Madeline's demands. Please tell me Polly has stopped crying."

"I think she has." Neil shrugs. "But it isn't going to take much to set her off again. Madeline has been pushing her all morning. She snapped at her for inputting the wrong location permit fee, then called her an idiot for completely forgetting to factor parking charges into our shoot budget. It's only a few hundred quid difference, but you'd have thought Polly had run over her cat."

This is not good news. Polly Jordan, my line producer, oversees the department's admin and operational needs. She's a very useful assistant, but she has the temperament of a nervous rabbit. No way in hell am I putting up with someone from client accounts upsetting a member of my team.

"Come on, time to head into the eye of the storm," I say, jerking my head in the direction of the others. Neil follows, but I detect a heaviness in the air around him and know something else is bothering him. "How are you feeling about Stella bumping you off BuzzPay?"

"Oh, I'm fine," he says unconvincingly. He stops walking and toes his shoe into a grassy crack in the pavement. His eyes connect with mine and a small smile tweaks at the corners of his mouth. "Okay, if you want the truth, I was pissed off when you first told me, but I swear I'm cool with it now."

"Ethan tried really hard, Neil," I say, resting my hand on his shoulder. I can tell he's really disappointed. "If it were down to me, you'd be running the entire shoot, and I have every faith that you'd do a fantastic job, but it's a massive client and it's just not the right time for you."

"Freja, it's fine," he says with a broad smile. "I'm frustrated because I really wanted to prove myself, but I can still do a great job. What do you say to us being co-producers?"

I stick my hand out for Neil to shake. "I say that's an excellent idea so long as you personally make sure I'm supplied with fresh espresso every twenty minutes when we're in Italy."

"You're on." He gives my hand a robust shake. "Actually, there's one more thing before we go over there." He looks apprehensively towards the group. "Nate Klein. What's the deal with him?"

My heart leaps. "What do you mean?"

"Well, he's almost as bad as Madeline. He totally chewed out my animated Bizzy Bee character, saying it was cheap, juvenile and would make him look like Dick van Dyke." Neil's intelligent blue eyes retreat under a frown. "I thought Violet had already signed off on the bee. I mean, I know Natalia wasn't completely sold on it, but when you think she proposed animating a freaking letter 'B' I don't think she's in any position to complain."

Neil's words enter my brain, then get lost in a jumble. "Wait a minute. Let's backtrack. Nate Klein said this to you when?"

"This morning." I'm not sure if he's still frowning or if he's squinting in the bright sunshine that has just broken through the clouds, but he's definitely not happy. "That's why I was so pissed off with you for being late."

"He called you this morning?" I ask, feeling my protection-radar kick into action again. Neil's my guy. Clients should bring concerns to account managers, not to my producers. "Why is he speaking to you instead of his account manager? At the very least, he should be complaining to me, or Violet."

Neil looks at me as if I'm stupid. "But neither of you were here."

"You mean he was here?"

"I mean he *is* here."

He looks over his shoulder, and my gaze follows to find Nate standing in the middle of the group, chatting to Madeline and our actress, Lexi Grant. I pull down my sunglasses as my body instinctively breathes him in. He's dressed casually today, but the way he holds himself never changes – strong, commanding, confident and unbelievably beautiful. Then, of all the stupid things to start worrying about, I remember I failed to force myself to put on any make-up this morning. "Shit. This isn't good."

"You're telling me," says Neil, irritation building in his voice. "You didn't prep me that we were going to start shooting today. I didn't know Lexi Grant would be here. Skye bit my head off when I called her at home to say we needed costume and make-up at the scene. I had to bribe Kwame to do the grip work, but I couldn't get hold of Kris, so I'm having to be cameraman for the day. I don't actually blame Nate for kicking off. We look like a bunch of bloody students on a field trip."

I don't even have to think twice, despite my brain being too sozzled to do any meaningful thinking. "There was no plan to start shooting today, Neil."

"Apparently they agreed the location yesterday afternoon and Violet emailed everyone about bringing the London shoot forward to today."

What the hell is going on? I didn't get that schedule. I take out my phone, search through my messages and fight back a sudden urge to vomit when I see not one but three unread emails from Violet. I click on the first one and wonder if anybody would notice if I choked myself. "Fuck!"

Neil's expression notches a few levels up the exasperated scale. "You missed her messages, didn't you?"

"Apparently. But she didn't say anything last night . . . at least I can't remember . . ." Oh shit, I do remember talking a little about working today with her. Just before she did that huge Dumbo sneeze. "It's my fault I didn't get my messages. But I wish Violet had checked that I knew what we were doing today."

"Maybe she didn't check because nobody has ever needed to check up on you before. You always know what you're doing and you never, ever fuck up."

I inhale a shaky breath because he's right. My life is totally screwed and it's getting worse with every day that passes.

Neil gently touches my arm. "What's going on?"

"Nothing. I . . ." I glance back over to the group. It looks like Skye has just arrived. Plus a tech van. And a council official with a clipboard who'll probably fine us for not completing the correct paperwork for the permit. Shit, how am I going to pull this together? "Okay, this is all my fault. You have to help me."

"I'm with you, but I doubt anyone cares what I have to say. After Nate Klein launched a full-scale takedown of Bizzy Bee before I'd fully digested my breakfast bagel, I've done nothing but look like a graduate trainee who doesn't have a clue what he's doing."

"Did you tell him creative backed the bee?"

"Yes, and he told me he didn't give a fuck." Neil steps closer and lowers his voice. "Between you and me, I think him and Madeline are made for each other. They're playing some kind of alpha death match. I'm not looking forward to spending a week in Italy with them. Maybe they'll get it on after this. Do you know if Madeline's single?"

Crap, how would I cope with that? "I don't know about Madeline, but Nate Klein is dating my ex-boyfriend's *General Practice* co-star."

His eyes spring to life. "Woah, wait. Who's

that?"

"Lucy Tonner."

"I knew about Lucy. I was talking about you. I didn't know you dated someone famous."

"It was a long time ago, but it was Richie Robbins. He wasn't famous at all when I first met him. We shared a house in LA." Christ, if he thinks this is big news, wait until he finds out the even bigger news. "Have to say, you don't strike me as someone who'd watch BBC2 daytime soap operas."

"I don't, but Rachel is a super-fan and my desk is next to hers. She's talked about Lucy all week."

Neil continues to relay Rachel's thoughts on *General Practice*, but my aching brain is far too occupied worrying about the impromptu shoot. I would never have drunk so much last night if I knew I'd be filming as opposed to scouting today. I glance back over at my assembled mini film crew. Everybody's doing everything they can to turn the shitshow around, and I need to do the same, so I close my eyes, take a deep breath and walk purposefully into battle.

I acknowledge Nate and Madeline's presence with a "Hi" and a very quick apology. Madeline makes her dissatisfaction known, but it's obvious her knowledge of my panic attacks is holding her back from giving me the ass-kicking I probably deserve. Nate, on the other hand, doesn't say anything at all. He looks off into the distance when I talk with Madeline, his jaw locked tight as if he's forcing himself not to speak.

We soon start working and I try to switch into professional mode, but it's a challenge because my body is craving another round of over-the-counter drugs and several hours of uninterrupted sleep. Neil starts filming, and I'm looking over his shoulder into the camera when I become aware of Nate watching me. I slowly turn my head and meet his gaze. His eyes are burning with the same intensity as a newly formed star. He looks away quickly, his skin flushed and his posture deliberately hardened.

Did I really see that? I daren't allow myself to believe that this means anything. Maybe he's staring at me because he's trying to work out why I look so goddamn awful. I keep my sunglasses on as much as I can, but I'm cursing myself for skipping out on make-up this morning. I spend nowhere near as much time in front of the mirror as Rachel and Jadine do every day, but I wish I had a tube of mascara in my bag at the very least. I came to terms with my ginger-ness when I was five years old, but I'm painfully aware that my pale copper lashes make my eyes look like they belong on a hamster.

Our London footage wraps in less than two hours and consists of Lexi, in a gorgeous pale-pink Stella McCartney mini-dress, walking out of the front door of the pink house with a huge, enthusiastic smile on her face. The ad's storyline could be ripped out of a nineties chick-lit book, which is strange because I know with absolute certainty that both Violet and Natalia, who came up with the idea, don't read those kinds of books.

In our story, Lexi's beautiful, but ridiculously ditzy, alter-ego buys cannoli from an Italian cake shop in London every Wednesday afternoon. It turns out that Lexi's character had a holiday romance with Nate, playing himself, who used Italian desserts to romance her. When Nate spots

Lexi leaving the cake shop years later, the chef tells him she's been visiting for years, but his cannoli aren't like the ones she used to buy in Italy. Being the genius proprietor of international cash-handling system BuzzPay, Nate orders the real deal from the café they fell in love in and hand-delivers them to the cake shop. The missing ingredient turns out to be honey, hence Bizzy Bee's proposed animated appearance, which links to the "Buzz" part of BuzzPay. I concede that this might have been dumb, but not as dumb as women believing all you have to do to find true love is live in a pastel-coloured house and frequent a cake shop. But what do I know? Most of the books on the Waterstones bestsellers shelves look like the scene I've set up. Maybe I should spend more time in cake shops and less time getting wasted in bars.

We wrap the first part of the shoot just before one p.m. and I'm thankful we've had good weather and a well-behaved general public. I'm helping Neil and the production runner, Kwame, load up the van when Nate finally decides to approach me. "Have you got a moment?"

"Um, sure, what can I do for you?" I glance at a group of twenty-something women gathered around us, and it takes me a few moments to work out that they're hoping for a selfie with Nate. Which is very weird.

He leads me around to the back of the van. Please let him be avoiding his fans' eager mobile phone cameras. My breath hitches in my throat as I brace myself for the worst.

"You know, Freja, I really thought we could do this." He crosses his arms stiffly and his eyes become dark, impenetrable boulders of rock. "I've heard phenomenal things about your work from Ethan, as well as from Madeline. I know you're supposed to be one of the best advertising film producers out there, so I was expecting you to blow away all my doubts that our past wouldn't affect your professionalism."

I know I've shot some great footage this morning, so I stand my ground. "Are you saying you have a problem with my filming?"

His gaze sweeps over the crowd. Nobody is close enough to hear him, but he lowers his voice anyway. "No, I'm saying I have a problem with you turning up to work still drunk from the night before."

I feel my eyes well up as his disappointment cuts through me. Damn it, I wasn't prepared for how much I needed him to have faith in me. I almost leap down his throat for daring to comment on whatever state he thinks I'm in, but then I remember he's our client. "It won't happen again."

"Does Ethan Fraser know about us?"

Shit. What do I say? If I lie, I'm sure the sunglasses will prevent my eyes giving the game away, but why should I lie? He didn't tell me not to mention our past to anybody. "He's my best friend's fiancé."

"So he knows how we broke up?" He runs a hand through his hair, gritting his teeth as the angry nerve that lives in his cheek pulses. "I knew he was being evasive when I spoke to him this morning. I don't want anyone else to know why we broke up, okay? I don't want to be known as a guy whose girlfriend cheated on him."

My voice disappears for a moment, before returning in a croak. "I don't want that either."

"Good," he says, his eyes betraying the extent of his humiliation. "I'm sorry for calling Ethan, but nobody knew where you were. Anything could have happened . . ."

My entire body gasps as my aching brain scrambles to come to terms with the fact he didn't call Ethan to complain – he called him because he was worried about me. "Well here I am, and the only thing that happened last night was a great night out—"

"You've changed. What happened to you?" The words leave his mouth in a disappointed whisper that shatters a previously unbroken piece of my heart. I want to scream the truth in his face because I can't bear the way he's looking at me.

"I have a life, Nate. All I'm doing is living it."

He stands tall, throwing his shoulders back. "You can live it all you like, just don't screw over my campaign because of something that happened a long time ago."

Crap. Why did he have to overstep? My blood soars to boiling point. "You think last night was about you? Are you fucking kidding me?"

His eyes anxiously search the crowd. "Will you keep your voice down?"

"Will you stop being an egotistical asshole?"

"What do you want me to think, Freja?"

"I want you to remember who I am!"

My words hit him hard. He stands before me, his chest heaving with each angry, shaky breath, and all I want to do is touch him. *I want you to remember who I am.* But I also want him to remember what my body feels like, what my kisses taste like, and how he used to love me. I want to know if what I think I see lingering in his eyes is really there.

"I'm sorry, but this is business. One more fuck-up and you're off my campaign."

I watch him return to Madeline and Lexi, then I get back to packing up the van.

When we're done I go home and sleep my way through Sunday.

# 15

TWO WEEKS HAVE PASSED SINCE I last saw Nate. I heard he was tying up loose ends in China, but then photos of him spending Easter somewhere hot and exotic with Lucy appeared in the press. I've tried to keep my mind clear of him, so I can concentrate on work, but he's become a frequent player in my dreams. Why is it that when you're trying to get a guy out of your mind, they pop up in your subconscious? And why are they always naked and yearning for sex?

The UK part of our filming was completed on schedule at the end of last week. I've shared preliminary footage with Madeline, who surprised me by liking it *and* requesting the return of the animated bee. She said Nate had changed his mind.

We flew to Milan from Heathrow first thing this morning, as a complement of thirteen. Thankfully, Violet recovered from her flu-cold-sniffle in time to come with us, although she still has a very persistent raspy cough. Frank and Natalia are operating as her creative sub-team during the shoot and will be spending the first day auditioning actors and film extras in Milan. Madeline and her assistant, Sophie, are here to represent the client, then there's actress Lexi Grant, my "co-producer" Neil, and my five-person technical crew. We've all been booked into a rose-bricked art nouveau-style hotel overlooking Lake Como, near the picture-perfect lakeside town of Menaggio.

As I unpack my suitcase, my mind wanders back

to Nate. I've spent so long trying not to think about him that it feels strange to give in and go there, but I actually have good reason to indulge myself this time. In a couple of days, Nate will be making his debut in front of the camera and I'm going to be directing him. I know that acting is something he's never done before, but much of BuzzPay's ad is entirely his vision. He's obviously going to look great on film, but the thought of directing him in a series of romantic scenarios with Lexi, including a snog and an embrace, is not something I'm looking forward to. I'm probably giving this niggle far too much freedom to run riot in my brain, but I still can't shake the feeling that this shoot has all the potential in the world to go horribly wrong.

I'm hanging the last of my clothes on hangers when there's a knock at the door. I open it to reveal a huge pair of bright-blue sparkling eyes. "You'll never guess what," says Violet, her entire body shaking with excitement.

I laugh as she bounces into the room like a real-life version of Tigger. "You look happy."

She pulls her mobile from the pocket of her denim shorts. "Just wait until you see this." She thrusts the screen in front of my face, and I want to throw up when I see the ugly red logo of Lord Klein's rag, the *Herald Online*. I always refuse to click on their garbage sensationalist stories, but I'm intrigued by Violet's bounciness, so I read the headline: *General Practice star's holiday bust-up with millionaire business tycoon.*

A smile explodes onto my face, followed by a horrible guilty feeling that I probably shouldn't be feeling as happy as I'm feeling. I scan the article, telling myself it's bound to be bullshit. There are quotes from an "insider" on Lucy's TV show, and there are photos of Nate holding hands with her on a sun-drenched Caribbean beach. I note with more giddiness that they have perfectly matching angry faces. "Okay, this is making me feel something I'm not at all comfortable feeling."

"Are you looking at his beach bod?"

My eyes do a cartwheel. "No." But then I scroll back up to the photo and take a moment to fully appreciate how amazing his tanned, olive skin looks in white surf shorts. His body is even more defined than I remember, and I spend a moment imagining running my fingers over the contours of his hard, sculpted chest. My womb goes all fluttery and I bite my lip.

"You're looking now, aren't you?" Violet says with a giggle.

"Firstly, maybe, and secondly, are you fifteen?"

"No, but you're both single now, so this couldn't be more perfect."

I hand her phone back. "It doesn't matter, Violet."

"Why not?" she asks, sitting down on the bed.

"You know why."

Her jubilant smile fades from her face. She sighs. "Look where we are. Could there be a more romantic setting?"

"We're here to work, but even if we were here for pleasure, it'd still be impossible." I sit down on the bed next to her, a knot of unhappiness swelling in my chest. "He could be devastated about Lucy, his brother said I broke his heart, he thinks I cheated on him, and if I need to remind you about the other huge elephant in the room, then it concerns his dad being a massive c-word."

She drums her fingers on the bed. "This is so fucking unfair."

"The one thing people all over the globe say about life is that it's unfair, but we just have to accept it."

"Well *I* don't say that," says Violet. She turns to face me and her eyes flash with fury. "If something in life's unfair, then you fix it."

"This is different, Violet. This can't be fixed."

She exhales sadly and rubs at her brow. "Maybe not, but sometimes the universe finds a way of fixing things all by itself."

Her hope ignites a flame inside me. I've always lived in the present. I never make plans. My life has always just worked itself out – even through all the bad times. I always felt that losing Nate needed to happen because there couldn't be a future for us, but what if we *could* find a way? Ugh. *What if, what if, what if* . . . What if I'd never met Nate Klein? I'd be living a very different life than I am now, that's for sure.

"We're meeting at Nate's villa in an hour. It's halfway between Menaggio and Azzano," says Violet. I nod at her instructions, but my mind is still whirring a world away, which she notices. "What are you thinking?"

"Hmm?" I gaze out of the window. The sun is so strong and bright that it's reflecting a field of white twinkling stars onto the calm water, and all of a sudden I want to go home – and I don't mean London; I mean Copenhagen. I need my dad, and my sister, and the people who knew me and loved me before the Kleins entered my world. "Being here just doesn't feel right."

She glides an arm around my back. "What do you mean?"

"You'll think I'm silly, and it's just a feeling, but the energy is all wrong. There's no balance, no calm, no *hygge* . . . Despite how beautiful it is here, I want to leave."

She rests her head against mine. "I'm sorry. I shouldn't have said anything about Lucy, and I definitely shouldn't have been so excited over the break-up. I want you to be happy. You deserve it more than anyone."

I take hold of her hand. Her sapphire engagement ring rests against my palm, and an envious ache spikes into me. I close my eyes and push the negative emotions out of my head *and* my heart. "Just be here for me this week. Glue yourself to me and keep my mind off him. That will make me happy."

Her eyes well up and she coughs on a sob. Then she coughs again, the remnants of the virus she's been battling for the last two weeks making her body convulse. "Jesus, I'm so sick of being sick."

I rub her back gently. "You're a lot better than you were."

"I know, but the cold is still on my chest, which means when I'm not coughing I'm snoring. Ethan says I sound like a strangulated goat. He wouldn't stay over at mine last night because he got no sleep on Saturday. I miss him, and I'm going to miss him while I'm here and . . . I'm sorry. I know I sound pathetic. Would you believe that this will be the longest time we've been apart since we met?"

"You're kidding. You've never been apart longer than six days? Even when you were just friends?" She nods, then starts coughing again. "You're not pathetic, but if you were a character in one of my favourite golden-era Hollywood movies and coughed like that, you'd be dead within an hour. Greta Garbo coughed her way through tuberculosis, cholera or typhoid in every movie she made."

She coughs again, covering her mouth with the back of her hand. "Thanks."

"You're welcome. Now get out of my room and take your germs with you. I need to get dressed."

\* \* \*

Villa Tramonto is located halfway up a small hill overlooking Lake Como. For some reason, I pictured Nate owning a centuries-old mock-Renaissance villa with landscaped gardens and marble statues leading up to the entrance, but instead I see steel, glass and modern geometric shapes. I shouldn't be surprised by this at all given Nate lives in a penthouse at the top of Heron Tower, one of London's tallest skyscrapers.

We're driven to the entrance of Nate's villa in one of the two minivans we hired for the duration of our stay. With half of our team out scouting locations in Menaggio, there are only six of us attending this afternoon's operational meeting. The villa is built into the side of a small hill, so we have to walk up some steps and sloping pathways to get there. On the way I notice that Madeline is really hitting it off with Lexi, which is pleasing because while the B-list actress is warm, friendly and engaging, Madeline is prickly, aloof and difficult. Last week, I learned that Madeline is so unpopular with the younger members of my team that they set up a WhatsApp group for the sole purpose of complaining about her. They said they were letting off steam, but as none of them would dare repeat what they'd written to her face, I tore strips off them and made them delete the group.

"What do you think about those two?" Violet asks, looking up the path ahead to Neil, who looks to be deep in conversation with Madeline's newest recruit, Sophie Page.

"I think he's definitely smitten. Sophie was struggling to carry a box of files up the stairs a couple of weeks ago and he nearly tripped over his own feet to help her out."

"They'd be adorable together." She makes what I can only describe as a "cutesy" face. The change in Violet since she and Ethan got engaged is both strange and frightening.

"Okay, calm down, Mills & Boon," I say as we climb the last few steps to the villa's front door. "This is work, not *Love Island*."

Violet nudges me with her elbow. "Now who's being cynical?"

Nate opens the door and greets Madeline and Lexi, then Neil and Sophie. They all enter the villa, and his gaze connects with mine.

"Are you okay?" Violet whispers.

A guttural, incoherent mumble leaves my body in response.

Nate looks at me only briefly. His dark-brown eyes are filled with warmth, but then he switches his attention to Violet. "How was the journey over?" he asks politely, before diving straight into the kind of small talk about gardens and the weather that only English people make. He ushers us inside his second, or is it third, home, and the topic of conversation moves swiftly onto the shoot, before switching to his newfound fondness for Lexi's back catalogue of movies, and then circling back to the weather. Apparently, Lake Como is enjoying a slightly warmer April than usual at a blistering twenty-five degrees. Violet, who is normally terrible at small talk, does her very best to sound fascinated.

The only thing I contribute to the conversation is a pleasant smile. I hate that I'm this insecure in Nate's presence. I definitely need a drink. Usually I enjoy getting to know our agency's clients, so it's bothering me that I can't relax and enjoy myself, especially given the beautiful setting.

A hired waiter carrying a tray stocked with bubbling champagne glasses suddenly appears before me. It's as if I willed him and his sparkling drinks into existence. I take a flute from him and try out some of my phrase-book Italian. A broad smile lights up his olive skin and he flashes an impressive set of perfectly straight white teeth. Yes, he's hot, and yes, if I wasn't in the company of Nate Klein, I probably would.

Nate leads us out onto a sunlit patio overlooking a square swimming pool with a spa feature. My brain immediately conjures up images of the various shades of after-hours fun that could be had in the pool, because that's how my brain likes to torture me. A stone wall encircles the villa and garden, with hedges, bushes, olive trees and cedars separating the property from the lake and surrounding mountains. It's all very impressive, but while everyone else comes together to take in the spectacular views, I can't take my eyes off Nate. His sky-blue shirt, rolled-up jeans and deck shoes don't fit the corporate-superstar version of Nate that the world knows today. Instead, his clothes and all the warmth and sunshine send me spiralling back to Nate from eight years ago – the one who kissed me on Santa Monica Pier and ate strawberries off my body in a Beverly Hills hotel room.

And, *åh min Gud*, I need another drink. I need to numb my anxiety and fill my veins with a lively alcohol buzz. I pour a generous amount of champagne down my throat before moving swiftly onto the next one.

I search for Violet and find her sitting at a round glass patio table with a sketchbook. "You look busy. What are you doing?"

"Tweaking the storyboard to fit the villa. I wasn't prepared for how awesome that view would be."

I look out over the lake to the horizon. There's a boat moored to the post of a short wooden jetty. I wonder if it's his? "It's all perfect for the shoot. He was right to use his own home. This place suits . . ." My voice evaporates when I spot Nate walking to the stone wall with Lexi. She's looking into his eyes, and he's smiling so widely that he looks like he has fifty teeth.

Violet looks up from her book and follows my gaze. "Have you heard about your team's WhatsApp group?"

"Yes, and I said I'd fire every single one of them

if they didn't delete it."

"Because of the betting?"

I'm confused. "Betting? No, because of the bitching."

She mirrors my confusion. "What bitching? They better not be bitching about me. Remember I told you what happened in New York? No way am I putting up with anything like that again."

Violet's New York story would give the characters from *Mean Girls* a run for their money, so I quickly put her mind at rest. "No, your name wasn't mentioned at all."

"Good, because I've had enough bitching to last me a lifetime." She lets out a sigh of relief. "The WhatsApp group I was talking about was set up by Kris the cameraman. Everyone in your team is taking bets on who Nate's going to bang this week."

"Please tell me I'm not on the list."

"Everyone who's female is on the list, except me." She holds her hand up and flashes her ring as evidence why she wasn't included.

"You mean Billie is on the list?" I ask. My young production assistant is a very proud lesbian who told me she would definitely sleep with Lexi if the offer was on the table.

"Hundred-to-one odds on Billie."

I roll my eyes. Why am I working with children? "Who's the favourite?"

Her voice goes quiet. "At the last count it was Lexi. Three to one. She's just broken up with some guy who plays rugby for the Harlequins, so with Nate fresh from dumping Lucy, Kris thinks they'll rebound with each other."

Why is she telling me this? "Not that I'm

remotely interested, but where am I on the list?"

"Fourth. Behind Madeline and Natalia."

What the hell? I don't think I could be any more offended. "I'm behind Natalia?"

She laughs out loud. "You know Kris is a plank."

This is sadly true. Kris Berg, my Norwegian cameraman, is a muscly giant who looks like he's just walked off a ninth-century Viking longboat. He possesses Tribe's biggest, ugliest tattoo, and his head is mostly shaved, with a long strip of light-blonde hair on the top – like a cranial Brazilian – styled into a long dreadlocked ponytail. Kris and I share Scandinavian ancestry, so I've tried very hard to like him more, but he definitely attended some kind of jerk finishing school. "I know Kris has the reasoning skills of a clownfish, but why the hell am I behind Natalia?"

Violet shrugs. "Natalia is quite striking up close. If you don't mind her hippie clothes and wooden jewellery. Her hair is gorgeous."

"I'm not saying she isn't pretty, and her hair is second in gorgeousness only to yours, but I'm just . . . Ugh, why the hell do I even care?" I take another drink, draining my second glass. Damn it, I need to slow down.

"I'm sorry, I shouldn't have said anything. I thought you'd find it funny."

"I didn't find it funny, but I should have." I glance back over to Nate and Lexi and know immediately why poop-for-brains Kris would make her odds-on favourite. She's beautiful, classy, talented and famous. And when I say beautiful, I mean ethereal elf-like beautiful, with creamy skin and a perfect petite body. Her dark-brown hair shines in the sunlight as she captures and holds every shred of the attention and admiration Nate is bestowing upon her.

Violet registers my mood by gripping my forearm and giving it a tight squeeze. "I'm sorry," she says again. I wave off her apology, then I let her get back to her sketchbook and go inside the villa to find a toilet. Madeline is sitting with Neil and Sophie in the open-plan living room, so I go over to ask if they know where the bathroom is. I don't hear what they're talking about as I approach, but when they see me, they immediately stop talking.

"It's not the right time to bring this up, that's all I'm saying," Madeline says.

"Now's not the right time for what?" I ask.

Neil throws Madeline a glare while Sophie casts her dark eyes to her knees.

"It's nothing," says Madeline, pronouncing each syllable of her words forcefully enough to let Neil and Sophie know that she's ending the conversation.

This makes my paranoia soar. "Are you talking about me?"

All three of them look at me at once, and all three of them are wearing confused expressions. My heart rate returns to normal – briefly – until I realise I've just made myself look like a complete fool. "Why would we be talking about you?" Madeline asks.

"I just thought . . ." I mentally roll my eyes at my own ridiculousness. "Just forget I said anything."

"Actually, Freja, you might be able to help." Neil's eyes shift briefly to Madeline, who gives him one of her most brutal death stares to date.

"I really don't want to make a big thing of this," says Sophie. She crosses her thin legs, straightens her red patterned sundress and fiddles with a gold bracelet that compliments her light-brown skin. I don't know Sophie, but it's hard to imagine anybody looking more awkward.

Neil turns to face her. "If there's anybody in Tribe we can trust with this, it's Freja."

Madeline cuts in. "I'm Sophie's manager and I have this under control."

"How do you figure that?" asks Neil, his eyes steely. Sophie's jaw stiffens as if she's battling to keep her cool. She looks away from both of them and my instinct is to leap in and rescue her. "How can you say you've got it under control when you're sweeping it under the carpet?" Neil demands.

Sophie leaps to her feet. "You know what? I actually don't need help from either of you and I wish I hadn't said anything." She storms out of the room, swishing past me with a brief, apologetic glance.

"Do I need to know what this is about?" I ask Neil.

Madeline opens her mouth, but he cuts her off with a wave of his hand. "One of Tribe's senior investors asked Sophie to apply for a position in his own company. He's been texting her on and off, and we both think his behaviour is inappropriate. But Madeline doesn't want to rock the boat."

I immediately know who he's talking about. And I know Madeline well enough to know her ambition would make her stop at nothing to avert conflict with him.

"Look, there's no harm done," says Madeline.

"Sophie declined Lord Klein's invitation to dinner."

What the hell? He invited a twenty-something client accounts junior to dinner? Ethan asked me if I'd ever considered that Klein could have hurt anybody else. I think of Sophie, who's barely out of university, then I think of all the women who must have worked with him over the years. A whole jumble of nightmarish "what ifs" slam into my brain. I feel like I've been punched in the gut. Why was I so naïve?

"It wasn't just dinner, it was a weekend retreat." Neil's frustration explodes into the room, and my worst worries are realised: I can't be the only one.

Madeline's bangles clank together as she stands to leave. I can't get used to seeing a dressed-down Madeline. Usually her light-blonde hair is straightened to within an inch of its life, a perfect style that complements her very polished manner. But today, her hair is wavy and she's wearing a casual tie-dyed maxi dress accessorised with clunky fashion jewellery. Which is the real Madeline? Corporate powerhouse or hippy chick? My guess is neither.

"This conversation is over," Madeline says. "Like I said before, Sophie is my responsibility and I'm handling it."

"But you're not doing anything." Neil rises to his feet. "You don't think it's inappropriate for a guy like Klein to pursue one of your team like this?"

"No, I don't think it's appropriate, but what do you want me to do? This is really none of your business, so I don't even know why I'm arguing with you. Sophie declined the invitation and told him she's happy in her current job, therefore the matter is closed." She takes a step towards him and lowers her voice. "And may I remind you we're in his son's villa and his son is our biggest client."

"And voila!" Neil's voice is thick with condemnation. "That's really all you care about, isn't it? As long as your clients are happy."

"Yes, Neil. Keeping my clients happy is my job." She walks past me in the direction of the garden, leaving my mind spinning.

"I'm sorry, Freja," says Neil. "I don't want to upset a client, and Nate seems like a great guy, but his dad's a creep. Sophie had to turn down his invitation three times and he's made her feel really uncomfortable. He only stopped texting her when she told him her dad is a former British ambassador."

A wave of nausea rushes through me. I don't know if I'm going to have a panic attack, or if I'm going to hurl, but I definitely still need the bathroom. "I'm sorry, Neil, I really need to find the toilet."

# 16

"I PROMISE THE GUY WAS the youngest actor the Milan talent agency had on their books," Natalia protests in her thick Russian accent. "Everyone else they sent was either over fifty or fat."

I push my sunglasses onto the top of my head and squint at Roberto. He wasn't what I was expecting – he resembles a skinned beaver. I'm tempted to suggest Violet fires him on the spot. I could call up the hot real-life waiter who supplied me with champagne at Nate's villa yesterday. "The brief said 'hot and sexy', didn't it?" It's a simple question, but it makes Natalia's face turn almost the same colour as her dark-auburn hair. Crap, she doesn't cope well with criticism.

"There's no real reason for the waiter to be hot and sexy," she says. Her voice is tight and anxious, showing me she doesn't cope well with stress either. "It isn't a plot point. We'd all go crazy if a female bit-part actor was sacked for her looks, so the same should apply to Roberto. His only job is to serve drinks to our main characters, so it doesn't matter what his face looks like."

"She has a point," Violet says with a sigh. She casts a glance at Roberto, who looks more pitiful with each passing second. "He may look like a rodent, but he has a lovely way of saying *ciao*."

I feel horrible because I still think we should let him go, for reasons entirely connected to his face. "It's not my call, but we work in advertising. Our job is to convince people to buy our clients' products, and it's a truth universally acknowledged that beautiful sells. We're not paid a salary to moralise over our clients' requirements or our audiences' buy-impulses."

"Well maybe we should moralise," says Natalia. "I shouldn't have to abandon my principles."

"You can be as ethical as you want in your personal life, but we are employed to sell." It's easy to see why Natalia drives Violet nuts. She doesn't seem suited to the cold, hard, capitalist reality of advertising. "Madeline created a client brief clearly stating that we feature beautiful people in beautiful locations, so if you want to feature Roberto's face, you'll have to run it by her."

"I think Roberto *is* beautiful," says Natalia. Her Russian accent adds a degree of sensuality to her voice, and I don't doubt she's genuine.

"Are you serious?" asks Violet.

Natalia rearranges her crocheted cardigan to cover her pale neck and chest. "I am always serious."

"Good god." Violet discreetly rolls her eyes. "And aren't you hot with that cardigan on? It's twenty-six degrees today."

Natalia folds her arms over the wool. "Yes, but I am Russian. My skin wasn't made for sunlight." She leaves us to join her creative team partner, Frank, who is seated at a shaded table covered by a bright-blue umbrella. Frank is the most laidback and accepting man I've ever met. He's probably the only person in the whole agency who could work with Natalia.

"She looks like Count Dracula's bride," says Violet, eyeing Natalia's blood-red maxi dress and matching weather-inappropriate knitwear. "Have you seen that cross around her neck?"

I play along. "I have, and if she really was a vampire, it would burn her alive."

The bridge of Violet's nose creases as she considers my point. "Okay, maybe she's just hot for Count Dracula and he hasn't bitten her yet."

"Again, crosses make vampires combust, so he'd be dead long before they managed to get it on."

"Maybe that's her plan. Maybe she's secretly a black-widow vampire slayer."

"Yes, Violet. That's much more likely."

"Okay, I'm going to head back to the hotel to run some last-minute script changes past Madeline. That woman is the absolute worst control freak. I honestly don't think I'd care if she gave all her best campaigns to Harry Hopkins after this. At least I would be free of her constant interfering with everything I do."

I say goodbye to Violet, then observe Neil setting up his next shot with Nate while Skye tends to Lexi's make-up. We're filming a date scene in a pretty pink café with striped awnings and sparkling white cast-iron furniture. The location, on the corner of Menaggio's main square, is absolutely perfect. We have Lake Como in the background, framed by a wall of mountains, and every half an hour a tourist tram dressed up as a train chugs its way up the winding hill to the next town. Nate and Lexi are sitting on seats decorated with flower garlands, and their lemon and turquoise clothing completes a summery palette of pastel colours that will look great on film.

The ad is going to be brilliant and, best of all, I

am feeling totally in control. Not just in control of the mechanics of the shoot, but in control of my emotions too. I survived yesterday's meet-and-greet, even after learning about Sophie. I managed to spend a pleasant afternoon with Nate and my work colleagues. I made small talk and I even laughed at their jokes. I can move on, I know I can.

"Freja, have you got a minute?"

Neil calls me over to the scene he's been prepping outside the café. I dive straight into work mode, checking over the lighting he's set up and the position of the dolly. "I wouldn't frame the shot on that level. Maybe raise the camera up a bit to block out the direction of the sun."

"I was hoping to make good use of the natural sunlight."

"Yeah, and that's great, but we've got a lot of shadow on Nate's left side."

I glance in Nate's direction, our eyes connecting over a vase of pink roses and columbines. He looks amazing. I smile at him and he sends a huge smile full of sunshine back at me. I ignore the throb between my legs. "I think it'll be fine like this, what do you think?"

Neil beckons cameraman Kris over. "I think we're going to try a dolly shot on this one."

"A what now?" asks Nate, with a spark of humour in his voice.

Lexi leans forward and lightly touches his forearm, making my very green, practically poisoned with envy stomach snarl. "Don't think too hard about the technical stuff; it's very boring. Just listen to Freja. She'll give you your directions."

We readjust the position of the cameras, and Kris

tries a couple of lead-ins to the café shot before I call Skye back for a last touch-up of Lexi's make-up. We do a couple of takes, but then it all gets weird.

"Nate, can you feed Lexi the cannoli off your fork and accidentally drop a little whipped cream on the end of her nose?" It's a simple direction, but I notice his jaw stiffen and his Adam's apple bob.

"Sure, um, do you want me to say anything?" he says.

I don't know why he's asking me this. "You have a script, right?"

"Yes, but you've just changed the script, haven't you?"

"No, I don't change the script. That's the copywriter's job."

"Oh, sorry." He looks perplexed. "I didn't notice the cream in the script, that's why I'm asking."

Lexi touches his forearm again. She's super friendly and helpful, but her touchy-feely gestures are bugging me for very bad reasons. "The director is just trying out a few options. Usually actors improvise."

"No, Lexi, I don't want any improvisation, thank you." I cringe inwardly at the harshness in my tone. "This is a purely visual take, so no words, just actions."

"No problem," Lexi says cheerfully. Everything about her is warm and genuine, which makes me hate my bitter soul even more. I rub out the chalk on the clapperboard, wishing it was as easy to rub out my jealousy.

"Acting is so bloody complicated." Nate takes a fork and prods the fresh plate of cannoli on the table in front of him.

"I'm sure it's nowhere near as complicated as the world of business." Lexi laughs and her eyelashes flutter in Nate's direction. *Åh Gud*, I hate that she bothers me this much.

"You've no idea how wrong you are," says Nate. "Just ask Freja – she gave up acting for business."

What the—?

"You were an actress?" asks Lexi, her eyes bright with enthusiasm.

"Yes, but it was a long time ago." Under normal work-based, bar-based or girls-night-in-based circumstances, I'd entertain everybody with tales of my acting career, but not now. Not in front of Nate. "Is the dolly in position?"

"I didn't know you were an actress." Kris's enormous tattooed bicep flexes beside me as he fiddles with his camera controls.

"I knew you were an actress," adds Neil. It's all I can do to stop myself shoving an entire plateful of cannoli into his big mouth. "Violet said you were awesome. Didn't you live in Hollywood for a time?"

"Briefly," I say, hoping my one-word answer ends the conversation.

"I spent a summer in LA. Whereabouts in Hollywood did you live?" Lexi asks.

"I didn't," I say, wishing Kris would hurry the hell up with his fiddling. "I shared a house with friends on the coast—"

"She lived in Santa Monica, and she worked in a diner on Route 66 wearing a cute little fifties waitress uniform and roller skates."

Oh my god, why?

The world stops turning as Nate drops his insider knowledge.

Everyone stops working. Equipment is put down on tables and, yeah, I pretty much think I genuinely want to die.

"Wait a minute," says Neil, his eyes as big as tennis balls. "You guys knew each other . . . before we came out here?"

"No," I say.

"Yes," Nate says.

Crap. *Tænk hurtigt, Freja.* Think fast. Hyperfast.

Nate's eyes darken to solid black orbs. "I'm sorry, I thought . . . You said Ethan Fraser knew and that his girlfriend's your best friend, so I just assumed . . ."

"It's fine," I say, wishing the ground would swallow me up.

"How do you know each other? Where did you meet? Why didn't you say anything?" Neil bombards me with questions I don't want to answer, and I wonder if there might be a psychological reason why he's missing all the very obvious social cues that everyone else has immediately picked up on.

"Looks like I'm going to have to narrow somebody's betting odds," says Kris, who is sitting at my feet knee-deep in camera attachments. Doesn't he realise he's within kicking distance?

I feel my face flush. I wonder if it's the mid-morning sunshine for a moment, but when my heart rate speeds up, I know it isn't. "We shared a friend in LA. That's how we met."

"It's imperative that I know if you shared more

than a friend, for, um, bookmaking purposes," says Kris. I wonder if I'd face disciplinary action if I hoofed him up the ass. It would be worth finding out.

"What are you talking about?" asks Nate, glaring down at the muscly Norwegian. "What are you taking bets on?"

"Never mind." There's a slither of disrespect in Kris's voice. If Nate decides to go for his throat, I'll let him.

"Why didn't you say you knew each other?" Neil sounds confused, but he looks like he's trying to suppress a smirk.

"There's no need to get weird about this," says Nate. "Freja and I dated, briefly, a very long time ago. Now can we get on?"

"Yes, let's bash on," says Lexi. She looks uncomfortable and a little bit disappointed. I wonder if I've upset her plans. And obviously, I thoroughly hate myself for wondering that.

"Yes, let's get on before we lose the light," I say, mentally thanking the object of my envy for presenting an escape route. "Places, everybody."

Kris sets up the camera on the dolly, make-up artist Skye dabs a fresh layer of lipstick on Lexi, our runners get in position with boom mic and light reflector, and a grinning Neil stands poised with the clapperboard in his hand. We're ready to go. I look back at Nate to make sure he's ready, but he's not in the zone. He looks distant and uneasy. After a few moments, our eyes connect and he mouths a very guilty "I'm sorry".

I'm not angry with him, so I send him a smile in return.

Then we get back to work.

* * *

We have dinner in the hotel at nine after finishing shooting at sunset. I resist drinks in the bar in favour of a hot bath and an early night, but I'm so tired when I get back to my room that I go straight to bed with my Kindle. I downloaded a book with a pink cover featuring cupcakes, cake shops and cottages to get me in the mood for the ad. Three chapters in, the book's heroine hasn't been able to make one basic life decision without having a nonsensical meltdown over it, so I decide to give up on her. She doesn't deserve to find true love in a cake shop; she deserves to have an allergic reaction to the cupcake and break out in hideous hives.

I'm just about to switch my bedside light off when there's a knock at the door. I pray it's not Violet with a personal problem, but I pray even harder that it's not Neil with a work problem, so when I open the door to reveal Nate standing before me looking tall and bronzed and gorgeous in a white shirt and smart, form-fitting trousers, I feel a certain amount of relief – until I start panicking.

"I'm really sorry for disturbing you." He looks swiftly up and down the hotel corridor before edging closer towards the door frame. "I tried to catch you alone in Menaggio, but it was never the right time."

Oh my god, what does he want? And why do I have to be barely dressed? If I had three wishes right now I'd waste them on a bra, some mascara and some pyjama bottoms, instead of shorts that reveal half my ass. "What is it?"

"I need to apologise about today. I can't believe I blabbed in front of your entire team. I honestly thought everyone knew about us, but I shouldn't have said anything anyway."

I cross my arms over my chest and cringe when I notice my nipples peeking through my silk camisole. Forget my earlier three wishes – send me a dressing gown. "Nate, seriously, it's fine."

His gorgeous eyes are darker in the dim light, but I can still see worry embedded in them. "Are you sure? I mean, I only said we dated, so it's possible they could think we only went out once—"

I shake my head. "There's no chance they'll only think that."

He laughs and his gorgeous sunshine smile warms my entire body, especially the place at the top of my thighs. "I guess not."

"It was my fault as much as yours. I told Violet and Ethan without checking you'd be okay with that, but I just figured I had to."

He frowns and sinks his hands into the pockets of his slim navy trousers. "Why would you have to?"

"Because Ethan is my boss," I say apprehensively, worrying whether I'm giving too much away. "I didn't know how you'd feel about working with me. There might have been repercussions for the agency, and this isn't just a job to me. Tribe is my life and the people I work with are my best friends. I've worked hard to get where I am and I didn't want this – you – to jeopardise that."

He holds his hands out in front of him. "Hey, I

understand. You're allowed to tell anybody you need to tell. Of course you are."

"Okay," I say, moving back inside my room. "All apologies accepted then."

I close the gap between me and the door, expecting him to say goodnight and leave, but he doesn't budge. "That's not all I'm sorry about," he says.

My churning stomach stills in anticipation. "Oh?"

His gaze is so intense that my womb starts beating in time with my heart. "I shouldn't have spoken to you like I did during the London shoot. It was none of my business."

I look hard into his eyes and see the raw emotion locked deep inside them. My nipples throb and, Jesus, why didn't I put the hotel's bathrobe on to open the freaking door? "I was late and hungover, so you had every right, but I'd already forgotten about that."

"And I'm sorry about coming to your office all those weeks ago too."

"It's fine—"

"But most of all I'm sorry about us."

Shit. What's happening? What does he mean?

He runs his hand through his hair and drags his eyes to the floor. "I shouldn't have cut you off eight years ago. I should have talked to you about Brett . . . I should have at least given you the chance to explain."

I swallow the panic back down and it feels like it pulls my heart with it. I can't do this. Not now. "Nate, I'm not in the right frame of mind to talk about this."

"I know, and I'm sorry about that too." He sighs from his gut as he leans on the door frame. "If I could go back, I'd choose to undo every action I took."

He looks at me as if he's waiting for a confession, and I want to cry out that none of this is his fault and none of it is my fault either. "I accept all of your apologies, but there's no real need for you to make them. Today was an accident, I shouldn't have arrived late at work with a hangover in London, and as for eight years ago . . ." I have to bite down hard on my lip to stop my tears falling. "There's nothing to apologise for about that either." My voice cracks. I force the desperate sadness out of my mind. "You're a good man. You've done nothing wrong."

My words land in his eyes with sorrow. He slowly nods as his mind accepts what I'm telling him. "I'll let you get back to bed." He manages to force a smile onto his face, but the rapid rise and fall of his chest tells me he's internalising much stronger feelings. "I'm glad I came to see you."

"Me too," I say.

I close the door and hold on to my tears until I'm positive he's not in the corridor, then I let it all out.

# 17

INSTEAD OF US EATING AT the hotel again tonight, Nate's booked us all in at a glitzy restaurant in Azzano close to his villa. The restaurant is usually frequented by international A-list celebrities, and it has a dress code, which was bad news for most of my crew, who'd only packed shorts or jeans for the trip. Nate managed to get the green light for a dress-down Wednesday evening if we switched tables to the terrace.

I needed to work by myself today. After last night's visit from Nate, I wanted to put some distance between us, so I delegated the filming of Nate and Lexi's romantic encounters to Neil, while I spent the entire day shooting lakeside scenery with Billie, my production assistant. Billie is a recent college graduate who thinks all "heteros" are fatally useless and tragic, so I knew she wouldn't ask any questions about my love life. I like Billie. She's a hard grafter, she gets on with everybody and she doesn't gossip.

As the day went on I felt more and more uneasy about tonight, and I've had to dig deep to find the energy to get ready. But now that I'm dressed, I'm worrying about my outfit. Black is usually my colour of choice for everything, sometimes grey and occasionally white. I don't know how my preference for dressing in monochrome started, probably something to do with being a redhead, but tonight I've chosen a blush-pink cocktail dress I picked up from Zara. The dress has blue and yellow sequined flowers along the hemline of the fluted skirt. I'm wondering how my very different look will be received when there's a knock at my door. I open it to reveal a violet-dressed Violet.

"Are you ready? The minivan is here to take us to . . . Holy moly! You look amazing!"

"Thanks. So do you." I laugh as I put everything I need for tonight inside my clutch. As usual, Violet is floaty and flowery, her long dark hair hanging in loose waves over a chiffon print blouse in dozens of shades of purple, with cut-out shoulders and puffed sleeves. She's teamed the blouse with a plain white pencil skirt and nude sandals.

"This isn't about me. It's about you in that dress." Her jaw drops so low that I start to feel a little self-conscious.

"Does it look like I'm trying too hard?" A wave of insecurity ripples through me, which is maddening because yet again I'm feeling things I never feel. If I were having dinner with a regular client, who happened to be just as famous, rich and hot-as-hell as Nate, then Violet's comments would be firing me up for a night of fun. "I really don't want it to look like I'm trying."

"Who cares?" She comes inside my room and sits down in the armchair. "Nate won't be the only guy in the restaurant tonight . . . Ooh, what if he thinks you're making an effort for somebody else?"

I look at her as if she's crazy. "Who would that be? Frank is a happily married father of four, Kwame looks like he's twelve and Kris is an idiot." She raises her perfectly defined eyebrows suggestively. "And Neil is like the kid brother I always wanted but thankfully never received, so don't even go there."

She laughs. "I know what you mean, but he's also the kid brother I wish hadn't moved out and got his own place. I miss having him in my team."

"You're not having him back," I say with faux smugness. "He's chosen his path and he's not going back to the dark side."

"Fine." She scrunches up her nose and pokes out her tongue. "So, back to the earlier topic of conversation – Nate. I think he was disappointed you weren't filming him. When I told him you'd be out shooting landscape with Billie today, I thought he might cry."

"Don't be ridiculous." I roll my eyes at her, but my stupid heart wants it to be true.

"Okay, maybe crying is stretching things a bit, but he was definitely disappointed." She leans back in the armchair, her bright-blue eyes looking at me intensely. "Neil noticed it too. Nate was a million miles away. It was hard work getting the footage we needed."

"What do you want me to say?" I close my clutch with a hard snap. "I don't know what to do, Violet. I don't know what he's thinking."

She bristles at the volume of my voice. "What do you mean? Has anything happened?"

"Aside from him outing me yesterday?" I say with a short, wry laugh.

"Was that why you took off with Billie today?"

"I know he shouldn't affect me this much, and I really don't want him to. But he does." I choose a very long, weary sigh from the large library of Nate-related sighs I've accumulated recently. "And I don't want my past played out in front of everyone

I know."

"Hey, it'll be okay." She comes over to me and lightly brushes my arm. "There was obviously some gossip doing the rounds this morning, but as far as everyone is concerned you dated a client a very long time ago, that's all. There's nothing newsworthy about that."

"Except he's a great-looking, ridiculously wealthy and extremely famous client." I shudder when I imagine the messages that will have already have winged their way to the rest of the agency back in London. "It's a wonder my phone hasn't been blown up by the force of incoming gossipy texts already."

"You'd normally love this kind of attention."

"I'd normally not be freaking out in case any more details from my past leak out." I walk to the door, but my hand freezes when I reach for the door knob. How am I going to get through dinner? "He came to my room last night. He wanted to apologise for letting the cat out of the bag."

I turn around and catch a brief glint of excitement flash in her eyes. "And then what happened?"

"He apologised for cutting me off."

"Wow," she says, a gasp of surprise floating from her body. "This is good news. You must be on his mind. Did he say anything else?"

The knot, or the niggle, or the ache, or whatever it is that's lived deep inside me all these years clenches the moment I think of him. "He said he wished he'd confronted me about Brett at the time and if he could go back he'd do everything differently. His brother said it took him years to get over my breaking his heart. He needs closure just as much as I do."

"Then you should sit down and talk to him."

"But what would I tell him if he asks about Brett? I would have to lie."

Her beautiful face stiffens. "You aren't going to want to hear this, but I think you should tell him the truth."

Her words hit me hard. "How can you even think that? Weren't you listening when I told you what his father did?"

"Yes, you know I was, but Nate deserves to know the truth – for himself as well as for you."

"It would destroy him."

"Or it might save him."

I shake my head. I have no idea what she means.

"Nate's relationship with his father has never been great, and if it were me . . ." She nips her bottom lip as she considers her own words. "Maybe I can see things from Nate's perspective a little easier than you can. I haven't seen my father in almost eleven years, and we haven't spoken a civil word to each other for longer still. If he'd done something terrible to hurt Ethan, I'd want to know. No question."

Her words cut into me, drawing fresh tears from my eyes. I want to scream out my truth almost as much as I want to move on, but I don't think I can do one without the other. "Nate would never forgive him."

"Good. He doesn't deserve Nate's forgiveness." She stands up to brush a tear from my cheek. "The only person who deserves Nate's forgiveness is you."

An angry, rage-filled ball of flame burns inside me. She's right. I know she's right. I rest my back against the wall and speak straight from my soul. "I still love him, Violet. I love him more than I've ever loved anyone, and the power of those feelings scares me far more than the prospect of telling him the truth. If I believed in fate, or in gods, then I'd think it was planned this way. It feels like we were cut from the same lump of clay or carved from the same tree. But what if—"

"He still loves you," she says quietly. "'Borrow Cupid's wings and soar with them above a common bound.'"

"Oh my god, don't bring Shakespeare into this, Violet," I say with a laugh that softens the air.

She grins. "You're an actress. It's appropriate."

"It's *Romeo and Juliet*, therefore I hope it bloody well isn't appropriate."

We both laugh again, then she gently grips my arm. "Come on, we'd better get going. Everyone will be waiting."

\* \* \*

The Ristorante Paradiso al Lago is a rooftop restaurant attached to the Grand Hotel di Lombardia. Our table is located on a lamp-lit terrace surrounded by marble pillars, art nouveau railings, swirling vines and a spectacular night-time view of the lake. Black mountains sweep over the horizon, and clusters of tiny twinkling lights mark the nearby towns and villages. This is my first ever visit to Italy and I wonder how on earth I could ever have felt well-travelled without experiencing this wonderful country.

The restaurant's antipasti was divine and, as I tuck into an exquisite bowl of seafood linguine packed with langoustines, mussels, crab claws and chunks of salmon, I feel like I could live here if I ever tire of London. Violet, sitting next to me, is devouring an equally delicious bowl of ricotta and aubergine gnocchi. We swap a little of each other's meals to compare and agree it's probably the best Italian food we've ever eaten. But then Natalia spoils the mood by letting her dissatisfaction over her unimaginative vegan salad be known, followed by Kris, who must have drunk a dozen bottles of Peroni already, complaining that his steak is too small.

I share a mortified glance with Violet. I already know that Kris ordered the filet mignon because he thought the most expensive dish on the menu would also be the biggest. He has no concept of quality over quantity, so this is how his brain will have made its decision. I watch him push the few remaining kale leaves around his plate before ordering a side of fries to "fill up on", and I make a mental note to choke the life out of him. He may be built like a ten-ton truck on steroids, but that doesn't entitle him to demand more food at the client's expense.

Half of us forgo dessert for coffee, as the talk switches from work to pleasure. I'm sitting at the farthest end of the table, with Violet next to me and Polly Jordan, my unfeasibly shy line producer, opposite. Nate and Neil hold court at the centre of the table, sharing stories from China. Neil worked for global advertising giant Evans and Rogers, who

Nate is convinced created a digital marketing campaign for KTech, so it's possible their paths crossed without either of them realising.

When the conversation moves on to what the non-Brits at the table miss most about home, Kris, Kwame and Natalia dive straight in with wonderful anecdotes about growing up in Tromsø, Accra and Nizhny Novgorod respectively. Then Sophie surprises us all with tales of her own exotic childhood, courtesy of her father, who is a former British ambassador to Guyana. Most fascinating of all, however, is Madeline's contribution to the conversation. I'm certain she said she'd once lived in Rome before we sat down to dinner, but by the time the desserts are served, she's claimed she'd never set foot in Italy in her entire life.

Even though Lexi Grant spent her formative years in Bedfordshire, none of us come close to competing with her tales of glamorous movie shoots in locations stretching from Alaska to Thailand. If it weren't for Nate being so annoyingly captivated by her, I'm sure I'd have been just as enthralled by her A-list name-dropping and tales of disastrous stateside auditions. She seems genuinely lovely, and I'm never wrong about people, so my brain's instinct to find a reason – any reason – to dislike her is making me feel like a terrible person. Jealousy suits nobody, but it suits me least of all. Although, it has to be said, I do look awesome in green.

"I can't believe Lexi worked with Tom Hardy," Violet whispers as she picks up her dessert spoon.

"Really?" I say. "I'd be very surprised if you could pick Tom Hardy out of a line-up of killer circus clowns."

"Ah, that's where you underestimate me," she says. "I watched four episodes of *Peaky Blinders* before I got bored by the violence."

"Wow, four whole episodes?" I say teasingly. "Was BBC Radio Three off air?"

She's just about to tease me back when Neil calls over to me. "So, Freja. Tell us something awesome about Copenhagen."

Up until now, I haven't felt like joining in with the conversation, which I'm sure hasn't gone unnoticed by my co-producer. "Well, I heard Copenhagen dropped down the ranks of awesome when I left ten years ago."

The table erupts into laughter. I catch Nate's eye just as a womb-melting sunshine smile erupts onto his face. I expect him to break the connection, just like before, but this time he doesn't. I smile back and my cheeks warm. I hope I don't look obvious. I sip my espresso, then I decide I need something much stronger, less caffeinated and more likely to get me at least to level three on the getting-pissed scale, so I catch the attention of the nearest waiter and order two more bottles of house white for the table, plus a very large Bellini.

"Did you act when you lived in Copenhagen?" asks Lexi. Crap. The conversation had moved on to Billie's plans to travel the globe with her girlfriend. Does she have to send it back?

"Yes," I say as all eyes return to me again. "Mostly in theatre, but I did one season of a Scandi-noir TV show."

"No way," shrieks Kwame. "Were you in *The Bridge*?" The young Ghanaian spends hours watching TV on every single possible outlet, but

I'm surprised he's managed to catch shows that aren't British or American.

"Sadly not." I shake my head and laugh. "I was in a show called *Den Store Løgn*. I'm pretty sure it wasn't shown outside of Denmark, so you won't have seen it."

"Actually, I think I've seen it," Frank says in his usual quiet manner. "I got hooked on Scandi TV when I was on paternity leave last summer. It's a police procedural, right?"

Crap. Frank is so calm and unassuming that I often forget he exists. "Yes, it is, but it was cancelled a couple of years ago now." The waiter returns with the wine and my Bellini, which is temptingly decorated with a slice of blood orange and a sprig of lavender.

"Did you say *Den Store Løgnen?*" Kris asks, in a perfect translation of the show's name from Danish to Norwegian.

"Not quite. It's *løgn*, minus the 'en'." He picks out his mobile phone and taps furiously away on the keyboard. I have a horrible feeling about this. "What are you doing?"

He looks up from his phone. "Checking you out on IMDB."

Double crap. I know I'm listed, therefore I know Kris is a series of very small clicks away from finding *that* clip of me on YouTube. Shit. *Okay, calm it, Freja, and think. Thousands of people in Denmark have seen your tits already, it's no big deal.* "Whatever you find on there, just remember it was a long time ago and—"

"Holy shit, boss!" His jaw drops and his huge blue eyes bulge in his skull. He looks like he's about to go into anaphylactic shock.

"What is it?" Lexi leans over a stunned Kwame to get a closer look at Kris's phone.

Madeline gets out of her seat and walks around to Kris's other side. She looks at the phone, then she looks at me. "Well, this I wasn't prepared for." She seems impressed, so I take the compliment happily.

"It was very artistically shot, if I remember correctly," I say.

Madeline's face glows as she grins. "You can say that again."

"I need to see what all the fuss is about." Neil fires up his mobile phone and leans in to watch with Natalia and Skye.

"I want to see too," says Billie.

The sound of my own voice, talking seductively in Danish and interspersed with some pretty obvious sex noises, blares out of three different phones as my colleagues watch the clip with various shades of shock written on their faces. I daren't look at Nate, because I can feel the distress radiating off his body. His stiff shape, with bowed head, is barely visible in the corner of my eye, but it's making me question whether I should have played along with this after all.

"Oh my god!" Frank says abruptly. I've never heard him talk so loudly, but I can still barely hear him over the cringey audio tracks playing in the background. "When I started working at Tribe, I knew there was something familiar about you. You played Inga Mortensen, didn't you?"

At last I'm recognised. "For ten episodes until I was murdered and disembowelled."

Frank's face flinches, then a slow crawl of dread

creeps into his eyes as he matches me up with my character and then the scene everybody is watching. My police officer character had a masochistic fetish compelling her to have sex with criminals. In the scene they're watching, she wrongfully arrests a bad guy, and screws him whilst handcuffed to the cell bars. "Hey guys, I think you should switch that off," he says.

"Relax, it's fine," I tell him. "I worked on that show a decade ago. I'm really proud of it."

Violet moves close so she can whisper in my ear. "Is this the episode where you had to pretend to blow off that seventy-year-old guy?"

"No that was a different show," I whisper back. "I did that when I was eighteen."

"Jesus, let's hope they don't find that one on YouTube," she says.

"I've already searched for it. It's far too obscure, so don't worry."

The scene playing out on Kris's phone comes to an end, but it leaves him with a barely concealed smirk on his face. Kwame, on the other hand, may never be able to look me in the eye again.

"Well, Freja, I have to say it, you're a really good actress," Lexi says enthusiastically. "I'm not sure I could have acted that scene so well."

Why does she have to be so bloody nice? "Thanks. I studied drama when I went to university in Sweden, but after that I guess I was called to work behind the camera."

I let my gaze flit to Nate for the first time. His concentration is fixed on his wine glass and his skin is flushed. I can't see his eyes, but I need to. I can't tell if he's embarrassed or angry. And I don't know why he'd be either of those things, but the energy he's giving off is entirely negative, and I know that Lexi and Neil, sitting either side of him, must have picked up on it too.

"So were you acting in stuff like this when you were dating Nate?" asks Kris.

"That's enough." Nate breaks his lock on the wine glass to stare daggers at the young camera operator. An unnerving silence settles upon the entire table. Unfortunately, Billie's phone is still playing, and the tense air is abruptly shattered by the sound of my very well acted orgasm.

Kris breaks into uproarious laughter. "Whoa, I bet you're sorry you let this one go."

Nate rockets to his feet, sending his metal chair flying backwards with a nerve-jangling scrape against the tiled floor. "You want to repeat that?"

Oh fuck. Kris swallows hard, and I'm not sure why he looks so nervous. Nate is undeniably fit, with a solid training in martial arts, but Kris has the stature and physique of a heavyweight boxer – mixed with the DNA of a mythical Norse giant. "Hey, I'm sorry. I thought we were all having a bit of fun. Freja didn't mind that we were watching the clip."

"Did you ask her?" yells Nate, staring down the brawny Norwegian.

Kris's pale skin reddens. "Well, no, but she'd have said—"

"She had no choice but to play along, you moron. If she'd told you to knock it off, how would that have looked?" He's not wrong in his thinking, but I'm taken aback by how protective he's being. Although Kris deserves an ass-kicking, I should be the one doing it, not Nate.

"I *am* quite capable of speaking for myself," I say, trying to sound as diplomatic as possible. Violet places a supportive hand at the centre of my back.

"I know that," he says defensively. My heart breaks when I see his body deflate. He knows he's overstepped.

"I'm sorry if I upset you, boss," says Kris. "I'll be honest, I'm a little surprised you've done stuff like this, but you look pretty damn great doing it, so what the hell, right?"

Jesus Christ, why won't he stop talking? Nate sits back down, his face as red as the Danish flag.

"I think we should maybe retire to the bar." Lexi glances at a few key players around the table, her eyes pleading.

"I think we should actually call it a night," says Madeline. "We've a busy day ahead tomorrow, right, Neil?"

"Um, yeah, sure," says Neil, looking completely flummoxed. "I've no idea what's happening, but sleep sounds like the best idea."

"Are you filming on location tomorrow?" Nate asks me tersely.

I reply in an even tone. "No, we captured all the scenic shots we needed today."

"So, how did you guys break up all those years ago?" Kris chips in from out of absolutely bloody nowhere. How many beers has he had tonight? A chorus of shudders and groans erupts around the table.

"You really think this is the question you should be asking me right now?" The layer of "highly pissed off" in my tone would be more than enough to make a normal person with finely tuned social skills shut their mouths, but Kris has poorer self-awareness than a crotch-sniffing dog.

"All of us were speculating over who dumped who this morning," Kris says with absolutely no sense of danger. "It wasn't just me."

"Nobody cheated on anybody," I say with a sharpness I hope will shut him up for good. But, oh hell . . . what the fuck did I just say out loud? *Åh min Gud!* My stomach sinks when I see Kris's expression sparkle back to life.

"Cheating wasn't mentioned this morning," he says. "Oh, but wait a minute . . . damn . . . he cheated on you, didn't he?"

Nate flies out of his chair again and Violet instinctively grabs hold of my arm. For a split second I'm absolutely terrified for Kris's safety, but all Nate does is gesture to the maître d', yank his suit jacket over his arms, then walk around the table to hand over his credit card to a waiter. "Charge the entire night on that. I need to get out of here."

"Wait!" I stand up and he immediately stops walking away. He turns around to face me, and I want to crawl into a hole and die because, with everyone's eyes on me, I have absolutely no idea what I'm going to say. His eyes search mine. His chest rises and falls in perfect synchronisation with my pulse. I have to do something. This isn't his fault. He isn't the bad guy.

"Nate wasn't the one who cheated," I blurt out.

He lets out a huge gasp of air, but instead of looking relieved at being exonerated in front of everyone, he looks even more furious than he did before.

Then I remember our conversation back in London. He specifically told me he didn't want people to know I cheated on him. He didn't want to wear that label.

Oh shit, I've done it again.

"I'm sorry," I tell him.

He doesn't reply. He turns his back on me, walks down the stairs and leaves.

# 18

THE ATMOSPHERE AT TODAY'S SHOOT could accurately be described as a dozen layers of shit piled on top of an overflowing cesspit. We're filming in Menaggio's small town square again, but today's weather has turned as dark as my mood. Goodbye, blue skies and sunshine; hello, blanket covering of thick grey clouds. The weather forecast said there was a seventy per cent chance of a downpour, so we're going to try for a very romantic kissing-in-the-rain segment. There's a risk that we'll have to call off today's shoot, meaning our schedule for tomorrow and Friday will get tighter and even more stressful.

I sent Nate a text message at some point in the night, after consuming half a bottle of wine I definitely didn't need. It consisted of an apology and a suggestion we sit down to talk, but he didn't reply. Meanwhile, Kris is certain he's going to be fired when we get back to London, which may very well happen, and Violet is doing everything she can to lift my spirits by suggesting a million and one ways I can fix the horrific mess that is my life. She's still annoyingly optimistic that I'm going to snag a fairy-tale ending, but what she doesn't realise is that my strong affinity with Hans Christian Andersen's version of *The Little Mermaid* has taught me a very hard truth: if you willingly give up your voice, then you don't live happily ever after with Prince Charming; you turn into sea foam. I'm pretty sure Andersen wasn't a nineteenth-century feminist living well before his time when he doomed his voluntarily voiceless heroine to a tragic demise, but the warning speaks to my soul.

Madeline crosses the square to greet me. "Rough night, huh?"

What does she expect me to say to that? "Yeah, I guess so." My throat cracks when I speak, and I grimace as a sharp pain wraps around my tonsils. Crap, that's all I need. If Violet has given me her deathly cold, I think I really will opt to live out the rest of my days as saltwater.

"What did you do to your hair?" I have no idea what she's talking about. I scraped it up into a ponytail this morning, but I often wear my hair up for work. "It's curly," she adds, no doubt noticing my confusion.

"Oh, right. That'll be the humidity," I say, combing my fingers through the orange frizz. "Pop me in a sauna for half an hour and I emerge looking like Ronald McDonald with tits."

She laughs and her brown eyes come alive. I think it's the first time I've ever seen her laugh, and it suits her. "While we're on the subject of tits—"

"Okay, you can stop right there. Last night just happened, but I really don't care that everyone saw my YouTube clip and—"

"No, you don't understand." She starts to laugh again.

"What's so funny?"

"I wasn't talking about *your* tits. I was talking about the colossal tit we have to work with." The warmth leaves her face and she switches seamlessly into her usual ultra-professional work persona. "Nate called me this morning. He wants Kris off his campaign, so get him on the first flight back to London. And it'll have to be at Tribe's expense, not BuzzPay's."

Kris Berg is very far from being my favourite person at the moment, but whenever a member of my team is threatened from the outside, my *mumie* mothering instinct goes into overdrive. "No."

Her eyes narrow. "What do you mean, 'no'?"

"I mean no, I'm not sending him home. He's a highly skilled camera operator. We need him."

"Can't Kwame take over?"

If there's one thing that makes my blood boil, it's people who know absolutely nothing about film production telling me how to run my crew. "No, Kwame is a graduate trainee. He doesn't even have one year's experience as a production runner. Of course he can't take over from Kris."

"What about Neil? Or Billie?"

I cough and my throat grates against my windpipe. Damn it. I'm going to kill Violet. "Neil is massively overqualified and as co-producer has about a billion other things to do, and Billie is even less qualified than Kwame, but hey, I know, why don't you do it?"

The sarcasm in my tone transforms her blood-red lips into a frustrated pout. "When I told you to bin Kris, I wasn't making a request, Freja. BuzzPay is bringing millions of pounds into our agency and they're practically funding Tribe's Far East expansion. If they want him gone, you need to make it happen."

I let out a brief sigh. "I'll talk to Nate."

"Are you kidding?" Her scoffing tone is matched with a glare of pure disbelief.

"I'm not kidding at all," I say. "Kris's offence was against me, not Nate, so I'll deal with him."

"He accused our most important client of cheating on his, um, whatever you were." Her hands are firmly planted on her hips. "I mean, you *were* there last night, weren't you? You *did* see the look on Nate's face when he stormed out of the restaurant, because from where I was sitting I think you're going to be the last person capable of talking him down."

I'm stunned by her lack of faith in me, but as I'm incapable of doubting myself, I brush it aside. "When I tell you I've got this, that means I've got it. You should know that by now."

She shakes her head and blesses me with a killer eye-roll. "Sorry, but I can't trust you with this. You didn't care to let me in on your history with my client, and it was only a couple of weeks ago you were sitting on your office floor having a panic attack. So no, I don't think you've 'got this' at all."

I square my shoulders at her insults. "You're really going to use what happened the other week against me?"

"To protect my client and my campaign? You're damned right I would."

Our attention is drawn away from our argument by the sound of screeching tyres. Nate's chauffeur-driven Alfa Romeo Giulia pulls up on the main road adjacent to the town square. He steps out of the car wearing dark shades, a crisp white shirt and tailored navy blue trousers that make his ass look like it's been sculpted by Michelangelo.

I briefly turn back to Madeline. "I'm going to talk to him now. Join me if you want, but I assure you my cameraman will not be leaving today."

Madeline mutters something inaudible under her breath as I leave her and make a beeline for Nate.

When he sees me, he stops walking. His broad shoulders stiffen, and he pulls his sunglasses from his face, sending me a warning glance in the process. "I don't think you're going to need those today," I say, pointing at his rather smart pair of Ray-Bans.

The vein that runs from his cheek to his temple bulges, but somehow his gorgeous face still makes my womb melt. He snaps the glasses closed and shoves them into his pocket. "In case you didn't take my not replying to your text message as evidence that I don't want to speak to you, then here's the message again: I don't want to speak to you."

*Okay, stay focused, Freja. You got this.* "I thought we were going to act professionally."

"That was before you humiliated me in front of a whole load of people." He starts to move away from me, but then he turns back. "Why do you think I didn't want anyone to find out you cheated on me?"

I flinch at his words and my heart screams out the truth. *I didn't cheat on you.* But I shrug it off. "I just assumed it was a guy thing."

He shakes his head. "A guy thing? Since when was I an insecure weak-arsed kid who couldn't handle locker-room jibes?"

"Talk to me then," I say calmly. "Tell me why."

"Because I can't have a private life anymore," he says, throwing his arms up in despair. "Everything that happens to me ends up in the press. I have prick journalists following me around London and I have paparazzi hiding out on Caribbean beaches taking long-lens photographs of me breaking up with my girlfriend. I didn't want you to become a target. I wanted to protect you."

His confession makes my soul ache. I think of the glossy photos and luridly detailed gossip articles that the girls in the office pore over, and I vow to never buy another trashy magazine ever again. "I said I was sorry. I couldn't let them think it was you who cheated. What did you want me to say?"

"Any one of a hundred other things," he says with a faint shake in his voice. "Just not the thing I specifically told you not to say."

The lump in my scratchy throat grows larger. I swallow, and the pain burns my ears. "Well, what's done is done, so we need to move on and get back to at least trying to act professionally. There's only two days left after all, right?"

The nerve in his jaw twitches. "Yes, thankfully."

"Okay," I say, ignoring the spitefulness in his tone. "While we're on the subject of being professional, I need to talk to you about my cameraman. Kris was completely out of order last night, and I promise I will go through the proper disciplinary channels when we get back to London, but we were all off duty and we were drinking, so—"

"It's fine. You can handle it."

"So you don't want me to put him on a plane this afternoon?"

He starts to walk away again. The stiffness in his posture is forced, as is his tone. He's trying hard to hide how hurt he is. "I said it was fine, didn't I?"

That was easier than I imagined. "Okay, I guess

it's time to get on with work. Skye needs you in make-up."

He nods briefly, then joins the rest of the team.

\* \* \*

The grey clouds stretching over the sky turn blacker as the morning rolls on, but we manage to take a couple of nice shots of Nate and Lexi strolling arm in arm along the short promenade, as well as getting some ice-cream-eating footage. I wasn't entirely convinced about the gelato, but Violet wanted to have a couple of filler options. I already know that I'm going to edit it out of my final cut when I'm back in the studio. We already have the café-and-cake scene, so we don't need more food. We're selling an online cash transaction service, not a dessert company.

With the threat of rain looming, Madeline, Sophie, Polly, Violet and the creative team return to the hotel to get a head start on some paperwork. Nate was called back to his villa half an hour ago for an urgent conference call. So, when the first drops of rain crash from the sky onto the pavement, there's only me, Lexi and my five-person crew still in the square.

"We need to get the equipment packed up pronto," says Neil, already unscrewing attachments from the cameras.

"I'll call the vans to pick us up," says Billie.

Kwame and Kris roll up our reflective screens, while I help Neil put the covers on the microphones and video equipment. Lexi and Skye take shelter under a nearby awning, and I'm just about to tease them over it when a giant crash of thunder rumbles through the mountains, followed by a burst of lightning.

And then the heavens *really* open.

Neil looks at me and mouths, "Oh shit."

"Sounds like someone pissed in Thor's cornflakes this morning," says Kris.

The rain pelts down, but I look on the bright side – wet hair is a much better look than frizzy hair, and thunderstorms are exciting. It only takes a moment before there are mini-rivers flowing furiously between the cracks in the square's cobblestones. A few tourists run to take cover in the shops, while others head for parked cars. Waiters from the restaurants and cafés bring in their menu boards and rush around removing cushions and tablecloths.

A few minutes later, we all breathe a sigh of relief when our minivan screeches to a stop at the edge of the square. We each pick up the most we can carry and start loading it into the van, but there's a problem. Only one van has arrived. The other driver took a trip to the nearest *supermercato* to pick up some personal groceries.

Once the equipment and bodies pile into the van, there's no room for our dolly car and track, which are still laid out in the middle of the town square.

Oh, and there's also no room in the minivan for me.

"You get in, Freja," says Neil. "I can pack the dolly away."

"No, it's fine, I'll do it. My hair is already wrecked."

Billie pokes her head out of the van doors. "The other minivan is on its way down the hill," she shouts. "There's a mass exodus uphill, so the traffic is rammed. He says he'll be five minutes."

"That's fine," I shout through another loud clap of thunder. "It'll take me that long to pack the kit up."

"I'm not leaving you here!" calls Neil.

"It's a thunderstorm not a bloody war zone," I shout back at him, laughing at the urgency in his voice.

He attempts to move the equipment that is piled haphazardly inside the van on top of seats and people. "I'll stay with you."

"There's no need for heroics, Neil." The rain is so heavy that every inch of my skin is already drenched. "I'm more than capable of packing up the dolly and there's no point in two people getting soaked through. Just get all of our gear back in one piece without drowning it."

He looks very unsure. "Okay, if you insist."

"I do insist, so go."

I hear the van doors shut as I start pushing the levers of the dolly car down into the frame to collapse it. I'm just about done when I realise I don't have the cover for the piece of track that the dolly sits on. Crap. The guys must have picked it up by mistake.

"Where the hell is everybody?"

I swing around so fast that I almost slip over. The last thing I expected to see was Nate standing over me holding an empty Armani carrier bag over his head.

"They're on their way back to the hotel. The other van is stuck in traffic."

"Here, let me help you." He throws down the

carrier bag and helps me fold the short legs on the track and pop the metal tube rails inside each other.

"They've taken the protective cover with them." I have to raise my voice over the thunder to be heard. "This is expensive tech. If it gets too wet it might rust."

Nate looks around the square. "Follow me."

"Follow you where?"

"There's an alleyway between the pizzeria and the bank."

He lifts the track and runs towards the arched entrance to the alley, which is set into the side of the pizzeria's mustard-coloured walls. There's a little window with green shutters and a box filled with pink zinnias above the arch, and the roof is made from chunky terracotta tiles.

I have to bend down to wheel the dolly car over the wet cobbles and through the puddles. The rain bombards my back with a volley of hard splashes. My cardigan is already soaked through and my thin white satin top is cold, heavy and stuck to my skin.

"Here, let me get it." Nate appears in front of me, his rain-soaked shirt stuck to every contour of his fabulous chest. He catches my gaze and I feel my cheeks flush. *Be less obvious, Freja, for crying out loud.* He pushes the dolly towards the alley and I follow behind him. Once I'm safe, I immediately throw off my cardigan. There's nothing worse than wearing wet wool. I decide that sheep must be permanently miserable. Then I look down and cringe when I find my top, when wet, turns completely invisible.

I have two choices: put the drenched cardi back on, or be grateful that I'm wearing a bra and own it.

I choose the second option.

"Oh, will you look at that," I say, gesturing to my chest. "Just when I thought the morning couldn't get any worse."

Nate runs his hand through his wet hair, ruffling it at the ends. My fingers twitch because I always loved his hair, and there's nothing I want to do more right now than touch it. "Actually, that kinda reminds me of the night we first met," he says with an approving grin.

Reminiscing about *that* night was the absolute last thing I expected we'd be doing after our altercation earlier. Am I embarrassed that I crashed into my living room to surprise my roomies wearing nothing but barely-there Christmas elf shorts and two strategically placed Mickey Mouse stickers? Hell, no. I was drunk, it was a prank, I didn't know Nate was there, and to this day it remains the best entrance I've ever made.

I laugh off his comment and try to get the colour back into my drenched top by yanking it away from my wet skin. "This might not be the best time or place to resurrect that memory."

"I would have to forget about it in order to resurrect it, and I've never forgotten anything about you."

I'm still half-laughing as I turn around to look at him. I let out a gasp when I see the hunger raging in his eyes. His breathing is fast. I can almost feel every exhale of air as it leaves his body, floating over my damp skin in soft blasts, leaving goose pimples in its wake. His warm olive complexion is flushed and his firm jaw tenses as he tries to swallow down his obvious desire.

I take a step back, knowing he's going to come for me.

And I want him to. It feels inevitable now.

I look hard into his eyes. Searching for answers. Wondering if he's sure. All the while my own desire builds deep and low in my pelvis, pulsing in waves of electric heat that make my flesh burn.

He takes five steps forward, crashes his lips onto mine and pushes me up against the wall. His hands tangle in my wet hair, then they pull and grab frantically at my clothing while his mouth moves from my lips, to my jaw, and then onto my neck. His teeth graze my skin as he nips and bites greedily.

I drag my fingernails down his stiff shirt, desperate to feel him but finding nothing but wet cotton. One of his knees manoeuvres between my legs and his groin grinds against my thigh. A flash of lightning lights up his eyes and makes the natural golden highlights in his hair glisten. I groan into his neck when I feel how hard he is, then I remember where we are. I glance around, making sure we're alone. There are three doors and windows at the exit of the alley – people's homes – and the entrance would be open to the world, if the town wasn't deserted.

"Don't worry," he says, as he licks and nips at my neck. He reaches for my hand and slowly entwines our fingers together. The gesture is all it takes for me to feel safe. "I had to do this. I don't care about the past . . . I want this. I want you."

I look into his dark-brown eyes and find every word he's just said written deep into his irises. Flecks of amber, copper and bronze light sparkle as a faint smile pulls at the edges of his mouth. I crash my lips on his, my tongue tasting every inch of his mouth until the heat pooling between my thighs transforms into a steady, pulsing ache. "Please," I say between raspy pants. "I need more."

I feel his hand reach around my back, before snaking under my top to find a cold, aching nipple encased in rose-pink lace. He kneads my breast as he continues to grind against my lower body, then he pushes the lace aside. I moan the second his fingers touch me, but when he bows his head and lightly bites my nipple through the wet fabric of my top, my moans turn into carnal growls.

"If I could fuck you here, I would," he says, grappling with my stiff linen skirt.

I wrap my arms around his neck. "I know, but please don't stop yet."

His fingers gently graze the soft flesh of my inner thighs, and my knees instinctively bend so I can push myself into his hand. "Nothing could make me stop."

One of my arms falls from his neck and he catches my hand, locking his fingers tight against mine again. His eyes don't leave me for a second; his focus is completely fixed and enthralled. He's enjoying how much my body reacts to his touch, and every sensual sound that leaves my throat emboldens him to keep going.

"I want you to come for me," he says. His hand dips inside my cotton underwear and he gently starts to caress my sensitive flesh.

I tighten my grip on his hand and mewl like a kitten. "I don't . . . think I'm . . . going to have . . . a choice."

"You could tell me to stop." His fingers trail through my wetness until he finds my clit.

My breath hitches high in my throat. "Don't . . . stop."

His face is so close to mine that our noses are resting against each other's. I wrap one of my legs around his, and he uses the extra space to sink two fingers inside me, while his thumb continues to make soft circular strokes on the most sensitive part of me.

"You have no idea how much I want all of me inside you." He speeds up the thrusting movements of his fingers until they synch with the rapidity of my breathing.

"I want that too."

He briefly breaks concentration to kiss the inside of my wrist, then his gaze returns with a new intensity. "I've never stopped wanting you. Not once."

His revelation takes me over the edge. A guttural, throaty shriek blasts up from my lungs as shockwaves of wild and furious energy ripple through my body. My hold strengthens around his neck as my legs shake beneath me, then just when I think it's over, Nate pushes his fingers faster inside my vaginal walls and another surge of pleasure rushes through me. I think this one might last forever. My legs weaken, but he holds me in place. My toes curl inside my shoes and my fingers grab wildly at his hair until the euphoria gradually fades away.

He holds me in his arms until my body stops shaking and my breathing returns to normal, then he helps me push down my skirt and straighten my top.

His sunshine smile breaks through the thunder, yet through my happiness I can still feel the same knot coiled tight in the pit of my stomach. What happens next? How do we get closure now? Am I going to tell him?

"What's going on in that head of yours?" he asks as he loops a bedraggled clump of wet hair behind my ear.

I look into his eyes again, and even though they're smiling, they're still filled with an intense desire. "We're not done yet," I say, grazing my hand lightly against the rock-hard bulge pressing against my hip. "I still want more."

"I do too," he says. "Do you think your minivan has arrived?"

"If it has, it's probably left without me already."

We both turn our heads to look at the scene outside our sanctuary. The rain is still lashing down, but it's lighter and the time lapse between thunder and lightning is several seconds longer.

"How much water do you think your equipment can handle?" he says, glancing briefly at the dolly.

"I don't even care anymore. If it rusts, it rusts."

"I think I could get it all in my car."

"You mean . . . ?" My voice dips seductively.

"I do," he says, kissing the top of my head. My nose twitches and I sneeze. He laughs softly. "Are you okay?"

"Aside from being very wet and very cold?"

He gives the tops of my arms a rub, then he lets me go. And my body groans at losing his warmth. "Come on, let's make a dash for it. My car is parked around the corner."

# 19

AS NATE DRIVES US BACK to his villa, I think there's enough energy inside the car to power the brightest star in the sky. I listen to the sound of the windscreen wipers battling the rain and notice that the air seems calmer outside. And I can't take my eyes off him. There's liveliness in the way he turns the steering wheel. There's determination in the way his hands pull back on the gearstick. He looks like happiness; he sounds like quiet acceptance. He wants to claim the person he left behind eight years ago, and I know this because I know him. He's always been so easy to read.

But what about me? Love doesn't seem a strong enough word for how I feel about him. There's too much power between us for it to be merely love, but I'm all too aware that I also have the power to hurt him. If I tell him the truth, will he break? If I don't tell him, will I break?

He uses a sensor to buzz open the electric gates to his villa, then he drives up to the front entrance and pulls on the handbrake. "I'm so glad you're here," he says. He tenderly cups my face and places his lips on mine. He tastes of rainwater mixed with joy.

"Shouldn't we talk?" I ask, pulling away but keeping my eyes buried in his.

He strokes my cheek with his thumb. "Not unless you want to."

I do want to and I probably should, but I can't, and not just because my stomach is filled with butterflies. I want this moment. I want him. Selfishly and fearlessly. I kiss him again, enjoying the soft growl that escapes his throat when my tongue slides into his warm mouth.

He opens the car door and steps outside. His cream leather seat bears his outline. I instinctively reach across and glide my fingers through the wet shapes his body's made, then he opens the passenger door for me.

We walk up to the little bank, then climb the stone stairs. His hand reaches behind him to find mine, and I smile because his hold feels safe and reassuring. But as we walk through the front door, the terrible Nate-sized knot that resides permanently in my gut squeezes tighter than ever, reminding me that we're going to need a lot more than love, no matter how powerful it is, if we're to make this work.

He scans my face. Uncertainty pulls at the corners of his smile. "How are you feeling?" he asks.

I speak straight from my heart. "Afraid."

He narrows the space between us and gently grips my shoulders. "What of?"

"Of how I feel," I say, searching his restless eyes. "And of what comes next."

His hand rests reassuringly on my shoulder and his anxious gaze relaxes. "I think I can relate to that."

My fingers skim the front of his wet cotton shirt then stop at the centre of his chest. I can feel his heart racing for me. "Are you sure about this?"

"I'm sure I don't want to keep living my life without ever finding out if I could have built something with you."

My body trembles at the raw honesty in his words. I inhale sharply. "I want to know that too."

"Then what are we waiting for?"

He takes my hand and leads me towards his bedroom, but instead of diving straight for the bed, he pushes me up against the wall and trails kisses on all the parts of me that are still bruised and tingling from our earlier encounter in the alley.

But his movements aren't nearly as wild and frenzied. He's taking his time, appreciating every kiss that I return and relishing every sound of pleasure that leaves my body. I undo his shirt, unfastening each button in turn with shaking hands. He slows down the pace of his kisses as if he's cherishing every second of us undressing each other.

He pulls my top over my head and removes the hairband from my drenched hair. I push his shirt down his arms and delight in finally being able to press my hands to his body. His chest is just as I remember: toned, defined and a shade perfectly between light olive and tan. He wraps his arms around my back to unzip my skirt while I unbutton his trousers. In perfect synchronisation, we kick off shoes and soaked socks until all that remains is my hopelessly mismatched underwear and his snug jersey shorts.

Taking hold of my hand, he leads me to the bed. I lie down in the centre, my head resting on gorgeous plump pillows and my body grateful for the warmth and dryness underneath me. He lies next to me, on his side, his head propped up on his arm. It isn't what I expect, but as I look up and watch his eyes move over me, settling on my stomach, then my breasts, and finally my mouth, I let him take the lead.

"What are you thinking?" I ask him.

"I don't know how this is going to sound." He forces a weak smile onto his face, but there's nothing but regret in his voice. "When I left LA I tried so hard to forget you. Then, over time, all I wanted was to remember every tiny thing about you. I was terrified that I'd allowed the best parts of you to fade from my memory. Then, when I was with Evelyn, and later Lucy, I couldn't stop comparing them to you. Their laughter wasn't as lively. They weren't as confident, or as smart, or as perceptive. Their bodies were imperfect because their skin wasn't dusted with freckles, or their legs didn't go on forever, or their hair wasn't the colour of fire . . ." His eyes dip under a frown and he sighs. "This sounds really unkind, doesn't it?"

"A little bit," I say, giggling softly. "But, if I'm honest, you had a huge impact on my relationships too. Looking back, I've definitely done foolish things because I couldn't accept that I'd lost you."

One of his hands rests eagerly on my hip. "Like what?"

"Like Richie," I say with a dose of guilt. "I think my subconscious chose him because of his connection to you. You were friends so we both shared part of you. But I never loved him."

"Weren't you ever happy together?" His frown deepens.

"We shared some good times, but . . ." I think back to the arguments, the misunderstandings and the disconnect. "He expected that I'd change. He wanted me to tick perfect-girlfriend boxes that he'd drawn up, but he never once communicated what he needed. He wanted a girlfriend who fitted in, and he grew to resent how my personality overpowered his. But it wasn't just Richie. Every man I've ever been with has tried to lock me up in a cage. You're the only one who let me fly."

"Because I fell in love with the way you spread your wings." He finds my hand and holds it tightly. He keeps doing that, entwining his hand with mine as if he never wants to let me go. "You're the only woman I've ever been with who wasn't afraid of falling."

I look down at our hands. "Because when I was with you, I knew you would catch me."

His hold tightens, but his expression darkens. "I was cruel for cutting you off and I hate myself for it. I wish I'd gone back for you. I wish I'd got on that plane. I would tell myself that we were only together a short time and we hadn't made any kind of commitment, but I just couldn't . . ." His voice disappears inside his chest. "I couldn't handle that you were with somebody else while you were with me."

For a brief moment I wonder if now is the time. *I didn't cheat on you.* The words should be easy to say, but as he leans closer, his legs and fingers entwining protectively with mine, I retreat. I don't want to light the match. My eyes fill with tears. "Do you trust me?"

"I want to," he says. He brings our hands to his lips and kisses my knuckles. When his gaze returns it's glassy. "You need to be free, so I wouldn't even try to tie you down. You said I let you fly, but I didn't, not completely. I decided you belonged to me, but you didn't make that same promise. I shouldn't have expected commitment so soon."

My heart aches at how hard he's trying to make excuses for what he thinks I did. He's convincing himself of my innocence so that he can finally forgive me. I feel a tear escape and run down my face. I try to hold on to the next one, but I can't. I unwrap my legs from his and curl them high towards my chest.

"Hey, it's okay." He sweeps his arms around me as I sob against him. "Let's put it all behind us. It doesn't matter anymore."

He wipes the last tear from my face with his thumb, then he leans down and kisses the wetness away. I run my hands around to his back. His muscles flex underneath my fingertips and I lightly trace my nails down his spine. I love him so much. I never want to stop holding him.

Our movements are small and soft. Our breaths are heavy. Quiet moans and gasps play like music as our fingers dance across each other's bodies. He unhooks my bra and kisses my breasts, letting his tongue circle each nipple until it's hard and begging for his teeth.

I sink my fingers into his hair as he licks a path through my freckles, stopping at the edge of my underwear. I raise myself off the bed so he can free me of the cotton. He kisses all the way down to my thighs, lingering briefly at my entrance, then he removes his shorts and moves on top of me.

Nate reaches for my hand again. His eyes are hungry yet tender as they connect deeply with mine. My body trembles in anticipation, impatience building in my groin as his cock rubs against the sensitive flesh between my legs. His hold tightens. His gaze strengthens. I raise my legs around his waist and he grinds slowly into me, filling me completely in one delicious thrust.

I let out a groan that could shatter glass, and the sound of my pleasure lights up his eyes. He slowly pulls out, then plunges back inside me. He kisses my mouth, my jaw, and my neck, then he resumes his deep gaze into my soul. Everything about his lovemaking is gentle, and different to before. When we were younger, there was a wild and chaotic urgency raging inside both us, but now he's deliberately prolonging the act, and I don't mind that one bit.

My hips move with his, gently beating a rhythm that joins with my moans to create a perfect melody. "Should I pull out when I come?" he whispers against my cheek.

"No, I'm safe," I reply, and less than a moment later his body jerks forward and we both shriek with enough electric energy to light up a hundred cities.

He collapses on top of me, adjusting his weight so he doesn't crush me, but half of his damp, breathless body is draped across me. One of his hands is still locked tight around mine, and my legs are still wrapped around him. "I want to stay inside you forever," he says, brushing my damp hair from my face.

"That might be awkward when we have to fly home."

He laughs and his breath tickles my neck. "Well, I'm not ready to climb out of you just yet."

I kiss the top of his head. "Then don't."

"I've never been so grateful for a thunderstorm." He runs his fingers across my neck and lightly massages my breast. "Will you stay with me until morning?"

My nerves electrify as he plays with my nipple. "As long as you keep doing what you're doing."

"Oh, I can keep this going all night."

We have sex again in his bed, then, hours later, we get up and shower. He orders a dinner delivery from his friends at the Ristorante Paradiso, and after eating we move outside to the garden terrace and talk into the night. We make love under the stars to the sound of crickets and gentle rainfall.

He finally falls asleep with his body pressed against mine, and I allow myself to believe that we can be together like this forever. We can forget the past and become something new – something built of who we are now, not who we were. But as his strong, protective hold loosens around my waist, I listen to his soft sleeping breaths fall onto the back of my neck, and I remind myself that even though he's a rich, powerful man, he's still breakable. His fragility is bound by his intensity, and thoughts of potentially destroying his world keep me awake. As the hours roll on, a dull pain develops in my head and every inch of my body starts to ache. I yearn to dream, but when warm orange sunlight breaks through the curtains and lights up the room, I have to resign myself to permanent restlessness. It's barely dawn when he stirs against me, and I know I've disturbed him. My skin is burning, my head is throbbing and my throat feels like there's a shard of glass wedged inside it.

"Are you okay?" he asks as I roll over to the far

side of the bed in search of coolness. His hand brushes my cheek and he bolts upright. "Jesus, you're burning up."

"Don't worry, I think it's just Violet's cold." A little of the concern embedded in his eyes fades away. "I'm sorry. I've probably passed it on to you already."

He lies back down and pulls me into his arms. "I can handle it. I'm a Klein. We're built of strong stuff."

*I'm a Klein.* His words wash over my skin like poison. What am I doing here? What was I thinking? I knew I'd crash back to reality at some point, but I didn't think it would happen this soon. Panic rises inside me and my brain thuds against my skull. "I . . . should get back to the hotel."

"It isn't even seven a.m. yet." His voice cracks with sleep and his expression is riddled with confusion.

I pull out of his hold, climb out of the bed and start putting on my underwear. I feel sick, and exhausted, and I'm not sure if my lungs are grappling for oxygen because of my cold, or because I'm teetering on the brink of yet another horrible panic attack. "I just need to go. I shouldn't . . ."

"Shouldn't what?"

When I turn around, he's standing at the other side of the bed wearing dark joggers, his chest bare. He looks completely lost. My heart aches as I look at him. It's what I feared. I'm breaking him already. "I feel like crap warmed up and I need some alone time. My head's just . . . not really working properly."

He opens his mouth to speak, but then he stops himself. He picks up a t-shirt off the floor and pulls it over his head. "I'll drive you back."

"Thanks, but I'd rather call our van."

"You're running away. Why?"

"I'm not," I say, putting on yesterday's clothes. My top is dry, but my skirt is still damp and my cardigan feels like it's just come out of a spin cycle. "I told you. I just need to be by myself to think."

"I saw your face change when I mentioned my name. Is this about my dad?"

My stomach feels like it's taken a ride on the waltzer in Tivoli Gardens. I shake my head and fumble with the zip on my skirt. Then I pick up my bag, take out my phone and text the minivan driver to come and pick me up.

"Freja, please. What's going on?"

I cross the room and stand in front of him. My head is pounding and my face is hot enough to fry an egg. How am I going to get through a full day's work in this state? "I don't know what's going on in my mind, Nate. I'm sorry. I'm just . . . really tired. I never worry about the future, but I can't stop thinking . . ."

He reaches for my hand, but I pull away from him. His shoulders sag. "Look, if you're worried about me forgiving you, I swear I have and I will never mention the past ever again. I meant what I said about forgetting you cheated on me and I . . ." He stops talking, and my blood runs cold. I know he saw my face change when he said the word "cheated". I tried to stop my eyes rolling. I tried so bloody hard. "What was that?" he asks. His tone is loaded with suspicion.

"Nothing." My phone beeps and I see a message from Marco, one of our drivers. He says he'll be outside in five minutes, which I hope is a speedier five minutes than yesterday's. "I have to go."

He grabs hold of my arm as I walk past him. "Not yet. Not until you talk to me."

I keep my back to him. "I can't."

"Tell me," he pleads. "Whatever it is, just tell me."

I turn around to face him, but I keep my gaze lowered. I think of her – the person I used to be. Would she be proud of who I've become?

*What should I do?* I ask her.

*Find your voice,* she replies.

I stoically raise my chin and look into his bewildered eyes. "I didn't cheat on you."

He exhales a sharp blast of air. "What?"

I say it again, but this time my voice is louder and stronger. "I didn't cheat on you."

"What do you mean? I saw the photographs."

"Where do you think the photographs came from?"

He shrugs. "Brett said they were stills from a video you'd set up."

I shake my head. Ever since I found out his father had shown him those photographs, part of me has felt betrayed that he believed what he saw without even asking me for an explanation. "I didn't know Brett's name until last week. To this day, I've never spoken a word to him."

"But . . ." He looks away; one hand leans flat against the door frame, the other ravages his hair. "Freja, you don't need to do this. I told you I was over it."

"You think I'm lying?" I feel my heart shatter. This is what I feared. This is why the coward in me chose silence so easily. Tears pour down my cheeks until I can't take any more. I step away from him. "I never lie, Nate. Never."

He doesn't respond. He looks at me as if I'm crazy.

My phone beeps again, and I take it as my signal to leave. I pick up my things, walk through the doorway, and I don't look back.

# 20

THE RIDE BACK TO THE hotel is a blur. Marco gave up trying to talk to me before we even joined the main road into Menaggio. I fold myself into a ball on one of the middle seats, my head pounding as it rests against my knees. I can't stop shaking and aching and I feel like I could sleep for a hundred years, so when the minivan pulls up outside the hotel, I make a beeline for my room. But I bump into Neil in the foyer.

"Holy shit, what the hell happened to you?"

I rake my hand through my unbrushed hair. "I've caught Violet's cold."

His blue eyes glare at me. "Where've you been?"

"Just getting some fresh air, you know, trying to clear my head."

He answers me with a sceptical glance. "Since yesterday afternoon?"

"Yes. In a way." I probably should have spent part of my sleepless night thinking up a decent excuse to explain my disappearing act.

"Violet has drawn up some last-minute scenes to shoot this morning. Madeline wasn't happy with the ice cream stuff, but agreed to let us try something else."

I knew those shots were dreadful. "Are you clued up on what they both need?"

"Yeah, we talked about it over dinner last night."

"Good, you're going to have to go ahead without me. I won't be much use today."

He nods. "Can I get you anything?"

"Do you have an axe to chop my head off?"

He laughs. "Not with me, but I do have some ibuprofen back in my room."

"Thanks, I have some in my overnight bag." I give his arm a light squeeze, then I walk over to the lifts.

"Um, Freja, one more thing."

I hit the call button. "What is it?"

He looks awkward as hell. "Where's our dolly car and track?"

The lift pings and the doors swish open. I step inside. "In the back of Nate Klein's car."

\* \* \*

I drink a gallon of water, take as many painkillers as I can without needing my stomach pumped, and wait for sleep to consume me. I'm interrupted several times by arriving and vacating holidaymakers in the corridor, noise from the streets below my window, and a wheezing cough which makes my ribs creak. I'd have better luck trying to sleep during one of my smelly neighbour's early morning drug parties.

I have no idea how long I've slept, or if I've slept, when the sound of impatient knocking at my door drifts into my consciousness. I groan as I roll out of bed, but I welcome the cool air on my damp, burning skin. I'm so hot and sweaty it feels like I've fallen asleep in the bathtub. I'm yawning when I open the door, so I don't notice Nate's facial expression at first. I don't see the pain, or the confusion, or the hopelessness.

"Can I come in?"

He doesn't wait for me to answer. He walks through the door and throws his jacket down on the back of the dressing-table chair. He looks like he's just been told he has six months to live, and a massive dose of guilt surges through my veins. I'm tired of feeling like this. I'm tired of carrying around shame that I didn't bring upon myself and lies that I didn't create. I need to put down this burden. I found my voice this morning, but now I've found something else: an all-consuming, unquenchable hunger to be heard and believed.

"What time is it?" I ask groggily. I rub my face awake.

"Three thirty."

"What? I feel like I've slept for thirty minutes, not seven hours." I sit down on the edge of the bed. "Did the shoot go okay?"

He nods stiffly. "We finished up just after lunch. I had a couple of urgent things to sort back at the villa, so I told your guys they'd have to make do with the footage they have already."

"Is Violet happy about that? She's responsible for—"

"Who cares?" I jump at the abruptness in his tone. "I'm paying for the work, so the only opinion that matters is mine."

"Ordinarily, I'd agree, but I know Violet was really keen to see her vision interpreted perfectly on film."

"Can we not do this?" He pulls out the chair and sits down, then he leans forward and locks his hands together. "I don't want to talk about work." The nerve in his jaw bulges and his shoulders sag. "I've known Brett Kirkman for years." I suck in a breath as I search his eyes. I know where this is going to end up and I'm afraid. *Really* afraid. "My dad recruited him when he was working as an analyst for Microsoft, just before Dad did that deal with your ex-Silicon Valley friend in LA. I've taken business trips with him, we've co-pitched for contracts together, and I've used him as a consultant for BuzzPay. He got married to an English girl a couple of years ago, and my dad is godfather to his baby. He comes to family birthday parties and, hell, he's even just arranged an internship at Microsoft for my half-brother this summer. He's been part of the extended Klein & Co family for years, but still, every single time I'm anywhere near him, I have to physically stop myself punching his teeth out."

I inhale sharply. If he's felt this strongly about Brett for the past eight years, then I dread to think how he's going to feel the next time he sees him.

"I called him earlier." He raises his head and looks directly at me.

"Brett?" He nods and my insides squirm. "What did you say to him?"

A short, scoffing laugh leaves his throat. "Same as I said to him eight years ago. I confronted him straight away after Dad showed me those photographs. He said he had no idea who you were when he slept with you, and I believed him. A couple of months had passed and he couldn't remember your name. He called you 'the redhead with the accent'. I wanted to knock him to the ground, and I almost did, but it wasn't his fault. He said he'd met you at the hotel bar. You'd had a conversation and then you came on to him. I didn't have any reason to doubt his story – the photographs were evidence – but then, today, when I told him what you said . . . that you *didn't* cheat on me . . ."

For a second I wonder if Brett might have confessed all, but the way Nate is looking at me – with anger and distrust – gives me my answer. I inhale a long, steady breath to settle my nerves, then I find my voice again. "I told you the truth."

"Brett says you're lying." His eyes flash defiantly. "He told me the same story as before. You met him in a bar, you came on to him, you invited him to your movie set, and then you set up a video to film yourself having sex with him."

"No." I shake my head and my eyes sting with tears. "That's not what happened. None of that is true."

He shoots to his feet and slams his fists down hard on the dressing table. "Then tell me! For fuck's sake, just tell me the bloody truth!"

I close my eyes. Tears crawl down my cheeks as I search for the right words. But there aren't any *right* words when everything is wrong. I raise my eyes to meet his. "He drugged me."

I've spent so long imagining this moment that when it arrives it's like finding an outtake I've cut from an ad. I didn't think his eyes would look like this. I didn't think the colour would drain from his face so quickly. In all the scenarios I'd played out in my mind, not once did he lose the ability to breathe. He falls back against the table. "What are you telling me?"

"I have a report, a medical report from a clinic in LA. If you need to see it, it's in a box somewhere in my house. The report says I had a high dose of

GHB in my bloodstream. It acted like a tranquiliser. I was barely conscious, I didn't know what was happening . . ."

"Wait a minute . . ." Nate catches his breath while his chest heaves as if he's just run a marathon. When he speaks again, his voice is crushed. "Are you telling me Brett Kirkman assaulted you?"

I shake my head. "It was all an elaborate set-up. He planned it every step of the way, and Brett, well, I guess he just did as he was told."

His eyes – red-rimmed and raw – come alive with fury. "You mean . . . ?"

I speak between sobs. "Yes . . . It was . . . your dad."

"Oh, god." He practically falls onto the bed next to me. My heart aches to hold him, but I'm afraid he might crumble.

"He came to my trailer. He wanted to pay me off, said he'd give me whatever I wanted providing I never saw you again. I said no, told him to leave, but he'd put something in my drink." He sits silently next to me. I reach for him, wanting his fingers to entwine with mine and hold me safe again, but his hand is unmoveable rock. "I didn't know what was happening. One minute I was passed out, the next I was naked and they were moving me around the bed. I remember their voices were raised, but I can't remember a word they said. I can still see the flashes of the camera and hear the clicks. There was never a video. It was just Brett lying with me, making it look like . . ."

My voice dies then. The moment he envelopes me in his arms it gets lost in my throat. He buries his head in my neck and holds me so tightly that I can barely breathe. Then he starts to cry. Just soft whimpers to begin with, but then sobs so deep and mournful that his tears soak through my hair and wet my skin. "Did they hurt you?"

I know what he's asking. "I don't think so. Not physically. I asked your dad, and he said they didn't, but I've never known for sure."

He pulls away from me but keeps hold of my hands. Pain burns in my chest when I see the horror in his eyes and the wet tracks his tears have made down his beautiful face. "When did you see him?"

I think back to that day. Glorious sunshine, palm trees swaying to a gentle breeze, my sneakers squeaking against the polished floors of the Beverley Wilshire Hotel as I purposefully made my way to his hotel suite. Pride balloons within me at how brave I was back then. "You'd flown up to San Francisco that day to pitch Aaron's tech to a Chinese company. I went to your dad's room and I asked him if he, or Brett, had hurt me. He said no, but even if they didn't rape me, they still *hurt* me, Nate."

His hands tighten around mine. "I know that, oh god . . . I know that."

"I didn't tell anybody until recently. I had to tell Violet and Ethan – I'm sorry. They won't say anything."

"That doesn't matter. You needed to talk. I can't believe you kept this to yourself for so long." His face crumples as he struggles to come to terms with what I've told him. "Why did he do it? I just . . . why?"

"Power and control. He wanted me gone. He

threatened to show you the photographs if I didn't disappear."

"So you just did what he asked?" His eyes cloud with disappointment.

I smile lightly. "All of these years I've been trying to figure out why I let you go, and I still come up short. I guess I just couldn't imagine having a future with you knowing who your father was, so there seemed little point wrecking your life on top of that. I loved you and I didn't want to hurt you. You and your father are roped together. You'll always be his son. I couldn't spend any more of my life tied up in knots between you."

His eyes melt with a desperate sadness, and I hate myself for doing this to him, even though I know I had to. "You're the strongest woman I know. I don't understand why you let him win."

"I was ashamed and I couldn't face what he'd done. I'm still wearing the scars. Years of nightmares and panic attacks and feeling like . . ." I wipe a tear from my cheek. "Like I'll never be good enough for anybody."

"You are good enough. More than enough." Grief sweeps over his face, and his words make my breath catch. "If you'd told me all this eight years ago, I'd have believed you."

I force humour into my eyes. "You've spent eight years believing I was guilty of filming myself cheating on you."

"And if you'd told me the truth, then I wouldn't have." His face is beetroot red. "Freja, you must have known that I'd believe you."

I shake my head and stand up, then I walk towards the tall window. The town is busy tonight. I wonder if that's normal for a Thursday. "You know what the world is like, Nate." I turn around and rest my back against the window pane. "I was a young Scandinavian girl in my twenties who didn't have a penny to her name. I got hammered every weekend, enjoyed one-night-only hook-ups with guys I'd only just met and, oh yeah, my work involved me taking my clothes off."

"You were much more than any of that. You were an amazing, intelligent, talented woman enjoying her life."

"I know what I was, and I have no regrets, but I also know how the world will choose to view me. People always go to the gutter first. Your father knew that, and that's why he chose shame and humiliation as a means to get rid of me." He sighs deeply, and I can hear the truth weighing heavily on him. "Even if you believed me, the world wouldn't. He's rich and powerful, and he's feared and respected in equal measure by other rich and powerful people. That world's alien to me. I was a broke waitress and student. I had no hope of fighting him." My gaze shifts to the floor. I can feel my temperature rise again and the ache returns to my muscles. I wonder if another round of painkillers would dull the pain in my heart too. "Sometimes I think I'm who I am today because of him. The only chance I had of surviving was if I shut everything he did out of my mind. I shut you out too. I thought I was doing okay, but then you came back and I couldn't hold on to it anymore. He stole so much of my life – my dreams, my happiness, my self-respect – but the worst thing he took from me was you because you're the only thing I didn't get back."

He joins me at the window. "What do you think our lives would look like today if all this hadn't happened?"

I raise an eyebrow. "If you're asking if I think there's a parallel-universe Freja and Nate out there, I'm not going to tell you they're married with two children, a home in Berkshire's leafy suburbs and four pairs of Hunter wellington boots sitting on the front porch."

The corners of his mouth curl and his cheeks dimple. "Two little redhead kids sounds great to me, but what about a dog?"

"I wouldn't accept anything less than a Great Dane."

"I can see that." Sunshine warms his face as his gorgeous smile returns. "You have me back now. Promise you won't leave me again."

I graze my bottom lip with my teeth, my doubts holding me back. "Nate, I can't make a promise like that. I can't see into the future." His smile fades in an instant. "I don't want to leave you. Will that do?"

"I want a relationship with you – a proper one with dates, romantic weekends away and DVD nights in with a pizza and a bottle of wine. I want it all – with you. Can we try?"

"Yes." I don't have to think for longer than a nanosecond. "You've no idea how much I want to."

"Then we'll find a way to get through this."

I wonder if he knows how hard this is going to be. "You've no idea how much I wanted to tell you the truth, but I knew how huge this was. The thought of ripping your family apart, or destroying your name—"

"Screw my name!" he says. His eyes are sharp under heavy brows. "The last time my name was important to me, I was using it to score points with the over-entitled dickheads at my boarding school. If it wasn't for my name, my mother would probably still be alive. My name made the simple act of falling out of love with my dad, and into love with someone who deserved her, a national scandal. I've never cared about my bloody name."

I shake my head, wondering how I could have got this so wrong. "But what about your family? Your brothers?"

"If it comes as news to them that our father is a wicked, depraved monster, they haven't been paying attention. Everyone knows what he is." He places his hands on my shoulders. "You're not carrying this alone anymore. I'm with you, I believe you, and we're going to make sure that bastard gets what he deserves."

I haven't thought about getting justice in years. I know it'll be practically impossible. "If we're together, then we have justice." I hold my hand expectantly to his chest. "If I could go back, knowing how much this hurt you, I wouldn't choose to keep quiet. But I don't want to give your father any more of myself."

He moves his arms around my back and pulls me close. "I want to tell him I know what he did. I want to watch him squirm. I want to see cold, hard terror in his eyes when I tell him I'm going to destroy him. I want to watch what happens to his face when I tell him how much I love you."

I smile against his shoulder. "I'd pay good money to see all of that."

"When we get back to London, the front-row seats are on me."

# 21

HE'S ALREADY DRESSED WHEN I wake up. Light-blue jeans and a cream shirt that contrasts beautifully with his bronzed skin. "How are you feeling?" he asks, setting down his cup of coffee.

"Not as bad as yesterday, but I'll feel better after another round of paracetamol." I seem to have lost the ability to breathe through my nose, so I sniff, and cough myself awake.

"I'll get you some." He disappears into the bathroom and returns with two tablets and a glass of water. He sits down on the edge of the bed while I take them, his arms stretched protectively across my legs. "Can I get you some coffee?"

"That would be nice."

He goes to the console table and clicks the button on the kettle. "What time is your flight today?"

"I'm not sure. Late this afternoon I think."

He pours hot water into the cup. "I'm not booked to fly back until tomorrow, but I can buy a new ticket. Do you take milk?"

"Not usually, but I do with crap hotel room coffee." I can see the side of his cheek bulge with a grin. He hands me my cup. "Do you really want to fly back to London with all of my colleagues? I mean, you've met Kris Berg, right?"

He sips his coffee with a smile on his face. "I don't want to spend a night away from you."

I rest my hand on his knee. "And that makes me feel pretty great, but there's a lot we need to sort out before we stroll hand in hand onto a plane together."

His mouth curls into a smile. "Are you worried about people knowing we're together?"

"In a way." I say, taking a sip of my drink. My mouth hates me every time I drink instant coffee, but any caffeine on a morning is better than no caffeine. "I'm probably going to sound a bit silly saying this, but I want to keep you to myself for as long as possible."

"Such as how long?" His voice is like velvet.

"Until I'm certain you aren't going to regret this."

He takes my cup from me and puts it down on the bedside table, then he takes my hands. My stomach flutters at the strength in his touch. "The only regret I've had in my entire life is that I didn't get on a plane eight years ago, fly back to LA and ask you to be mine. Well, that and the haircut I got when I was nineteen." His smile widens until his cheeks dimple. "There's more chance I'll wake up tomorrow and see a blue sun than there is of me regretting loving you."

Loving me? *Min Gud*, this is really real, isn't it? "For this to work, you're going to have to choose me over your dad."

"I've already chosen you," he says defiantly. "Wholeheartedly and unequivocally. And if he'd hurt a stranger instead of you, then I'd choose the stranger. I don't want you to worry about that, okay?"

His words sting my eyes and I feel a lump form in my throat. But there's some frustration too. Could this same conversation have happened eight years ago? "Okay, I'll try, but there's more." I don't feel any vulnerability sharing my insecurities with him. "Having a relationship with somebody you work with is always difficult, and you're a client, a famous and good-looking one, who every woman in the office kinda notices."

A look of pure mischief sweeps over his face. "Are you calling me handsome?"

I have to twist my mouth to stop myself laughing. "You know you're handsome. What I'm saying is people will talk. You wanted to fire Kris two nights ago for crossing the line, and the gossip about us being in a relationship is going to be much worse than that. Then there's my CEO. Stella Judd wanted to fire Ethan and Violet when they got together. She hates when her people's personal lives mix with work. And all this is *before* we bring your dad into the equation."

He lets out a long, laboured sigh. "Can we get back to talking about me being handsome?"

I chastise him with a hard glare. "This is serious."

"I know it is, but it isn't important. I didn't think you'd care about what people think."

"Neither did I," I admit, feeling a little foolish and a lot insecure. "Maybe I just need some time."

"Okay, I get that." He stands up and passes my coffee back to me. "I'll put these terrible, lonely" – he glances at his watch – "almost twenty-four hours to good use by planning out our happily ever after." He bends down and kisses the top of my head. "Do you want me to pack for you before I go?"

"Thanks, but no." I say, climbing out of the bed. "I'm actually feeling a bit better, so I'll manage."

He kisses me before leaving, and I'm already

counting the minutes until tomorrow morning.

\* \* \*

I'm dreading the journey to the airport. I check out of the hotel late and make sure I'm the last to take my seat at the back of the minivan. Neil tells me that I still look terrible, Violet apologises for loading me with her germs, and Kris bemoans the fact he's sixty-five pounds out of pocket because Nate didn't sleep with Lexi.

I'm relieved that Madeline is in the other minivan, and when we get to Milan Malpensa airport, I make sure I check in last and ask to be seated on my own. I spend the entire flight playing an addictive but pointless amusement park app on my phone, but I can't stop my mind wandering back to the last few days in Italy. Or rather, I can't stop thinking about Nate – his body, his gorgeous smile, his beautiful words. I should be walking on air, and I almost am, but I also have a horrible, gnawing feeling of dread knotted deep within my abdomen.

We split into teams to take taxis back from Heathrow. Violet heads off with the North Londoners. She promises to give me a call as soon as she's spent some time with Ethan, so I don't expect to hear a word from her for the rest of the weekend. After we drop Kris and Kwame outside a block of council flats in Kennington, we head for Bermondsey, where Billie apparently still lives with her mum. Finally we take Frank to his modest semi in East Dulwich. I have no idea how he manages to fit all of his children in such a tiny house, unless his 1920s three-bed semi has the same supernatural properties as Doctor Who's Tardis.

With all of the stop-offs, it takes over an hour and a half to get home. I don't mind the long journey one bit, because I have three beautiful text messages, complete with heart emojis, from Nate to read. I reply to each one and promise to call him before I go to bed.

I don't bother to unpack, opting for a candlelit bubble bath and another try of the pink-cake-shop-in-Cornwall-near-a-romantic-looking-rundown-cottage book. But I give up on it, again. The heroine, inexplicably named "Decca", is an insipid idiot and I hate everything about her.

I'm just about to order a takeaway when my doorbell rings. I sneeze, then plod to the door with half of my face buried in a tissue.

"Surprise!" It's Violet, with wine, and Georgie, with a huge bowl of something covered in tinfoil.

I flop against my hallway door. "I was just about to call for a pizza."

"You can forget about that," says Georgie. "I've brought chicken soup, darling." She carries her precious container straight to the kitchen and, judging by the ping, pops it into the microwave.

Violet smiles apologetically. "She was worried about you."

"I've only got a cold," I say, as I follow her through to the living room. "And why aren't you with Ethan?"

"He has a business dinner," says Violet, not even trying to disguise her devastation. "We haven't seen each other for six days, so of bloody course he decides to celebrate my return by wining and dining prospective clients." She sits down on her usual spot on my sofa. "Also, Georgie isn't worried about your cold. She's worried because I told her I know something dramatic happened between you and Nate."

I don't bother denying it. "How did you find out?"

Violet's eyes swell to the size of saucers. "Oh my god, you mean we all guessed right? Something *did* happen?"

"Wait a minute," I ask her. "Who is 'we all'?"

"Me and Neil mostly," she says through an enormous grin. "And Sophie – who's really nice, by the way. Oh, and Lexi thought so too. Did you sleep with him?" Her eyes come alive when they scan my face and settle on my barely disguised smirk. "Oh my god, you did, didn't you? What was he like? Was it wonderful?"

Georgie dashes through the door from the kitchen, carrying soup and a spoon. "What have I missed? Were we right, Violet?"

"I'm just about to get the rundown, but yes," says Violet.

Georgie squeals, and for the longest of moments I'm very worried about the soup. She lurches, splashes some of the hot creamy liquid over the side of the bowl onto her hand, then squeals again. "Shit, shit, shit! That burns like hellfire." She places the bowl on the coffee table.

"Do you need some ice?" I ask, slightly amused.

"No, I'm not leaving the room in case I miss something." She sits down in an armchair, holding her splashed hand as if it's about to fall off her wrist.

"Okay, I'm glad you're both sitting down for

this." I try not to laugh at their eager expressions. They look like two five-year-olds on Christmas morning. I build up a silent drum roll in my brain, then I make my announcement. "Nate and I are together."

Two very strange and very different squeaky, shrieky noises leave their bodies. If they both start to cry at this point, I'm sending them home. "Tell us everything," says Violet. "How did it happen?"

"It was totally unexpected actually. He just made a move."

"Oh, dear god," says Georgie, clutching her sore hand to her chest. "You mean, he took you by surprise? But how? You're never surprised. You always know what everyone is going to do even before they do it."

"George, please," I say with a comedic eye-roll. "My spidey-senses are only ninety-nine per cent flawless. I am not an Avenger, although I would totally rock a rubber superhero suit. Preferably a black one, with perfectly sculpted double-D cups."

"You wouldn't fill double-D cups, sweetie," Georgie teases.

I glare at her. "Do you want me to continue or not?"

"*I* want you to continue, so stop swaying the conversation and focus," says Violet.

Georgie hisses under her breath. "I need ice." She gets up and heads for the kitchen. "Don't you dare start talking until I get back. And eat your soup!"

"I'll wait a while if you don't mind," I say, gazing at the thick, steaming liquid sitting on my coffee table. "I'd rather not set fire to myself."

Violet is so excited that she's practically bouncing on the sofa next to me. "You have to tell me. Where were you when he made the move?"

I can't help but giggle. "Jeez, I don't think I've ever seen you this jiggly before, Violet."

She curls one leg up underneath her and sits like a puppy waiting for a treat. "Just spill, will you?"

"Okay," I say, trying not to laugh. "We were in an alley."

"Oh my god," squeals Georgie, returning from the kitchen with a bag of frozen Mediterranean vegetables and a tea towel. "You did anal?"

Oh Christ, that's it. She's finally lost the plot. "Georgie, how on earth did you jump from getting frozen veg to anal sex? Are you out of your mind?"

"No, it's just where my brain went when I heard you say 'alley'." She still has a shocked look on her face. "You know, as in 'back alley'."

My eyeballs jump out of my skull. "Yeah, I got it!"

Violet collapses into a fit of giggles. "Oh god, this is priceless. Keep talking, Georgie, please."

"It was an easy mistake to make," she says. She sits down and straps the veg to her hand with the towel. "And don't tell me you haven't ever done it, because I won't believe you."

"No, I haven't done it," I say with absolute sincerity.

Georgie's eyes narrow. "Truth?"

"Yes, of course it's the truth." I pick up the soup. The plastic bowl must conduct heat, because it's still boiling hot. I sandwich a cushion between it and my lap and stir the gloopy liquid with the spoon.

"Wait a minute, Georgie," Violet asks. "Are you telling us that you and Mitchell have dabbled in the dark arts?"

Oh god no. Rewind! "Don't ask her that! Are you crazy?"

Violet laughs. "Why not?"

"Because she has no filter and she'll tell you." I'm just about to open my mouth to eat when Georgie realises my worst fears.

"Mitchell wanted to give it a try," she says with a shrug. "I didn't enjoy it as much as he did."

I throw down my spoon in defeat. "That's it, I'm done."

Violet looks like she's going to have a heart attack.

"Just forget I said anything," says Georgie.

"How can we do that, huh?" I stretch out on the sofa and pull my legs onto Violet's lap. "Last week you told us Mitchell's dick was bent like a boomerang, and tonight you've revealed he prefers to dance the chocolate cha-cha. I didn't need to know any of this information."

"We're friends, we're supposed to share," says Georgie, with a wounded look on her face. "But just forget about it and tell me about the alley."

Memories flood my mind. Mouths, tongues, stone walls, rain, his strong hand holding mine, the wild, hungry look in his eyes. I lie back against the cushions and a huge smile spreads across my face. "It was the best sex I've ever had. Each time."

"Wait, more than once?" exclaims Georgie.

I hold up my hand and slowly count up to five on my fingers.

Violet gives my ankle a squeeze. "I am *so* happy

for you."

"I am *so* jealous," says Georgie. "Happy, but jealous."

"So, how did you leave things? Is he still in Italy?" Violet asks.

"He's coming home tomorrow." I pick the soup back up and start eating. Yum, roast chicken and vegetable. This tops pizza. How did she know it was just what I needed? "He wanted to swap his flight for today, but I told him I needed some alone time."

"Why? You've had eight years of alone time," says Georgie.

I sigh and glance at Violet. She smiles encouragingly. "It's all going to work out, you know. I don't have your spidey-senses, but I know this was written in the stars. You were always destined to find him again."

Georgie inhales sharply. "That's so beautiful."

Violet eyes twinkle as she grins. "Words are kinda my thing."

"We need more words, but first we need wine!" Georgie puts down the frozen veg and picks up the bottle of red. "Don't talk until I get back again." She goes to the kitchen.

"Did you tell him?" Violet asks as soon as we're alone.

I put the soup back down on the table. "Yes."

She lets out a huge sigh of relief. "How did he take it?"

"Badly at first, but he came through for me in a big way. Still, the truth really hurt him. I think part of me will never forgive myself for telling him."

"You had no choice, Freja. He needed to know."

I nod sadly. "I know that, but I can't stop blaming myself for not finding a way out for us that didn't hurt him. Or end up with him losing his family."

"Has he confronted his dad?"

I feel sick at the thought. I hope I don't lose my soup. "Not yet, but he will."

Our conversation is interrupted by a knock on the door. My nerves jar because I have no idea who it could be. "Want me to get it?" asks Violet.

"No, it's okay. It's probably someone bringing me news I never knew I needed about how God loves me."

I open the front door to find Madeline Westgate, also known as the absolute last person in the world I expected to see. "I'm really sorry to bother you," she says in her northern lilt. "Can I come in for a minute?"

"Sure." I stand aside so she can enter. She looks totally different tonight, having swapped her usual sleek, polished business suits for a grey zip-through hoody, black leggings and trainers. Her platinum blonde hair is tied back in a short, swishy ponytail. "Did you run over here?"

"No, I took a cab when I got back from the gym." She walks through to my living room. "Oh, you have company. Hi, Violet."

"Yes, it's just a girls' night," I say. Violet looks as surprised as I am.

Right on cue, Georgie appears carrying three glasses, the bottle of wine and a bagged-up frozen chicken breast. The veggies must have started to thaw. "Oh, um, hi, Madeline. Do you want a drink?" She's clearly flummoxed by the frosty blonde's sudden appearance.

"No, thank you," Madeline says with an uneasy smile. "I don't plan on being here long."

She looks around the room anxiously before finally sitting down in an armchair.

"Is everything okay?" I ask her.

"I need to ask you something." She's speaking with her usual directness, but she still looks awkward. "I apologise in advance because this is personal and I wouldn't normally ask, but are you sleeping with Nate Klein?"

My pulse starts to race. I hope she doesn't give me any of her self-important "he's my client and this could mess with my career" nonsense. "What has made you ask that?"

"Trust me," she says. "I have a good reason." I don't trust her, but I also don't lie. And I also have a very horrible feeling about this.

Violet clears her throat. "Should we leave the room?" she asks, with a small jerk of her head towards the door.

"No, it's fine, stay." I sit back down on the sofa. The energy is tight and uncomfortable. My instincts are telling me to send Madeline home with a fib, but I'm intrigued by what possible reason she could have for showing up at my house this late on a Friday night to ask me that question. "Yes, Nate and I are in a relationship."

Her face doesn't react. Damn, how is she so infuriatingly impenetrable? "Does his father know?"

My stomach tenses. I can't breathe. "What?"

"Lord Klein's my client," she says. "I'm pitching for all of his businesses. I want KTech, Cask and

Cork, and the chain of Statten bars. I need to know if he knows."

Oh my god, she *is* going to launch into a work rant. "Look, Madeline, I know your job is very important to you, and I respect that, but if you've half-jogged and half-taxied your way over here to warn me off having a relationship with a man I knew long before I got my first job in advertising, then you can leave right now. My relationship with Nate is none of your business."

"You don't understand," she says in a strong, even tone. "That's not why I'm asking." Her enviable full lips thin with unease.

"Then why are you here?"

Madeline shakes her head, but there's a quiet rage burning in her eyes. "Claire Hill resigned from Klein & Co yesterday. She's a friend and she's a phenomenal marketer – the absolute best I've ever worked with. She called me this morning, just before we left for the airport, to tell me she's suing for constructive dismissal and she's also going after Lord Klein for sexual harassment." Her jaw tenses, and her usual impenetrable façade gives way to genuine concern. "I told Sophie to bury those messages Lord Klein sent her. What kind of a boss – no, what kind of a friend – does that make me? My instincts were minimise, deflect and preserve my client's reputation. I could have stepped in at any point, but instead I chose my own comfort and ambition."

My brain whirrs. It wasn't just me. There *are* others. But how many? Could I have stopped this? I felt sick when I learned how Lord Klein had pursued Sophie, yet I didn't do anything either.

Madeline isn't responsible for this, I am.

Madeline's dark-brown eyes remain glued to me. "Klein & Co's board have suspended him while they investigate Claire's accusations. When Klein called me earlier tonight, I assumed he'd want to talk about Claire, but all he talked about was you. He asked me if anything had happened between you and his son in Italy." My body starts to tremble. Has Nate told him? I know he spoke to Brett yesterday. Violet takes hold of my hand. "I told him the truth – that I didn't know anything – but he was rude, and aggressive. I came here tonight because I need to know just how messy this is going to get. He said you almost destroyed his business and his family back in LA, and he wasn't going to let you destroy Tribe. He didn't say it outright, but he made it sound like he wanted you fired."

"He can't threaten her job," says Violet.

"Why would he even do that?" Georgie asks.

"I guess he doesn't like me very much." I try to inject lightness into my tone, but I can't disguise the shake in my voice.

"What's he got on you?" Madeline asks. "I know this is serious. He sounded scared on the phone."

"Oh, he's got nothing on *me*," I reply confidently. But then I remember the photographs and I start to imagine the worst. What if he shows them to Tribe's board? Or gives them to the press?

Madeline's eyes look straight through me. "Why do you look so petrified?"

"Why are you interrogating her?" Georgie snaps.

"Because I need to know what he's done and what he's capable of," says Madeline.

I draw up my legs and rest my chin on my knees.

"I can't tell you what he did, but I can promise you that I'll do everything I can to make him pay for it."

# 22

*"I DON'T KNOW WHO I AM! Woooh-oooh-oooh."*

Oh my god, not again. I crack open an eyelid and stare at my alarm clock, willing the numbers to say something other than six a.m. "*Gå ad helvede til, dit røvhul!*" I scream at full volume, pointlessly, because Derrick won't know Danish swears, and because he can't hear me. I wish my scream was strong enough to reach through the wall, grab Derrick by the throat and fix it so that he never troubles the world with his torturous singing ever again.

If I were a superhero, that would be my superpower – the ability to telepathically throttle my enemies. I don't care if I receive the power via an insect bite, radiation or some kind of alien mutation, but please, just let it happen. I'll have the black rubber suit with the double-D cups too. Oh, and the tits to fill the suit would be a well-deserved bonus.

I shove my head under a mountain of pillows and pray for a power cut. This is not how I want to spend Saturday morning when I have a stomach full of worries. I get up after ten minutes and let the sound of my shower drown out the noise.

I think about last night while I'm showering. After Madeline left, I filled Georgie in on the whole story, and gave Violet an update. Georgie was upset I hadn't told her before, and I don't blame her. We've been best friends for seven years, but I gently explained why I'd tried so hard to lock the pain out of my head until it got to a point where I couldn't.

Derrick is still inflicting his vocal cords on my eardrums when I finish blow-drying my hair, so I decide to have another word. Which undoubtedly means I'm going to yell at him and call him a pig – or much worse. I get dressed, plait my hair and I'm putting on my shoes when there's a knock on my door. I open it unthinkingly, expecting a courier or the postman, so I'm taken aback when I see Nate with his suitcase and a holdall.

"Hi," he says, sending me a huge bolt of sunshine. "I got an earlier flight." He drops his bags inside, kicks the front door shut, then sweeps me up into his arms. His kiss is everything I need to make me forget about last night's news and my horrible morning. His hands smooth down my hair as his lips press tenderly against mine, as if he's savouring every second of our reunion. "God, I missed you."

"It hasn't even been a day," I say with a soft laugh.

"I know, but I couldn't wait to see you." His fingers stay in my hair, twisting loose strands of copper behind my ear. "Christ Almighty, what's that awful noise?"

"Ah, that would be Derrick. He thinks he's destined for rock stardom."

"He's destined for me going around there and kicking his arse if he keeps that up."

"Funny, that's just what I was going to do, but it's probably best to ignore him. After a while it becomes white noise. He usually goes to bed around eight a.m."

"He sounds like he's being tortured." His face

contorts in disgust, but then his expression softens. "How's your cold?"

"Still there, but much better, thank you." I kiss him again, but when I pull back, I see hesitation in his eyes. "You flew home early because you were worried I'd had second thoughts, didn't you?"

His anxious eyes turn suspicious. "How do you . . . do that?"

"My spidey-sense?" I casually wrap my arms around his neck. "It's a finely tuned skill."

"Well, it's kinda scary," he says, his arms tightening around my waist. "It's a good thing I'm always upfront."

"Oh, you're not," I say jokingly. His forehead crumples into a frown. "You aren't alone though. Very few people are completely open. I get much more from a person's body language and facial expressions than I do from their words."

"Should I be worried about this?"

"Not at all," I say with a giggle. "If I always know what you're thinking, and you know that, you're much more likely to be honest with me."

"Okay," he says with a cheeky lilt. "So, what am I thinking right now?"

Our noses brush as he kisses me again. "Firstly, you want sex."

He opens his mouth ready to protest, but swiftly changes his mind. "No prize for guessing that."

"Okay, then how about this?" I say. His hand moves from my waist to my hip. I kiss him softly, letting my teeth graze his lower lip. "You're worried about me. Your eyes are full of doubt, meaning you want to make sure I haven't had second thoughts about us." He exhales deeply and rests his forehead on mine. "I haven't had second thoughts." His breathing accelerates – short blasts of air tickling the top of my chest. I run my fingers across the nape of his neck, and his entire body shivers. "You're also hurting and you want to talk to me about your father."

"I don't want to talk about him." He pulls away, his arms falling to his sides. "That is ... I don't *think* I want to. Can we go back to talking about sex?"

"No, we can't." I look hard into his glassy eyes. "As much as I want to, we can't fix any of this with sex, because something's come up."

Fear flashes in his eyes. "What is it?"

I take his hand and lead him through to the living room. "Violet and Georgie came over last night, and before you ask, yes, I told them about us, and yes, they know everything. They're really happy."

He sits down on the sofa and I join him. "That's fine, Freja. I don't mind you talking to your friends."

"Madeline was here too."

His face changes instantly; a mix of curiosity and concern creeps into his eyes. "I didn't think you two were friends."

"We're not friends." Saying those words out loud sounds strangely unkind. "She's impossible to read and her priorities suck, but I think she's a good person deep down, and I think she cares."

"You think?"

"I haven't been able to penetrate her ice armour yet, so I can't say for sure, but often the people who consciously hide their empathy for others are the people who care most."

"Hmm, okay, I can see that," he says thoughtfully. "And she's a really great client manager, if that helps. She's incredibly hardworking."

"Work's part of her problem. She's ambitious and driven to succeed, but she lacks balance. She guessed we were together, but she came here uninvited to tell me your father had called her wanting information about us. Have you spoken to him yet?"

He's immediately on edge. He shakes his head and shuffles forward on the sofa. "No, not yet, but I will. What did he say to Madeline?"

"Apparently, I was the sole topic of conversation. He wanted a rundown of everything that happened in Italy, including if we ever spent time alone together."

He balls his hands into fists. "Freja, I know you said you didn't want to take this further, and I respect that, but he's not getting away with what he did to you. It's not enough that I get to shut him out of my life forever. I want him behind bars. Hell, I want to tear the bastard apart."

I place my hand on his arm, wishing I could absorb his rage. "I've always known he couldn't be prosecuted, Nate. There isn't enough evidence, and it happened in the States."

"Then what do you suggest?" he says anxiously.

"Madeline told me Claire resigned yesterday. She claims your father sexually harassed her, which forced her out. He's been suspended by Klein & Co's board pending an investigation."

Nate swallows hard. "I believe her."

"I do too." I strengthen my grip on his arm,

drawing his gaze to mine. "And your dad has been sending messages to Sophie Page."

"The kid working with Madeline?" He looks like the world is closing in on him. "Why?"

"He asked her to dinner, then he invited her to spend the weekend with him at a getaway for his execs. He said he wanted her to work for him, but she felt really uncomfortable about it."

"Why the hell didn't she say something?" His confusion is genuine. As is his anger.

"Because she's young, black and female, and he's a rich, powerful man," I say. His expression registers his frustration at not getting the dynamics at play straight away. "Have you ever noticed him behaving inappropriately at work?"

He shakes his head. "He's definitely a misogynist, but I just attributed that to his age and the company he keeps. He's surrounded by yes-men, pompous establishment politicians and borderline fascist *Sunday Herald* hacks. He's unpleasant and condescending to everyone, but with women he's definitely worse." His eyes glisten as he tries to hold back his tears. "I'm always going to be that scared little kid listening to his mother crying herself to sleep – begging her to smile instead. But when it comes to work, I've distanced myself from him for years. Even before I launched KTech and moved to Hong Kong, I spent as little time working with him as I could. I've heard the odd rumour, of course, but I haven't witnessed anything . . ." His voice gets lost as his breathing becomes unsteady.

"What is it?" My heart rate speeds up as I watch him struggle to order his thoughts.

He stands up suddenly and walks to the window. "I could have stopped this." The room suddenly feels smaller. "There was a girl in the year above me at Oxford, Imogen Curtis. She was a maths geek with a brilliant mind, but she was also funny and sweet and beautiful." He smiles when he talks about her, but his sadness is evident on every line of his face. "She had this great way of building you up if you were down, and this one time, after I'd split with my girlfriend for probably the tenth time, we stayed up all night drinking cheap beer and talking about *Star Wars*. When she graduated, my dad got her a finance job at Klein & Co, so we kept in touch. After I moved to Hong Kong, I heard she'd resigned. There were rumours Dad had something to do with her leaving, but he denied it. He said she was poached by headhunters for Morgan Stanley and she moved into banking. I tried to contact her, but she didn't return any of my calls or messages." I touch my fingertips to his cheek and he closes his eyes. "What if he's hurt her too? What if I could have done something?"

"You would have done something if you'd known, or if you'd seen."

He takes my hands in his. "What if I didn't see because I didn't want to see?"

"I don't believe that. You'd have stepped in if you'd known." I let my thumb play against his jawline. "This isn't your fault."

"Isn't it?" His dark, soulful eyes swim with guilt.

"Don't go down this road." I move my hands to his shoulders, but his gaze is firmly planted on the river view outside my window. "I've been blaming myself for years, and when I heard about Sophie, then Claire, and god knows who else, it was too much. But there's only one guilty person in all of this. I'm not carrying your father's guilt around with me anymore. I've already put it down, in Italy, when I told you what he did to me. I'm not letting you pick it back up again."

"You're saying that as if I have a choice." His hand locks against my hip, anchoring me to him.

"You do have a choice, just like I do." I take his hand and lead him back to the sofa. When he sits down next to me, he seems calmer, but the vein in his cheek is still twitching. "Just before I left for the airport yesterday, I told you that I didn't want to give any more of myself to your dad. But now, knowing about Claire and the possibility that there are others . . ." I try to order my thoughts, but part of me is afraid of giving them life. "If it's going to cause trouble for you, or for Tribe, then I won't talk, but I've been thinking maybe I should try."

"You mean you want to go after him?" he asks.

"I mean I want to help the other women he's hurt."

"Then you should." He raises my chin and kisses me softly on the lips. "I'll back you all the way. Whatever it takes."

"I'd have to do a full risk assessment first. I couldn't bear it if anybody else gets hurt."

"I trust you," he says. His fingers dance against mine until all I can think about is undressing and feeling all of him on my skin.

"Can I ask you something?" I say, heat building between my legs.

"Of course. Anything."

"In the alley, back in Menaggio, what made you

come for me?"

He runs his hand through his hair. "I just knew that I wanted you and I was tired of waiting."

"Waiting?"

He nods. "Ever since that night I saw you in my building, all I could think about was getting you back. Seeing you again felt like a dream, and I knew in that moment that all I wanted was this moment."

He moves forward to kiss me, and the second I taste his warm mouth against my tongue, I know that this is real. He's my "one" and I'm his.

He makes love to me on the sofa, then we move to the bed for the rest of the afternoon. Then, as Saturday turns into Sunday, and we spend another whole day together, I think I finally accept that each other is the only thing we both need. I needed to lose him so that he could find me, and as I fall asleep with my hand locked firmly in his iron grasp, I know that this could be forever.

# 23

WE SPENT THE ENTIRE WEEKEND together, culminating in my first stay-over at Nate's penthouse apartment. I guess this officially ends my "no sleepovers, no dates, no commitment" rule. I should be happy. It should have been the best weekend of my life. If somebody had told me a month ago that I'd be sleeping soundly in Nate Klein's arms with the twinkling lights of London stretched out all around me, I'd have told them they were crazy. But the niggle is still there. Dark clouds are still blocking out the sun, and no matter how hard I try to enjoy the present, I can't shake off the feeling that something terrible is waiting around the corner.

Nate left for his Shoreditch office at six thirty, leaving me with my very own key for his place. I guess this means that not only is my no sleepovers rule broken, but I officially have a boyfriend. A smart, charming, rich, successful, famous and unbelievably good-looking boyfriend. I don't think I'll ever stop pinching myself.

It's just after nine when I arrive at my office. Rachel greets me at the doors to the studio, wearing a smile so big I imagine she's going to tell me Jadine has resigned. "Oh my god, finally. Why are you late?"

"Late for what?" I say, walking past her and onto the studio floor.

"Erm, for work," she replies, matching my pace.

"I had a thing to do, plus I'm the boss." I take a

giant swig of my latte.

"That's what I wanted to talk to you about. You may be *a* boss, but *the* boss is waiting for you in your office."

I stop dead in my tracks and grip her arm. "Stella is back?"

She screws up her brow. "No, Stella is still in Seoul. Ethan is in your office."

"Jesus, don't do that to me."

Her eyes pop. "Why are you so jumpy? And why didn't you answer my email about this afternoon?"

Shit, I've no idea what she's talking about. "Run this afternoon by me again."

"My JET presentation?" she says, hurt in her voice. "Wendy is adding some final touches in post-production and Rory has licensed the most fabulous soundtrack . . . Please tell me you had a chance to review the footage I sent you over the weekend."

I fail to keep the confusion from my face. Rachel grits her teeth. "I'm really sorry, Rach. I've a lot going on."

"I can see that," she says. "And judging by the way Ethan snapped at Billie for offering to get him a drink while he waited for you, there's a lot going on with him too. Did something bad happen in Italy?"

Oh crap, why is he in a bad mood? "No, the shoot went really well. Just let me see what Ethan wants and we'll catch up later. What time's your presentation?"

"At two in Conference Room A."

"Great, I'll be there."

I leave her looking lost, which makes me a colossally shit and unsupportive boss. This is

Rachel's first huge campaign and she needs far more from me than what I'm giving her. I make a mental note to give her at least an hour of my time before lunch, then I head for my office.

Ethan is sitting at my desk, the colour of his face blending into the whiter-than-white shade of paint on my walls.

"Oh Jesus Christ, what is it now?"

He jumps slightly, then gives up my chair. "Here, sit down."

"What's happened?"

His jaw clenches. "Lord Klein is here."

"He's in the office? On the exec floor?"

Ethan nods and sits down opposite me.

"Okay, what do you want me to do?"

He inhales sharply. "I'm sorry."

I see terror and guilt written in the worried lines of his face. Panic rises high into my throat. I swallow it back down. "Ethan, what have you done?"

"He arrived an hour ago with a face like a melted welly." He's struggling to make eye contact, which serves to make my pulse skyrocket. "The atmosphere was horrendous. He threw a shit-fit at his PA, then he literally threw a box file at her. There's only me working up on the executive floor at the moment, and Stella's return can't come quick enough because I need Klein out of this building." He leans forward in the chair, his eyes heavy with guilt. "I'm sorry Freja, but I told him . . . that I knew."

My throat goes dry. "Knew? About . . . me?"

"I'm so sorry. He said something and I snapped."

I inhale a lungful of air, trying in vain to quell

the panic that is rapidly engulfing me. "Please tell me you didn't tell him you know about LA . . ." I catch the look in his eye and I have my answer. He's told him everything.

"You should have seen the look on his assistant's face, Freja. She was terrified. So I went in there and the next thing I know we're yelling at each other, he's threatening me and I tell him . . ." He looks like he's going to be sick. He is struggling to hold my gaze, and every line and angle on his face is strained. Shit, this is bad. "I told him I knew what he did to you and I wasn't going to rest until he got what he deserved."

My chest tightens. "You promised, Ethan. You promised you'd wait."

His blue eyes swim with guilt. "If I could go back and un-say it all, I would. It was like it was before, back at BMG. There was this guy who was threatening Violet. He had some dirt on our boss and he said he'd back off if she slept with him. He hurt her, and she was scared, and when she told me what he did, I just saw red. I ended up beating the shit out of him in the men's toilets."

Violet told me about Ridley Gates. She said she'd never been so afraid in her entire life. "I'm not Violet, Ethan. And this isn't the same as that. You had no right to charge into my life and play the hero."

His creamy skin flushes and his jaw tenses. "This is my agency. I have a duty to protect everyone who works here – people I care about. I'm not letting him treat my people the way he treats his own."

"I get why you did it," I manage to say while grappling to get enough air into my lungs. "But you have no idea what you've done."

Concern blasts onto his face. "Freja, are you okay?"

I shake my head. "I don't know. Just . . . don't let him come down here."

"That's why I'm here," he says keenly. "I knew I'd messed up straight away, so I called Nate. He told me to get down here and not let you out of my sight. He's on his way over."

Usually I'd protest that I can watch over myself, but that would seem ridiculous given my current state. I swing my legs out from under my desk and focus on the ceiling. I try to inhale through my nose; I count the white bubbly tiles; I feel my throat closing up and my lungs burn. "Can you get some water . . . please."

Ethan is on his feet and out the door by the time I take another breath. I bend forward, then lie back against my chair. I wish Madeline were here, I wish Nate would hurry up, but most of all I wish I could control my stupid emotions.

"Shall I get someone?" Ethan asks, as he crashes through my door holding a plastic cup full of water. I can't answer him. I sip at the water, wishing it had the power to course through my veins and cleanse me of my fears. "Freja, you don't look too great. Violet told me about the panic attacks. Should I call an ambulance?"

I shake my head. "No, it'll go."

He looks like he's fighting panic of his own. "Oh god, I'm so sorry. This is all my fault."

Nausea surges through me. For a brief moment I think I'm going to throw up, and I reach for my bin. I breathe in and count. Then I do it again. Somehow

I manage to convince my stomach to hang on to my morning coffee, but I can't convince my brain to calm down.

Ethan comes around the side of my desk and falls to his knees. "What can I do?"

"Just need . . . to wait."

He places his hand on top of mine. "Okay, then we'll wait."

Less than a minute later, my door flies open and Nate storms into the office. "Thank god you're both still here. What the hell were you thinking? . . . What's going on? Freja, are you okay?"

"She's having a panic attack." Ethan stands up so Nate can take his place.

He reaches out to hold me but stops himself. His dark-brown eyes are alive with worry. "Please, Freja," he says, smoothing my hair from my face. "How can I help you?"

"My chest hurts so much . . . I can't . . . just help me to breathe."

He cautiously takes hold of my hand. "I'm here now. It's all going to be okay. Everyone believes you and we're going to beat this together. He can't hurt you anymore." His eyes glisten as he looks at me. God, I don't want to scare him. Why can't I get it together?

"That's not why . . . I'm not scared of him . . . I'm scared of . . . of sea foam."

The words leave my body before I have a chance to wonder if I'll sound stupid saying them. I look at the utter confusion on Nate's and Ethan's faces and I have my answer. "What's sea foam, darling?" Nate asks.

"The Little Mermaid . . . She turns into sea

foam." I close my eyes. I can feel my heart slow thanks to his magic hands. Who'd have thought that all I needed to beat a panic attack was to feel his touch?

"I thought she lived happily ever after," he says, his mouth curving into an adorable smile.

"Disney did that." I inhale a pain-free lungful of air and start to relax. "The real Little Mermaid sold her soul to the sea-witch in exchange for her voice and endured never-ending torture for the chance to walk on human feet. She risked everything for a shot with the prince, but because she couldn't speak he didn't fall in love with her. In the end, she transforms into sea foam." Nate's thumb moves softly over my wrist as he strengthens his hold. "I chose to stay quiet, and I have panic attacks – pain – that won't stop. I nearly left London, you know. When I heard we were bidding for Klein & Co's advertising I was just going to pack up and leave. I could have gone back home to Denmark."

Ethan edges towards the door. "I'll give you two a moment and keep watch outside."

As soon as we're alone, Nate pulls a chair around to my side of the desk. "What made you stay?"

"I remembered who I was. Freja Larsen is not afraid of anything. I didn't want to be a person who ran away. I wanted to be brave."

"And you are. You found your voice and you won." His face lights up with a smile, but it doesn't reach his eyes. "And I'm not anything like that stupid prince, because I fell in love with you all over again. Before you found your voice."

"What if it's too late? I've spent eight years

trying to forget all this happened, but now I want to be speak, and Nate, I think I want to be heard too."

"Then we'll find a way." His hand reaches behind my neck and he pulls me close. Our foreheads rest against each other's and our legs fit together. "But, I think we need to swap out the real Little Mermaid for the Disney version."

I laugh softly against his cheek. "That's the most offensive thing I've ever heard."

"Well, the Disney story is closer to ours." He laughs, and I finally see some warmth and sparkle return. "I fell in love with you at first sight. I never thought that would ever happen, but it did. You must remember it the same way – how quickly everything clicked into place in LA as though we'd known each other forever. I was intoxicated by you. Your humour gave me life, your insightfulness made me feel safe, your confidence inspired me, and the way you care so deeply about everybody made me want to be the one who cared deeply about you. Those weeks we spent together were the best of my life, and last week, in Italy, I enjoyed every single second of falling in love with you all over again." He nudges himself closer, both hands bolted to mine. "I never fell out of love with you and I wanted you back before I knew the truth – before you found your voice."

Tears run down my cheeks as the truth finally settles into my heart. I tell myself – again – that this is it, this is everything and this is forever. I lean in, my mouth yearning for his, but as our lips almost touch, the door opens and Ethan steps inside.

"I'm sorry, I knew I'd be interrupting." His awkward expression would be comical under other circumstances. "Lucille has just called me. Your dad is on his way down."

Nate shoots to his feet. "Does he know I'm here?"

"I don't think so," Ethan replies.

"I thought I could do this." I inhale and exhale as slowly and deeply as I can. I don't want to have another panic attack. "Fuck, I'm sorry, I don't want to let you down again."

The expression on Nate's face changes as he watches me try to pull myself together. A darkness creeps over his skin until his eyes burn with intensity. "Stay with her," he says to Ethan. "I don't want him anywhere near her." Then he storms out of my office, swinging the door shut behind him.

I can't let him do this alone. I take a step forward, then another, then another. Until Ethan's body is a rock in front of me. "I know what you're thinking, but don't. If I let you out, Nate will kill me, and if I tackle you to the ground to keep you in here, he'll probably kill me for that too. Do you want my death on your hands?"

"This mess belongs to me, Ethan." He sighs deeply and I know he's already resigned himself to the inevitable outcome. "Could anything have stopped you going after Ridley Gates?"

He shakes his head. "The hounds of hell couldn't have stopped me."

"Multiply that feeling you had by a million and you might be close to where Nate is." I walk past him and open the door. "This is his dad."

"Fuck's sake," he says with another sigh. "Okay, but I'm coming with you."

\* \* \*

We climb two stairs at a time, reaching Tribe's reception in seconds. Both of our receptionists are standing at their desks; one of them has her hand over her headset. "Mr Fraser," she says with a panic-stricken expression on her face. "I was just trying to call you."

"What is it, Priyanka?" Ethan asks. His voice is unsteady, but my gaze is focused on a trail of employees leading from the lobby of the main building to our reception area and back towards the east stairwell. Some of them are talking in hushed tones. Most are standing around, gaping in shock.

"I don't know why, or how, but Nate Klein – the guy off TV – has just grabbed Lord Klein by his throat."

It feels like the air is sucked out of the room. "Where are they now?" She doesn't need to answer. I follow everyone's gaze to the east stairwell and we head for the double doors, with Ethan yelling "Get back to your desks" at the bystanders – some of them from other companies – who are standing to attention with mobile phones clutched eagerly in their hands. "If any of this finds its way onto social media, the person responsible will be rewarded with their P45 tomorrow, you got that?"

The crowd disperses behind me, but my focus is entirely on getting to Nate and stopping him from doing something stupid. We barge through the doors and find a burly security guard holding Nate against a wall, palm flat to his chest. Lord Klein is standing at the opposite wall, with Julia Hinckley, his loyal advisor, at his side. His assistant, Sandy, the timid-looking woman I remember from LA, cowers in a corner. I assume she's the woman who Klein threw the box file at earlier. Why the hell does she still work for him?

Lord Klein shifts out of Hinckley's grasp and walks towards me. "The second I found out you worked here, I knew you'd stop at nothing to finish what you started."

"Don't you dare speak to her!" Nate yells from underneath the security guard. The man's dark-brown face is full of determination as he grips tight to Nate's arm. "Freja, go back downstairs."

"No, let her stay," says Klein, tugging down the sleeves of his jacket and straightening his tie. "I've a few things I want to say to her."

He takes another step towards me, but Ethan blocks him with his body. "What did I say to you upstairs?" he growls at the older man.

Klein raises his chin, looking Ethan square in the eye. "Keep out of this, Fraser." His tone is full of power and authority. "Keep out of it and I'll forget what you said to me upstairs, and that way you get to keep your job."

"You think Stella is going to take your word over mine?" says Ethan.

Klein doesn't flinch. "I think Stella Judd will do what I tell her to do. I'm her biggest investor and I could destroy this agency in a heartbeat. You must know I'd do it."

Nate battles to break free from the security guard's death grip. "Dad, I swear to god, if you take one more step . . ."

"You'll do what?" Klein says, his steely grey gaze unwavering. "Are you going to hit me, son?"

He narrows his eyes in disgust, then he turns back to me.

My breath catches in my throat, but I hold his gaze. "I'm not afraid of you. Not anymore."

"Well you should be," he says. Julia Hinckley clears her throat. Klein raises his hand to dismiss her non-verbal warning. "I'll assume you've filled my son full of the same lies you fed Fraser."

"I told both of them the truth." My voice shakes when I speak and I hate it.

He laughs in my face. "You told them a pack of lies, and if you ever dare repeat them, I'll have you up in court faster than you jumped into bed with Brett Kirkman."

I dig deep and pull a stronger voice from my lungs. "No, I told them the truth, and they believe me because they know what a sick filthy bastard you are."

"Everyone knows who he is," says Nate. His father doesn't look at him. "And if anyone didn't know before, they sure as hell will when I'm done." The security guard relaxes his hold on Nate, but he keeps one hand on his shoulder. "You drugged her, you abused her, you forced her to leave me, and then you told me a lie knowing it would kill me." His voice quivers slightly. It's barely noticeable, but I can hear it and it makes me ache. "Me and Freja are together, stronger than ever, and your time is up. You are no longer my father. I'm severing all ties with you, and if anybody ever asks me about you, I'm going to talk as if you're dead."

"We'll see about all of that." Klein speaks in an even tone, but when he turns back to look at me, his gaze is scorching. "You haven't changed, have you, girl? Still the same dirty money-grabbing whore you were all those years ago."

It happens in an instant. Nate overpowers the security guard and lunges at his father, knocking him to the ground with one hard punch to the side of his head.

A blur of voices and movements rush into my line of vision. The security guard is shoved into the wall, Ethan is knocked out of the way, Julia screams for help, and Sandy flees the scene. Hard, sharp thuds echo around the stairwell as Nate delivers blow after blow to his father's face and upper body.

"Please stop. Please." I don't know if I'm saying the words out loud or whether they're in my head. Tears run down my cheeks as violence transforms the man I love into someone I barely recognise.

And then it's all over. Somehow Ethan manages to wrestle Nate to the floor, holding him in an armlock. Nate's eyes are lost and unconnected. Julia bends over Klein's bloodied face, still shouting for help. Three police officers rush into the space. The security guard helps them apprehend Nate. He looks down at his father briefly, then he looks at me. "I love you," he says, as an officer handcuffs his arms behind his back and takes him away from me.

# 24

IF I DON'T STOP PACING up and down my living room I'm going to need a new carpet. After I'd given a full statement to the police, and with my mind totally consumed by Nate's arrest, Ethan sent me home. This means I've missed Rachel's presentation, but I can't dwell on how shit that makes me feel at the moment. I'll have to strap on my Scarlett O'Hara bloomers and think about being a woefully useless boss tomorrow.

Ethan asked Violet to come and sit with me, but she had an important team meeting and I refused to let her skip it. Besides, if she knew what I planned to do, I'm certain she'd have spent all day trying to talk me out of it. I love her dearly, but her fixation on fixing things in the way she thinks is best is predictable and exhausting.

Nate's personal lawyer, Celine, has been updating me with news throughout the afternoon. We expect he'll be charged with grievous bodily harm, but the detective investigating appears sympathetic to the mitigating circumstances – namely me.

I don't blame Nate for lashing out. I blame myself. And I know there are a million and one reasons why none of this is my fault, but I still can't shake the guilt and I'm frightened that I won't ever be able to.

It's almost six p.m. when they finally arrive. The butterflies in my stomach have been replaced by spiders with razor-sharp fangs, and when I open the door and show them to the living room I wonder if I'm doing the right thing after all.

Kevin Conroy, Lord Klein's number two, takes a seat on my sofa. Julia Hinckley, bearing an expression made from cold, hard steel, takes a seat next to him. Then finally, Brett Kirkman, the guy I'm most surprised to see turn up, sits down in the armchair adjacent to me.

"Before we begin," Kevin says in his harsh yet melodic Northern Irish accent, "would you care to enlighten us as to why you requested Brett's presence?"

My gaze flits to the American, but he can't look at me. His shoulders are slumped and he's preoccupied with tracing a thread that has come loose on his suit jacket. Good. He's unnerved. "I wanted him to witness this."

"Why him?" asks Kevin. "He's an analyst. This has nothing to do with him." His tone is laden with suspicion.

Is he pretending not to know about Brett? "I have my reasons. Can we proceed?"

Julia Hinckley places a briefcase on my coffee table, opens it with two clicks, then removes a bundle of papers. "This is a draft copy of the agreement. Look over it. We are able to amend it, but obviously time is of the essence."

I take the papers from her and stare hard at the title. *Non-disclosure agreement*. My blood freezes as the symbolism of this moment cuts into my flesh. I came up with the deal – Plan A – this afternoon, but as I hold the document in my hands, I realise I'm actually making a deal with the sea witch. I didn't do it eight years ago; I'm doing it right now.

I'm trading my voice for Nate.

"This says that I'm prevented from speaking about what Lord Klein did to me to anybody, not just the press or police."

"That is correct," says Julia. "Although you'll note the wording refers to an 'alleged' accusation."

"What you get in return will be worth it," Kevin says derisively. "Two hundred grand for pretty much nothing. I'm guessing you could pay off your mortgage with that."

"Maybe if I didn't live in London. But I don't want Lord Klein's money. I've told you what I want."

"And you're getting that too," says Kevin. "Leonard – Lord Klein – has already agreed to prevent the police charging his son with assault, which, considering he will be very lucky if he gets out of hospital by the end of the week, is far more than Nate deserves."

Julia's pale face becomes even sterner. "At least three people have informed the police that Nate told his father he was going to kill him while he was beating the living daylights out of him. I visited Leonard a few hours ago. He has concussion and a broken jaw, but I'm more worried about the damage that's been done to his good name than I am the cuts and bruises. I've advised him the police should be pursuing a far more accurate charge of attempted murder, but he wouldn't hear of it, so if I were you, I'd sign that document and take the money – before Leonard changes his mind."

"Attempted murder? Really?" I study her reactions. Her posture is stiff, her pupils contracted, and her glare is intense. Her cool professionalism can't mask her fury. "You know what kind of man he is."

"I know nothing of the sort," she fires back at me.

"Do you know what Klein did to me in LA?" I ask her. She glances uneasily in Brett's direction, and I see red. "Of course you know. You've known from the start, haven't you?"

Her mouth thins as she forces blankness onto her face. "I've worked for Leonard for over twenty-five years. Like all successful men, he goes after what he wants and he's tough when he needs to be."

"You call that being tough?" I can't bear this. I fight hard to keep my eyes from watering, but I fail. "He drugged me, removed my clothes and took photographs of me. All I ever did was fall in love with his son."

Her jaw clenches as she holds my gaze, but I'm more interested in Kevin's reaction. His eyes are filled with anger too, but when he wrings his hands and hunches his shoulders it all becomes clear. He didn't know. *Min Gud*, he didn't know.

"No man of his stature is devoid of enemies," says Julia. "I must say I never thought I'd count Nathaniel as one of his enemies. He's always been a chip off the old block."

Fire rages inside me. "Nate is *nothing* like his father."

Her lips curl into a scornful smile. "They're both men who will stop at nothing to get what they want. You barely know him."

"I know I'm not the only woman you've attempted to buy silence from. Have you forgotten about Claire Hill already?"

Kevin intercepts. "We are not here to discuss ongoing Klein & Co legal matters."

"You mean you haven't managed to pay her off yet?" I feel a surge of admiration for Claire. I hope she holds out. I hope she nails him to the wall.

"Like I said, we're not here to discuss Miss Hill." Kevin's tone is clipped and he still looks very angry.

"But you believe her, right?" I raise my voice as my frustration builds. "You know that Klein sexually harassed her, just like you know what he did to Imogen Curtis."

Kevin freezes. His blue eyes widen. "How do you know about Imogen? That was a very long time ago."

"I'll tell you about Imogen," interrupts Julia. She crosses her arms defiantly and fires Kevin a warning look. "Leonard gave her an amazing opportunity to learn from and work with the best people in the field. I'm not going to sit here and tell you that Leonard isn't attracted to pretty young women, because in all the time I've known him, that's always been his greatest weakness. Imogen was more than happy with the leg up the career ladder Leonard gave her; in fact she used his infatuation squarely to her advantage. Her skirts became shorter, her eyelashes fluttered when he talked to her, her hips swayed whenever she walked past him. She knew what she was doing, but when he returned her advances she decided to play the wide-eyed virgin. It's exactly the same with Claire Hill, except this time Leonard chose to flatter a girl who lacked charm, as well as good looks." I can't believe what I'm hearing. The internalised misogyny is staggering. I feel my jaw drop. "I've been telling Leonard for years that the world has changed. A wealthy man cannot even look at a woman these days, let alone tell her she's pretty, without her crying sexual harassment."

"Do you really believe that?" I'm honestly lost for words. This woman is a dinosaur. "There's a word for women who'd take a man's side rather than support the women he's hurting. Do I need to spell it out?"

"Oh, don't give me any of your politically correct feminist rubbish," she says with a sneer. "I suppose you think I'm 'letting the side down'." I offer my raised eyebrows in response. She lets out a short, mocking laugh. "In my experience, certain types of women need to evaluate how they present themselves. If they act and dress like they're going to open their legs for a career boost, they can't complain when powerful men follow through on the promises made. These are the cold, hard facts, dear, and I've warned Leonard about it for years, but to no avail. He'll continue paying hush money to women like you until he's in his grave."

"You're both as guilty as he is," I tell them, my blood boiling in my veins at the extent of the damage their complicity has caused. "How many women's stories have you turned a blind eye to? How many women have you coerced into signing gagging orders?" Julia remains stony-faced, but Kevin's expression wavers again. "If any of Lord Klein's indiscretions find their way into the press I expect you'll both be rushing to proclaim your shock and deny you had any knowledge of what he was doing." I scan more of the document's pages before deciding the time is right to reveal my hand. "As I said, I don't want the two hundred grand. I don't want Klein's money and I never did; however, his capital investment in Tribe has created a huge problem for me. I want his senior partnership in the agency I work for transferred to Nate. Consider the two hundred grand he was throwing my way as payment."

Kevin tilts his head and lets out a scoffing laugh. "That investment is worth a hell of a lot more than two hundred grand. No way will Leonard agree to that."

I turn to face Brett. Up until now, he's been quietly observing, no doubt worrying why I requested his presence. "He'll agree, otherwise I make it my life's mission to go after him, as well as Brett, for sexually assaulted me."

Brett shrinks into the armchair. He looks terrified. "You can't prove anything."

It's the first time he's spoken tonight. His Californian accent wasn't prominent in my nightmares; it was always just a noise I didn't recognise.

"What's she talking about, Brett?" Kevin asks. There's a discernible grain of wildly escalating distrust in his tone.

"You really didn't know any of this, did you?" I say, mildly amused that Lord Klein hasn't bothered to brief Kevin, his attack dog, before sending him in to do his bidding. Julia steeples her fingers on top of her knee. My eyes connect with hers. Her guilt is palpable. "Why don't you fill Kevin in, Julia?"

She doesn't answer me. She briefly glances at Brett, before turning to face Kevin. "Call Leonard.

There *might* be a chance he'll agree to hand over his stake in Tribe to Nate."

Kevin's pale skin is beaded with sweat. He abruptly stands and picks up his mobile phone. "A word outside please, Julia."

They leave me alone with Brett. My stomach turns in on itself. I pull my knees up to my chest, then I realise how obviously scared I must look, so I place them back on the floor. I'm not afraid of this man. *I'm not afraid. I'm not.* I force myself to look at him. He's still sitting with hunched shoulders, his back moulded into the armchair as if he needs something to prop him up. His body is a fortress built out of shame.

"Nate tells me you're married and have a daughter?" I roll my eyes at myself. Great time for small talk, Freja.

His gaze meets mine for the briefest of moments. "Yes, her name is Jinnie. She's eighteen months old. My wife is expecting our second child in July."

Anger bubbles through me. He doesn't deserve to be loved. He doesn't deserve children. "Does your wife know what you did?"

His brow crumples. He places his fist to his mouth as his face slowly cracks. Jeez, I didn't expect this reaction. He's absolutely terrified.

"I'm sorry," he says, tears glistening in his light-blue eyes. "I was young. I didn't want to do it. He told me . . ." His chest heaves as he inhales a huge breath in an attempt to compose himself. He grits his teeth and shakes his head. Physical signs that he's stopping himself from talking, but I want to know. I've needed to know for such a long time.

"Why did you do it? I deserve an answer."

He shakes his head again. "Usual story; I'd gotten into trouble and I needed money. My mother was sick, and her insurance wouldn't pay out as she hadn't disclosed a pre-existing condition. Everything snowballed from there. I was in deep, but Lord Klein offered me a way out. All I had to do was pose for a couple of photographs. He said you were a gold-digger with dirt on his son and you were going to rip his family apart. He paid me to do it. He paid for all of my mother's treatments, and he's still paying for the medicine she needs."

"Oh my god." It's actually worse than I thought. All these years I assumed Brett was totally complicit in Klein's plot. I never gave Brett an identity, or a life. He was just an extension of Klein – an appendage, a part of the same nightmare. I stare at him as he slumps awkwardly in the chair. He has no idea what to do with his body.

"Please don't tell my wife. Not with the baby due. I don't have much, but I have some savings, and—"

"Are you freaking kidding me? You think I'd take money from you?" I feel nothing but despair – for him and myself. Then I check my feelings. The guy's worried his wife will find out he assisted in sexually assaulting a woman – me – and I'm actually sitting here feeling empathy for him?

"What do you want from me? Why am I here?"

My senses buzz into life. For eight years I've been desperate to know the truth. Now, finally, I have my chance. But what if I hear the news I've been dreading? My pulse starts to race, as if the last eight years have been building up to this moment, but I hold my nerve. "I want you to tell me the truth."

"What do you mean? I have told you the truth."

"Because of the drugs he gave me, I can only remember pieces of what happened in the trailer: the clicks of the camera, your face, the feeling of being moved around the bed." He swallows hard, then he slowly nods when he realises what I'm asking him. "Did either of you hurt me?"

His head snaps up, his eyes focused on the ceiling. I expected him to say no. I expected him to jump straight into defence mode. Why isn't he saying no?

My breath catches. My body starts to shake. "Just tell me what he did to me. Please."

"When I got there he was undressing you. I didn't think he was going to do that." His eyes are downcast, but he keeps glancing at the door, no doubt willing Kevin and Julia to return. "We argued. I told him he didn't need to remove all of your clothes, but he said you were a porn actress – that you spent every day with your clothes off and it was nothing."

My blood pressure rises and panic surges through my veins. "I was never a porn actress," I say, tears rolling freely down my face. "But even if I were, how the hell would that make it alright?"

"It wouldn't. I'm just telling you what he said." He glances at the door again. I can just about make out Kevin's voice talking on his mobile in the hallway. "I was relieved I was there in the end."

"You were . . . relieved?"

His breathing is shallow and rapid. "I'm sick of feeling like crap over this. It was for my mother – it was her life." He runs his hand through his dark hair and grimaces as if he's trying to stop himself breaking down. "Eight years I've lived with this. I can tell you I'm sorry a thousand times and I know it'll never be enough . . . I'll never make up for what I did. When Nate confronted me I could see how much he loved you, and I knew then that Lord Klein had fed me a pile of bullshit, but if he'd used someone else instead of me . . . or done something alone . . ." His breathing slows and his eyes connect with mine. "I wouldn't do what he asked."

"What did . . . he ask?"

"He, um, told me . . . to touch you."

My heart is beating so fast I think it might explode. I inhale as much air as I can, slowly breathing out through my nose. "Touch me where?"

His voice is small. "Everywhere. He wanted my hands everywhere and he wanted to take photographs of me doing it. But I refused. I convinced him we didn't need to go there – that lying in bed next to you was enough. He was really pissed about it, but at least he gave up trying to force me."

I close my eyes as the full horror washes over me. I always knew it was a show of power. Klein was only interested in control, not in sex, but how far would he have gone if Brett had complied? "And later? When Nate asked you if we'd slept together?"

"I lied." He shrugs as if he's a naughty child. "And then I spent eight years trying to forget what I did."

Kevin and Julia come back inside, and the atmosphere immediately turns from freezing to hypothermic. They share a glance, but neither of them acknowledge the obvious change in our demeanours. Kevin launches straight into business mode. "Changes are being made to Section F of the agreement to remove the payment to you and replace it with a transfer of the Tribe investment to Nate." He removes a small wireless printer from a case and sets it up on my coffee table. He taps through some screens on his iPhone.

"This agreement is between you and Lord Klein," says Julia, returning to the sofa. "It is not connected to any of Lord Klein's business interests or any of his other investments, outside of Tribe advertising agency. Once you've signed your part of the agreement, we will take it to the hospital for him to sign. Kevin can witness on your behalf, or you can choose me or Brett."

Plan A went better than expected; now it's time to unleash Plan B. "Actually, I think I've changed my mind."

Julia purses her lips. "You've what?"

"You all came here knowing I'm a film-maker, right?" I watch with glee as the colour drains from all three of their faces.

"What have you done?" Kevin asks, his eyes scanning every corner of the room.

"If you're looking for a camera, it's over there," I say turning my head in the direction of my bookshelves. Kevin immediately jumps to his feet and strides over to the corner of the room. It takes him less than ten seconds to find the Blackmagic Micro I borrowed from work. He snatches it off the shelf and throws it against my wall. "If breaking the camera will make you feel better, then knock yourself out. But every word spoken in this room this evening has already been uploaded directly to the Cloud. Isn't technology amazing?"

"You fucking bitch," snarls Julia, taking to her feet. I almost laugh at how ridiculous, and completely lacking in self-awareness, she is. Yeah, lady, I'm the bitch in this scenario.

Brett starts to panic, his body twitching in the armchair adjacent to me. "I can't believe this is happening. I just told her everything. I told her that Leonard tried to force me—"

"Shut up, you idiot," Julia bellows. "Is that damn thing still recording?"

Kevin picks the camera off the floor, fiddles with the controls and switches it off. The colour has returned to his skin, but his anger is still bubbling underneath. He sits back down on the sofa, his head bowed. "What do you want?"

"Same as before. Get Lord Klein to drop the charges against Nate and transfer Klein's Tribe shares to him. But I'm not signing the NDA."

"I can tell you now that he won't agree to that," Kevin says.

"Well I suggest you give it your best shot, because I'm in possession of information that Claire Hill's lawyer will definitely be interested in. Plus I have a very convincing confession from Brett which implicates Lord Klein in a sexual assault. Which newspaper would pay the best price, do you think?"

Julia's jaw bulges as she grits her teeth and stares down Brett. "You idiot. What in the name of hell were you thinking?"

"What's to stop you using that video after we give you everything you want?" Kevin asks.

I consider making some sort of agreement, but

then I think of the Little Mermaid. *They're not having my voice.* "I don't think there's anything stopping me, but there was nothing stopping Klein from showing Nate those photographs after I'd agreed to his demands either. Tell him he can have my word, which is worth far more than his."

Julia and Kevin agree to bring my offer to Klein. I hope they feel like the walls are closing in around them. I hope they know that their days enabling Klein's foul behaviour are numbered.

After they're gone I think I could collapse into panic again, but I don't. Maybe the closure I received from Brett's revelations was what I really needed, regardless of what did, or nearly did, happen. I even manage to make myself a gorgeous cup of Blue Sumatra coffee. And drink it. And keep it down.

As the hours roll on, I start to worry why it's taking so long for the police to release Nate. Has Klein refused to comply? Has Kevin Conroy finally found some balls and taken a stand against his nefarious boss? But when my doorbell rings shortly before ten I forget everything in an instant because I know it's him.

# 25

I THOUGHT IT WOULD BE NATE.

I rush to my front door ready to throw my arms around him and tell him everything is going to be okay, but when I'm confronted by Ethan and Violet my heart drops.

When I see the look on their faces, it drops even further.

"What's happened?" My pulse is racing. "Just tell me. Is Nate alright?"

"We haven't heard," says Ethan. I step aside so they can enter, then we all go into the living room.

"My stomach is in knots. I need to know if he's okay . . . Why do you both look like the world is about to end?"

Violet shares an anxious glance with Ethan. "Come and sit down, hun."

Hun? Since when did Violet call anybody "hun"? Jesus, this is bad.

Violet and I sit on the sofa, with Ethan in the armchair opposite. "What did you do, Freja?" he asks, his voice deliberately gentle.

"What do you mean?" I reply.

He takes a lengthy sigh. "Stella called me. She signed a deal with Hong Jun-hee this morning and was due to fly back to London tomorrow, but then she got news that Lord Klein has sold his investment. After being in the Far East for over a month, she's spitting more than a few feathers. Ms Hong's nephew, Go Kang-sik, was lined up to roll his Seoul advertising agency into Tribe Asia &

Pacific, and when he hears the news, she's convinced he'll pull the plug. Can you imagine how weapons-grade pissed off she is? How has Nate inherited his father's share of my agency?"

Oh my God. He agreed. But . . . crap. Why didn't I foresee the consequences? I knew that Lord Klein's internationally renowned name, plus his role in the government and links to the royal family, were a huge selling point for the South Koreans. "They wanted me to sign a non-disclosure agreement in exchange for Nate not getting charged with assault—"

"You really did that?" says Ethan. His disappointment is palpable. "You traded the truth for Klein's stake in Tribe?"

"No, let me finish," I say. Violet rests her hand on mine. I hope at least she understands. "That was just Plan A. I wanted to sign in exchange for getting the assault charges against Nate dropped, and to get him out of Tribe. I had no idea if they'd go for it, so I had a Plan B too. I filmed the whole thing, and I got confessions out of all of them, but I'm sorry. I didn't consider the consequences for Tribe of removing Lord Klein's name."

"You filmed them?" Ethan's face lights up. "What did you get out of them?"

"Enough. I hope."

"Ethan," says Violet, drawing out his name. "Now mightn't be the best time for this."

His eyes flash with realisation, his expression finally softening. "Shit, I'm sorry. I'm sure it'll all die down with Stella and . . . God, I'm being a selfish prick, aren't I? It's just with all of this going down when she's away I've proven myself to be the weakest link in the chain of command again."

"She'll understand if you explain what's happened," I say. "If you need to tell her you can."

"Are you going to do anything with the video?" Violet asks.

"The only thing that matters to me is Nate. I need this to end." I don't have to fake a smile, but I don't think everything has sunk in yet. "But it feels good that I have the video."

"We're here for you," says Ethan. "And we'll help. Whatever you decide to do, we'll back you."

Violet's hand moves to my shoulder. "And I have a very special request to make."

I catch another shared look, but this time both of them are smiling. "You're pregnant and you want me to be godmother?" I say in jest.

"Don't you dare start that again," says Violet.

Ethan's jaw twitches. "We're doing things in the right order, remember?"

I laugh. "Well, what is it then?"

"We've set a date," says Violet, raising her chin proudly. "You can say no if it's not your thing – I promise I won't be offended – but how would you feel about being a bridesmaid next summer?"

My face erupts into a huge smile. "Yes, absolutely. Oh my god, why on earth did you think this wouldn't be my thing? This is totally my thing!" I gather Violet up in a huge hug that I never want to end.

"Hey, are you okay?" she asks, gently pulling away.

I wipe my eyes. "I'm just so happy you finally set a date."

She glances at Ethan. "It was actually all his

doing."

Ethan gives me a cheeky wink. "Bet you didn't see that coming."

"I didn't," I tell him, trying in vain not to laugh. "Those big-boy pants finally fit, huh?"

"They're actually kinda snug," he says. "But if you start talking about babies again, I will leave this room right now and never come back."

"One step at a time, eh?" I say teasingly. "Now, what are you going to make me wear?"

"Anything you want," Violet tells me. "I intend to be the least bridezilla-like bride in the world, so you can choose."

"And before you start, I'm not wearing a kilt," Ethan says.

"Why not?" I ask. "You'd look good in a skirt."

"He's saving the skirt for the stag do," says Violet. Ethan twists his face at her.

"So have you picked a venue? How many guests? Oh, and what about a honeymoon?"

Violet is just about to throw herself into an enthusiastic description of her wedding plans when my doorbell rings. All three of us freeze for a moment. I know it's him this time. It has to be. I stand, walk into the hall and open the door.

"Hi," he says, tucking his hands into his pockets. His eyes are downcast. He's probably expecting me to start yelling at him about the pea-brained stupid thing he did this morning, but I'm not even a little bit angry. I'm just overjoyed to see him.

I rush forward, wrap my arms around his neck and hold him so tight I think I might crush him. "Thank god you're okay."

"I'm not okay," he says quietly, his breath

tickling my neck.

"Oh god, sorry." For a second, I think I must be squeezing the life out of him, but when I pull back and look into his devastated eyes, I find him broken and shattered. "Have the charges been dropped?"

"For the moment." He closes the front door.

"Violet and Ethan are here," I say as he follows me into the living room.

"We're just leaving." Ethan takes hold of his fiancée's hand. "It's good to see you," he says to Nate.

"Um, yeah, about that . . ." Nate rubs the back of his neck. "I'm sorry about this morning. I didn't mean for you to get caught in the crossfire."

Ethan waves off his apology. "Don't mention it. I'm sorry for wrestling you to the ground. I think you got me with a right hook, so we're equal."

Nate's eyes jump. "Did I? God, I'm really sorry about that."

"You don't need to apologise," Ethan says. "You didn't ask me to leap into the fray."

"Well I'm glad you did." Nate's face falls. "Or who knows what could have happened."

All the happiness from Ethan and Violet's wedding news floats away, and we're left with the cold, hard reality of what could have been.

"Take the day off tomorrow," Ethan tells me. "I'll cover your workload."

"And if you need me, don't hesitate to call," Violet adds.

I show them to the front door. Part of me wishes I could hold on to them, because I don't know what to expect from Nate. "Thank you for coming round."

Violet smiles as Ethan places his arm around her shoulders. "Look after each other," she says.

When I go back to the living room, Nate is setting out glasses and a bottle of wine. "How did you guess that's just what I need?"

He unscrews the bottle top and pours. "Sixth sense."

I take the glass he passes me and we both sit down.

"Seems I inherited a huge investment in an advertising agency alongside my freedom," he says, his mouth curling slightly.

"You certainly did," I say with a measure of pride. "And I hope you're not angry with me, but I sort of blackmailed your dad to get it."

His eyes almost leap out of his head. "You blackmailed him into giving up a several-million-pound investment? How?"

"I secretly filmed Kevin Conroy and Julia Hinckley talking about Claire, and Imogen, and the NDA they wanted me to sign. They admitted everything." His eyebrows shoot skywards. "And then I got Brett Kirkman to confess what he and your father did to me. The film uploaded directly to the Cloud."

His jaw practically drops to his chest. "Oh my god, are you MI6?"

"I'm better than MI6."

His beautiful dark eyes melt. "So let me get this straight. You completely fucked over my dad's top execs, then you strong-armed them into giving me a several-million-pound share in a business, and then you got me out of jail?"

"Yup," I say, with a huge grin.

"You're fucking amazing." His eyes glisten, but his smile still holds. "But, now that I own a sizable chunk of your agency, this technically makes me your boss."

"Well don't get any ideas," I say with a giggle.

He laughs and picks up his wine glass. "Wouldn't dream of it, but I don't know the first thing about advertising."

"Neither did your dad. You don't have to be involved in the operations. Just attend board meetings and receive a nice fat dividend once a year." I pick up my glass and take a drink. The spicy liquid calms my nerves. "Have you spoken to him?"

"My dad?" He shakes his head. "No, and we won't be talking. Not ever. Like I said this morning, we're done."

He takes a drink, and when he places the glass back on the table, his hands are unsteady. I instinctively reach forward and hold them, but flinch when I see the cuts and grazes on his knuckles.

"I'm sorry you had to see that." He turns his hands around so that he's holding mine. "I've never hit anybody in my life before, except during karate and taekwondo. I couldn't control my rage, and I should have been able to."

I reach up to stroke his cheek. His skin is warm, but clammy with stress. "I understand why you did it. You don't have to explain your feelings or apologise to me."

"I wanted to kill him." He rests his arm on the back of the couch and runs his fingers over the bumps in the fabric's pattern. "I wasn't thinking of my family, my career or you. There was nothing in my head but rage. Red-hot, uncontrollable fury, and it would have been all too easy to just keep going. If nobody else had been there – if it was just me and him – then I don't think I'd have stopped. I took everything he did to you and I pushed it all into my fist and rained it down on him."

"Any one of us would have done the same," I say, hoping I can allay how distraught he is. "Your father has done terrible things."

His body stiffens as he slowly turns his head to face me. "What did you find out? How did you blackmail him?"

Is now the right time to tell him? I don't want to bring yet more heartache into his world. I sigh, realising silence is what got us into this terrible mess in the first place. "Kevin and Julia have been covering for him for years. Claire Hill, Imogen Curtis, Sophie Page our accounts junior, and I'm sure there are many more women out there just like them." I take another calming drink. "But we'd guessed this was going on, right?"

"We did." Nate's eyes fill with a deep sadness.

I stare at my lap as I process all the possible word choices available to me in sharing the rest of what I learned. "I invited Brett this evening because I wanted to know, once and for all, what happened in that trailer." His eyes lose focus and he swallows hard. His grip on my hand grows tighter. "Your dad paid him to do it, and ordered him to do more while I was unconscious, but he refused. I think I always knew deep down that he had at least tried to hurt me."

Nate's body jerks forward. His head is bowed

but I can see his limbs tremble. "How do we make him pay?"

"I gave my word that I wouldn't . . ."

Confusion fills his gaze. "You think I can live out the rest of my days knowing my father hurt a whole bunch of women, and assaulted my girlfriend? I should have listened to the rumours, no matter how ridiculous they seemed, or how unsubstantiated they were. I should have persisted in finding Imogen. I should have fought for you."

"You have me now," I say. "It's over and we won. The evidence I have will make him think twice about ever putting a foot wrong again. We're done with the past, now we need to let the past be done with us."

"Why are you saying it's over?" he asks. I don't understand why he doesn't want to walk away. We could have our lives back as well as a future. "You got the ammunition you needed. You could go after him."

"I didn't choose to be one of his victims, but I *am* choosing to be a survivor. I'm free of him now. I'm free of the cage. I want peace in my life."

"But he's free too. And he'll go on hurting people the way he's always done: using his power and wealth to get whatever he wants. It's our duty—"

"No, stop, just stop, because what you're suggesting isn't easy. It could have a catastrophic effect on your family, your business and on our relationship." His breath hitches and he looks at me in shock, despair flooding his eyes. "Rich powerful white men control everything in this country, and the structure of every institution – from politics to the press – is designed by them and for them. Men like your dad hate and fear people who are different. What do you think would happen if a shitty tabloid like *The Sunday Herald* got hold of my story? Within half an hour they'd have found the G-rated TV show I made back in Denmark. An hour outside of that and they'd know the name, job and bank balance of every man I've ever slept with. I'd deserve everything your father did to me for the clothes I wear and the fact I enjoy drinking and partying and having sex. If you're envisaging a fair trial where your dad is brought to justice for all of the crimes he's committed against women, you can think again. That isn't how the world works."

"I understand all of that," he says. He takes hold of my hand again and kisses the inside of my wrist. "And I wish the world would change for you, but I also want to make him pay."

"Loving me and living the best life we can – together – is making him pay." I shuffle closer to him and rest my head on his shoulder. I thread my fingers through his and we fit together again. "I want everything, Nate. I want to make good use of that key you gave me to your place. I want dates and weekends away and couples' dinner parties. I want to take you to Denmark to meet my family this summer, then I want to spend all Christmas holed up in your apartment watching old movies while snow falls on the city around us. I want my life to be about you, not him."

He crashes his mouth to mine and I respond instantly, tasting his lips and feeling my way around his body. "I can't promise to make snow fall at Christmas for you," he murmurs, "but I can promise everything else. Plus lots of orgasms."

I laugh. Then I almost cry, because everything about us really is perfect now.

I let Nate go eight years ago, and now I'm letting the past go.

I unlocked the cage, I culled the monsters, and I made space for a second chance at life.

"We're going to have the time of our lives," he tells me as he leads me into the bedroom.

I smile because I believe him. "I hope you're not just talking about sex."

"First things first," he says with a wink.

He kisses me, then I tug him towards the bed.

*The End*

# A MESSAGE FROM GUNTHER
## (Max's cat).

If you enjoyed this book, then *purr-lease* would you consider leaving a positive review on Amazon?

Reviews help other readers find Elizabeth's stories and open up different ways of marketing to all the millions of humans out there who will love her books.

She says I (or rather my idiot owner) might get my own story if I can *purr-suade* you. I personally don't know how this will work. Max is a liability. He still hasn't realised that I'm the one who steals the serrano ham out of the fridge. I've been doing it for seven years! Seven!

Mee-ow

## When Freja met Nate

Freja is a live-for-the-moment kind of girl. She knows who she is and what she wants, and what she wants is to be a world-famous actress, drink a lot of cocktails, and enjoy all the fabulousness life in LA has to offer. She's not looking for love. She's been there, done that, and left the T-shirt behind in Denmark.

But then she meets Nate Klein, and suddenly Freja wonders if she really does know what she wants. She obviously wants his delicious body, but maybe, just maybe, she wants something more…

Nate is handsome, funny, kind - everything Freja could ask for. But his father is a wealthy, powerful man. A man who is determined that the heir to his empire will not end up with a part-time waitress who wants to be a movie star. And he will stop at nothing to get his way.

## FOREVER YOU – a Novella

It's been two months since Nate Klein stormed into the offices of Tribe advertising agency and punched his father to the ground. That was the day he made a simple choice: Freja. She was all that mattered to him and, after eight years believing a lie, he was going to protect her – whatever it took.

Since then, Nate has lost his company, his TV show, his reputation and his family.
But that's fine. He can cope with losing everything - as long as he doesn't lose her.

Nate's story, coming late 2019.

AVAILABLE NOW
The Agency Series
Available to buy now – priced from FREE ☺

# CAST OF CHARACTERS

Tribe is based on several real life advertising agencies. Here's a quick reference guide to help you figure out the organisation of the company:

## SENIOR PARTNERS

| | |
|---|---|
| Stella Judd | Partner & CEO |
| Sir Arthur Lovett | Partner & Chairman |
| Dylan Best | Partner (CEO of BEST) |
| Kenneth Ives | Partner (CEO of Helios Travel) |
| Saul Brown | Partner (silent) |
| Lord Leonard Klein | Partner (investment) |

## JUNIOR PARTNERS

| | |
|---|---|
| Daniel Noble | Managing Partner (Clients) |
| Ethan Fraser | Managing Partner (Creative) |

## PRODUCTION DEPARTMENT (Film)

| | |
|---|---|
| Freja Larsen | Film Production Director |
| Zain Haddad | Film Producer (senior) |
| Neil Dawson | Film Producer |
| Rachel Hart | Film Producer |
| Jadine Clark | Film Producer (junior) |
| Polly Jordan | Line Producer |
| Euan Morris | Sound Mixer |
| Rory Fraser | Music Supervisor |
| Skye Peters | Costume & Make-up |
| Kris Berg | Camera Operator |
| Kwame Agbeko | Production Runner |
| Billie Moon | Production Assistant |

## CREATIVE DEPARTMENT

Violet Archer — Creative Director
Harry Hopkins — Creative Director
Natalia Salnikova — Art Director
Lily Xu — Art Director
Will Thornton — Art Director
Frank Hughes — Copywriter
Sean Blackwell — Copywriter
Pinkie Pinkerton — Copywriter

## PRODUCTION DEPARTMENT (Print)

Georgie Ravencroft — Studio Manager
Max Wolf — Designer (Senior)

## CLIENT ACCOUNT MANAGEMENT

Phillip Lovett — Account Director
Lennox Jackson — Senior Account Manager
Madeline Westgate — Senior Account Manager
Sophie Page — Account Executive

## PR

Anais Tremaux — PR Manager

## ADMINISTRATIVE

Lucille Monroe — Executive Assistant
Priyanka Sharma — Receptionist

## ABOUT THE AUTHOR

Elizabeth Grey spent a sizable chunk of her childhood in North East England locked away in her bedroom creating characters and writing stories. Isn't that how all writers start?

Following a five year university education that combined such wide-ranging subjects as fine art, administration, law, economics, graphic design and French, Elizabeth entered the business world as a marketing assistant before moving into operations management.

Marrying Chris in 2007, Elizabeth now has three young children and runs a small, seasonal business selling imported European children's toys and goods. She is active in local politics and campaigns tirelessly to improve the UK's education system.

During her time as a stay-at-home mum, Elizabeth rekindled her love of writing and thinks herself lucky every day that she is now able to write full time.

When not working, Elizabeth finds herself immersed in her kids' hobbies and has acquired an impressive knowledge of Harry Potter (thanks to the big boy), Star Wars (thanks to the little boy) and Barbie (thanks to her daughter). She loves European road-trips, binge-watching Netflix series and doing whatever she can to fight for a better world.

She's been told she never loses an argument.

**Elizabeth's top quotes:**

*"Real courage is when you know you're licked before you begin, but you begin anyway and see it through no matter what. You rarely win, but sometimes you do."* – Harper Lee

*"In this life, people will love you and people will hate you and none of that will have anything to do with you."* – Abraham Hicks

*"Be who you are and say what you feel. Because those who mind don't matter, and those who matter don't mind."* – Dr. Seuss

*"I am no bird and no net ensnares me. I am a free human being with an independent will."* – Charlotte Bronte

*"I am not afraid of storms for I am learning how to sail my ship."* – Louisa M. Alcott

Printed in Great Britain
by Amazon